To Wendy
Make sure you always
sleep with one eye open!
Duncan Moron
aka
Christopher C. P.

Duncan's Diary

Birth of a Serial Killer

Duncan Moron

iUniverse, Inc.
New York Bloomington

This is a work of fiction. All of the characters, names, incidents, organizations, and dialogue in this novel are either the products of the author's imagination or are used fictitiously.

iUniverse books may be ordered through booksellers or by contacting:

iUniverse
1663 Liberty Drive
Bloomington, IN 47403
www.iuniverse.com
1-800-Authors (1-800-288-4677)

Because of the dynamic nature of the Internet, any Web addresses or links contained in this book may have changed since publication and may no longer be valid. The views expressed in this work are solely those of the author and do not necessarily reflect the views of the publisher, and the publisher hereby disclaims any responsibility for them.

ISBN: 978-1-4401-7516-9 (sc)
ISBN: 978-1-4401-7517-6 (ebook)
ISBN: 978-1-4401-7518-3 (dj)

Printed in the United States of America

iUniverse rev. date: 11/2/2009

Dedication

I would like to dedicate this book to my three daughters and my once-good friends Sudhir, Janine, and their three children. I also dedicate this to all of the people whose lives that I have affected in a negative way and to the lives that are no longer with us because of my direct or indirect actions. Kids have the unique ability to see the world from eyes of innocence with a love that cannot be matched. While I do enjoy the notoriety and status that my newfound infamy has afforded me, I also have a small twinge of guilt that I have forever changed and altered the lives of so many.

I truly love my children, and if I could be a normal citizen capable of going to work and leading the life that most people survive I would do so. Unfortunately, once I started down my path I was forever unable to stray from who and what I had become.

This accounting of my activities is dedicated to my children. I can only wish that after they have read this they will at least understand the pain and confusion that I went through. I had no intent of malice when I started this journey. Some things in life are chance, and some things in life are preordained. I think my transformation was a mixture of both. My struggles are no different than others who struggle with who they are and what they become. As long as we are alive we are all in the process of growing, adjusting, and adapting.

I don't think I had a choice but to become who I am today. Like the butterfly that takes flight, it was only a matter of time before I started my transition. My path has drastically changed the lives of others, and for that I truly feel sorry. I hope they will be able to forgive me at some point. "I am what I am," as Popeye used to say, and while I might feel badly for my actions I will never be able to alter the direction of my past life.

My story is from my own experiences, but I have taken the liberty of interjecting my assumptions on what took place when I was not there. It was easy for me to gather and document activities from the parties I was closely associated with.

So my story is dedicated to those whose lives are intertwined with mine by no choice of their own and are now a part of this telling as well. My life is their life. I might play a more active role while others are more passive but we are all a piece of the same puzzle. I hope that somebody can find something positive from this but I am afraid you will have to look deep.

I wish you luck.

Additionally, to Jennifer Love-Hewitt. If you would like to go out sometime please call me.

CONTENTS

Prelude

Once an animal takes its first bite and its tongue has been saturated with that initial drop of blood, is it possible to ever go back and forget the appetizing spice of life as God originally intended? Hunt or be hunted, is that not a saying from a book?

The newness of my separation from my wife hung over me like the plastic vault of a new toy recently pried open with those damn metal ties that cling to its contents. You try painstakingly to unravel each one only to find there are still more hidden in the back. I was looking for a release for my newfound freedom. Sitting in a bar with my close Irish friend Martin, I was contemplating what new adventure I should embark on. He casually suggested the Dominican Republic, which I myself would have never thought of. From the picture he painted, it sounded like a good idea.

The Dominican Republic is an island filled with sandy beaches, a warm tropical climate, and a calm serenity. It is an undiscovered oasis of tranquility. The clouds seem to float in the air like cotton balls randomly strewn about the sky. The beaches are not crowded, and the ocean is a bluish green tint, as warm as in Los Angeles. Sharing its small locality with its close neighbor Haiti, the island is approximately split in half between the two, although they are governed in widely different standards. It is also well known that the locals (both men and women) freely open up to travelers and show them the warmest welcome imaginable. They have an island sensuality of exotic abandon frequently prevalent in third-world countries. Everything comes with a price though—STDs are rampant in third-world countries—so buyers beware.

I'm now on my third Stella. I am listening to my pal's tales of basking in the warm, intensely soothing heat while bathing in the nude with supple, twenty-year-old women. I must admit that I'm intrigued. Martin had purchased a couple of lots down in the Caberete area and had the intention of building homes down there for retirement. I realized that I might not ever have his financial standing, but the thought of spending a few days with beer and women on the sandy beaches had me convinced that this could be the perfect spot.

Martin was a big, burly guy you might imagine as being typically Irish with his oversized arms and protruding belly. He was his own general contractor and had been in the construction business all his life. He spoke with an Irish accent, and at times it was difficult to understand him. I found the closer we became that most people mistook his accent as a lower-level of intelligence. They discounted him rather quickly upon first meeting him, but in reality he was smarter than anyone I knew. Well-read, politically active—there were few current or historical events that he did not have an in-depth knowledge of.

I will always remember a trip he and I took to Las Vegas. In a cab, he told the driver he could guess the general locality of his origins. The driver accepted the thrown gauntlet, and Martin commenced to tell our foreign born guide what country and region he was from. Upon the agreed acknowledgment, he then discussed the recent elections in said country, and what he felt about the winner's political views. I wondered how I had never heard of this country and had no idea who or what elections were exuberantly being discussed. Luckily for me, most cab drivers are Indian, so predicting nationality in those situations rarely is a challenge.

Martin was my one friend that remained after the parting of ways with my wife. He was a castoff, along with me, from the group of alcoholic, coastal socialites that teamed up with my wife. Their little group felt they were the upper echelon of society in our coastal San Francisco community. It is odd that the one intelligent person in our mix was too intimidating to be included in the drowning, self-important cliquish circle their cellophane world had created.

So when Martin said Dominican Republic was a great place to sew my renewed wild oats and forget about the hulkish grip my wife imposed on me, I swallowed the bait and hook in one gasping gulp of renewed vigor. No matter what my marital status our kids would always keep me connected to that bitter woman. With my destination in place I immediately kicked into high gear. I made my arrangements and found myself on a plane preparing to land at my desired destination a short few weeks later.

Martin had hooked me up with a friend of his who had helped him acquire the property he had purchased. He had informed him that I could be a potential investor. With this introduction I was soon to find I had a five-day, personal tour guide that would be my butler—for a few drinks and some inflated exchange rate purchases. It made the navigation of this little third-world island country much easier.

I arrived at the airport in Puerto Plata and a blanket of heat smothered me when I stepped out of the confined air-conditioned airport enclosure. It was like walking from civilization into a generic concrete construction site. There was a row of rental car attendants and various random vendors that sold beer at every available corner, including the ice cream stand where Jean stood.

Jean was Canadian and had lived on the island for the last twenty years. I never completely understood how he had ended up down here. Once he had stepped foot in paradise he had designed any scheme possible not to leave. Neither one of us knew what the other looked liked; so I was surprised to hear him call my name as I walked down the pathway in my sandals, khaki shorts, and out-of-place faded polo shirt. I turned, assumed this was my greeting, and held out my hand for an introduction.

Jean graciously said hello and pointed to the ice-cream stand. He asked me if I would enjoy an oversized Presidente to drink while we became acquainted. We guzzled down three large beers as he gave me the lay of the land. We decided upon finishing to move over to the Hertz car rental desk to start the next stage in my journey. I paid for the drinks (expected and a common theme of the trip), and we then started the process of acquiring my car.

Jean was extremely gaunt with the sunken eyes of somebody who has enjoyed alcohol to an extreme for several years. Upon first seeing him I thought how easily he would fit in with my wife's circle of friends. They only cared about clouding their pointless existence from one day to the next. Alcohol was always an easy choice for aging America. Jean's genuine ability to open up and be himself made him different from them. His casual accepting demeanor would not fit in well with the plastic society of the hierarchal standing in my wife's pretentious gathering of acquaintances.

Jean had married a local woman, had a few kids (this part was a little foggy to me), and his oldest son lived with him in Caberete. For some reason he and his wife did not live together. From the sounds of their agreement she was not completely faithful as some of her children were not the direct product of Jean. Apparently, this was easy to see, at the birth of their third child when he came out black as coal. Jean laughingly recanted the story, revealing his surprise when he held his wife's and some man's child for the first time in the hospital.

We rented a little SUV. It appeared to not have been washed since it rolled off the assembly line in some foreign country having made its way to this little island via an ocean vessel. The floorboard was strewn with the remnants of the dietary nourishment from several past patrons. We still went through the fifteen-point inspection required by corporate central. It is very odd how guidelines are established and pushed down to every known location regardless of local customs or even common-sense standards. Have neckties cut off the oxygen to corporate executive's minds?

I decided to let Jean drive. He was familiar with the area and had lived here for several years. I had seen him drink three beers and felt pretty confident that these were not his first for the day which made me a little uncomfortable. He grabbed a couple more from the ice-cream stand, I promptly paid, and we popped a couple open for the drive. Not only can you drive after drinking—apparently you can drive while drinking in this little island sanctuary.

We made a quick stop in Sosua at a local restaurant where Jean had an acquaintance. Guzzled down a couple of more beers and talked for about thirty minutes. We then headed out to the house that he had set up for me to rent. Again, just to hone in on the theme of the trip, we stopped at the local grocery store for a twelve-pack of beer before heading to the house. I quickly settled in to my second-story two-bedroom townhouse and was amazed at the view and proximity to the ocean. I had two balconies overlooking the constant ebb and flow of the scenic watery view and was at most ten feet from the sandy edge. The vastness connecting all continents swirled and churned in chaotic abandon.

The sound alone was amazing— listening to the constant breeze blowing and berating the beaten sides of the brick barricade that tentatively held the soil in place. Living here would be an easy transition as the peacefulness seeped into every pore of my being within minutes of my arrival. I had already lost track of what time it was and cared little of what was going to happen next.

We hung out in the living area that connected to the main balcony and drank several more beers. After some time had passed we decided to move to the local bar where Elvis ruled the roost. I wondered if Elvis was a popular name in the area, or if by some odd way the name had made its way from the states several years ago at the timing of his birth. The bar was really an overhang that had four to six plastic tables strewn about with some seats. Beer was poured from behind a bamboo bar-like structure. I continued to think how odd it was that I felt so at home in this world so different than my confined environment. The iron shackles I was used to enduring in my marriage from hell would never fully evaporate.

At the bar Elvis introduced a couple of local girls both young and beautiful in a tropical-flowered-dress sort of way. Both were simple but held flawless beauty afforded only the truly youthful with skin that flowed smoothly almost without blemish that bless those of darker tones. I had been seamlessly flowing Jean money, and he was brokering the purchase of beer (for most of the bar I think). Later I would discover for my extracurricular activity as well. He had been made aware of my desires and purpose of the trip—drinking was high on the priority list but not number one.

I was asked to simply make my choice. Once I decided we were driven back to my perfectly placed home on the ocean and I enjoyed the local culture in a passionate hour of sexual release. I had purchased a local phone with a prepaid card and called Jean afterward. He came over to pick me up and arranged for her to be taken away. We once again moved back into the second tiered priority: drinking more frigidly cold beer. In retrospect I am unsure how cold the beer actually was but in the twenty-four-hour blazing heat of the tropics anything slightly cold was pleasantly accepted. Satisfied in all ways possible on day one, I was content to let the rest of the evening flow in whatever direction it happened to sway.

Jean decided that he would take me over to his place and introduce me to his son and another gentleman who was staying with him for a couple of days. I spent most of the trip never sure if what was being told to me was factual or fabricated or completely false from my new found friend. I constantly tried to figure out how to decipher what was real, but the company was so pleasant and the environment so satisfying who really cared.

Jean had continued drinking while I had partaken in the sultry palate pleasing taste of youthful succulence. He now seemed well into his final stage of daily inebriation. He drove me the short distance to his small two-bedroom hovel that was just one step above sleeping outdoors. It was sparsely furnished. There were a couple of beds, a couch, and one simple bamboo/wicker chair with a faded out green cushion. I met his son Jean Junior (or Junior for short) who knew only a few select words in English. Jean's friend was easily forgettable.

We sat around for about an hour, drank some more Presidente, and mixed in a shot or two of the local paper-bag-covered whiskey. Jean's friend was close to being passed out on the couch. I finally decided I needed to call it a night and head back to the world of the living to get some sleep. It had been a very long forty-eight hours and was now starting to catch up with me.

Jean offered to drive me home. He stated that he would come by around 10 AM to pick me up and start the next day's events. I would soon find out this would mirror my first day. A recurring agenda for all the days of my stay. We stumbled into the SUV. As Jean was pulling out, he thrust the car into reverse, hit the gas, and with a sudden jolt that rocked the car I realized he had rammed a tree stump. This had placed a nice sized dent in the passenger door. This was a rental car wasn't it? I was beginning to understand the no drinking and driving rules of the United States.

As sudden events often do I sobered up instantaneously and promptly told Jean he had lost his driving privileges. I removed him from the driver's seat and said goodnight. I then drove myself back to my rental house only a short ten minutes away. Only one main road travels through the coastline. It would be virtually impossible for me to get lost. The rest of the evening was uneventful, allowing me to get much-needed rest and gather back my energy for the rest of my stay. Jean arrived the next morning around 10 AM with beer in hand left over from the night before. We then started the pattern anew.

The only deviation in the drunken, sexual-oriented routine was Jessica. She was a lovely nineteen-year-old dark skinned native Dominican who exuded a self-assurance unnatural for anyone her age. She was vibrant, stubborn and lively, and carried herself with such an air of self-importance that one could only ponder its origin. Her smooth skin and perfect, porcelain smile held only a hint of the tortured background that had been thrust upon her out of family obligations.

I would later find out that she had only recently been severed from her obligation to marry the owner of the house that I was staying in. This was due to the couple's inability to come to an agreeable finality on the structure of their mutual obligations. He was a sixty-plus-year-old man that wanted the daily satisfaction of a twenty-year-old's attention. She was from the Dominican Republic and wanted the monetary rewards that only came from foreign connections. They had not been able to find a desired resolution, so she had been forcibly released from her commitment. The two were now moving on to other conquests.

I am by no means rich or even exude the appearance of being wealthy. In this country you need very little to vastly leap over the bounds of normalcy. I met Jessica at the house in which I was staying. She was the local masseuse, and on that specific sun-filled day a massage on the beach had seemed like the perfect afternoon treat. I spoke to her briefly as she stroked my legs, arms and body. She effortlessly pushed on the soft cushiony appendages that were now the combined parts making up my forty-one-year-old middle-aged body. I asked her if she would like to go to dinner in-between the pokes and prods.

She agreed, and I picked her up at her parent's house which was about a thirty-minute drive out of the civilization known as Cabarete. She lived in the country dwellings that most locals trekked back to each day. She jumped in the car and we made our way back to a tourist styled dining establishment in the city. We both had a fat juicy blood-rare steak and drank some tropical mixed drink designed to sweetly move you into a softened mental state. I convinced her it was time to head back to the house. She reluctantly agreed. We then made the awkwardly silent ten-minute drive and grabbed a beer from the fridge upon arrival. We sat out on the balcony listening to the waves rhythmically pound the shore in never ending succession.

After a couple of drinks I moved over to join her in her reclining lawn chair and started gently stroking her coarse jet-black hair. I kissed the sides of her cheeks and neck. She was surprisingly unresponsive and stoically stared out at the ocean as I clumsily fondled her perfectly hand-sized breasts then moved over on top of her. She weighed at most 100 pounds and was all of 5.3 in height. Possibly from the daily routine of massaging over aged men she was extremely strong. A sudden shock of reality hit me when I felt the backhanded slap across my cheek. I waddled backward slightly and stared disbelievingly into her dark brown eyes.

She then cradled my face forcefully with both hands as she violently pulled my mouth to hers. She stuck her tongue out like an arrow driven into the inner recesses of my reluctantly accepting throat. I grabbed both her hands forcing her back against the chair and reciprocated the exchange in reverse. I explored the inner parts of her mouth with the abandon of a heat-seeking missile desperately looking for its target.

She violently grabbed my hair with both hands and yanked my head backward smacking me again this time with her left hand. She continued to control my head with her fingers that still had a firm grasp of my hair. My survival instincts took over, and my hands went instinctively around her neck. I began choking her and pushed her on her back. A devilish smile slowly crept over her face as I realized she had provoked the reaction she was looking for. I slapped her hard across the cheek, then backed off her and grabbed both of her legs. I twirled her over so she lay face down and yanked off her skin-tight pants smacking her repeatedly on the ass in the process.

At some point we moved to the bedroom, where we continued the sexually violent exchange for another two hours until we both lay spent and bruised. We were exhausted and face up on the bed—oddly a couple of feet apart. We did not intimately connect beyond the sexual encounter. Although I had a tumultuous history growing up, I had never physically hit or come close to striking a woman. I had never even contemplated hitting a girl, nor could I understand why a man would do such a thing. I had trouble understanding why anyone would inflict pain for pleasure on a physically weaker person, whether it was from a lack of self-control or other reasons.

The exchange I had just encountered was completely out of character and went against all my natural instincts. It set off flares and alarms that rocked my very being and warned me of the dangerous grounds I floundered in. It was like the Hoover Dam, imposing and huge, but once the gates opened and the water rushed forth, it stayed the course until calmness returned. My only worry was wondering if the calmness would ever return.

I was confused and struggled to grasp what had just happened. Jessica got up and started talking in Spanish in a subdued tone. Even if I knew the language it would have been difficult to understand her. She got dressed in a quick burst of energy and closed the door with a soft click of the latch. I was left alone to ponder the ramifications of my actions. I remember thinking I should be more prepared in the future. Sexual activity without a condom makes little sense today.

I spoke to Jessica a couple of times after I returned home to the United States, but after a while my e-mails to her were not returned. I had not seen her on the island after our one encounter. I guess she had gone back to her daily activities, and from my little knowledge of her the sexual explosion could have been part of her standard routine. I, on the other hand, felt different. I felt changed in a way that I couldn't understand. I fell back into the grind of deadlines and requirements that are a part of our hapless existence but would remember this encounter forever.

A few months later I realized this was a key that had unlocked and opened an entirely new world I would navigate to like salmon swimming upstream. Life throws curveballs at times, and if you concentrate and are prepared you might get lucky and hit one out of the park. You might also strike out—so be ready.

The Beginning

I sat in a non-descript airport seat in San Francisco Airport and looked up at the generic monitor that stated my flight to Boston was on time. God, I can't believe I am flying to Boston again. I thought I would not be doing this for a while but here I am. My name is Duncan. Yes, I have heard all the jokes: Duncan Hines, Duncan Donuts, etc. The name was mine and seemed to fit my aimless personality.

As I sat there I couldn't help but think of the girl in airport security as I trudged through the maze of tape and temporary poles, herded like cattle one by one. Yes, here is my ID and boarding pass, yes here it is again, and again, and again. She was a beautiful brunette with long, cascading hair walking three people ahead of me. She wore a pair of black leather shoes pointed to a severity, a sleek tight pair of black slacks, and what appeared to be a thin soft sweater underneath a white fitted sport coat.

She looked just like a young Jennifer Love-Hewitt, I remember thinking as I saw her pass to another lane. We were both waiting in the same lines as the other two hundred people moving through security. I have always and probably will always have a thing for Jennifer Love-Hewitt. I don't agree with the current tabloids that call her fat. I think she is full-figured (large breasts) but in no way is she fat. I remember staring at her look-alike as she handed her identification to the obese security guard with a nice mustache. Since when should our protector look somewhat Asian and somewhat African-American, both? Not sure whether the security guard was actually a female or a male but in San Francisco we don't ask and in reality we don't care.

As I made my way through the gate I collected my keys, change, phone, XM radio, etc. in a massive buddle. I then put on my brown leather boots, thinking how athletic I must look while I managed to balance successfully on one leg while zipping up the side of my boot without even losing my footing.

As I walked into the non-descript airport bookstore I remember fretting about never again seeing the wonderful Jennifer Love-Hewitt look-alike again. I looked for a non-fictional book to read so I could keep up my recent pretense of being sophisticated.

As I breezed through the books, my Jennifer (I was already possessive of her, which is a problem of mine) walked into the same store, picked up a newspaper, and headed for the check-out lady. She must have followed me in, I thought. She must have thought I was somebody she would have to meet. I should walk over to her, say hello and see where the conversation went. Instead I again, as always, chose to stare, gawking like a perverted peeping Tom, thinking of what might be as she checked out and walked away.

If chance would have it that she was also going to Boston and she was seated next to me on the same flight, then I would spark up a conversation and we would live happily ever after. I was sure of that. Then again, lightening might strike me as well. I stared up at the two-toned airport monitor again, which stated my flight to Boston was on time.

How had I managed to get here? I am forty-one years old. Average build (five to ten pounds overweight perhaps). Short brown hair (mixed with some slight graying and some heavier gray on the sideburns). I am 5' 11" or in reality 5' 10" and a half (but that sounds pretentious to say), and in average shape. I am two months into a separation from my wife of fifteen years. I have three daughters, who are age fourteen, eleven and six. My favorite TV show is *Californication*. I have been having an affair for the last two years with my close friend's wife, and I am getting a little worried that she wants to get serious. I find this a little more than frightening.

My father was mentally and physically abusive to me (and to my stepmother I found out later in life), and I did not speak to him much. I had basically cut my family out of my life seven years ago when my father went on his last rampage. He would no longer hit me, but in a psychotic fit he accused my stepmother of being a lesbian. He told her he would kill her if he ever saw her again. She, of course, stayed with him and received her beating, but he did not kill her. That was the end for me. I remember telling him at the time that he could either get help, or he would never see me and his grandchildren again. He of course chose the latter.

I have worked in a corporate finance job at the same company for the last four years. My boss must have been born with a corn cob stuck so far up his ass he has not been able to get it out for forty-five years. I am sure that he picks his nose on the way to work, flicking the remains on the floor mat.

All in all I live what must look like the typical suburban broken family life, yet I feel there must be more. There must be some rush of excitement. There must be something out there in the world that would provide me with fulfillment. Anything I could look forward to and count on that would change me forever.

But, today, all I got was the attendant bellowing over the loudspeaker in broken English that our flight was now boarding. We could yet again get in another line and feed our broken lives onto a plane. We would then sit for hours where most of us would go to another city and stand in a line waiting for our very existence to be extinguished. Like a simple fire that burns itself out at the end of a long cold day.

Is this what life is about? Sitting in lines just waiting for it to end. Endless lines, moving us into more lines, until we lose track of who and what we are. I can't help but think there must be something to bring the spark back into the lifeless, endless nothingness that had made up my forty-one years.

I must interject that my world was not total misery. I did have three wonderful daughters who meant everything to me. They were smart, beautiful, and full of energy. My eldest was not speaking to me, since I had left our house. She was having a difficult time adjusting to the divorce. The middle one was simplistic and a little immature for her age, but this quality added to her innocence that I hoped she would never lose. My youngest was the sassy one. I was convinced she would give me the most trouble of the three. She would be tough to handle down the road with her blonde hair and Californian upbringing.

I also have a wonderful black lab named Delilah. We named her after the song "Hello Delilah" that had been on the radio the night we picked her up from the breeder. Her fur was not just black, but a shiny black like the sheen on a car after it had just been waxed. She was a beautiful dog, a little over one year old and a great companion. I would later find out she also had the ability to eat anything, endless energy, and unbelievable enthusiasm.

As I approached my seat on the plane I was excited to see that although I had a chair in the exit row it was also the last row in the exit aisle. This meant it most likely would still recline. I sat down, and sure enough. Not only did I have the extra spacious legroom, but I also still had a reclining seat. This made my day. I would have to work very hard to surpass this fantastic turn of events. My life really did suck.

I placed my computer bag and my overcoat in the overhead bin. My next order of business was to pull out the in-flight magazine and find the featured movie. The video on a six-hour cross-country excursion can make for a quick or a long trip depending on its quality. As I reach for the magazine, the attendant's voice crackles through the speaker and tells us cows (we were all herded to our seats) that we should use the space under the chair in front of us as our primary storage. This always annoys me. I think to myself, why I should do this? I check my bags. I don't carry on three suitcases that weigh over one hundred pounds and expect to somehow jam them into the overhead compartment. Why don't people ever check their luggage? I choose to ignore this direction and keep my computer bag and overcoat in the bin above my head. I am thoroughly convinced that airlines do not want us to check our bags. The more suitcases that are checked the more baggage handlers have to be hired. This means less money the airline executives can place into their overstuffed protruding pockets. Everything in life is a racket.

Alvin and the Chipmunks. What luck. I don't mind kid movies, but *Alvin and the Chipmunks*? I might as well shoot myself right now. It is bad enough that this movie takes away all my joy from my given seat with the extra legroom that still reclines. I would rather remove my eye with a spoon than see *Alvin and the Chipmunks*, and yet here it is. How people are allowed to make movies of this nature and then get paid for making them is beyond my ability to grasp.

I placed the self-promoting airline magazine into the pocket on the back of the seat in front of me and picked up one of the three books I had purchased from the bookstore. The first of which was titled *Tips for Girls*. It was my middle daughter's birthday in nine days, and this seemed like a very appropriate present. The other was about some Indian girl and her hopeless childhood, but it was a bestseller and therefore something I should force myself to endure. The third book was something on our current political system that seemed appropriate for me to read.

I started with the Indian girl story, lasted about forty pages until I could no longer keep my eyes open, and then feel asleep. The last ten pages I had spent doing the inevitable head bob. My head moved like one of those bobblehead figures on the dashboard of a New York cab that rocks with every pothole. As I woke we were now in the air and a good thirty minutes into our five-hour flight. I really wish I could have slept more. That damn attendant was blaring on the loudspeaker with her booming voice about the movie we were going to watch. I picked up my Indian girl book and took pleasure in a life that might be more depressing than my own.

I was distracted by the young couple sitting next to me. The man was in the middle seat, the woman was in the window seat, while I was in the aisle. My guess is they were in their twenties. He had very short, cropped hair, blonde and was slight in build. She was not big, but was not thin either. Still young, but the ass was blooming and would blow up nice and round after the first child popped out. She had slightly curly blonde hair with streaks of sandy brown. Her teeth were not perfectly aligned but seemed to go with her middle-class face. I believe they were not used to flying all that much as they read the escape plan diagram from the seat pocket in front of them. Does anyone really look at this?

As soon as the seatbelt light turned off she stepped across us both heading to the rest room. It seems odd to me that people instantly have to go to the rest room on planes once the seatbelt light goes off. It is almost like the opportunity presents itself so they suddenly have to take advantage of it. Has anyone ever heard of crossing their legs and holding the shit in? Strangely, I felt myself getting up as well and following her. It was as if I was in a cloudy vision and suddenly had lost control of my body.

As she entered the restroom and closed the door, I forced myself in behind her. I jammed my arm into the small enclosure, and it shut behind me easily and locked with a small flip of my fingers. She faced me with horrified eyes that were wide open. I could sense the scream welling up from her stomach, which would soon erupt. I grabbed her head with both of my hands and slammed her face into the mirror over the shrunken airline sink.

I crushed her head repeatedly over and over again as it hit the mirror. I felt her skull turn to mush as it caved in and flattened out like a piece of cardboard. The bones in her face rattled like a baby's toy as I slammed it repeatedly and watched the blood squirt through the cracks in her face covering my hands and body like a fountain. With the rush of excitement, my palms were sweaty, and my labored breathing erupted out of control.

She was now limp in my arms and her hips fell against me in the small enclosure. I felt myself growing excited with every push. I shoved her head into the wall and let her ass thrust back against my throbbing member as if we were making love. As the banging on the door began I felt like I would erupt any minute. I heard a deep voice yelling, "Hey dude, are you okay?"

I laughed to myself, thinking I had never been more okay. I had never felt more alive than I did right now. I felt like my life had just begun. Like a baby as it takes its first step. I was just now feeling the potential of who and what I could be. The feeling of euphoria swept over me yet the annoying voice continued without pause as I slammed my trophy one last time. I felt the moisture envelope me as my sweat mixed with the blood of my beautiful creature sagging lifelessly in my arms.

Again, I heard "dude, buddy, are you okay? Wake up." The shaking of my arm was involuntary as if somebody were grabbing me. My eyes felt weary as I pried them open with all my strength. I hazily saw the boy sitting next to me. His girlfriend stared over his shoulder. There was a flight attendant in the aisle, and I heard the guy on the seat opposite of me whisper to the lady next to him, "that guy is screwed up." My mind slowly grasped that I was still sitting in my chair, soaking wet with sweat, and the guy next to me was asking me again if I was okay. I was dreaming. I heard myself mumble, and I shakily got up and went to the restroom. I splashed water on my face repeatedly, trying to bring the color back to my skin and slowly come back to reality. It had seemed so real. I couldn't believe it was simply a dream. The feeling of ultimate bliss clung to me like a tattoo. I realized that I couldn't continue living without experiencing something like this for real.

My life was soon to begin. I felt alive and nauseous at the same time as I violently threw up in the silver toilet expunging my just eaten meal. The feeling of sickness swirling with the vibrant awareness was an odd mixture and difficult for me to balance. I slowly made my way back to my seat, as people stared at me from their cowering positions. Leaning back in my chair, I relaxed again, allowing my breathing to return, and noticing that the couple next to me quietly kept their distance.

The rest of the flight was uneventful. Read, sleep, read, sleep, and then I watched the second movie *Enchanted*. A kid's movie, but tolerable. The "fasten your seat belt light" dinged off, and I gathered my belongings from the overhead storage unit. As I yet again waited in line crammed in the aisle between seats that were shoved together. The only goal being increased profits versus any comfort for the patrons. An older lady in her sixties looked over my shoulder with that "will you help me" glint in her eyes. You know the look—they can't actually verbalize the request of asking for help with their bags, yet they sit and stare at you then at the bag then back at you again.

"Ma'am, do you need help with your bag?" I asked her politely.

"Yes," she said. "That red one right there." She pointed her veined bony finger above my right shoulder. I grabbed her bag with one hand and braced it with the other, as I navigated it over the heads of the two people standing between us. "Thank you," she said, and then turned toward the front. We waited expectantly for the doors to open so we could be released from the stuffy confines of our plane.

I trekked down to the baggage claim, picked up my bag rather quickly, and headed off to the Hertz car pick-up. They seemed to have mixed up my reservation, thinking I would be coming in at 9 AM versus 9 PM. This forced me to go through the process of verbally dealing with the counter girl instead of just grabbing my car and leaving. No SUV. Still winter in Boston, and I get stuck with a large American-made car that some might say fits my age and status. "American Made." I hate that phrase. Means so little nowadays. "American Made", might just be another way of saying crap pieced together as quickly and as cheaply as possible in order to maximize the profit companies can suck out of the American people.

The trip to Meredith, NH, (where my company's office is located) is about two hours north of Boston. It is a straight shot up freeway 93 to exit 23. Unfortunately, I am not sure that I will ever forget the exit number. The only reminder of civilization outside of Boston on the drive to Meredith is Manchester, which you don't even pass through. The rest of the drive is shrouded in darkness. There are no street lights, few cars, trees on both sides of the roads as thick and endless as the ocean, and very little sign that people actually live there. My journey is an endless jaunt through a state about the size of my thumb. I searched for a radio station every twenty minutes, and weeded through the static-filled airwaves. "Live Free or Die" is the New Hampshire motto. I think it's appropriate only if you are allowed to exterminate the people who deserve the latter. "Die"—do they really know what they are saying?

I do remember this time to call in my dinner order to Giuseppe's, the Italian restaurant associated with my hotel. They have one of the best seafood pasta dishes I have ever eaten. Spicy yet not too hot, full, flavorful with bits of lobster, crab, and prawns (I usually hold the mussels so the dish is not overwhelmed by a fishy taste). It comes with a Caesar salad if you remind them several times, and bread as well. The entire town closes at 10 PM. If you forget to order anything for dinner you go to bed hungry or are forced to eat the greasy tasteless options at the local fast food establishment.

I get to my hotel (it's really a bed and breakfast) and walk through the hallway to the checkout counter. It's not a typical place to stay on a business trip. Older couples often come to enjoy a weekend getaway at the best spa environment a small town can provide. This is the kind of place where puzzles rest on tables in the hallway, quilts hang on the walls, and a fresh bowl of bright red apples in an oversized bowl sits on the wood laminated counter.

The slightly overweight yet somewhat attractive lady at the counter checks me in. She has a bright, warm smile that you would expect from a small town girl.

"Hello and how are you?" she asks. She has soft straight brown hair and brown eyes to match. She wears a frumpy hotel outfit. It is odd that places of business can never pick out clothes that flatter their employees. Her tight-fitting grass-green blazer must have been made of the finest nylon and synthetic material that $20 could buy.

I wanted to say I was feeling great now that I saw her, and would she be interested in a quick romp in my room? Instead I only managed "Fine. Just tired and ready to relax in bed while masturbating as I look at porn on my computer."

Okay, admittedly, I stop at the relaxing in bed part. No need to freak out the simplistic check in girl. I go through the registering process, put my bags on the window seat, and grab my dinner from the restaurant downstairs. I then settle down with my computer for a night of *Seinfeld* and Seafood Frivoli.

Going forward, I anticipated my fantasies being different, as I contemplated my dream on the airplane and the feeling of life that it had instigated.

REFLECTION

I awoke the next morning slightly jet-lagged, not wanting to get out of bed, and still lamenting how sad my life was.

What road did I take that led me to this end? I remember as I was growing up my goal was to retire when I was fifty-five with a great nest egg. I would relax on the beach, sip drinks with umbrellas, and shit like that. What the hell happened to me?

I don't hate my life or who I am. I don't hate my actions or what I have become. I just think by society's standards I am the definition of a loser—or at a minimum I have some serious issues.

My idea of a great evening is eating a salad, watching a little TV, and looking at all the porn on Craigslist lamenting that I can't even afford a car date for $80. That is the going rate for the cheap ones now. Interestingly enough, I am not even sure that sex is the most important thing in my life. At one time I thought I was a sex-a-holic. Okay, that might be wishful thinking. Sex is about all I ever think about. Probably has something to do with my upbringing, which was anything but traditional.

My family background is a mess by *Leave it to Beaver* standards. I try to explain this on dates and still to this day have no idea why I don't just say I have a few brothers and sisters, and I talk to them infrequently.

My mother was married before she married my father. She had a son in this original marriage (Peter), which would make him my half-brother. She then married my father, had me, and in a couple of short years they divorced. I originally went with my mother but my father did not think that was the best idea so he took me away from her. He informed my mother that he would beat the shit out of her if she ever attempted to contact me in any way. My mother seemed to follow the rule fairly well, as I never saw her again after I turned one. I have had contact with Peter, who must be as messed up as me since he also has some dysfunctional ideas about appropriate sexual behavior. This probably helps support genetic dysfunction versus environmental influence on deviants I would assume.

My mother remarried after she divorced my father, (which I learned from my brother Peter) and had several kids. I'm not sure how many, as I don't have contact with any of them. Meanwhile, my father married a lady when I was about nine. She had two children from a previous marriage. This is important in the grand scheme of things, as my stepsister played a vital role in my sexual growth. Her name was Sarah.

My father was only married to Colene for a short time, and then they divorced. My lasting memory is the two of them having a heated debate, her in the kitchen and he in the living room. Colene was hurling plates and obscenities at him while he played duck and cover. My stepsister Sarah and I hid in our bedroom but snuck a peak now and then to see the show. My father would later marry another lady named Elizabeth, who had a child before she married my father. Stepsister number three. This opens a question that nobody has really ever answered for me. If your parents marry and you have a stepsister, and they divorce, is she still considered your stepsister? I don't really know how to answer that question.

That is the end of my family tree. My father is still married to Elizabeth and they will be celebrating their thirtieth wedding anniversary on October 31. Who in their right mind gets married on Halloween? Seems unbelievable to me, but congratulations to them. I don't know that I could define the marriage as happy, but it seems to have worked for their lifestyle so who am I to judge.

I lie in bed, not wanting to force myself into the cold frigid air of the hotel room. Preferring the warmth of the overstuffed down comforter, my mind travels back in time to my first kiss. Sharon Gillmor was her name, in the small town of Desoto, IL where I grew up. That was the beginning of my obsession with the opposite sex that would later lead me here (today).

I was eight years old, and it was the summer after my third grade year. Sharon was a decent looking girl with the kind of hair that you might think of from the '60s. You know, the kind that doesn't really move. Just stays in place and will remain that way for her entire life. Her facial features will grow old, her body will deteriorate, she will move into adulthood and then into old age. Her hair is most likely the same now as it was then. Immobile.

There was just something about Sharon. Still can't place my finger on the button, but there was something special. Teachers liked her, she was bright, and answers flowed from her rather easily. It was simple for her to overachieve. She had the ability to look wonderful in a dress for a school function, while still being athletic enough to hang with the boys—we would chase each other through the streets of our small town, which had a population of 1,600.

Our town was the kind of place where everyone knew everyone and you were related to most people you saw on any given day. Kids could ride their bicycles to school, go to a friend's house in the afternoon, and parents didn't have to worry. We hung out in fields and played down by the river. Everything seemed simplistic. One didn't hear of drugs or alcohol at all in our little town. Not in grade school and middle school anyway.

It was a bright day with the sun shining and a slight breeze rolling through the manicured lawns. Sharon and I were running and playing. Chasing each other seemed like a way to gain physical contact without the issues of what physical contact might mean. We were kids who still had the innocence of not knowing what we were doing or how fucked-up the world was outside of our little town. Simplicity.

I chased her through the grass, finally catching her behind her house, as we both fell next to a hay bale that was sitting in her backyard. Hay was littered all around the large brick that had been slightly pulled apart. Somebody had used a small portion of its contents to insulate plants.

As we lay there, a few strands of hay in her hair, we were close enough to touch legs. I still remember the electric feeling of her body slightly making contact with mine. I wish that I could say I took my hands and gently cupped her cheeks, as I slowly pulled her close. Gently pressing my lips to hers as she met my kiss and closed her eyes, slightly purring as we engaged in our first romantic moment.

Instead it was more of a quick in-and-out peck that lasted less than less of a second and was over before it even really started. We never spoke of the kiss, or of that moment again. As we grew up and went to high school we moved into different crowds and went our separate ways. I will always count that as my first kiss and therefore always remember Sharon Gillmor as the girl who started me down the path of sexuality.

Sharon might have instigated these feelings, but my formal education, as with all kids, occurred in school. My dad was not the touchy feely kind that exists today. He was more of the "don't talk about it and keep your deviant desires hidden" type of father. Most of my sexual education began in school at the sixth grade level. As with most good sixth graders we had the pleasure of gaining our formal sexual knowledge in the middle of health class, or when I was a budding child in my twelfth year.

The process is easy really. Like most subjects, you are given a book. You then read the chapters that are assigned. You go to class the following day, and you then discuss the topic. Once this process is completed you are given a test on the subject to ensure that you did not screw anything up. The goal is to enable you to firmly grasp the concepts you were charged with learning.

My roadblock was the discussion section. I truly could not grasp how the parts of the opposite sex worked. My sexuality was relatively easy to understand. I had a penis, and at times it would get hard. I would get excited, and then shit (not a good choice of words probably) would fly out of it. Life would feel wonderful for a few seconds. Somewhat like the Fourth of July when the fireworks reach its finale, and the lights spray throughout the sky, and everyone around you oohs and ahhs. There's nothing like the feeling of ejaculation.

Mrs. Johnson was my sixth grade teacher. I don't remember the names of all my teachers, but I do remember her. Not because she was smoking hot, or anything. That would have been Mrs. Reynolds. She was hot, her daughter was hot, and everything about her family was hot. Not the kind of hot where you are stunned by her beauty although she was very pretty. Hers was the kind of hot that oozed sexuality in a way that made her movements fluid and graceful. I would have definitely loved to have a mother daughter encounter with them. She is most likely still hot to this day although my guess is she would be in her sixties.

Mrs. Johnson had the arduous chore of trying to teach my class and specifically me the process of how our bodies were made. How they worked in the reproduction cycle. In my defense I don't think there are very many males that truly understand how the female body works. We might have several of our group that get the mechanical specifics. Very few of our kind truly understand the overall functioning physics of putting all the pieces together to a female satisfying conclusion.

I dutifully went home, read my assigned chapters in my health book, and came to class not knowing what the hell was happening. Completely mystified by the entire make-up and functionality of my sexual counterpart I was prepared to ask specific questions. I would not go through life unsure of the instrumental aspect of the opposite sex.

Mrs. Johnson started her speech. She explained body parts, and how things worked both separately and together. She dutifully explained the interactions of how an erection occurred and where the penis would be placed in the process of intercourse. Intercourse naturally was for the purpose of procreating, but it could be a source of pleasure as well.

The tricky part for me was the process of ejaculation, penis penetration, orgasms for woman, and how all of this occurred without accidentally getting urinated on. I continued to ask the question how could there not be inadvertent urination, while in the process of intercourse, since the parts were used for both purposes. This had the affect of annoying my teacher to no end up to the point where I heard her talking to another teacher. She stated the class overall went very well, and she was really only disappointed in one student.

I took the honors for disappointing, but it would be several years later before I truly understood the concept of how things worked. I say that from a man's point of view, as again I don't think any male truly understands the inner workings of the female anatomy. Who the hell knows what's up down there?

THE PLAN

The most meaningful event that happened on my five-day stay in Meredith, NH, was my experience with Match.com. A co-worker had told me about the Web site, and I had decided to sign up. One evening I went through the procedure. If you have not done it I would highly suggest it even for those of you who are married. It is self-reflective to put down on paper who you are, what are your likes and dislikes, what you enjoy doing/not doing, etc. You also analyze who you are interested in and then list the same qualities in a future partner that you want to find. It is a meaningful and interesting process for all of us desperate, lonely, losers in life.

My current motives were somewhat different. I was familiar with Craigslist (thanks to my brother-in-law) that offered the opportunity to pick your partner for an hour (if you were willing to pay). Match.com was not dissimilar. For both sites, the seller lists out their positive attributes, places pictures to entice you, and then you pick who you are interested in. One site just gives you a sure thing, while the other site (assuming you pay for dinner etc.) costs about the same. The glaring difference is you most likely will go home unsatisfied that evening. It is really a choice between short and long term. Craigslist, being short term, guaranteed immediate gratification and Match.com, being long term, not guaranteed somebody "special." Both sites are really nothing more than a conduit allowing us to prostitute ourselves for a chance at happiness.

My goal was simply to look for a likely candidate to meet, torture, and then murder in a slow deliberate way. This might sound sadistic to say out loud, but it is truthful nonetheless. I debated about which site would be better, as I was familiar with both. Craigslist might seem like the site of choice, but after thinking about it carefully I realized the women on this site were much more street savvy. Although they tend to be young, they are also connected to people you do not want to piss off. My site winner was Match. com. Having chosen my venue I would now enlist the time to find a good candidate.

I could not stop dreaming and fantasizing about the possibilities. What I would do, how things would work—my constant state of anticipation had me in a frenzy. Why could you not carefully and consciously pick somebody out from a crowd, seduce them to be your friend, and then take them to a secluded spot and do what you would like to them? Avoiding the obvious answer to the question—it is against the law. Books are written all the time about the aspects of killing and how to elude the police. How hard could it possibly be? I wonder if they have anything at the library titled Killing for Dummies: 101 Ways to Murder Somebody.

My plan would be simple. I would disguise myself, making slight changes in my face and body, and then take pictures in this altered state. I would have to keep a completely separate wardrobe, which I would purchase only with cash. I would have my online clothes, which I personally could never wear; my online pictures could not be taken anywhere that I myself had recently been. In a nutshell, my online self would have to be completely and totally separate from my real identity. The two could never cross.

I would then have to set up a P.O. Box under a false name for billing information. I would use this name to set up a profile on Match.com, and then attempt to find the first person to share in my new experiences. All of this was truly the easy part. The difficulty was where I would take them once I had managed to ascertain a prize, and what to do with them when I was done. I owned a house up in Twain Harte (a quaint community near Yosemite), which seemed like an adequate spot. I would just need to figure out how to modify the house, transportation, and disposal. I realize this sounds emotionless and mechanical but keep in mind that the logistics of killing somebody needs to be mechanical. You really need to think it through, as you would an equation. If you are careful, consider all the possible outcomes, and plan accordingly you can really do whatever you want. Luck is also a good tool, as long as it is on your side.

Most people who see my house in Twain Harte reference its likeness to the Winchester House—with its many twists and turns and endless rooms. People have a tendency to get disoriented in the house. The house is over 4,000 square feet, and has four bedrooms, four bathrooms, two kitchens, two living rooms, a TV room, a pool table room, and a dining room. It is brightly colored (we bought it that way) and has themes in different areas. The living room for example is the red, white, and blue with flags, decorations, blankets, knick knacks, everything red white and blue down to and including the furniture with the blue couch and the large, overstuffed red chairs. I am as patriotic as the next guy, but a blue couch and red chairs? What the hell were these people thinking? Still it was beneficial having everything in place. Purchasing a house in a vacation community, it is normal to have furniture included in the house sale.

We did not redecorate the house once we purchased it (slightly over a year ago) because we rented it quite often as a vacation home and did not want the disruption. The house was split into two sections. The main part of the house contained the bulk of the square footage. There was a small apartment with an entrance up the back steps that contained one bedroom a functional living room kitchen and one bathroom.

The trick was going to be how to keep the main house rentable, keep the bulk of the apartment intact , and section off a room in between that could be completely hidden and soundproof.

I decided to drive up to Twain Harte the following weekend and see what I could do. The house was not rented for the month of April. I was not going to see my girls much, so I could actually work on the house unnoticed. It was now the end of March, so my plan could not be shelved for reflection at all. In retrospect, had I more time to contemplate, it might have swayed me from the path on which I was about to embark. I personally believe that most people are capable of doing things that are horrible. They end up not doing them because of the time frame in which they have to talk themselves out of it.

I was lucky enough in my childhood to have been forced to work in my dad's rental property empire. He had purchased several houses in the surrounding small community of DeSoto, IL, and had accumulated upward of thirty-five homes. Keep in mind most of these were in the 50k range as a purchase price. Housing costs in that area are almost as depressed as you might imagine living there could be.

I was the designated flunky on many projects including roofing a house, installing a sewer line, hanging drywall, painting, siding, etc. In-between the open hand slaps to the face, and the balled-up fists to the head, I had at least learned a trade that might be able to help me in my current endeavors.

Friday, April 4,[th] I went home, picked up my black lab and drove my Volvo XC90 SUV the twisty route to Twain Harte. Traffic was a little heavy so the trip actually took me closer to four hours versus the normal three but was relatively uneventful. As I pulled into the driveway, my next-door neighbor Ron was out walking his dog Buddy for his evening shit. He waved hello. Ron and Darlene would be my biggest obstacle in my planned activities. I still remember when I first purchased the house and Ron introduced himself. He stated that he had keys to all the houses on the block, with he and Darlene watching most of them for the owners. My first task as a new homeowner was to make a spare key and give it to Ron and Darlene.

This actually turned out to be a lifesaver. One weekend in the middle of winter I woke up early to let Delilah take her morning stroll. I ran outside in my usual bedclothes of running shorts and nothing else. Delilah paced back and forth looking for the perfect spot to make her mark. As I turned to go back inside and escape from the 20 degree frigid air I realized I had locked the door behind me and could not reenter. After ten minutes of attempting to break into any crack in the exterior, I ran across the lawn and beat on Darlene's door. She reluctantly opened up after several minutes, and upon seeing me reached over grabbed my spare house key, flung it in my direction, and closed the door. Most likely saved me from frostbite and breaking a window to reach the safety of warmth. I thanked them profusely later that morning and several times after.

I did smartly have the upper apartment and the house keyed separately so although Ron and Darlene had access to the main portion of the house they did not have the ability to enter the apartment upstairs. They could only come and go in the rentable portion. Still, I would have to carefully plan not only the changes that I had in mind, but how to mask them so they were as unnoticeable as possible.

I pushed the button on the garage door opener, pulled into the garage, and let Delilah out of the back of the SUV. She hopped out, full of pent-up energy from the four-hour drive. Immediately she lost her water intake from hours earlier and then went about reacquainting herself with her surroundings. The house was on two lots and had a semicircle drive that entered in one side of the parcel and then emptied out on the other. My neighbor (Charlotte) had just recently painted their house the same color (exactly, is that not freaky?) as mine. It was a bluish gray that had a wafting smoky affect. I actually share the driveway with Charlotte. Our houses were originally built by sisters, and they were relatively close together.

I closed the garage door after corralling Delilah and unpacked the few items that I had brought (I kept a second set of most things at the house). I walked up the stairs. It was a little cold in the house. It was still chilly there at night, and we kept the heat off to save on the energy bill. I turned on the heat and lights, put the overnight bag down, and went immediately to the refrigerator for a beer. A nice cold Stella always hits the spot no matter what frame of mind you are in. I chugged down a nice big gulp, stretched, and went to survey the house with new motives.

I walked down from the apartment. It ends at a wall, and you can either turn left or right. Turning right leads to a short hall that opens up to the renter's area with the pool table room on your left and the TV room on your right. Turning left takes you either down more stairs to the garage or up a few stairs to the kid's room. It was the kid's room that I felt held the most promise. I would need access from the garage, and access to water that was close from the bathroom. The ability to section it off in a non-obtrusive way would prove to be more difficult.

As I sat there in a chair five sizes too small for my frame, drinking my ice-cold Stella I waited for an epiphany. It came quicker than I would have imagined. The room was about 18 x 45. A very large room. When you walked up the stairs you came to a cupboard on your right with a shelf about waist high. The shelf held a dollhouse and other miscellaneous toys on top. As you walked ahead there were three stairs leading into a pass-through bedroom that then led to the rest of the rental portion of the house. The room continued past the three stairs and contained two bunk beds (full on bottom and twin on top and a futon that was folded most of the time into a couch). At that end of the bedroom was a window seat spanning the full width of the room. Everything was directly above the garage.

I could section off the portion that contained the dollhouse, wrap the stairs from the garage upward, have a door leading into my section of the house, and let the hallway move forward into the bedroom. This would require the slightest structural changes to the house, and could be explained away by changing a portion of the apartment as well. I could simply add on some of the space to the apartment. Keeping most of the area for a hidden room would be easy. It is not like anyone ever measured the dimensions.

I now had a plan for my personal playground. Since the main house was not rented, I went down to the TV room, flipped it on, and started a fire. That room contained an old-fashioned wood-burning stove, which was used for heating, not aesthetics. It was made from solid iron and had a large handled door on the front that once shut increased the heat in the stove to unbelievable levels. The stove could heat the entire house when it was stoked to full capacity. This meant the TV room became unbearably hot as the heat sifted through from there to the rest of the house. My second epiphany was disposal. I was sure that this stove could faithfully rise to a level that would allow me to disintegrate bones. Why not put it to the test?

I ran back up the stairs, grabbed a couple of my dog's thoroughly used and completely chewed beef bones, and threw them in the fire as it was reaching full capacity. My job now was to sit back and watch a DVD entitled *Hostel II*. It was about the ability to pay for the pleasure of killing people in a small village in Europe. How ironic.

As the movie ended—and three beers into my evening—I decided that the fire idea would work (the bones were about 30 percent gone). It would take a long time, and I would have to be very diligent in my burning efforts but that was a small price to pay. This meant that I would not be able to have mass amounts of people flow through my new procedure. I would have to take my time on the experimentation and fun and then slowly dispose of the remains.

I spent the next four weekends, taking an extra Friday when possible, working on the project. It was slow going at first but went relatively quickly after the structural portion of the renovation was underway. I put four layers of soundproof drywall and insulation into the walls floor and ceiling. This cut into my space of the room but I felt it was necessary for the end result. I slightly expanded the upstairs apartment, and must say the finished product was something of a modern-day masterpiece. I had successfully added a room approximately 10 x 10 that was completely hidden—off from the rest of the house.

On the outside of the newly built cube I had placed finishing strips along the seams of the wall that successfully hid the door from anyone who might be looking. The door was in the upstairs apartment in the back of a closet. I felt extremely confident that there would be no way that anyone would ever be able to find it. I had added a self-release lever that worked by pushing a button at the baseboard. This then released the hook holding the door allowing it to open in. It was perfect.

The inside of the room held a tiled floor with rubberized, washable walls. The tiled floor had a drain in the center that vented out to the back yard. The entire room was all in bright white. Tile, walls, ceiling, everything was bright white. The room simply contained a metal-framed twin-sized bed with a rubber mattress, a metal side table, and a metal table like you would find in a veterinarian clinic used for examining dogs or smaller pets.

All in all I felt very pleased with the finished product and all the possibilities it held. I took a boom box in the enclosure turned it up full blast with some rap song and firmly secured the door. As had been the case throughout the testing and building procedure, once the door was closed you could hear nothing at all from any part of the house. The final stage was now to paint the outside area to completely hide any remnants of the newly built studio. Nobody would ever know anything about this room and it would be for me alone save the few select people that I invited on special occasions.

In between my weekends working on the project and the added dimensions of the house, I spent my days at work and my evenings on Match.com. I went through a trial and error process where I sent out eloquent e-mails telling ladies how our profiles agreed. I talked about their desires and how we shared common interests. In total I had sent out seventy-one e-mails, and I had received zero responses. Each of my e-mail attempts varied slightly until finally my realization came upon receiving a few responses at one time in one week. Women simply wanted a direct invitation, no small talk.

They were desperate to begin with and had no desire to push out the process any longer than they had to. I should start my own dating site someday and call it "desperate woman over thirty-five who will do anything to get a date." Okay, a little long in the title and redundant. I don't think you have to say desperate and woman over thirty-five both.

Once I realized this I had three dates set up almost instantly, one on Friday night, one on a Sunday afternoon, and the last one on the following Thursday evening. Jill was going to be my first shot at seeing how my plan would progress.

Preparation for My First Date

I really needed to get some fashionable clothes that would afford me the luxury of dating a higher class of women. I had been married for fifteen years and had fallen into the typical pattern of spending most of my money on my house, kids, wife, cars, and all of the typical crap that married men work so hard for that makes no sense. Buy a big house to have room to buy a bunch of shit that you will never use. Have a garage sale to get rid of all the shit to make room for more. My life was nothing more than a meaningless assembly line of factory-producing crap, but on a positive note, I was apparently efficient at it. I should put that on my business card: "Efficient Shit Producer."

So I embarked on an adventure to the mall with my oldest daughter. Even without talking to me she was always up for a trip to wander aimlessly from rack to rack perusing any form of bodily coverings that were marked up 400 percent. As with all teenage girls, she was up to the task of buying clothes on all occasions.

Jeans were the place to start. Lucky Jeans, or Tommy Hilfiger. I had no idea what to buy or what was in style but every single pair that my daughter picked out was a minimum of $100. Whatever happened to the $20 Levis? They looked as good to me as these designer jeans with makeshift holes and pre-made faded patterns, and I could buy five to one.

I ended up with a pair of Lucky Jeans, a pair of Hilfiger, and one pair of Calvin Klein. My main decision making criteria was how athletic my ass looked in the mirror, and these three seemed to be my best bet. I did have a nice ass. The next item was shirts. Seems like the style is a black t-shirt under a dress shirt, but you really have to go with black on black of some pattern. I picked a few out, was politely reprimanded by my daughter, and she then went about picking out several choices for me. I spent about four hours in total going through items and trying on outfits. This is about four hours longer than I could tolerate in that environment. Again, typical of the suburban man, I didn't enjoy shopping at all. I did end up with a variety of colors in the shirt area although predominately black.

We couldn't leave the mall without ensuring that my daughter was compensated for her fashion expertise. We ventured down to Nordstrom's to look at jeans for her in the high end section Denim section. Shortly I realized that her jeans started at the $200 level, and worked their way up from there. What a great time to be in the denim business.

As we walked into the money sucking pit designated designer clothes a middle-aged woman approached us and asked if we needed help. She had short black hair that was naturally curly, just short of being kinky. She dressed very fashionably in a pair of slacks and a pair of black leather shoes that most likely cost more than my entire outfit. She was probably around 5' 4" and weighed a very slim 100+ pounds. She had a smile that lights up a room. The smile always gets me. When I woman has a nice smile it seems like everything else fades into the background. It is, in my opinion, the most expressive part of a woman. Give me a woman with a great smile, and I can overlook anything else. Always makes me wonder how I married my soon-to-be ex-wife. Her smile was severe and painstakingly sharp. I always used to secretly joke to myself that her words came out so edgy because they had to work their way out of her taunt stretched mouth that sharpened every syllable as it micro pressed its way through the angled opening.

We began the process of my daughter trying on jeans. I ended up buying three pair, four shirts, t-shirts, and a belt all in the time it took my daughter to find one pair of designer labeled denim fashion statement. I can't believe the process that a woman young or old goes through to find perfect-fitting clothes.

The good news is it allowed me time to get to know Sherene, the woman who helped us. She had two kids, was in the process of getting a divorce, and was looking for a place to live. Apparently, her husband's family kept their house in trust to avoid losing it in just this situation. Good for them, but it sucked for her. Her husband was a member of the National FBI team that investigated serial killers. I thought at the time how ironic it was for us to share this oddly placed connection. He was gone most of the time on business trips, was very distant, and had grown into a sullen odd man. At least this was Sherene's take. She had just gotten a day job at a venture capital company as an assistant and worked evenings and weekends at Nordstrom's.

Sherene is one of the women you would marry on sight: fashionable, pretty, bright, and extremely personable. So I asked her out to dinner while my daughter was in the dressing room. She unfortunately stated that she was not dating at all during the divorce proceedings. She preferred to wait until it was final and spend time finding herself over the next few months. As a guy you are never sure if this is a nice way of getting blown-off or a legitimate statement. I chose to believe the latter and would periodically stop by Nordstrom's to see if she was working to say hi.

After my shopping spree, I still had a few additional logistical issues to work out. How to get my new found date in my SUV, how to keep my SUV from being recognized, and how to transport her to Twain Harte. For my SUV I had a brilliant idea. In the parking lot of the mall, I simply slipped behind a car and removed its back license plate. I then removed its front license plate and placed it on the back. This meant that I now had a license plate with a current sticker, and the owner would most likely never notice his front plate being gone. I additionally removed the front plate from the car in the next slot. Even though they did not match, I now had two plates. This process cost me another $100. I had to ship my daughter off to do more shopping while I played musical chairs with the plates in the parking lot.

All of the preparation had finally gotten me to Friday, May 23 and my first date. My plan was to stop at a local gas station then switch from my casual business attire to my newly acquired chic stylish wear. I was nervous with anticipation throughout the day. My palms were sweaty, and I found it difficult to eat anything at lunch.

I had chosen a pair of Lucky Jeans (slightly faded and with pretend holes in several spots), a Claiborne textured greenish shirt, a new set of black boots, a new black belt, and new black t-shirt and athletic briefs (which I commonly wear). Everything was new, trendy, and hip (although I am not supposed to say that, as "sick" is now the appropriate terminology). A far cry from my normal attire of Levi jeans (that my female coworkers swore were tapered even though they were not). It had been a long time since I had purchased modern-day wear, so this was a definite change from my normal everyday attire.

I left work around 5:30, stopped by the local drugstore, and purchased some chloroform which was simple and easy to attain. I now had my clothes, my car was prepped, black leather gloves in the glove compartment, and the means to render my date unconscious. My disguise was simple: very slight reddish dye through my hair and some slight prosthesis added to my nose altering its shape minimally but effectively. I inserted some teeth enhancers that altered my bite a small fraction but had the affect of adjusting my jaw line so my facial expression looked remarkably different. It is amazing how tiny adjustments can affect your look just enough to throw off how somebody will view you from memory.

I had been exchanging e-mail with Jill throughout the afternoon about the logistics of our meeting. She had suggested three places in Palo Alto, which were all close to her Menlo Park home. I picked a pub she had listed as one of my available choices. Her last e-mail to me left her phone number, and since I had failed to give her my name, she had also requested it not knowing what to call me when we met. She stated that she would prefer to know if I was going to be on time. She was uncomfortable waiting in a pub by herself. This was not something she was prone to doing. I had sent her back a brief reply with my number and name: "Lewis."

She was a perfect candidate. She was in her mid thirties, had one daughter, and was slight in build. She ran frequently for the enjoyment of running as well as keeping herself in shape. She was very conservative in her profile. She grew up in Palo Alto but only recently had moved back. She had fair skin with a few freckles around her face and arms and looked a little uncomfortable smiling. Her hair was brown but with a hint of reddishness throughout, and it was cropped about a couple of inches above her shoulders. She exuded a sense of uncertainty and self-consciousness about who she was, and what she was looking for. She stated she was separated versus being divorced but had not elaborated any further.

She reminded me of my stepsister, Sarah, from my father's second marriage to Colene. Sarah afforded me the fond memory of being the first girl that I ever touched, and the first girl who ever touched me. We had lived in a three-bedroom house in Johnson City, IL. Sarah and I had to share a room at the ripe time of our sexual awareness.

I can't remember the first time that we started exploring each other. I do remember Sarah enjoying it even more than I did if that is at all possible. She had the budding of very small breasts forming and did not have her period at the time. Her arousal was still from curiosity more than anything. She was as pure and fresh as a girl her age could be. I was just entering puberty. I had the ability to get an erection, but really didn't know what that meant. Like her, I was simply curious about the opposite sex.

We spent many nights with her coming over to my bed, touching and feeling while we were both naked. Never really doing anything other than learning what our bodies were like. There was never any penetration or ejaculation or anything sexual. We were just two young, curious kids getting to know each other and growing to the next level. Playing doctor would be the appropriate terminology used in prepubescent lingo I believe.

I will always remember when I got hard for the first time with her touching me. She was so curious and excited. Her touch was soft and sensual, but again we were young and had no idea what this meant.

One day my father came in and caught us both naked. After a long talk from her mother our episodes stopped, and we fell back into the normal routine of being kids. Since my father was only married to Colene for less than two years, we moved on, and I did not have much contact with Sarah after that. I did find out she posed for *Hustler* magazine at one point in her life. She didn't make the main spread, but she did open up to the world. I remember feeling sad that the innocent girl I knew and explored my first beginnings had moved to magazine porn, but who am I to judge?

The self-conscious way that Jill carried herself reminded me of Sarah, and my first experience seeing and touching the opposite sex.

My Date with Jill

After arriving in Palo Alto, I drove around for a while and finally decided to park in an underground garage close to my designated meeting point with Jill. I parked in a corner spot close enough to the stairs, not really knowing how the night would progress, or how I would get her back to my car. I would have to remember to go by my Match.com name of Lewis versus my real name as the night moved forward.

It was in the mid nineties and I was not used to the heat. It was still very light out even at a little after six, and the heat showed no signs of letting up. My new clothes were rather heavy so I was worked up quite a sweat by the time I arrived, but I did look good. I think the nervous anticipation did not help. That and the temperature made for a long, hot stroll.

The pub was a small local Irish bar. A few stools were in the dark small room, and some tables were over in a corner. There was an even smaller outside sitting area, which was crowded—a very large party spilled inside the bar as well. I ordered a Stella and looked around for Jill. Standing over in one corner drinking my beer and watching the small TV hanging above the bottles in one corner.

Most of the group in the bar seemed to know each other. Not as locals would in a dive bar, but as a large group who just attended a wedding and were at an after-party. They were loud and boisterous, making sure that everyone heard them and knew of their presence. Not really a crowd strewn with cute women but more of the overweight variety that drank beer, enjoyed it, and didn't care for offsetting this with any form of exercise. They must all be married women, I thought.

Jill finally called about twenty minutes after our agreed upon meeting time. She said she was sorry that she was late but would be there in five minutes or less. I described the scene to her, and we both mutually agreed it might be easier walking down to Gordon Biersch and see what the crowd looked like there. Talking in the pub would be next to impossible. I told her I would meet her out front, and we could make the short walk together to our new destination.

Jill arrived in a black pair of tight shorts. Something close to biking shorts but without the extra padding in the ass. She had on a tight sleeveless shirt that was colorful and did not quite match the shorts. She wore a pair of tennis shoes with ankle socks and as true to her picture her hair was brown, cropped short and had a hint of reddishness running through it. Her freckles were more predominant than I remembered from her photos, but all in all not a bad likeness. She would not win any beauty contests, but she was not ugly at all. Very fit, in fact, and she had a smile that would slice through steel. Not a "come here and talk to me" friendly smile, but more of an "I have been through a lot so don't hurt me" smile. It would be interesting to get to know her and figure out what had happened in her life to make her first impression seem so bitter and sad.

We made the walk to our new bar and started the obligatory small talk that accompanies a first meeting. She informed me that she did not work and was currently beginning college courses. She was going back to school, (her husband was going to pay for all of this) find a career, and start a new life. This got us down to the bar where we found a table and began the dating ritual of discovery.

Her husband was now a doctor. She had apparently put him through school, supported him while he was doing his residency, and just when he finally was ready to start his practice he met a nurse. He screwed her and dumped Jill to the side as he started his new life. This definitely explained the bitterness part. This woman was going to be damaged far into eternity and well beyond this life.

This was the uplifting conversation that we began the evening with at the bar. We managed to get through a couple of drinks, and I suggested that we go find a place for dinner. I was hungry, and at least eating a nice meal would give me a distraction from Jill's sadness.

It was growing dark but was still in the between stage of night and day. The heat was lingering in the 90s like the bad taste a spicy bean burrito might leave, but the setting sun added a peaceful calm to the evening. We walked up to University Street and made the turn to find a quiet restaurant to share some dinner and talk about our miserable lives.

We agreed on a little Italian place. I do love a good bowl of pasta, and I immediately ordered a mediocre bottle of red wine. Jill gently protested She was not a drinker, but I didn't think I could make it through a whole dinner without my senses being numbed. She was killing me, and in all honesty I was probably doing the same to her.

I had to forcibly concentrate my conversation keeping it centered around my kids, and my recent split from my wife who I hate beyond all sensible reasonableness. Hate is a strong word, I know, but truthful, as sad as that is. I am not sure what happened to my wife along the way to turn her into the bitter nag of a woman she had become. I do know that when I finally decided to make the break it was one of the happiest days of my life.

My mind kept wandering to what I would be doing with Jill later in the evening and the pleasure she was being set up to provide. If she only knew that this was her last supper would she savor each bite a little longer. Chew each morsel slower to remember the sweet taste of normalcy.

Her grand offering to the conversation, beyond her own bitterness about being dumped, focused on her only child who was autistic. The challenges that she faced on her own as a single parent were immense. What a pair the two of us made that evening. I did manage to get out of her that she loved to run, had joined a running club, and up until a couple of weeks ago ran almost every day. The only thing stopping her was a pull in her right thigh muscle that was not allowing her to go full speed, so her running had become limited. She was hoping the injury was short lived, and she would soon be back to her routine.

Between dinner and our pathetic attempt at a conversation the evening inched along. Finally we found ourselves at the end of our meal. After paying the check we started the stroll back to our cars. She had parked relatively close to the garage, but above ground, so we walked together. We arrived at her car first, and I asked her if she would mind driving me into the garage a few blocks away to my SUV. She reluctantly said okay, but it was easy to see that she did not want the evening continuing much further.

As we were driving I eased my right hand into my front pants pocket and felt the rag I had doused with chloroform in its plastic bag. It was fairly simple sliding the zip-lock seal and removing the rag out of my pocket and holding it between the door and the seat. I was beginning to feel the nervous anticipation of actually making the next move. There was no going back now. A turning point in my life was very quickly approaching. It would be the end of who I was; the rebirth of myself into somebody I did not know but was dying to explore.

There was a parking spot right next to mine, and she pulled in slowly. She was a careful person, a careful driver, and very reserved. As she inched forward I casually readied the rag in my right hand. She put her Volvo (ironic we both drove Volvos) into park as I scanned the surroundings, ensuring nobody was near.

I forcefully placed the rag over her mouth and nose. I used my left hand to hold down her upper torso by her neck. The move was precise and very quick. Unfortunately I had underestimated her strength. As she fought back, she scratched my left cheek, flailing wildly with her arms in all directions. At one point she hit the windshield wiper lever, starting them in a frantic motion. Our interaction of pushing and flailing went on for what seemed like hours but in reality was less than thirty seconds. Still much too long for something of this nature. She slowly subdued and fell into a restless slumber. I again looked around to see if anyone had witnessed our interaction.

Unfortunately there were three long fingernail scratches across my left cheek that would take a while to heal. Chloroform fumes were filling the car and it was starting to smell. I would have to do something about the vehicle—my DNA and hair was everywhere. Seems like it is getting harder in today's society to have any fun doing anything. I also made a mental note that getting into shape would have to be a priority. I was now forty-one, and I would need to ensure that I had physical advantage over anyone that participated in my new game. It was one thing to look good, but I would need strength as well.

I got out of the passenger seat of her car, opened the back seat of my SUV, and went around the back to pick her up. I slowly grabbed her under her shoulders by both arms and heaved her out of her car. I pulled her toward my open door. Her feet scraped the ground as I dragged her the few feet, and she lost one shoe in the process. I picked it up, placed it in the back of the SUV, and moved into the back seat. I tied her arms and legs quickly (I would have to stop later and do a more thorough job) and placed a piece of duct tape over her mouth. Isn't it odd how useful duct tape is? If you are ever in doubt of what kind of tape to use duct tape always works. I wonder who invented duct tape, and if they still receive some kind of royalty every time it is sold. I doubt it. As with most things the company the person worked for probably took full credit. Made all the profits, and then when they went bankrupt the individual found out the company had squandered his retirement plan. He is now most likely living on a park bench somewhere.

After securing Jill in the back seat, I casually placed a blanket on top of her admiring again the freckles that pre-dominated her facial features. She seemed much more at peace now than at any time throughout the evening. Luckily I had a lighter in the front mid-section of my SUV. Lucky seemed an odd term—if you looked into the tiny compartment that separated the two front bucket seats there seemed to be an assortment of odds and ends that would do a Boy Scout justice.

I tore a piece of blanket using my pocket knife (yes I carry a pocket knife, which was a remnant of my military days) and placed the end of the long strip into the gas tank of Jill's car. I lowered it into the hold as much as possible then lit one end. Once I was satisfied that it would indeed burn I got back into my car and started driving toward the exit. I paused long enough to hear the explosion as the car burst into flames and slowly pulled into traffic making my way to the freeway. I stopped on a small side road to secure Jill slightly better (I also changed the license plates back to my own) and made my uneventful trip to Twain Harte, which would be Jill's last home.

The entire process did not go well. It would be a miracle if I did not get caught. I would really have to plan the details better next time, as there were far too many loose ends that could expose me. I wasn't going to worry about that now. I had my prize, and all I could think about was driving the three-plus hours, and what fun awaited me at my destination.

Two Days of Fun

I arrived later that night, used the garage door opener to raise the door, and pulled into my home. The drive up was uneventful, and Jill still remained fast asleep in the back seat with the blanket nicely tucked around her peaceful face. I went upstairs and cleared out the closet, opening the door and adjusting the bed and bindings slightly, getting them ready for their new guest.

Downstairs I was surprised to see Jill rolling around in the backseat of the car, apparently attempting to flee. Her bindings were well in place making it impossible for her to really move. She did have a look of terror on her face, but I was surprised how calm she had remained when I glanced at her just a few moments ago. She surely must have been awake. I was in a slight dilemma. I preferred her to be awake, but her current state made it almost impossible to move her. I decided to give her another slight dose of chloroform and knock her out yet again.

This did the trick, and she was quickly fast asleep within a couple of minutes. I picked her up tossed her over my shoulder. Her head dangled down my back as I carried her up the stairs. I carefully laid her down on the rubber mattress and started the process of preparing her for the next couple of days. I slowly undressed her so she was completely naked and admired her body as I removed each article of clothing. Her breasts were very perky, reminding me of two small torpedoes as they projected out from her small torso. The freckles, which were a strong facial feature, also traced their way throughout her body masking her nipples in a barrage of coloration. I do love a woman's nipples: different shapes and sizes. Hers were small pinkish and appeared to be the type that would grow an inch or so upon stimulation. Her pubic hair was a little unkept. I assumed that she must have not expected us to move to this level of intimacy on our first date.

I laid her back on the bed and securely fastened her hands with metal handcuffs, which were attached to a pole imbedded into the wall. This allowed her some movement back and forth so she would not completely be immobile. Unfortunately they did not allow her to turn completely over. This was disappointing to me, as I thought through all of the things I would like to do with her, but in this position I would not be able. I would have to try and work through that issue later.

I next fastened her ankles much in the same fashion as her hands, but the handcuffs were attached to the bed frame (the end of the bed did not go from wall to wall). Now, with her lying naked, I admired her for a few more minutes then left to start a fire. I wanted to destroy our clothes from the evening as quickly as possible. It took me close to thirty minutes to get a fire going in the stove. I began wondering how to explain the fire to my neighbors if they inquired. Which they surely would. It was chilly but nowhere near chilly enough for a fire. I would have to suggest to them that I decided I wanted a fire to make the room more cozy as I drank a bottle of wine and watched TV.

The heat grew from the roaring flame. I went upstairs, changed out of my clothes, took a quick shower, gathered everything up, and started the process of burning them a few at a time. Within an hour I had all the clothing in the fireplace and would have to wait for it to burn down. I torched everything but the boots— I didn't think the rubber soles would be great in the fireplace and decided I could keep them in my special room for future use.

I grabbed an electric shaver, some shaving cream and a razor, went back upstairs, and entered my room. I closed the door behind me. Jill was still sleeping (I thought, anyway) so I started the process of shaving her pubic hair. I slowly sprayed the cream on my hand, the kind that comes out something like lotion and then creams up once you rub it in. I gently spread the greenish substance between her legs, after using the electric shaver on most of the hair directly on and around her innermost personal area. I noticed that her pubic hair also had a slightly reddish tint similar to the hair on her head. I then slowly shaved every strand of hair from between her legs, being very careful not to cut her. Again I admired the run of freckles that sprayed over her body— randomly congregating in some areas and sparsely populating others.

After I was done I took a cloth, wetted it with slightly warm water, and cleaned the rest of the cream off. I had never shaved a woman before so the experience had left me aroused beyond my wildest imagination. I was now at a point where I wanted her to wake up. I lay down next to her. My naked erection firmly pushed up against her leg in anxious anticipation, quietly willing her into consciousness. With the tape now removed from her mouth it would be interesting to see what her reaction would be when she realized where she was.

Minutes passed by and she did not move. I could wait no longer. I slowly started sliding my hand between her legs gently nudging one of my fingers inside her, stroking her, hoping this would arouse her. As I thought, she started stirring, making a soft purring sound as she gentle moved her legs in rhythm with my finger firmly implanted inside. She slowly opened her eyes and as saw me she turned her head and started to scream. I guess I should have anticipated this reaction, but it took me off guard at the time. She was hysterical beyond control, sobbing and wailing with her arms and feet flailing against her bindings so severely that I was afraid they would start to bleed.

I tried to calm her down, but she was beyond self–control, and she had worked me into a frenzy. I grabbed a towel and planted it over her face, yelling at her to stop. She would not or could not, would be more appropriate. After several minutes of this, I held down both her arms and put a fresh new piece of tape over her mouth firmly closing it. At least I would not have to listen to the constant screaming.

Since I was already worked up, and would not be able to sleep in my current state, I quickly entered her and held down her arms so she would not be able to scratch me. It took me only a few short strokes before I finished. The preceding activities had gotten me so excited I was ready to explode before I started thrusting.

I rolled over and lay there for a few minutes. Jill's movements had stopped now and she was lying still. I could hear a slight muffled crying coming from beneath the tape, and I felt sad and alone even with her next to me. I had never wanted to hurt her. I only wanted to be with her. To be with somebody who loved and cared for me in a way that I wanted them to. To stop with the incessant bitching and finger pointing, but to simply be with me and do what they were told.

I could no longer look Jill in the face. I left the room, turned off the light, and went upstairs. I had to take a shower and spent several minutes washing and scrubbing the dirt and filth off of my body. As the water streamed down my face, I began to cry. Sobbing uncontrollably, and losing my ability to stand, I squatted down in the shower in a small ball wondering about what I had done. It reminded me of the scene in the movie from the '70s where Glenn Close hears of her friend's death and huddles in the shower crying from the news of the recent passing.

My daughters have always made fun of my inability to cry. They often comment on why, when things are very bad, I don't cry. Why didn't I cry when their mother kicked me out of the house? Or when I sat with them and told them about getting a divorce? Why did I not have the ability to show my emotions as they did?

I was never sure how to answer them, but at this point in time I knew I had the ability to cry. It must just take something extraordinary to move me to tears. I stepped out of the glass enclosure and grabbed a towel. After drying I put on a pair of black nylon running shorts and went to bed. I was wiped out from the day's events and the sexual release had taken almost all the energy I had left. I really needed a good night's sleep and wished with all my heart that closing my eyes would erase the blackness that was enveloping my mind.

I felt as if I were lost in the woods wandering aimlessly but had lost the ability to see. I was waving my arms in front of me, cringing at the scratches the branches were inflicting as they grabbed at me from every direction. When one can't see where they are going, and with the sudden attack of panic, the loneliness is as suffocating as being alive in a coffin. You see the first shovel full of dirt being pushed down on your face while the blackness descends.

You are helpless, and there is no longer anyone who will help. You have used up all your favors from what few friends you had, and you are now left to face the ramifications of who and what you are. Is it worse to die yourself or to live the death of somebody you have killed over and over again. Feeling their pain and their suffering, knowing it was you who was the source of the very infliction you feel?

THE DETECTIVE

Sudhir Takhar was born and grew up in Foster City, but that did not erase his Indian heritage. His mother and father had both come from India, and his father spoke broken English at best. He had married an Indian woman (Janine) as was tradition. She was Sikh and he was Hindu, so the marriage was frowned upon—the two types did not mix gracefully. How prejudiced are we as a society? Not only do we have to be of the same nationality, but we have to be from the same specific region. Granted, India is a big place, but it seemed odd that the two religious factions were that opposed to each other both being from India. Maybe we are at greatest odds when we are close enough to intimately know each other, yet still harbor ill will. Sounds like the definition of marriage.

Sudhir still tells the story of skipping school on several occasions. Even with his flawless mastering of the typical Peninsula English dialect he could do a great Indian accent. He used to recount the times with fervor of calling his school, pretending to be his father. Speaking in the native broken English that is common in most American big city cabs. He would hysterically tell how once on the phone the answering attendant would quickly agree to his excused absence as she had trouble understanding what he was talking about. He mimicked his broken native tongue flawlessly.

Janine, Sudhir's wife, was attractive, smallish at about 5' 4" and around 110 pounds. She was lighter skinned than Sudhir and had long thick black hair that she normally wore down. She worked as an HR contractor and traveled periodically for whatever reason Sudhir never understood. She made decent money though, and that kept Sudhir from having to excel at his own job so he never questioned her actions or her whereabouts.

To make matters even more complicated his wife had a boy, Warren, who was twenty years old, from a previous marriage. Sudhir adopted him. They now had a boy and a girl of their own, Matt, twelve, and Tracey, nine. His kids were quiet and unassuming, much as Sudhir was himself. The family tended to keep to themselves, although Sudhir was close to his brother-in-laws and brothers and spent most of his spare time with his immediate or extended family or watching TV. He was a TV fanatic. Last year at the station there had been a departmental party, and one of the activities was TV trivia. Sudhir knew all the questions from cartoons such as *Shazam,* or what was the cat's name on *The Brady Bunch,* which was only in one episode in the first season and never reappeared.

You were either impressed by his vast array of useless knowledge or saddened at the realization of how he gained it. Sitting for hours in front of the TV, drinking scotch endlessly, to escape his reality. He wasn't a happy man. He tolerated life and was pleasant on occasion.

Sudhir had just made detective a year and a half ago. It was his sixth time taking the examination, and he had resigned himself to never taking it again. He only signed up the last time at the insistence of his captain who had urged him to try yet again. Sudhir had passed at the bottom of his class and apparently (due to some minority quota) had made detective. Four of his fellow police officers had scored substantially higher. This further made him an outcast within his department and ended up driving him to drinking even more than he previously had.

He had been on the Palo Alto police department for twelve plus years now. He had graduated from San Mateo community college, and wandered aimlessly through a few dead end jobs before falling into his current occupation. He had never aspired to be a cop, had never removed his gun from his holster, and had no desire to move up in the world. His wife seemed to suck all ambition out of his existence. It took everything he could muster to get up each morning and make it through the day.

His one saving grace was his kids. He loved them unconditionally and spent time with them whenever he was sober enough to muster the effort. He always had dinner with them in the evening unless work kept him out late. Since he was never given a case of any significance this was usually not a problem.

His oldest adopted son, Warren, had just turned twenty and attended the local San Mateo Community College. He was average in school, making Bs and Cs, and really was unsure of what he wanted to do in life. He had inquired several times about quitting school altogether and starting an apprenticeship program at the local garage where his uncle Thomas was a mechanic. He could make more money being a mechanic than he felt he would ever make after completing college and getting a job. He really felt college was a complete waste of his time and effort.

His two younger ones were still in the age of innocence. Dad was looked up to and respected, and as long as he hung out with them it didn't matter who or what he really was. Looking through the eyes of kids who are still naïve is a great tool to keep things in perspective. Once innocence is gone there is no getting it back.

Matt was small for his age; smart but introverted like his father. He had recently had surgery on both of his ankles. He was pigeon toed to the point where he had to wear special shoes and could only walk, not run, as he tripped over his own feet. The surgery had cut the tendons in both ankles, placed braces on his feet (not allowing them to push back up and pull in). This would let the tendons heal by stretching back together and reconnecting. It meant wearing leg braces for more than a year, but he would run and play as a normal child once complete. He was just recently allowed to start walking without his braces, and it appeared the surgery was a great success.

Tracey was very quiet, kept to herself, and was a straight-A student. She was helpful around the house and loved watching TV with her dad. She spent most of her spare time doing homework and playing with her doll Patricia, which was named after her grandmother's cat.

At the ripe age of thirty-eight Sudhir was about sixty pounds overweight to the tune of 260, about 5'11". He had not seen hair on the top of his head in about ten years. Along with drinking he also smoked (the one thing his wife could not force him to quit) and dipped now and then a nice pinch of Skoal up to about three years ago. That was when the cyst in his gums had appeared. Luckily it was not cancerous, but it still had to be removed and the process of doing so continued.

To remove the cyst the doctors had to cut out a large part of his gums, the bone structure in his mouth, and three of his teeth. They then took a chunk of bone from his hip, and grafted it back into his mouth so the jaw could keep its form. The bone had to heal for approximately one year before he would be able to put some sort of tooth structure back into place. Unfortunately the first round did not take so he had been without the lower left part of his teeth and jaw for the last year plus.

This made lunch awkward, as not only was it difficult to chew, but every time he ate anything he had to thoroughly rinse out his gums to avoid infection. None of this really bothered him much, as his goal was really to coast through life and get to death with as little turmoil as possible. The only issue he had with the process was after each surgery he had on his mouth he had to take antibiotics for about thirty days to ensure no infections occurred. During that time period he was not allowed to drink. When Sudhir was not allowed to drink he went from being an ass to being somebody nobody could tolerate being around. The family and the department all preferred him to drink over the alternative.

It was amazing that somebody of his nature ended up being on the police force. It was a fluke really. When he was between jobs at one point and had no idea what to do he had read an article in the newspaper about an opening in the city of Palo Alto. It had stated how you could retire with a nice pension and spend most of your day outdoors. Seemed at the time the city was having difficulty recruiting so they were actively trying to get bodies into the system. Sudhir went in and applied only to find out the job was really on the police force.

He had managed to pass the test, made it through the academy, and decided to stick it out as it was better than anything he had previously done. He had never been in great shape but at least back then he was able to pass the physical portion easier than some. If he had it to do now it would be a completely different story. He had no ability or desire to run, lift weights, or exercise in any way. He was the complete opposite of the new level of officers in the system that seemed to thrive on being dominant, physically fit, and controlling of theirs and other peoples actions. It takes a rare person to be in the force these days.

This made it odd for him to receive a call at 11:00 PM on a Friday night to look into a car exploding in an underground garage facility. He just didn't get calls in the evening. He normally didn't get calls for anything. He always thought it wasn't because he was incapable, but merely because he just didn't have any desire to do more than what he needed to get by. Do the minimum and do it to the minimum level was his philosophy. Just well enough so you don't get fired but not so good as to get noticed and raise any expectations.

He sat up in bed and listened on the phone sitting in his boxers exposing the black course hair that filled his back like a blanket. He grunted to his wife that he had to go out and investigate an issue with a car fire. Tonight had been a typical evening so he was still inebriated from the scotch. He rolled into the shower, trying to sober up, threw on some clothes, and grabbed a cup of coffee at the Seven Eleven that was a few blocks from his house.

Every time he went into the Seven Eleven he thought of all the jokes he had heard over the last twenty years. Cab drivers and Seven Elevens. Indians come to America and they all work driving cabs and doling out coffee and overpriced snack cakes. He often felt that he as well would have been much happier doing something of this nature. Little responsibility, and no real direction. Simply taking money to drive somebody where they wanted to go or handing out change and stocking food on shelves.

He could do that and not ever have to worry about carrying a gun or—

"oh shit" he had forgotten his gun back at the house. He grabbed his coffee, went back to the car, made the short drive back home, and pulled his gun out of the locked cabinet. He heard his wife mutter something, but he ignored her and headed off to University Street and the car garage.

THE CAR

When Sudhir arrived at the car garage a small crowd of people had gathered around a yellow police taped section in one corner. The facility was an unassuming structure, mostly underground. It had been constructed to contain the vehicles of everyone who now visited the built-up area of bars and restaurants. The eight-block set of streets made up the downtown entertainment area of Palo Alto.

With Stanford right around the corner the students, visiting parents, and community provided a never ending supply of money and patronage to the small businesses. You had everything from local Irish pubs where the regulars tended to go. They could hang out on a balmy afternoon drinking several pints of Stella. Gordon Biersch was where the more hip (sick) younger crowd tended to congregate before they ventured off. Evenings were spent in downtown San Francisco or a dance club along highway 101.

It had a mixed array of restaurants and high-end shops focused on University Avenue, but several side streets had built up as well. Sudhir had parked outside the garage on the street above ground. He walked below down one of the sets of stairs that were on each corner of the garage. Then ventured over to where he saw the small crowd and walked directly toward the police officer who was ensuring nobody pressed too close.

The fire inspector, Jeff was poking around at the car and holding up a small piece of cloth. He placed it in a plastic bag carefully holding it with his latex gloved hands. Sudhir had known Jeff most of his life so he walked over and asked how things were going.

"Nice" Jeff said. "Family is good, kids are doing well. Same ol same ol." Jeff stated that his guess so far was a piece of cloth was used to start the car on fire. It had been placed in the gas tank and lit from the outside. It appeared to be arson of some sort, but the owner was still not here to claim her vehicle. They did not have any idea why the car would have been set on fire. They were trying to track the owner down now. Her name was Jill Hammel and she was a local lady in her thirties who had grown up in the area. She now lived with her parents less than a mile away.

Sudhir's eyes were slightly glazing over as he heard this news. Information was so easily available to anyone in today's society, he thought. He found this amazing. The fire inspector had been here less than an hour. Most of the team had been here only slightly more than an hour, and he already knew that Jill owned this car. She lived relatively close to here, with her parents, arson was involved (or highly suspected anyway), and the cloth was most likely the tool used to start the process. How is it possible that such information can be ascertained so quickly without putting too much effort in? Big brother was indeed watching all of us, he thought.

So with arson being likely, Sudhir pulled out his notebook (seemed like something he should be doing) and wrote down a few notes. He asked the junior officer standing guard over the crowd if anyone had seen anything.

"No sir" the officer responded in a gruff tone. He was definitely one of the new breed of officers. Buff-toned gym types who looked at Sudhir as a nuisance more than anything. The officer had asked around, as he had been first on the scene. Nobody had seen anything. They were only gathered to observe the event and gawk at the unknown as most in society do.

Isn't it odd, our obsession with gore and mishap? How many times do we drive down a freeway only to be forced to stop and sit through hours of traffic because an accident has occurred? The odd thing is when the accident is on the other side of a freeway, blocked by a divider. The only reason traffic is slowing down on your side is everyone has to stop and look at what happened. Are we really so preoccupied with death that we slow down just in the hopes of seeing somebody else's misery?

Sudhir was able to get the phone number of Jill's house. Since it was approaching 1 AM he was now concerned that he was staring at a blown up car, and Jill was still not back. Most of the garage had cleared out with only a few stranglers remaining to gawk at the crime scene. The tow truck was here, and the car was being loaded up for transportation to the police impound lot. The scene was about to be closed. He decided he would stop by Jill's house, and see if the lights were still on.

The ten-minute drive was a short one, and he wondered why somebody would drive such a short distance. He then remembered he himself could barely walk up a flight of stairs without losing his breath so driving seemed logical. It would have also been dark when Jill was returning home. It seemed to make sense that she would have felt safer in her car.

The porch light was on when he pulled up to the curb in front of the address he had been given. He could also see a light on in the house, and it seemed like there was some movement. He felt that gave him the green light to call them and feel them out under the circumstances. Is it normal for Jill to stay out this late? Had they expected her home?

He called and assumed it was her dad that answered. Sudhir introduced himself as a detective on the Palo Alto police force. He interjected that at this time there was no cause for concern but wanted to inquire about their daughter Jill. He asked if she was home. Jill's dad said no, she was not currently there, but they were worried as she had been expected home a couple of hours ago. She never stayed out this late. She was very conservative, prompt, and never would have left them wondering where she was. They had tried to call her several times on her cell phone, and she was not picking up.

Sudhir suggested he come inside, as he then informed them he was sitting out in front of their house and would like to talk to them in more detail. He told them of Jill's car. He could sense the worry and anxiety building with each of his uttered words. They were now somewhat frantic (probably with good cause, Sudhir thought) and were wondering what the next step was. Sudhir also wondered what the next step was. He had never been down this path before, so he had no idea what to do next.

He spent a few minutes with them discussing the details. He tried to fill them in on the facts without alarming them any more than they already were. He did not stay long, and after the short discussion left their house promising to call them the next day. He wanted to help them proceed if they had not heard back from Jill. He also had them agree to call him immediately if they heard from Jill, or from anyone that knew her.

On the drive home Sudhir wondered about his wife and kids. How he felt about them, and what they meant in his life. He had never been faced with the possibility of somebody being abducted and or killed. He felt a sickness in the pit of his stomach at the thought of his own family and how fragile the strings were that held your existence together. The slightest crack or smallest fragmentation could drastically change everything you lived for. He decided he would have a drink when he got home before slipping back into bed for the two hours of sleep he could still get.

Drinking remained the one comfort that without fail could return him to the restful numbness that isolated him from reality. What was reality anyway, and who is to say what you have to face. What can you choose to ignore and sweep under the rug? As he swallowed the first gulp of scotch, he couldn't help feel the tugging pull that this night was going to change him somehow. Divert his path down a new road. He wasn't sure that he was ready to step up and face the challenges and blockades that might appear. As he took another drink, the familiar relaxing warmness started to spread throughout his body. He settled down into his recliner to finish before heading off to bed.

The Next Day

Sudhir woke up at his normal 7 AM time and rolled out of bed. He stumbled into the shower and quickly washed his close to hairless head. Bright green bottle, he thought. Odd that he washes his head with shampoo when there is more hair on his back than on his head. It seems like he should use soap on his head and shampoo on his back. Everything in life is a marketing scheme. Our society is programmed to use shampoo on our head no matter what, so that is what we do every morning, even if we don't have one damn hair.

The kids were already rummaging about getting ready, so he threw some waffles in the toaster and started pouring milk. They both liked Egos in the morning, and he always sprinkled a little cinnamon sugar to go along with the syrup. Sweet way to start the day. He poured himself a cup of black coffee, informed the kids that their mom would drop them off today. He took pride in their yelps of protest at his not being the designated delivery boy this morning, and headed to his car.

When he arrived at work he started preparing the report from the night before, and after only ten minutes he was beckoned by his captain to come down to the office. Rarely did anyone speak to him, so he assumed it was serious. When he arrived in the small glass enclosed square a couple of the newer detectives were in the office as well with his captain. It was a non-descript box, the obligatory photo of the wife and kids on the desk, and couple of awards in plain wooden frames hanging on the walls. A couple of generic metal framed chairs with worn green padding sat in front of the plain metal desk that was now and always covered in papers.

The two detectives were a couple years ahead of Sudhir in the promotion line so they had more experience with the detective title than he did. In Sudhir's mind that was really about all they had going for them. Sudhir was sure he would be removed from the case, and it would be placed into the hands of more seasoned detectives, but he had reservations about handing it over to these two. They were not known for their ability to carry most things through to resolution and were labeled as inadequate at best. Again this was all Sudhir's opinion, and his opinion of most people was negative.

"Please grab a seat" the captain said as Sudhir walked in and closed the door behind him. The discussion started around the car explosion the night before as Sudhir was prompted to explain the evening's activities. He went through his interaction with the fire inspector, his visit to Jill's house, and his promise to them that he would call them today. He needed to let them know what the next steps were if Jill had not returned.

The captain listened intently, nodding and muttering on occasion, until the story reached its conclusion.

"Sudhir, you realize with your lack of experience and the fact that the case is turning into a missing person and a possible homicide that you are not really qualified to move forward on … this?" Sudhir nodded. "Unfortunately, with the work load that we have in house right now, I don't really have any choice but to let you take the lead with the investigation and see how you perform. I would like you to utilize Mike and Scott as consultants, and they have agreed to help out as needed."

Sudhir sat thinking to himself how he could possibly be in a position to learn something from two guys who were ten years younger than himself. Their combined IQ could be no higher than ten but he said that would be fine, and he appreciated being given a chance. All three left the captain's office together and headed down to the pit (the large room where all the detectives' desks were crammed together). He listened as Mike filled him in on his role. Mike was the leader of the two. He was a big, burly man who had to spend a minimum of four hours every day in the gym. Sudhir guessed that two of those hours were probably spent looking at himself in the mirror.

Mike filled Sudhir in on appropriate protocol. He provided a step-by-step approach or checklist to moving forward in a case of this nature. A detective for dummies checklist, if you will. He also agreed to help Sudhir out, and scan the area with him, and thought it might be best if the three of them went to the parent's house together. He made it clear that this was Sudhir's case, but didn't want to have him feel like he was out there on his own. They would help him and lead the investigation as a team, with Sudhir doing most of the detailed follow up.

The conversation moved Sudhir into thinking he had been too quick to judge the two, and he found himself gaining a new found respect for Mike as the day progressed—he hoped of Scott as well. Both looked like the Arnold who won Mr. Universe, versus the Arnold of today that spent his time ascertaining loans from the Federal Government to bail out the state of

California. Not saying Arnold doesn't look good for his age mind you. He was just not the buff, look-at-yourself-in-the-mirror-all-day physical specimen that he once was and that Mike and Scott now enjoyed being.

They arrived at University Avenue around 10 AM and started walking around. Most of the restaurants and bars were not open from the night before as of yet, and Sudhir thought to himself it was a little stupid coming here so early. Mike had decided he needed to walk around the scene to get a feel for the specific area. He very much believed that you had to get in tune with the crime. Visiting the actually scene where it took place frequently during an investigation had always helped him keep in sync with the direction he needed to head.

Their next move was to call Jill's parents, and see if she had yet arrived, and if not would it be okay if they stopped by and spoke to them for a few minutes. Since Mike and Scott had not spoken to Jill's parents yet it was decided that Sudhir needed to make the call and see if they could come over for an update. As he was dialing the number he continued to feel a hole growing in his stomach as his concern for Jill grew. He had difficulty thinking of her all alone sitting in some dark room waiting for something horrible to happen. Scared, isolated, and confined is a horrible way to look beyond this world and contemplate what your next step is as you play out your role in this universe or another.

He dialed her parents' phone number, and her father answered. No she had not come home yet, and they were worried sick, and yes please come over. Any help the police could be at this point would be very much appreciated.

When the three arrived it was clear to Sudhir that he had a lot to learn about what to ask and how to proceed, but when the conversation went into a lull he spoke up and let his instincts take over. He asked to see Jill's room, if she had a computer, if she was dating anyone (she was not) if anyone was currently angry at her, where did she work (she was going to school), did she have any hobbies (running).

The three were allowed to look around her room and see if they could find anything. Since this was not officially a missing person's report, as Jill had not been gone more than seventy-two hours, they still were required to ask permission and had to be careful not to upset anyone. They were allowed to take Jill's laptop. They received a list of phone numbers and addresses of her friends, running mates, and everyone the parents knew that she had contacted recently.

They split the tasks up between themselves of contacting the cell phone company, scanning the restaurants, polling friends, and looking through the computer. The next twenty-four hours seemed critical in the development of activities. Again, the feeling that Jill was taking control of his life was overwhelming. Sudhir did not like saunas that much but the few times he had been in one the initial suffocating feeling as you opened the door and made your way over to the wood bench was overwhelming.

A sauna seems to suck the moist fresh air out of your body and replace it with a heat that to him was unbearable. He had never lasted more than ten minutes in a sauna and felt the feeling must be similar to that of having your head forcibly placed in a plastic bag closing off the air as you gasped continuously for breath. The helpless feeling of being out of control, not afforded the luxury of one of your basic rights of breathing clean fresh air. He didn't like this feeling, but unlike the sauna he couldn't leave. He was trapped in this airless enclosure and felt his only release was to track down this killer and stop him before he had a chance to do anything else.

Sudhir had never met Jill and couldn't understand why he felt this connection, but he mourned for her and if he was alone might have started crying right then. God, he could only hope that she was okay and that his ineptness would not be the cause of her being harmed in any way.

The Next Day

I awoke around 7 AM. Still spent from yesterday's activities, but as usual I was fully alert. The flagpole was at attention, as they say. I immediately thought of Jill lying there anticipating what might await her and decided there would be no way that I could not take her again. I jumped out of bed and quickly maneuvered the obstacle course through the closet to the hidden room behind the door.

When I turned on the light I noticed that she was lying still on the bed. She had apparently relieved herself as there was a yellow tinted liquid circling its way beneath her butt and thighs. A slight stream had apparently rolled into a pool on the floor. She must have continued in her struggles to break free as the redness around her ankles and wrists were raw with dried blood and swelling.

I poured a bucket of warm water with a little soap and started cleaning her up the best I could, as a mother would a child who was ill and bedridden. She made some whimpering sounds as the warm water streamed over her taunt stomach and cascaded down the drain in the middle of the floor. It had been ingenious to install the drain, I thought to myself. It really would make cleaning things up rather easy.

Once I had her as presentable as possible, I slowly entered her for the second time. There was no struggle and no sound as she lay there silently. I tried to ensure that the movement of my love making was pleasant for her, but I could not get her to react at all. I started talking to her about how beautiful she was, and how the freckles on her face were flattering. I complimented her reddish hair, but still nothing. I started to lose the ability to continue as I slowly shriveled back into stagnation, and with every fraction of shrinkage my anger began to build.

Who could she possibly be to reject me? Who did she think that she was? She was average-looking at best. She was in decent shape but she was a leach on her previous husband. She did not even have the ability to support herself. She was worthless to society. Who would even miss this small grain of sand that contributed nothing to the world?

I had not even noticed that I had begun striking her with my hand, smacking her across the face. Her cheeks were now a bright red rosy color and seemed to be swelling before my eyes like a balloon being inflated for a birthday party. I must have done this several times, slapping back and forth as my right hand crisscrossed from cheek to cheek over and over again. I was shaking violently and uncontrollably and started to shiver as if the room had suddenly dropped twenty degrees instantaneously.

I jumped off her and ran from the room, hearing her sob quietly as I closed the door shutting her in the darkness. This would be the last time that Jill would speak to anyone, see anyone, or have any verbal or emotional connection to anyone on this planet. A slow bubbling sob that whispered quietly in a lightless room as her wrists and ankles were fastened into place. The last thing she would see was my smallish soft white naked body as I ran away from the rejection that I was facing yet again.

I slammed the door shut and ran to the shower. I lathered myself with shampoo and soap over and over again trying to wash the grotesqueness from my body. Who am I and how could I have ever done something like this? I just needed to get away. Go back to my house and forget that this ever happened. I went back to the closet never opening the door but ensuring that everything was closed tightly shut. I placed the contents of the closet back into place, concealing the door. This closed the life of Jill away from me and away from everyone she had ever known.

It didn't take me long to straighten up the rest of the house. I dutifully cleaned out the fireplace and the remnants of the night before seemed appropriately destroyed. The house itself was in decent shape as I packed up everything I had brought and ensured it was all in order before taking the baggage to my truck. As I opened the garage door my neighbor Dan was outside letting his dog Buddy do his morning duty. He called out to me, saying hello, and then he asked me where Delilah was. God Delilah, I had forgotten my dog back home. Like a tidal wave of reality hitting me all at once it was everything I could do to remain standing upright. I felt engulfed by the recent events hitting me again and again.

I shakily replied back to him that she was safe at home, and I was definitely going to bring her up next time. I had only made a quick trip up to grab a few things and was heading back now as I heard my voice quivering in a broken reply. I told him to tell Darlene hello, and I started up the truck and headed out.

I had made so many mistakes. I had not really even enjoyed the final prize. Everything was so wrong. It was supposed to be my greatest experience ever. Make everything worthwhile. Give me back my reason for living. My essence of being. My ability to feel whole and worthy to society. Instead I was driving through the arch of downtown Twain Harte shaking and crying uncontrollably. My tears were streaming down my face as my nose was running freely like the water from the faucet I had used to fill the bucket to wash off Jill's body less than an hour ago.

God, why did she have to be like that? I was nice to her. I was going to clean her up and give her food. I would have been a servant to her, washed her face, and gently brushed her hair stroke by stroke carefully and slowly. I am human, I have feelings, and the ability to be hurt and cry. If anything I am superior to her in that I was willing to give her life had she but tried to be nice and polite to me.

I remember very little of the first two hours of the drive, but at some point I could no longer stay focused on the road. I had to pull over on a small dirt lane, the same dirt lane that I had pulled over on the night that I had gotten Delilah. I had picked up Delilah for the first time from a breeder in Pleasanton. She had been returned as the owner thought her too insane to keep. Truthfully it was the poor sap's wife who thought this and had forced the guy to return his new best friend to its origins.

Finding the breeder on Craigslist, I had contacted her and one evening on my drive up for a weekend in Twain Harte had picked Delilah up with the girls and driven her to the house in the mountains. I had been afraid with her being in the car for three hours that she might have to let go of her small puppy bladder so I had pulled over on this very road and walked her for the first time. She never actually went but had acted crazy running then choking from her collar only to run again and choke again. That was the beginning of a pattern for her, as she was very loving and affectionate but not very bright.

I pulled over on this dirt and gravel road and parked under a tree that was about one hundred yards from the highway and cried. I curled up in the fetal position with the car shaking from my violent movements as I hysterical and uncontrollably let go of all my pent up despair. I must have drifted off to sleep as I woke up with my phone ringing in the passenger seat next to me.

It startled me, as this was the phone I had purchased at Wal-Mart. The kind of phone where you can pay for it with cash then activate it with no contract and no name and use it anonymously. It always seemed odd to me that these phones existed, as gangsters and drug dealers used them all the time. They were untraceable. To circumvent this, Wal-Mart only allows you to purchase these phones two at a time. It seems odd that this is our solution to gang violence. Limiting your purchases.

The phone rang again so this time I picked it up. "Hello, who is this," came across the line.

"Who is this" I responded.

"This is detective Takhar of the Palo Alto Police Force," came the response. "Will you please tell me who this is?"

I hung up the phone, turned the power off, and threw it on the floor of my SUV.

How could this be happening to me?

At times in my life I lost connection with myself. To state it clearly I completely lost all ability to form movements with my limbs and direct my actions consciously. It is as if I left my body and observed myself from a distance as somebody else seems to control my physical being. While these episodes are infrequent, and last briefly, this time was different. It was as if somebody completely took control of my being yet it was not me. At that time I realized I was changing and that my issues were deepening. I realized that I needed help but also realized that I would never allow myself to go back to who I was. The only way that I would ever be hole was in death as my essence was now broken forever. It is like walking in the woods on a quiet day. You are all alone and suddenly you step on a small brittle branch, and you hear the crack as it breaks resonating, echoing, throughout the trees as it bounces from one to another. Once you break beyond repair there is no going back.

MAKING PROGRESS

Sudhir's task had been limited to the computer and the cell phone company. Mike and Scott had taken the friends, family, and restaurants. The computer was very simple. Sudhir dropped it off at the precinct software guru's desk and asked him to find out any recent activity. Look for dating services, contacts or a diary, anything that might give him a clue as to what Jill had recently been doing or who she might have recently been with. The computer guy said "no problem," give him three or four hours, and come back.

Sudhir's next task was the cell phone company, and that proved slightly more tedious. First he had called the 1-800 line and asked to have the most recent activity for the phone number he provided. The generic attendant that answered stated that was against California privacy laws, and she was not authorized to give out that information. He then asked to speak to a supervisor, and was told there were none available.

Has there ever been a supervisor available when you needed to speak to somebody at a cellular phone company? Do supervisors even work at cellular phone companies? Finally in anger Sudhir started screaming into the phone that somebody's life could be in danger. He needed to get the activity on this phone number immediately. If not, he would be coming down there personally and making sure that everyone who impeded his progress paid the price that the victim might be paying by these delays. The vein in his forehead protruded out marking a long dark brown line, which occurred often when he got angry. He was then told to hold for a minute and she would see what she could do.

After several minutes she came back on the line and asked Sudhir to continue holding as a supervisor would speak to him shortly. After a total of forty-three minutes on the phone, a man (who sounded like he might have been twenty years old) picked up the line and asked Sudhir how he could help him. Sudhir then went through the entire story yet again as he was requested to start from the beginning. The supervisor politely said he would fax Sudhir a form. The form needed to be filled out and returned and once approved the data could then be given out. The whole process could be done within thirty minutes as this was an emergency.

Sudhir gave out the precinct fax number and hung up. He waited for the form and finally twenty minutes later it arrived. Simplistic enough, it took about ten minutes to fill out and was returned back to the same machine from which it came. Sudhir typed in the fax number and pressed the send button hearing the familiar squeaking tone informing him that the machine had made its desired connection. He had asked for the last thirty days of listings for phone as well as texts. He was most concerned with the previous night's activity and needed that immediately. Ironically, as Sudhir would find out later, the computer sitting on his desk was tied into this very database. If he had known how to access it everything he was requesting was there waiting for him.

Finally after another forty-five minutes of waiting the return fax arrived. There were a few numbers from the afternoon in question so Sudhir started calling these as priority number one. The first was to her parents, and he politely informed them of who he was again and apologized for calling. It was an awkward conversation, but he was moving quickly, and had not realized who he was calling before they had answered the phone. The second two were friends of hers, and he responded to them saying he was sorry but was calling them by mistake.

The fourth didn't answer on the first try so he called again. The second try somebody picked up the phone so Sudhir politely said "hello, who is this." There was a pause at the end of the line and the response came back of "Who is this." Sudhir gave the obligatory answer of "This is detective Takhar of the Palo Alto Police Force, will you please tell me who this is?" At that point the phone went dead. Sudhir was immediately convinced that this was a bad sign. A very bad sign. He repeatedly tried to call the same phone number again and again but it went straight to the recorded message stating that this phone's voice mail was not set up.

He then called the phone company and told them the story and after another hour plus on the phone was told that the number he was calling was pre-programmed. It was sold in retail stores across America and there was no way to track down the owner or the phone in any way. The panic was beginning to set in as Sudhir now knew for certain that Jill was in trouble, and he had no idea how to help her.

He had a nagging feeling in the back of his head that he was missing something. There was an oddity about the voice, a familiarity of some kind that he couldn't understand or place. It was almost as if he was talking to a friend in the brief verbal exchange and that instant bond was baffling. Could he be so far removed emotionally from society that the one connection he felt subconsciously was to a killer, and if so what did that say about himself. Is it true that in order to catch a murderer you have to feel and connect on a level lowering yourself to who and what the killer has become?

He went and told his captain immediately to ensure that he was aware of the pending doom he felt would have to be conveyed to Jill's parents. His captain tried to put a calmer spin on the synopsis, but he too had to admit that the likelihood of Jill returning was growing slim. Shit, this was more than Sudhir had signed up for when he became a small-town police officer in a college area known for parties and corralling underage drinkers.

He decided to drive down to University Street and meet up with Mike and Scott so he could inform them of his discoveries. It was their investigation as well after all and, he did not want to make more enemies than he already had. He made the short drive for what seemed like the one hundredth time in the last twenty-four hours and parked in the exact same spot he had the night before. He then called Mike's cell phone number, and was informed they were at Starbucks a couple of blocks away.

At this point they had not found out much. Sudhir was not thoroughly convinced they were even trying. They stated they had walked around to several of the local restaurants and bars in the ten-square-block area, but as of now they were not having any luck. Sudhir asked them for the picture of Jill they were using, and Scott stated they had just placed the entire file back in the car less than ten minutes ago. He could retrieve it if Sudhir did not have his own.

Sudhir opened his file and had remembered to include the photo of Jill that had been given him by her mother earlier this morning. He then decided he would walk the same path and ask around himself. He was gaining (as he had hoped) a little more respect for the two detectives but he just wanted to look as he had nothing else to do that afternoon. He couldn't face the fact that he was incapable of helping Jill.

Sudhir spent the next few hours going from store to restaurant to bar to store showing the picture to anyone who would listen. He finally did get a slight nod of acknowledgement at a local Italian restaurant where a waiter was pretty sure that he remembered her from the night before. It seemed that she had been in having dinner with a gentleman who was very nondescript. The waiter could really give no details other than Caucasian, average build, brownish hair, and an odd bite.

He seemed to remember Jill as the two had ordered a bottle of red wine and he remember the gentleman had drank most of the bottle while Jill only had one small glass. Either the guy in question was a heavy drinker and could hold his alcohol or maybe he was inebriated enough to have made a mistake. So far Sudhir was not finding out much that would lead to a conclusion.

He did talk to somebody by chance in the garage who apparently worked in one of the local restaurants. The man parked in the same spot most every evening and did remember the night of the exploding car. He also remembered a green Volvo XC90 SUV that had been parked in the corner close to the stairs. He remembered it because it was the same car that his sister drove and had the same small dent on the back of the trunk that his sister had. He had thought at the time in a laughing way that maybe the dent came as part of an option package. Leather seats, Bose speakers, and a small dent on the trunk lid in the back of your car. Sudhir did not think much of it at the time but noted it anyway.

As it was now well into evening, and he was not used to staying out late he decided to head home. The kids would be going to sleep soon, and Janine had already called him several times trying to figure out why he was not performing his daily tasks. What was he thinking by not being there to function as a father, watching the kids and checking homework? She could not and would not be the slave of the house. She was a working woman as well and earned more money than he did in his thankless job.

He was actually looking forward to getting home so he could have a glass of scotch. The day had really worn him down, and he was not used to getting this far into the evening without a little kick to help rejuvenate him. Sometimes he was surprised at just how reliant on the taste of alcohol he had become.

He made it home in time to grab his kids and give them a couple of big hugs. He heard about the fight that Matt had been in today, and how he had to sit on the wall. Sudhir might define it more of a scuffle than a fight as twelve-year-old boys are not quite ready to make the jump to fighting yet. At least Matt was not. He also heard about the bad mood that mom was apparently in, and how she did not like the fact that he was not home when he was supposed to be. Kids get the brunt of a lot of conversations that a rational, non-married person might think they should be left out of.

After getting them tucked in, and telling Tracey her bedtime story, he plopped down in his favorite worn brown leather lazy-boy recliner and turned on the TV. *Bonanza* was on Nick at Nite, and he would be able to catch the last forty minutes. He had always loved little Joe. He had remembered growing up wishing he was left handed so he could pull a gun out with the blazing speed and accuracy that Little Joe could.

He managed to get through about ten minutes before Janine laid into him. She chewed up fifteen of her own going through the long list of things that he had managed to screw up in the fourteen hours since he had last seen her. It was amazing to him the things that he could do wrong in the span of one day. He let her vent, and once she finished, he got up and poured another glass of scotch, sat down in the recliner until the next thing he knew it was 2 AM. He must have fallen asleep in the chair again. He seemed prone to doing this the last few years as the alternative (his bed) was occupied by his wife. He was not at all happy dealing with her unless he was forced to.

He got up, turned off the TV, and headed off to the warmth and comfort of his down pillow hoping that his wife had not taken that again as well. Another day would begin tomorrow, and he would have the pleasure of doing it all over again. Day in and day out. God, life was monotonous and unfulfilling. As impotent as he felt in his marriage, he now was transferring that same emotion to his job. He needed to find Jill and hold her in his arms. He wanted to tell her everything would be okay and see the eyes of her parents light up as he pulled in front of her house seeing her run to their waiting embrace. He knew that Jill was not a child, but every time he conjured up her image it was of a little girl, scared and all alone.

Instead he lifted his legs and felt with each step he was heaving concrete bricks attached to each of his feet. He trudged down the hallway to the cold bed awaiting him. He couldn't remember the last time he looked forward to slipping between the sheets next to his wife. It had been several years and no amount of synthetic heat emanating from the furnace would warm the widening gap of freezing unspoken words that were sifting between them at this point.

FREAKING OUT

I finally arrived home hearing Delilah barking in the back yard. She must have heard me shut the front door and was most likely wondering where I had been. I rented a little two-bedroom in Burlingame after I split with my wife. It was right off of El Camino Real next to a church of some denomination unknown to me. The church actually owned the three houses on my block and rented them all. They were reserved for the pastor, but apparently he thought the homes were not quite up to his standard and preferred to live elsewhere.

It was a charming old house. The windows never really shut all the way so you had a constant breeze filtering its way throughout. I had purchased a bunch of used furniture on Craigslist and had made it into a casual, slightly modern place to hang out. My oldest daughter has a bedroom, and the little ones sleep in the sunroom. The only down side was to get to the sunroom you had to pass through my older daughter's room. She really did not like the intrusion of her sisters coming and going as she busily went about her fourteen-year-old activities.

I split custody with my wife 50/50. I have the kids two days a week, and she has the kids two days a week. We split three-day weekends every other weekend. While it sounds reasonable, it was hell on the kids being transported back and forth. My wife would not listen to any other option. Once she made her mind up there was no swaying her—so why try. Probably the biggest reason I am no longer married to her is because she is neurotic about having things her own way. Then somehow she twists the blame back to me when things go wrong. She is like an evil little psychotic yo-yo.

I stripped off my clothes and headed directly to the shower. I was still shaking uncontrollably and did not possess the ability to stop myself. It was a miracle that I had made it home at all. I turned on the hot water full blast, quickly adjusted the temperature to a reasonable level, and jumped in. The warm, caressing water did manage to calm me down, but I was not able to fully relax. There is something so therapeutic about the steam of a hot shower as the warm water runs over your body. After a long twenty minutes curled up on the bathtub floor, under the steady stream that washed away my concerns, I finally shut off the faucets and toweled off.

I went straight to bed, lying on my back staring up at the ceiling. It was off-white and the walls were a slight taupe color. It was very similar to poop after you feed your baby a jar of ground up turkey or some other unrecognizable meat product. I lay naked, vacantly transfixed on the painted drywall above. Not really sleeping, but not fully awake. My mind wandered to my three daughters and back to my childhood playing with my cousins to work issues and to my soon to be ex-wife. I hated her with a passion. I focused on anything other than Jill, and what I had done. I couldn't bring myself to believe that it was really me who had killed somebody.

It seems odd that the first person I murdered I didn't actually see die. I wondered if Jill did die. I was not present for her death—was I actually a killer or was her death simply something that occurred. I did not stab her or shoot her or choke her with a rope. If she were smart enough she should be able to escape. In truth it was more her inadequacies that killed her. I didn't feel like a killer, and I didn't even see her die. I probably was not a killer at all.

Is the president a killer if he orders the deaths of several people in an air raid? Should I be punished any more severely than him, as he is not punished at all? I was struggling to see the difference. My mind then began another journey, and I started thinking about an attractive girl I used to work with. She was Asian and very thin. She had nice, dark skin but her face was still prone to acne even at her age, which my guess was late twenties at the time. I am not sure why I started thinking about her but I had a huge crush on her and often fantasized what her tight small perky breasts must look like underneath the form fitting shirts she wore. It was the schoolboy kind of crush where my tongue would fold up every time she was around, not allowing me to form words. My palms would become sweaty when I saw her in the hallway. I would have easily slept with her had I been given the chance. I later found out that would have been a mistake. She had a severe case of herpes. Can you imagine me trying to explain to my wife how I contracted herpes during our marriage?

I wondered if Jill had any sexual issues. I had made love to her without any protection. How was I to know what kind of person she was? I remembered hearing that when you sleep with somebody it is as if you slept with anyone and everyone she has. I started thinking about her husband, and his lover. How many people had they slept with? How could I have not used protection? The last thing I needed was to catch herpes or syphilis or God forbid something worse. Six degrees of separation is a real pain in the ass.

I turned on the light and examined my body for any signs of infection, or a small opening that might have allowed the entry of a virus. Not having ever done this before, I was not sure what I was looking for. I decided to get my laptop, go online, and do some research. I was appalled by the pictures of sexually transmitted diseases that popped up. Syphilis is a horrid disease, but there is a cure. It is simple to rid yourself of it once you have contracted it. The key is to catch it quickly. Apparently I was to look for a small, reddish sore that resemble a pimple. If not treated this pimple would grow into a much larger puss-oozing sore that would not hurt, but was disgusting to look at. The sore itself is whitish, surrounded by a reddish encrusted border, which continually oozes a puss-like substance.

I moved into the bathroom and started the exam all over again to take advantage of the higher wattage bulb. I hoped a more thorough viewing might put my mind at ease. I carefully looked through my nicely manicured hair between my legs, being careful to slowly and systematically review every square inch. As I painstakingly performed my physical I did notice a very small red bump in the upper-right section of my pelvic area just below the midpoint of my torso. It was bright red, like a ripe tomato, and about the size of a quarter of a raisin. I had never noticed this before but that is not to say it could not have been there. I had never given myself an exam of this nature.

I couldn't handle this. It was Saturday night, and I went to the liquor cabinet and poured a glass of scotch with a few ice cubes. I gulped down the first glass and poured another. This one took a bit longer to digest, and by the end of it I was starting to relax a little. I just had to get my act together.

On Monday morning I called my doctor first thing at 9AM. I told the receptionist it was an emergency, and I had to see my doctor that day as soon as possible. I was told that 11:30 was the earliest, but she would fit me in at that time. I had spent the rest of the weekend doing continual examinations. My pattern was to do my self-exam, find a spot or an issue that concerned me. I would then look at pictures online of all the possible outcomes, drink two or three glasses of scotch, and start the process over again once I sobered up. By Monday morning I was a complete psychotic mess.

Getting through the waning hours beginning the day while pretending to work was difficult, but I tried to be my normal flirtatious self. For a corporate accounting geek, I was always told that I was quite forward with most of the women that I came into contact with in the work environment. There was one girl specifically that was drop-dead gorgeous. She had a dark-skinned, creamy complexion and had an angelic personality. Late twenties, long, dark, black hair, she shifted between being about ten pounds overweight to perfectly fit. Currently, she was leaning more toward the perfection mode. She was full-figured despite that fact that she was only 5' 0". To top all of this off, she was the nicest, most pleasant person you could be around. I often told her that her biggest issue in life was going to be that she was too perfect. How or why she was not already married was beyond my ability to understand. I would marry her right now if she would have me but I seem to say that about a lot of women.

I made my usual morning stopover to say hi on the way to my office. Made the normal pleasantries "how was your weekend," "fine," etc. I finally arrived at my brightly lit home away from home and turned on my computer. Once settled I headed off to the bathroom for yet another self-examination, and the ensuing panic attack that came shortly thereafter. I had managed to find two red spots that seemed worrisome and one dark spot that very closely resemble a mole. I was interested in the different perspective that the changed lighting at my work bathroom would give me and my problem.

Lighting can alter your perspective drastically, given the different wattages, different types of bulbs, and even placement. It is like that *Seinfeld* episode where the lady looks gorgeous one time only to look horrible a few hours later due to the effects of lighting. It makes you appreciate the lighting crew on movie sets a little better. They have a tougher job than anyone gives them credit for in my opinion.

God, I wish that I could have a drink right now. I muddled through the next couple of hours then headed off to see my doctor, which was a quick fifteen-minute drive away.

My doctor was a petite Jewish woman who had a practice with her father and two other physicians. She was a smallish woman, about 5'3", with brown hair, and she was well-rounded. Not what I would define as fat but round. She was very pleasant, and matter of fact. She had been a referral from my boss two jobs ago, and I had kept her as I moved on now three jobs into our relationship. She was reasonable and knew me well as I had been visiting her for over ten years. I went into the building, strolled up to the desk, noticing the normal clientele of three people all in their seventies sitting in the waiting room. Have you ever observed that every time you go on a doctor's visit most everyone waiting for their appointment is sixty plus years old. My guess is that you must spend half of your retirement years trying to extend your life as long as you possibly can. Is it the older age that drives the smell in the waiting room as well, or is it simply the smell of sickness and decay? It is an aroma of sweetness, but not like candy. As if something you know is rotting, but still has a semblance of its former wholeness.

I signed in as instructed with my name and time of entry and the mundane admitting lady asked me what the appointment was in regard to. I had no idea how to respond to the inquiry, so I simply said it was a private matter I would only talk to the doctor about. She looked at me as if I had the plague and ushered me to my seat with a brushed-off wave of her hand. What was I supposed to tell her, that I was afraid my penis might be falling off due to my odd activity the last few days?

Twenty-five minutes later I was ordered into the examination room and told to wait yet again. A few moments later the doctor came in and sat down on her rolling stool. She navigated toward me and directly asked what the issue was. I explained to her that I had been with another woman, and I was now concerned that I might have contracted a STD. I was not familiar with how to know for sure, I told her, as I had never been exposed to this type of thing before. She went through the list of standard questions, how was my marriage, how were the kids, how was my personal health, did I have smoke detectors in my house, etc. Why does a doctor ask me if I have smoke detectors in my house? That seems like such an odd, random question as I wait to bend over and grunt like a stuck pig.

Once the questionnaire was filled in completely she asked me to drop my pants and show me the focus of my concern. I reservedly did so and pointed out the two reddish sores and the brown one, while trying to control the shaking feeling that I was able to contain mentally but barely control physically. She went through her examination, looking at the spots, adjusting my member back and forth with her latex covered cold fingers. She then asked me to raise my pants.

She informed me that the two red spots were something called "cherry moles" and that I most likely had them all over my body. I guess they are quite common. As she was talking to me she spotted one on my arm. "See you have one here as well," she commented. The brown spot was indeed a mole, and I had nothing to worry about.

She asked me if I had any painful urination or severe itching, which I happily responded to her I had not. She stated that I seemed fine, most likely had no issues. She advised me to try and refrain from any activity that would cause me concern or worry going forward. I agreed and left.

I only wish that this would have been the end and my mind would have returned peacefully back into place, but unfortunately this did not happen. I returned to work that day, and was fine for the next couple. By Thursday morning I noticed another spot and began to panic yet again. I spent the next four weeks visiting my doctor once each week for a spot on any part of my body that I felt might be some form of STD. I had blood tests taken for every STD that I could think of, and that my doctor would allow me to take. Everything came back negative. At one point I walked into the doctor's office, and the generic admitting lady simply responded to me by saying "you will be happy to know your tests are negative." I think everyone in the office thought I was crazy, and at this point they were most likely correct.

During the last visit with my doctor she asked me if a visiting physician could sit in on my examination. She stated that he was evaluating her examining skills as part of her ongoing education requirements. She hoped it would be ok if he listened as she discussed things with me. A very short five minutes into our dialogue on my current issue I figured out he was a psychologist. He was spending more time asking me questions and writing down notes than he was observing my doctor. It was at that point I decided I really needed to move on. The only way for me to do that was to go back to Twain Harte and bring closure to the entire issue. That meant disposing of whatever was left of Jill. God, I thought I would throw up right there in her office.

I decided that I would make the drive this weekend and finalize this chapter of my life. It was time to escort Jill out of my conscious thinking for good. I had not been contacted by anyone from the police since that initial call. I had destroyed my phone, and I just needed this to be over. Maybe I was not the serial-killer type. Maybe I was just a plain ordinary guy who made a mistake and needed that mistake to be buried. Again, it was not like I had killed anyone. I was not even there when it happened.

I already felt more comfortable. I left my doctor's office, promising that I would not be returning, feeling like I had just turned a corner. My neurosis was healed and I truly felt that I was on the road to recovery. I went back to work feeling better than I had in a long while and made plans to go to the mountains over the weekend.

Removing a burden that has been weighing you down is a refreshing, wholesome time in anyone's life. At that exact moment it feels like someone injected you with pure oxygen as the flow of youthful energy rejuvenates your essence. I felt reborn with a new outlook on life, and even though I knew the feeling was fleeting it was nice to sit back and enjoy it today. I did not want worry about possibilities and maybes that could or might occur down the road.

Nothing New

Sudhir spent the next few weeks canvassing the local establishments, talking to Jill's friends and relatives, and reviewing the same data and facts over and over again. They had set up a small task force and spent several days at the Hammel's house going through all of Jill's belongings. Sudhir had gotten to know Jill's parents (Bob and Rae) and her autistic daughter Riley. He felt like he was part of the family and therefore was sharing in their pain and the same sense of loss as if Jill had been his sister. Mike and Scott had long gone from the case. Although they were still listed as primary detectives Sudhir was the only one spending any time or effort to find Jill or figure out what happened.

The computer had proven helpful. Jill definitely had gone out to meet somebody named Lewis for an initial date. Sudhir had tracked down the profile and found it led to a lock box address that had been opened for a very brief period and had not been used since. The person who had opened the lock box paid in cash, and there was no other current mail being delivered there. He had the forensics team come down and look for anything around in or by the lockbox but they had come up empty. They had managed to pull the fingerprint of the local mailman, and he was quickly dismissed as a non-factor.

Sudhir had slipped back into his old routine of kids, drinking, and miscellaneous minor work related duties. He continued to spend all his free time on the data surrounding Jill's disappearance. He just could not accept that it would be written off as one of the hundreds of unsolved cases pushed aside by the many undermanned and underpaid police departments across the country.

Janine had taken to more business trips the last few weeks. It seemed that she was gone two or three days every week. He still could never figure out what the hell she did in HR that required her to be gone so much, but the last thing he wanted to do was ask. That would require a conversation between the two of them, and he avoided talking to her at all costs. Once you got her going there was no real way to stop her, and her monotonous rambling was more than he could stand.

Sudhir was looking forward to this weekend. He was having a barbecue at the house, and several families were coming over to hang out. He was planning and implementing most of the associated tasks, but it would be nice to hang out with the gang again. They really didn't get together enough. Ken would be there, and several other guys ranging from the local corporate accountant that Sudhir had grown up with, to his brothers and his wife's brothers who he saw most every weekend anyway. It was a good excuse to eat some grilled chicken and drink beer. He was Indian so his barbecues did not consist of the traditional hamburgers and steaks, but nicely grilled chicken and turkey dogs for the kids, which were always a big hit.

Lately, he had fallen into drinking more than normal. He even had reverted back to his old ways of slipping a squirt or two of vodka into his coffee at work. He was well aware of his problem drinking, but seemed to lack the ability to control it. He was pretty sure that he no longer cared. He was still able to devote energy to his kids, even when he was several drinks into the day. His sobriety was never questioned, as he liked the numbness that alcohol could bring, but never pushed himself over the edge to inebriation. He was always in control, but could never muster the energy of facing the day or evening without the fogginess that a quick sip helped provide.

Nobody other than himself was really aware of his excessive habit. He kept it well hidden. Everyone knew he enjoyed his gulps now and then, but not to the everyday extent that was reality. He really had his mouth to thank for even giving him the brief respite from his normal routine. If it wasn't for his doctor's advice he might not have ever tempered his habits, but the medication had forced him to slow down and so he had. He had given up dipping completely, cut back on his smoking, and slowed his drinking. His drinking and smoking had reverted back to their old ways, but he would never dip again. The growth in his mouth had cured him of this, if nothing else.

Isn't it odd to refer to a cyst as a cure? It had enabled Sudhir with the strength to stop dipping once and for all. His wife, of course, hated it. That was not always a good sounding-board, as she tended to hate everything. She was turning bitter in her middle age, and if the trend continued it would push her over the edge at some point. His love for his wife was genuine and he knew he didn't believe or condone divorce but ….Marriage in his mind was for better and worse. While the worse part had taken control of the union and dominated the relationship he held out hope that better would resurface at some point down the road.

The difficulty of staying married over an extended period of time is mostly challenged by the changes faced by couples as each one grows and adapts to new circumstances. As Sudhir got older, he realized that the metamorphosis needed to occur as a couple, so you alter as a team and a union. He now realized, and hopefully not too late, that they had started leading separate lives long ago. As they started changing individually that is where the rift threatened the foundation that began when they first said the words "I do."

Sudhir was surrounded by divorce and it seemed several couples he knew were splitting up. With the spoiling of children in today's society, it was most likely only going to get worse. Our humanity seems to be built on the "me" and the "now," and marriage cannot work if both parties are focused on themselves and not their partners.

He had no idea how to convey this to his wife, who he still loved deeply despite their current state. If Jill's case did nothing else it was reminding him how important his family and marriage was. He still held a passionate desire for the person she used to be. They both needed to refocus their energy, and he only wished that he could help guide them back to that directional path. He was going to look into counseling again, see if they could go back to weekly sessions, and maybe the dialogue would help foster a catalyst to better times. As soon as this case was concluded he would refocus on his marriage, and with the reprioritization of energy maybe they could find a way.

BACK TO TWAIN HARTE

I finished packing my car Friday evening after work. I again did not need a lot of items, as I kept the house in the mountains well-stocked. I did bring my laundry basket of dirty clothes as my new mini-mansion in Burlingame did not contain a washer and dryer. I seem to have a roadblock against buying them. The biggest obstacle was financial, but that had not stopped me from spending freely in the past. Since my separation from my wife the financial burden of keeping two houses running was having its toll on my credit card debt, and each month the mountain continued to grow.

After loading up I ushered my dog from the basement, and she excitedly made a beeline for the back of the SUV. She had her spot on a very well-worn moving blanket nicely folded for a bed behind the third row of seating. Not much room for her to move around, but she loved the prospect of going anywhere and was always exuberant to make a trip. She leaped into the back of the truck, and I closed the hatch right after throwing her a rawhide bone.

As with most labs, I imagine, Delilah could chew through a single large rawhide bone a day. She ate them like candy, but the more she chewed on them the less she chewed on furniture or shoes or anything else within her reach.

I jumped into the front seat, started the SUV, and headed out. I turned on the music and listened to the songs my oldest daughter had recorded on my XM radio. I sang along with most of them as the trip to my cabin home progressed. I am one of those individuals that must be moving and/or active at all times. I am constantly flicking a pen, tapping my foot, or padding my hand. The music and singing helped me divert my overly active energy in a positive direction.

I hit traffic at the 880 Interchange, which happens more times than not, and instantly knew that this would be a nighttime drive. I was already leaving toward the end of the day but had hoped to make the bulk of my journey in the waning light. It was not to be the case. As I sat in traffic, I contemplated what I would find and tried to block it out of my mind. It only made me anxious, and I was starting to lose the ability to control my anxiety. My neurotic preoccupation with fantasy STDs was just starting to lapse, and I did not want to replace this with anything else right now. My nerves really needed time to heal.

As I finally made it through the Los Angeles-like congestion of Pleasanton/Dublin/Tracey the evening was now well into night. It was approaching 8:30 and the sun was a good hour into its round trip on the other side of the world. That was when I received my first e-mail from my ex-wife-to-be. Our current mode of communication was e-mail. We had attempted face-to-face discussion that never ended well. We then had moved into phone conversations that always erupted into a brawl that could be turned into video game, and had finally ended contently with e-mail as our only conduit for discussion.

You can say whatever you like through e-mail and vent your frustration in a one sided conversation. If you chose you don't even have to read the response. Her monologue started off blaming me for taking files, two pictures she had thrown in a closet, my grill, and two lawn chairs from our house. When I had picked up the rug the other day I had also grabbed a few other items.

I was a little taken aback at first on how to respond logically, which my wife does not understand the definition of anyway. I took our files as I had told her I was going to since in the few months after I had moved out she had not looked at them once. Ironically she continued to ask me questions about their contents even while they were in her possession. I had finally stated in e-mail that I would just pick them up as it didn't seem to make sense for her to have them if she was never going to even look at them.

I took a grill, which she had never used. I took two of the nine lawn chairs, which seemed reasonable, and two paintings that she hated and kept in the back of a closet. This was the kind of person that I was trying to deal with in a reasonable manner. I stated the above to her as nicely as I could and kept my response brief and to the point. I think that is how you are supposed to try and reason with crazy people.

She replied, calling me a thief and a liar. Telling me how underhanded and sneaky I was, and how she couldn't believe I had sunk so low as to steal things from her house. Keep in mind that the divorce was still not final. I had taken relatively nothing from the house at this point, and she was calling me a thief. The conversation took a negative spin from there, and we continued to banter back and forth calling each other names and genuinely being childish.

God, she really is the definition of insanity. I only wish that I was low enough to forward these e-mails to her group of alcoholic friends, so they could see the instability that I had to deal with for fifteen years.

My wife had become a deranged sperm bank for anything with balls on Match.com, and now she was accusing me of pilfering leftover junk that she didn't even want. Apparently too much semen intake through the mouth starts to rot your brain. It must be something like eating too much candy rots your teeth. Her head had liquefied into a slushy, salty repository that was devouring her ability to think clearly.

Unfortunately, this interaction reached its crescendo just as I was exiting the freeway at Manteca. I was now on the little two-lane highway that twists its way up the mountains toward Yosemite. During the twenty-mile stretch between Manteca and Oakdale I happened to see on the side of the road a car pulled over. A lady waved her arms frantically. Since my blood was at a boiling point I pulled over in front of her car and backed up to within inches of her front bumper.

As I exited the car it was very dark. The streetlights were nonexistent, but the road was instead lined with pecan trees neatly stacked up in never ending rows. She informed me that her car had broken down, and her boyfriend had left fifteen minutes ago to jog ahead to the nearest gas station and ask for help. She anticipated him being back in another thirty minutes or so, but was growing apprehensive being on the side of the road by herself.

She was in her mid-twenties would be my guess, very slim, with what appeared to be sandy blonde hair. At one point it had obviously been dyed blond as you could see her root structure in the dark of night lit by the glow of her headlights. She was around 5' 3" and about 110 pounds. There is no way that the large protruding breasts that shot out of her skin-tight tank top could be real. Not sure why she didn't have a coat on, but the chill of the night had added a perky benefit pointed in my direction. Her nipples protruded straight ahead like the tip of a ballpoint pen that has just been ejected from its resting place.

I walked up to her, balled up my right fist, and cold cocked her right in the head. It was like slow motion. I watched my hand slowly moving forward my fingers clenching in a tight round ball being shot through the air. My knuckles became redder with each inch of motion as I compressed my fist into a small sledge-like sphere. My middle finger knuckle connected first, as my fist flattened out against the left side of her nose and cheek. The cartilage and bone seemed to cave inward with a snapping sound that for some reason brought back the memory of the rice crispy commercial where "snap crackle and pop" were featured.

She went straight down like a tree that has just lost its roots, and has no ability to stand on its own. I still had the chloroform in the car from my previous encounter and dumped some on my hand and quickly pounced on top of her covering her mouth and now bloody squirting nose with my hand. She was groggy from the shock of the moment and did not even put up a fight before she lost consciousness. My hand smothered her face with blood shooting between my fingers. Her nose was like a little volcano that was having a small eruption.

I moved her to my car and threw her in the back seat, not even bothering to tie her down. I ran to the driver's seat and jumped in throwing it into gear and slamming on the gas. I squealed off of the curb throwing gravel into her headlights as the car twisted onto the road and sped off. What in the hell was I thinking? It was one thing for my wife to push me over the edge, but another thing to act stupidly without thought of the future. My goal from the beginning was to always be smart, and I was being anything but.

Delilah was standing up in the back staring over the row of seats at our new addition. She had a quizzical look on her face, as if she was wondering what had happened—and if I knew how ludicrous I had become. I looked back and did not see anyone behind me. As I did so I caught a glimpse of the blonde's belly button ring protruding out from where her tank top had bunched up underneath her large supple breasts. Her tight designer jeans were about two inches too long and frayed on the bottom covering her sandals of which she only had one remaining on her left foot.

God, she was beautiful, even with the swelling and redness that now covered her face and was seemingly dying her hair an unnatural reddish color from the blood. The eruption had already slowed to a steady trickle. The color of her skin was turning a dark purple and grew each minute as the swelling moved over her features. She was going to be very sore in the morning, or at whatever time she gained consciousness.

The additional hour drive through Oakdale along the twisting, curving highway toward my house in Twain Harte was uneventful. I again pulled through the main street underneath the arch that proudly displayed the town name welcoming you to this sleepy quaint village where kids could play on the street and nothing of any significance ever seemed to occur. If they only knew the acts that were now being committed, I wondered how many of them would remain or if the town would be forever tainted by the memories that would be instilled.

I hit the garage door opener as I pulled into my driveway, and watched the door slowly being sucked back into the garage by the chain installed on the roof overhead. Delilah as normal was antsy to relieve herself and bolted from the back immediately upon my raising the rear hatch. As usual she reacquainted herself to the area sniffing and zig-zagging back and forth. She finally found that perfect spot that had been reserved this day for her and her alone to saturate with her bodily fluids.

Everyone needs that one true connection to reality that keeps you grounded and focused on what is real, and what is just sheer fabrication. Delilah was my link. She was the source of my connection from the brink of moving into another world to understanding the lines that were being crossed. My kids were my only hope at being a whole person, and the love that they projected was a gift that cannot ever be taken for granted, but Delilah was always there for me. Dogs are the perfect companions because of the non-judgmental unconditional love that they will always have every single time you open the door—no matter what kind of monster you have evolved into.

God What a Mess

I closed the overhead door to the garage so I could do the rest of my activities in privacy. I opened the door to the house and trudged up the stairs with Delilah dancing around my feet half jumping and half bounding taking the stairs quickly only to stop and pause at the landing above. I thought it was odd but with every step I began understanding why she was acting unusual.

Once when I was younger I remember eating a potpie with my cousin and my father for dinner. The three of us sat around the brown, laminated kitchen table on the brown vinyl covered seat cushions. With our utensils we dug into the circular aluminum foil turkey/beef filled crust-encased $1 meal. I can't believe these things were ever invented, and that people actually ate them. For a man with no idea how to cook my father thought they were a staple in the dietary growth of myself and anyone else he needed to feed.

As I brought my fork to my mouth about three quarters of the way into devouring my tasteless generic bite, I remember seeing a one-inch cylindrical shape. It was a slightly darker color than anything else in the creamy filled wasteland of my plate. I held it out in the middle of the table and my cousin instantly labeled my current find, screaming, "Oh gross, a worm!" In reality it was only a portion of meat product that had not completely been ground up, and was compressed into something that was labeled beef. It must have escaped the processing cycle enough to remain in some semblance of its original shape.

I stared at the lifeless two-inch worm-shaped object and felt a rumbling in my stomach. I thought about what else I had just begun to digest. The rumbling very quickly rose to a frightening level, and I knew that I was going to be in trouble. I dropped my fork instantly, covered my mouth with both hands, and bolted through the living room. I aimed for the bedroom and the bathroom that was beyond. Unfortunately my ten-year-old body was not quick enough. Midway through the living room the creamy non-digested substance sprayed through my enclosed fingers covering my mouth in a multi-tiered fountain. I left a trail through both rooms all the way to the bathroom.

By the time I reached the toilet and raised the lid everything had already evacuated my body. I simply heaved a couple of last gasps. My father, who was disgusted with my inability to contain myself, screamed that my stupidity was beyond childish. He stated that I would be required to clean up every drop of undigested pea, corn, and creamy substance off the walls, floors, and furniture.

There are some memories that remain with you for your entire life. They are formed like hardened concrete into your psyche, and once there are forever embedded into your foundation as immovable as the concrete forms of a football stadium. The smell from this episode in my childhood was one of those memories. It took me two hours to clean the sprayed chunky mess that was seemingly everywhere. With every wipe and dab my nostrils filled with the putrid smell of the partially digested remains.

This is what I smelled as I moved upward. With each step the smell intensified until it was overwhelmingly the only odor that I could consciously recognize: the putrid, decaying smell of rotting death. I opened the closet door and walked through the hidden entrance in the wall in the back, and the gust of rot knocked me to my knees. All of this did nothing to prepare me for the sight that lay on the metal bed.

I have been to funerals and have seen the death of older people. The wrinkled soulless shell of what had once been a person. Nothing I had ever been through could have prepared me for what I saw. I did not even attempt to hold my mouth, as everything I had eaten for the last two days violently spewed into the room and surrounded what at one point I had called Jill. I didn't stop to be thankful in the moment but in retrospect continue to think how lucky I was yet again that nobody had rented the house in the last few weeks. How could I have ever explained this smell emanating from inside the walls?

This entire episode took a few short minutes, and I remembered the blonde. As disgusted as I was, I knew I still had to act quickly. I surprisingly felt little remorse. Possibly because the thing I saw held such little resemblance to a person. I filled a bucket with water, kicked Jill's blackish purple body off the table, and watched it bounce down to the floor like a helium-filled balloon that had lost its ability to maintain flight. I threw the bucket of water on the bed, washing the remaining residue of Jill's body from the rubber mattress. I then went to retrieve the blonde from the back seat of my SUV.

I threw her over my shoulder and easily carried her up the stairs. Gently placed her on the bed, and fastened her hands and feet in the same fashion as Jill's. What an improvement the new model was compared to the last. Even in the moment, I felt aroused by the beauty of this girl.

Now I had to address the overinflated monstrosity that was once Jill, and how to purge the smell and memory of her current state from this room forever. I luckily remembered that over the summer I had moved eight gallons of muriatic acid that had been at my now ex-wife's house in El Granada. We had a pool at that house, and when we made our original purchase the previous owners had left much of their cleaning equipment and supplies behind as part of our house closing gifts. Since I had not needed it for cleaning the pool I had decided to bring it to Twain Harte. I had thought I might be able to use it to remove the stains off the garage floor from some bad car experience that must have leaked out over the years.

I went down to the garage and retrieved a large plastic bucket. After a couple of trips I also lugged up four gallons of the acid. I carefully poured all four gallons into the orange home depot all-purpose bucket and then turned to Jill. Since my house was surrounded by trees—like a mini-forest in the middle of my small town—I had a nice serrated hand-saw for cutting limbs. This seemed logically like a good tool to start dismantling Jill to a size that would fit in the bucket. I did not want to try and move her in this condition, and I was definitely scared to touch her. She seemed like she might burst with any prodding.

I went down to the garage yet again for what seemed like my twentieth trip and retrieved the saw. I then began the dismantling, cleaning, and slow disintegration of Jill. The initial cut was quite interesting as a fountain of yellowish puss squirted from her body in a never-ending spray. I literally saw her start to shrink as the liquid pooled around her and headed in a rippling stream down the drain in the middle of the room.

I carefully removed parts of her body by cutting the joints as you would when you carve a baked chicken, yet this was easier as the sections were barely fastened together. I felt like a surgeon must feel but instead of trying to configure pieces I was the maker of the puzzle deciding where and how to cut each slice. Creation comes in many forms, and I honestly felt whole for the first time in a long while. After placing each apportionment in the muriatic acid and watching the skin dissolve I realized I would not have enough to do the entire body. I did feel I could get it down to a manageable level.

About halfway through the process I went down below to the fireplace and stoked an inferno from the wood set off to the side. Next I prepared to place what was left of Jill (which would not dissolve in my container) into the fire. I attempted to break her down into an even smaller pile of remains.

It took me around five hours to stuff the entire contents of Jill into the fireplace, and then I started the painstaking task of cleaning the room. Her bones were burning rather quickly as the few weeks of deterioration and the acid seemed to have softened them, making them more susceptible to the flames. I used a gallon of bleach trying to remove the smell of my past meals and the leftovers of Jill. They had mixed together in different spots forming a bond of pools throughout the room. Through all of this my new addition had remained still, slowly breathing in broken gasps but not moving nor showing any signs of realization to her new situation.

After everything was completed I shut off the light, closed the door, letting the last trickle of evidence sift down the receptacle in the center of the room, and went to shower off. The glass enclosure was a relaxing solitude where my thoughts seemed to drift away, and as always I felt calm and secure. I toweled off and fell into the large king-sized bed and was asleep in less than five minutes.

Nothing during the day had gone as planned and my mental instability seemed to be growing with every twenty-four hour interval that clicked like the timer on a bomb waiting to explode. I was confused and unsure of what I was becoming. I wondered in half conscious half subconscious thought if this is how a caterpillar must feel. It wraps itself tightly into a cocoon and drifts off to sleep not fully aware that when it awakens it will be to an entirely new world. Its life will have forever changed. How can you begin to understand with a rational mind the transformation of turning into a creature that can fly after having a simple relaxing slumber? Waking up as if just being born, a new being who can now and will forever be able to see the world in an entirely new perspective. I felt as if this would be my last night as a caterpillar. Tomorrow would be the awakening of a butterfly that would have the abilities both mental and physical to conquer this world.

Starting to Have Some Fun

I awoke the next morning feeling refreshed and opened my eyes to the brilliant light flowing through the windows. I felt exhilarated and renewed and wondered what I should do first. I thought about the beautiful blonde girl awaiting me in the next room. The feeling of an early morning rise of energetic manhood become taut with the anticipation of the wonderful treat of which it was about to partake.

I reflected back on the previous evening and wondered why my activities no longer bothered me. I could no longer deny that I had dealt a fatal blow to a human being that had meant no harm to me or anyone. She was innocent to the extent that an adult can be and had a child that would be at home wondering where her mother was and why she would never see her again. How would it feel going to bed every night without a comforting warm hug or a kiss goodnight from mother? "Please read to me mommy," would be words that the child would never again speak, or even if she did would remain unanswered as her mother would never again utter a single phrase.

How would her soon-to-be ex-husband handle the responsibility of being burdened with an autistic child? Would he consider her an albatross, or would he relish in the ability to be the sole comforter in the child's life forever? Jill's mom and dad would still play a role, I am sure. There is a huge leap from parental love and affection to grandparents who at this stage assumed their direct child rearing days were beyond them.

How would they all react to the knowledge that there was not even a remnant of Jill left on this planet? A few decaying bones that were half dissolved from liquid acid, and the ferocious heat from the furnace in the TV room downstairs. Nothing left. What must that feel like to be completely removed from the world in the short span of a few hours? I am not sure what to think of the sadness to lose somebody forever and have the gnawing feeling of not knowing what happened. No ability to say good-bye to your loved ones or have them say good-bye to you would be an eerie feeling.

I again felt the tenacious clawing feeling of despair creeping back into my conscious thought, threatening to gain control and cloud what had started out to be a gorgeous, warm sunny day. I had plans to implement, and I was not going to let myself be swayed from having fun and letting loose.

I had now gone further down the path of darkness as I was sure dismembering and disposing of a person was evil. It was an act worse than simply killing somebody. I don't really understand why this is but in the grand scheme of commandments the slow disintegration of a human being must be pretty close to shutting all light out of my current psyche.

I finally rolled out of bed, no longer content to reflect on my actions, and had no energy left to decipher who I was or what direction I was headed. I jumped into the shower, quickly washed, wrapped my towel around me and headed into the closet. With every step closer to the door I felt the familiar rise of manhood growing tense with anticipation.

My beautiful blonde girl was awake when I opened the door and turned on the light. Her face was still swollen and now contained the familiar streaks of blackness running down in streams of tears from her near perfect green eyes. Even with her makeup smeared and splotchy she was a gorgeous specimen of the human race. I seemed to have renewed her anxiety upon entering the room and felt that my being naked was probably causing her great concern.

I slowly started removing her clothes and had to use a pair of sharp silver scissors to cut through her skin-tight jeans. I was not able to pull them over the metal handcuffs that firmly held her small, perfectly smooth skinned ankles in place. She remained still during the surgical procedure of being undressed, and continued to sniffle and whimper as her layers of protection were removed.

The naked body is an amazing thing. The skin is the single largest organism that a human being has. A living protective layer that acts as a barrier to so many different intruders over the span of a lifetime. My current blonde fascination had a milky white complexion, and I admired the small moles and marks that sparsely covered her near-perfect body. Her breasts were amazingly spherical, again leading me to believe that she must have purchased them at some point in her life. Nobody could possibly have two masterfully aligned breasts that were firmly implanted in exactly the right location.

I decided that I would try an experiment. I was curious as to what level the human body overrides the mind and takes control away from logical thinking. She was obviously very distraught, and in no way was thinking sexually, I imagined. Having an orgasm at this point was one of the last things that she could possibly be dreaming of. I wondered if I stimulated her long enough would her body allow her to feel pleasure?

I slowly kneeled down, gently spread her legs, and kissed her on each inner thigh delicately running my tongue up circling until I zeroed in on my target—teasing and attempting to please her. I rhythmically used my tongue and fingers and began to taste the familiar moistness that comes with the excitement of arousal from every woman's inner sanctum. I felt her begin the rhythmic rocking as her body started keeping time with my fingers as they probed deeper and more forcefully. My tongue, fingers, and her body flowed together in unison like an orchestra reaching the crescendo of a wonderful symphony.

She came in an explosion bursting forth going in all directions as natural as spring water being shot from a tube at point blank range. Apparently a woman's body can orgasm even in the worst situations—our sexual drives seem to have a mind of their own. Her body began to relax, as her butt and legs settled back into the black rubber mattress that felt somewhat more like plastic.

My own excitement had been building with each thrust of her hips, as I was also ready to explode from the fifteen-minute episode of satisfying such a beautiful creature. I moved into position, and with a few short strokes, reached my own apex of happiness as I burst forth and shot all of my pleasure inside her, filling her with a part of me. It seems that once you make love to somebody you will always have a part of that person. Joining somebody in this intimate contact is more giving than anything else physically you can do.

I looked into her light-green eyes as I removed myself from our recent connection and saw the sadness welling up within her. She had a blank far-off stare that seemed to be saying she was disconnected from what was occurring, and although her physical being was participating the rest of her was in another land far away where life was simple and without pain. I rolled over to the side of her—letting my right leg straddle hers—and rested my head on my hand, propping it up with my elbow. I looked into her eyes and pondered her vacant expression. I wondered what her thoughts were and why she did not utter a single word.

The sadness was coming back to me, and I now hypothesized that the blood flow from making love once completed reversed back and the emptiness left a hollow feeling in the pit of your stomach. As boys go through those teenage years the guilt of masturbation must be the byproduct of this same scenario. I hypothesized that prostitution is not the sole source of man's physical affection because a woman's true love has the ability to make you feel good in those moments after climax when men are most vulnerable.

I felt sorry for this girl with no name. She was just standing by the road. Not bothering anyone. Stranded by sheer bad luck that drove circumstances in a direction that she could not control. Where would she be now, and what would she be doing if I had not happened along and taken control away from her and now forced her down the path that I chose. Is that what God must feel like, with the ability to force things and events, shaping them in whatever form he chose?

Did this make me a god of some sort? Knowing that I held all of the power to destroy or reshape the life of this person? I was now all that she would ever know. I was her sole source of sustenance and interaction. She would never again hear anyone else's voice or talk to anyone other than me. I was her beginning middle and end from now and for all of her future as short as that might be. I felt like a god with the power to grant or end life. I could do anything I wanted.

Another idea popped into my head that seemed to perk me up. I had recently gotten a tattoo in the form of a cross that was composed of intricate loops weaving their way around my bicep. The process of getting a tattoo hurt like hell, and I vowed that the next time I got one I would ensure it was in the middle of a lot of alcoholic drinks.

I decided it would be fun to brand my new-found toy much like you would a cow to ensure that everyone knew it was my property. This seems to be the same concept that vampires have in most movies, as they talk about their human helpers and in some cases mark them somehow. This would give me a fun project for the day. I quickly kissed my blonde Barbie doll on the forehead and headed out to look for something that would do the trick.

I bounded upstairs with new-found energy letting my manliness dangle and flop around like a balloon blowing in the wind. There was no need to put on clothes or clean off, as I wanted to spend the rest of the day completely devoted to playing with my toy. I looked for something metal with my name on it, or my initials, or something that would just be cool to imprint on her perfect soft, white skin. I pulled open the top drawer of my dresser and luckily found one of those small toy license plates with Duncan emblazed across its perpendicular blue background. Lucky again, that should be my nickname, I decided as I was really having a good run of events going my way.

I turned on the gas stove, got a pair of salad tongs, and held the license plate directly over the heat. I don't think the metal was made for this kind of temperature. It very quickly started to soften and bend and was well on its way to liquefying. I ran through the closet door, and held my new branding equipment in front of me.

My blonde prize was lying still, staring into the ceiling, and did not seem aware that I had again entered. I quickly lowered the license plate directly on her stomach, firmly holding it in place with a towel that had been lying nearby. Wherever this girl had been for the past several hours, she quickly returned with a shrill, high-pitched scream that resonated off the walls and threatened to shake them like a miniature earthquake. Her legs and arms rocked against her bindings, and her movements reminded me of *The Exorcist* where Linda Blair violently vibrated on the bed when the demon took control of her small body. The only difference was I did not get to see the blonde's head turn a full 360 degrees, but it appeared at times to come close.

At least if nothing else she was now going to be a part of the rest of the day. She had a frightened, panicked look in her eyes as if she were just now starting to comprehend what position she was in. Her screaming continued until I took a rolled up piece of duct tape and forced this ball into her mouth, and then took additional pieces and tightly closed it into position. I enjoyed her joining the party, but I was in no mood to listen to the screaming banter of a girl who understood far less about the world than she would ever comprehend.

I put down the tongs. Carefully, using a corner of the towel, I pried up the license plate. It had embedded itself into several layers of skin on her stomach. The detachment was like trying to separate one of the grocery store tags from a pear. You always end up with a 1/8 of an inch into the pear removing a large chuck of the fruit upon the separation. I don't know how far in the new opening went, but the letters of my name seemed to be rising from her stomach surrounded now with a slowly forming pool of blood. Wow, this was truly amazing. I was again getting aroused but knew that I would very quickly tire of this game. I was already starting to think of what the next girl would look like, and how I would get her into my new fun land.

For my final treat of the day I decided it would be interesting to find out if I could possibly time my climax with the exact moment that this young girl's life ended. She seemed somewhat lethargic right now, as the pain from the branding experience must have been too much for her, and she was soundly passed out. Isn't it odd how your body shuts down when it comes to the realization that it cannot tolerate the level of pain that it is being forced to endure.

I again jumped up, ran to the bedroom, and grabbed my pocketknife from my pants pocket that had landed on the floor next to my bed the night before. I ran back to the blonde, and again my stiffness began protruding upward with each step closer. I took the blade and slashed a nice two-inch cut on the wrist of her right hand and watched as the blood started a steady stream to the floor below as her hand dangled over the edge of the bed.

I then entered her and began to feel her squirm beneath me as she slowly awoke from her pain-induced nap. She looked at her wrist and watched me as I moved back and forth. Her newly found panic only further enticed the building of my excitement as the realization of what occurred flowed into her facial expressions. She was flailing her arms but could not reach me to do any physical harm. This had the added affect of spraying me with her blood. I bathed in the thick red liquid while continuing to thrust in my methodic action.

Her arms began to lose energy, and you could sense that she was literally being drained of her life force. Her eyes began to lose any kind of light. At this time I was fully covered in her blood and exploded inside her like a shotgun blast rips into the flesh of a deer at point blank range. It felt like I was in an orgasmic state for hours while the sheer pleasure of the moment seemed to be never-ending. When I did finally look down into the face of my little blonde Barbie doll it was only to see the life at its final stages. Although my timing was off by a few minutes I had indeed reached my goal and realized that from this point on I would have to kill everyone in this very fashion. I could only hope that the second time around continued to hold the same level of pleasure as this.

I removed myself from my now lifeless partner and decided to leave her there for the rest of the day and go take a quick shower. I toweled as much of the blood off that I could, threw the towel in the corner, and headed into the tranquil relaxing refuge of my warm water flow that I enjoyed so much. The day had been perfect, but I was spent. I needed to relax, watch some TV, and figure out how I could spend the rest of my time in my quaint little home away from home.

SHE IS SPECIAL

I had known Sarah for a few years and it was through her that I met Hannah. We were not close friends but acquaintances. At times we found ourselves having a drink together but our relationship was strictly platonic. I found it funny that Sarah on a night where she had consumed a huge amount of alcohol told me Hannah's story. Sarah was a good friend of Hannah's and on most occasions would not have divulged so much. I doubt she even remembered telling me all that she did. Alcohol can make you do funny things sometimes.

Hannah would be turning thirty-one in a few weeks. She had two girls. One was fourteen and a freshman at Burlingame High School, and her younger daughter had just turned eleven and was in middle school. Hannah worked a low-paying job as an assistant that her friend Sarah had gotten for her three years ago. It was Sarah who had convinced Hannah to move up to the bay area from her then current location of Alabama.

Hannah had lived a charmed life in the beginning. She was the prom queen, the head cheerleader, the homecoming queen, and she was still drop-dead gorgeous although admittedly she did have to work at it now. She had grown up in a small town outside of Huntsville, Alabama, and most of her family still lived in the area. All her young life, she had dated Eric. He was a football legend in her area and had led their high school to two straight state championship titles. He had a scholarship to USC and had been the newest great arm that was supposed to lead the Southern Cal Trojans to their next championship. It had all seemed like such a blur for Hannah.

When Hannah was a junior in high school Scott had been a senior, and it was during that year an episode occurred that would change her life forever. Scott was having a few people over to his parent's cabin down on the lake and had asked Hannah to come along. At the time Hannah did whatever

Eric told her to do. She had truly felt lucky to be a part of his life. Hannah described Eric as having an energy that would rival the little pink bunny on those battery commercials. She felt he held a seemingly hypnotic power over everyone around him.   His touch and his personality were like magic that people and things fed from to make their lives meaningful.

Eric should have felt lucky to have somebody like Hannah, and apparently have her he did. Hannah had given herself to Eric freely since the end of her freshman year. She did as she was directed, and there was no limit to what she was willing to do if he but snapped his fingers and gave her the mandate. Sarah had disgustedly described Eric and the adoration that Sarah had felt for him before that evening. It was easy to see how much she hated this man.

Eric had driven them down a rocky road, which left a permanent impression on Hannah's memory. It had been odd for Eric to take Hannah to his retreat with four of his closer friends. She was normally not included when the boys decided it was a night out on their own. She had known that boys needed to have their space to roam and vent to give them an outlet for their endless energy and exuberance.

The long, gravel road had been bumpy and uneven in the four by four Ford truck that was given to Eric by the local dealership after he had won the first state championship. The truck had been a black, sleek symbol of what was wrong in the small town. Grown men worshiped a local hero who was still a boy and allowed him free will about the town as if he were somebody to be placed on a pedestal instead of a juvenile in need of guidance and mentorship.

Hannah had ridden in the passenger seat. Two of the boys had been in the back, and two others in the bed of the truck with Rocky, who had been Eric's mongrel dog. Crippled since birth with a shorter right front leg that only allowed him to hop around, Rocky had been Eric's constant companion and the only real thing he loved. Everyone else to Eric was just a means to an end. He was destined for greatness, and the rest of the world was just parasites along for the ride. Hannah had been naïve and trusting of Eric, but that night changed everything for her as the kids made their way to the destination.

The overhang next to a one-story two-bedroom house that must have been built about two hundred years ago was imprinted on Hannah's memory. The house had been musty smelling with a creaky wood porch that held a three-seated swing. It must have come straight off the set of *Gone With The Wind*. At the time Hannah had felt a little tinge of the cold night air as she waited with her white cotton shawl dangling over her shoulders. She remembered hoping that Eric would hurry up and manage to get the key in the right spot, as he had always struggled to open the creaky door.

Once the doorway was breached, the lights immediately were switched on, and the old console wood-laminated TV was tuned to the local Alabama game. As usual, Eric had grabbed a beer from the refrigerator, waited for the door to latch shut, and then pointed to the bedroom that was just off the living room. Hannah had known what the signals meant. She had dutifully went to her place and started to disrobe so she could make love to the boy she had adored her entire young life. She had realized he wanted to finish before the game started, as it was the highlight of the week to see Alabama University play football.

Eric was not your typical youngster from Alabama, nor was he typical for anywhere. Hannah described him as having the ability to shrink a room to the size where he was the only thing that mattered. He was always the center of attention, and was totally and completely the focus of everyone he knew. Unfortunately he had and most likely still does care only about himself. He had grown to believe what everyone said and thought and now felt that he truly could do no wrong. The world had been his to command as he saw fit.

Hannah performed her girlfriend duties that night, making sure that Eric was pleased in any way that he needed up until the point where he was spent and could be pleased no longer. As was normal, the entire process from beginning to end took no more than ten minutes, and then he lay next to her telling her how special he felt she was. Their relationship would be the one to last through all eternity. He had a way of saying things that could make anyone believe they now had the ability to conquer the world. They too were going to be the one carving destiny versus being a cog in a wheel that turned and moved as it saw fit.

As Eric left Hannah that night, he leaned over to her and said how much he loved her and was so proud that she would do as he said. He had whispered to her how much it meant to him to be able to trust her to play the role that he had instructed and devised. At that point, after Eric pulled on his jeans and walked out of the bedroom door barefoot and shirtless, he raised his hand, pointed his thumb in the air, and yelled out "next." Hannah quickly understood what that night was meant to be.

There were four other boys that had accompanied them to the cabin, and Hannah was to know all of them intimately, and some of them more than once. Who was she to question what Eric had commanded. Who would even believe her if she had tried to tell the world what kind of person Eric was and what he really did to humiliate her and degrade her. She had been just a tool to be used for whatever purpose he desired. Hannah had done as instructed that evening and ensured that each boy was pleasured and fulfilled to his climatic finale. Each boy had the experience that he needed and was gratified to his endless rapaciousness.

Sadly enough, Hannah married Eric a few months later, as she had become pregnant from that evening. Despite their misgivings Eric's parents had insisted he do the honorable thing, since he was the father of the child. Nobody knew any differently. It was the south after all and there was a code that needed to be upheld. She had then followed him to USC, where she attended a junior college for one year. She ended college after her first year to follow Eric back home. It had only taken Eric two years to get kicked out of school, and lose his scholarship for conduct detrimental to the team.

He had taken poorly to not being the star that he was projected to be, and apparently everyone was a little bigger and quicker in the college arena. His skills were not able to compete at quite the level everyone had predicted. He and Hannah moved backed to their small town, had another baby, and she watched Eric disintegrate into a lowly drunk with no goals—only a huge belly and a smell that seemed to emanate from him at all hours of the day.

It is amazing that Hannah had ever made it out of that hell, and if it were not for Sarah she most likely would still be there today. Hannah had met Sarah in her one year of junior college. Sarah had gone on to graduate, transferred to USC, and got her degree in accounting. She now worked at a corporation in Foster City. Sarah's friend had owned a company and needed an assistant. Having kept in contact with Hannah, Sarah gave her a call, had her move to the Bay area, and got her the job.

Hannah lived in a small two-bedroom apartment off Broadway in Burlingame. She worked for the last three years in her current job and went out periodically with what seemed to be a long list of losers. Her past dates were either married and wanted a fling or were themselves past heroes of some level or another but who were now just alcoholic wannabees waiting for their life to end.

Hannah attempted to be a good mom and provide for her kids to the extent she was able. The small two-bedroom apartment was the maximum her low paying job would allow, which meant her two daughters had to share one bedroom. The schools were great in this small bay area community, so at least both her girls would get a good education. Hannah's parents had both died a couple of years back and would never know the sadness her life was and continued to be.

The oldest daughter Laura was perceptive and picked up on the bleakness that oozed from her mother's pores. They were both good kids who gave Hannah little trouble and had to fend for themselves much too often it seemed as of late. After Sarah had introduced me to Hannah it was through our daughters that we became better connected. They both attended school together and had become friends.

Laura was my biggest advocate to her mother. She continued to comment on how funny I was and how cute. I had made the kids pancakes one morning when Laura spent the night, with crumbled up chocolate bars which was amazing to her. Sarah was intent on fixing us up and Laura was helping my case immensely.

Pancakes prepared by a father in the morning were something Laura had never been exposed to. Even the concept of a man in the kitchen who was doing anything other than preparing to leave was foreign to Hannah's daughter.

Hannah's dating life continually found her sitting in a bar across from another failure who might even be married. Her experiences in that area were less than pleasant. She tended to wander off during conversations lately, as they all seemed to roll together. There was nobody left that was interesting in her mind. It seemed everyone did the exact same job and lived the exact same life as everyone else. It was all meshing into a jumbled ball of Playdoh.

Hanna's mom always warned her not to mix the colors. Don't roll everything together, Hannah. It will all form into one big ball of colorless brown goo and you will never again be able to untangle it and see the bright spectrum that you were meant to enjoy. Ah, such is life. The colors had long ago faded for Hannah, and she described her life as a brown mess and would never amount to anything more.

The odd thing is, the cycle that we all find ourselves in seems to closely match that of our parents. Whose parents did not always want more for their children than they had for themselves? We all want our children to succeed in ways that we never dreamed. Holding themselves above the group and status that they were born. Every little girl dreams of being a princess, but in reality we all know that is just not the case. Most slippers get tarnished at a young age, and once the dirt gets embedded it seems impossible to ever get clean again.

INTERESTING EVENTS

Sudhir woke up early as usual in his recurring slightly hung over still somewhat drunk stage. In the last several weeks he had found that the closest to sober he ever seemed to get was in the morning right before he had his cup of coffee with a little vodka kicker. He recently could not even make it until after his shower, but preferred to grab a cup with his jolt before jumping under the soapy water.

He was still unable to get Jill her out of his mind. It had now been several weeks since she was last seen, and he knew the odds of her ever returning were minuscule. He had kept in touch with her parents, who had also given up hope. They were starting to plan a ceremony for her friends and their relatives so they could all say good-bye. Under normal situations it might still seem too early to give up all prospects completely, but with the evidence in play it seemed she was not coming back.

He had downed his first cup of coffee, and it was settling in to his system warming him to his inner core. The comforting spray of the shower ran down his head and settled in a pool circling his partially plugged drain below. He watched the swirling water as it continued to build, but eventually found its home in the unknown black hole down the drain. His almost hairless head was most likely to blame. He would have to work at unplugging the jumbled mess this weekend.

Sudhir continued to feel there was something more he could or should be doing. Even if Jill was murdered, he had to bring the responsible party to justice. He didn't feel like he could continue without having some conclusion to this madness. He must have drifted off into one of his daydreams which were lasting longer than normal lately. He heard his wife outside the curtain and knew that if he didn't exit soon he would be berated for taking more than his allotted time.

He waited for her to leave then jumped out, quickly toweled off, and threw on his polyester slacks and faded plaid shirt. He then went in for another cup of coffee, as he began preparing the kids' breakfast. He could already hear the rumblings of bickering coming from down the hallway, as they awoke and immediately began the debate from the night before with refreshed vigor. As he placed the waffles on the table Rachel turned on the TV, which had recently become customary for breakfast. A Volvo commercial advertised the new model of the safe and secure XC90 SUV. How ironic, he thought.

He turned to the TV, and began to wonder how many Volvos were sold in the Bay Area. He wondered how many XC90s were in the Bay Area and additionally how many were green. He felt for the first time that he might actually have an idea to move forward with. It was a long shot, for sure, but worth a try. He hurriedly fed the kids and shuffled them into the car as he herded them to school. Once in the office he began his search.

He had gone through some training since the phone incident and was becoming more comfortable with the information available online. There was an extensive car database and registration information available. He should easily be able to pull up how many models were registered in the surrounding area—exactly what he was looking for. Five thousand, one hundred and seventy-eight XC90s of the green color. Sudhir felt that within this list somewhere was his guy. He pored through the registry of names briefly, but realized this would not be the correct way to move forward. He decided to shrink the list down by using only male-registered vehicles, as it would seem odd that a woman would be performing this type of crime. This only narrowed it down to 4,187—most cars are registered under a male's name it seems.

His next thought was to focus on crimes where a XC90 was involved. Maybe that would narrow it down. He canvassed the recent crime reports involving missing women, referenced a Volvo XC90, and was surprised at a recent occurrence. Apparently near the town of Manteca just a few days ago a Volvo SUV was seen pulling away from a car. A woman had been abducted. She had not been seen since. Her boyfriend had been picked up and questioned, as he has a record for some minor incidents, but nothing had added up for him to be further detained. Sudhir decided he would drive up to the local police station and see if there was any chance that this crime was in some way connected to Jill's disappearance.

On the drive up he realized this morning was the first morning in a long time that he had not had a shot of anything to start off his workday. Not counting the pre-shower pick me up, of course. He simply felt driven and purposeful at the thought he might actually have found a lead. He called ahead to make an appointment and to be sure the local detective assigned to the case would be able to see him. He was assured this would be acceptable and continued on with his trip.

Once in Manteca he headed to the local station and discussed the case with Philip, the detective assigned to investigate. There was an incident with Brenda's car (Brenda being the missing girl in question), and at the time her boyfriend was with her. They had been out at a local bar, but were actually heading home early. He stated that she was feeling extra open-minded, and he had wanted to take full advantage of the timing, so they were in a rush. On the way home they had an issue with the car and pulled over on the side of the road. He had jogged ahead to the local gas station and just before he made it back to the car he saw a Volvo SUV pulling from the side of the road where Brenda's car remained.

When he arrived she was not there, but he had found one of her sandals on the ground in front of the car. He did not have a cell phone on him at the time, he had forgotten it at home. By the time he had jogged back to the gas station and called the police a couple of hours had passed. He was questioned and everyone at the bar was questioned and everything followed his story. She seemed to have just disappeared. No note, nothing just gone.

Sudhir shared his own case with Philip, and they both assured each other that they would keep the information flow going if and when anything came up. Sudhir was given a copy of all the case notes and interviews that had occurred and he left with his stack of new documents. He spent the rest of the afternoon and evening scouring through the details, hoping that something would enlighten him, but nothing connected. Finally around 9 PM (and after several calls from Janine) he called it a night and headed home.

He again realized that he had now gone the entire day without a drink—save the good morning sneak. He took his vocal beating upon his arrival in good spirits, went to his solitude in the living room. He relished in the comfort of his visual and auditory escape again with *Bonanza* on Nick at Nite. He really was not paying much attention as his mind continued to float around today's findings and he instinctually felt sure that the two incidents were connected. This meant that he now not only had a killer he was tracking but he had a serial killer of at least two victims.

Sudhir decided he would start over tomorrow. Look through his case details and the now connected incident of Brenda, and see if anything seemed linked. Jill and Brenda, two girls that might not be able to live out their lives as they expected—and were due. Who has the right to take a life that is not his or her own. For the first time in his existence, Sudhir had known in his heart that given the opportunity he would be able to use his gun. He had always wondered if at the moment he needed to react if he would be able to actually pull the trigger. He truly felt that not only would he be able to, but if given the opportunity, he would enjoy it. This person needed to be removed from earth, and he needed it to happen quickly.

He couldn't conceive of having to add another folder to the stack of two in his lap. He couldn't even remember placing the folders in his lap, but he now held them as he would his own daughter Rachel close to him. He wished he would have been able to protect the two women and keep them out of harm's way.

The helplessness one must feel as they see their child taken from them in an act of violence must be one of the most heartbreaking experiences that a parent can face. The only thing worse would be the forced ineptness a parent feels as his or her child becomes addicted to drugs. The parents are forced to watch the painful demise of the child as they deteriorate into nothingness consumed by an inability to say no. The only positive thing he could think of is this was at least a faster move into death.

The slow demise of a son our daughter over an extended period might be more than he or anyone should have to handle. In the end both arrived at the same location. Death of a child leaves a hole that should never exist and can never be filled. A hole that can rot the insides of a parent until they too might find themselves falling over the edge never again having the ability to return.

A CHANGE

I awoke the next morning disappointed that I had nothing to play with. I now wished that I had allowed my new found toy a one day reprieve so I could appease my appetite again. As usual, I woke up ready to start my day off with a bang. Unfortunately, this was not to be, so I started the process much in the same way that I had cleaned up the remains of Jill. With my blonde toy there was at least a semblance of her former self, although it was marked with a hollow vacant stare. She was as cold as the frigid air outside, completely drained of her life fluid.

Cleaning up took me the better part of the day, and once completed I piled the remaining bones in a corner of my special playroom and marveled at what a diminutive pile the two women had now become. There was not much left of my ladies in waiting and hopefully during my next trip I could whittle them down to nothing.

I arrived home on Sunday afternoon, unpacked, and decided to do some grocery shopping. My three girls were going to arrive again on Monday evening, and I did not have any of the basic staples in the house. I shopped, did a few additional mundane chores, then sat down to catch up on some work and watch a little TV.

It was odd making the transition back to "normal life." I felt the familiar twinge of guilt at times when I dropped off my girls, and relief swelled in my bones at having peace for a few minutes. I can only describe the emotion as a few seconds of calm and serenity shortly replaced by a longing emptiness when I immediately wish they were back. They have a way of keeping me grounded with their wholesome, non-conditional love. The eyes of a six-year-old telling you she loves you is a moment that should be preserved.

The girls arrived in their normal chaotic manner. As usual my fourteen-year-old was in her same teenage moody way. She was so hormonal, and taken to attitude swings, it was difficult to try and decipher what was going on in her head. We went through the routine of dinner, homework, showers, brushing hair, which is never a great activity. For a six-year-old girl especially, it is constantly filled with screaming and crying with every knot that is detangled. My attempt at sensitivity makes the exercise last for thirty minutes or more. How could I be so caring at times, and yet so callous in my other life, I thought as I put the two little ones to bed and settled down for the evening.

My oldest wanted to talk so we discussed the current living arrangements. She has continued to ask over the last two months if she could live with me exclusively. I had always tried to discourage this, as I feel it is important for a child to have a positive influence from both her mother and her father. I personally feel her mother is incapable of positive influence—but nonetheless felt she should have both. She began crying and explaining how I didn't understand how bad it was there, and how her mother was constantly screaming at her and making it unbearable to live.

Eventually I caved and said, okay. I would give it my best shot and see what I could do, but it would be a difficult battle. This was the umpteenth time we had this conversation, and it seemed that she felt strongly and genuinely was having trouble living there. I would later learn I should have stuck to my original thinking, as teenagers change their mind like the wind shifting around a bonfire. No matter where you stand you tend to get smoke blown directly in your face. There is no winning.

I had a court date set up that week anyway, and was expecting to receive my wife's filing very soon. Sadly, this came the next morning. My attorney had warned me that in the process of getting a divorce I should expect my wife to blatantly lie about one major thing in my life. Not embellish or extrapolate, but completely and totally lie. Since I was the petitioner and asking for the divorce he stated it was a very common occurrence coming from the respondent. As I read the filing that he faxed over, I was astounded at the contents.

It was a ten-page document focused completely and totally on what an ass I was, and how I had spent the last fifteen years making her life miserable. I had apparently stolen all her money from her (but I had no idea where I must have put it). Every decision ever made was my fault, the kid's problems and issues were all derived from my immaturity, and I had an inability to see or do anything correctly. It was hard for me to contain the explosion in the pit of my stomach. It is like a volcano in a cartoon where the top is plugged by an artificial cap. You see the mountain trying to explode, but the cap holds it secure as the mountain gyrates up and down, attempting to let the pressure escape. My attorney had warned me how odd a filing it was. Once he completed reading it, he was still unsure what she was asking for. Normally there is some kind of request—her entire goal seemed to be only to disparage me in public.

I immediately called my attorney to say how disappointed I was. He stated that she would lie but other than her name, I was not sure if anything else was factual. She continued to surprise me in terms of low she could sink. Just when I thought she might have hit bottom, she found the ability to dig her hole deeper and move further down into the sewer where she seemed to enjoy working. The only time she refused to bend over in our entire marriage was when I had requested oral sex. For that she stood up straight and firm, resolved not to ever cave to something so disgusting.

One of the lowest points in our divorce was when I found out she was reading her boyfriends profiles from her dating service to our eleven and six year old daughters. She actually sat down with them, reviewed her dates, and showed them pictures. This was long before our divorce was even final. Her inability to think logically and beyond her own selfish interests astounded me.

To make matters even worse, the document she filed was public. This meant that everything she had written could be viewed by anyone with a computer and a desire to look it up. She had written personal stuff about our kids, their activities, and issues that could now be viewed by anyone. If I had not hated her with every fiber of my body already, I certainly did now. I am not sure what level of emotion runs beyond hate, but that is now what I felt for her. Hate, although a strong word, was nothing compared to my feelings at this point in time.

This of course goes against all the counselors' advice on getting a divorce. You should try and have as positive a relationship with your ex-spouse for the sake of the children. This seems to be the key to keeping the children as whole as possible. What the counselors failed to realize was this is the same woman who, on the day we had set aside to tell the kids we were getting a divorce, lay in her bed with the TV on. Upon my arrival she stated "This is your show, you can do whatever you like." Leaving it up to me to explain to the kids what was happening and why their mother and I thought it best that we no longer remain together. This was with *Friends* blaring in the background, as she lay on her ass and watched TV.

I only wish that her so-called friends and family could see the real woman they thought they knew and respected. If only I had a camera and could videotape a few of her select episodes, everyone's opinion of this insane two-faced lady would change drastically and immediately. Her own family would be appalled at what kind of person she truly was and had become. She could rival the late Heath Ledger and be cast as the next villain in the Batman sequel. She was that far-gone and apparently that good at acting.

I decided to allow my older daughter the luxury of staying with me full-time, but this would now change my continuing plans. My pent-up anger was building, and no release seemingly possible with my daughter as a constant companion. I really needed to change my mode of operation and try to discover a new outlet. I was intelligent enough to realize that if I did not find a new avenue I would one day explode, and my sadistic ex-wife would be the recipient of years of pent-up anger.

This was and would always be unacceptable. My children needed a mother, no matter what. Even if she was twisted, and her favorite mode of communication was warped facts and deformed truths, they still adored her. I could not allow myself to use her as the outlet for my anger. I would have to find another release.

Unfortunately, my preoccupation with my long-term married lover was also starting to take its toll. She was continually demanding more and more of my time as things with her husband deteriorated. She was becoming increasingly paranoid that I was going to leave her behind and move on now that I had my newfound single status. She was correct in the last assumption, but I knew the only true way to rid myself of her completely would be expiring her as well. She would need to go at some point. I just had not figured out a logical solution as of yet.

My first two participants in my newfound hobby had been unique and allowed me to explore on a very personal level my hidden desires and fantasies. Unfortunately I knew that my living arrangements would now drastically minimize my free time. I needed to find an outlet for my bottled-up anxiety, but I needed to do it in a way that would be over quickly and concisely.

Hobbies were something that I was becoming more and more familiar with. Upon the decision to get divorced, I had decided to explore things that my controlling, perverted ex-wife would never allow. One was looking for a new job that I could truly say I enjoyed, two was spending more time snowboarding that I had taken up only last year, three was kite surfing, four was scuba diving, five was writing a book (which I am now doing in my memoirs), six was taking control of my life. I no longer was willing to accept the verbal abuse that I had for the last seventeen years and this meant finding an outlet for my frustration as well. I also enjoyed the fact that my children were able to participate in snowboarding, and I hoped that they would one day take to kite surfing or scuba diving. My youngest was already a very accomplished skier.

I often think of how Atlas must have felt in the tales of Greek folklore. How he was responsible for holding up the world, and his sole job was ensuring it remained propped up on his shoulders. What a huge responsibility it was to provide an environment for everyone to feel content. They could move about their lives and do as they pleased. This had been my marriage. To prop my ex-wife up and hold her hand through every decision that was ever made, only to have her point a finger at me and blame me when anything went wrong. She manipulated me into making decisions so she did not have to, but I was only allowed to make the choices that she stipulated. This allowed her the luxury of blaming me for anything and everything that ever went wrong in our household.

Number six on my list was the most important to my sanity, and since I now had to find a new avenue to move into I decided I would try something unique for me. The two things I kept from my military days were my pocketknife and my 9MM Beretta pistol with a suppressor (silencer). My wife never knew about the latter, and I was never able to keep ammunition in the house for my fear that I would load the gun one evening and shoot her point blank in the head. I would have to aim for the mouth, though, as I am not sure that she used any other body part from her shoulders up. Her ears were simple receptacles for her earrings—she had never listened to anything I muttered in our entire marriage.

This was an unregistered weapon. At the time of my purchase several years ago, it was still relatively easy in the southern states to purchase a gun of this nature. You did not have to tell twenty plus government agencies and ask permission. I got the gun out a few weeks ago and commenced shooting it now and then at a local range. I kept it in my SUV in the floorboard underneath the mat in the back by the spare tire.

My decision was to drive to San Francisco, guilelessly pull out my gun, take a walk in a couple of dark alleys, and shoot the first homeless person that I saw. I would then casually walk back to my car, get in, and drive away. I was concerned with this plan for two reasons.

One, I of course could be seen and identified by somebody. This didn't seem to be a major issue, but was a consideration all the same. I couldn't imagine anyone caring if one less homeless person was on the streets of San Francisco. There seemed to be an abundance of them every time you walked down any sidewalk. It was difficult going to dinner and seeing a play downtown, anymore, without partaking in the pleasant aroma of street urine and pot smoking that could be seen openly on any block anywhere.

The other issue was release. This would be different than my first two encounters, as I would not be able to sit and relish in the death or get to know the person before I became their gateway to another world. It would be impersonal, and I was concerned I would not gain the same level of elation that I had from my first two activities. I was willing to try this new idea, but I did not hold out a lot of hope that this would appease my growing hunger.

I was continually remembering the movie *American Beauty,* and the random scenes of death the boy character helped institutionalize. How he had taped the brown paper bag as it randomly flittered up and down, while seemingly going nowhere. Just floating along, entranced in it's own world. How he stopped and peered into the dad's eyes, as he lay there having just recently been shot. The preoccupation with suburban society had been overshadowed by the look at death from a new angle.

I decided to give it a shot, so to say, and since I had a dinner plans later that week would try it out on short notice. Unlike my first two events, this was really doing a service to the city. Everyone was trying to continually find an answer to the homeless problem, and maybe I had stumbled upon the perfect resolution.

A NEW RESOLUTION

Sudhir decided he would give himself one week. He would go through every name on the Volvo list and see if there was any way that he could narrow down the possibilities. He felt strongly that the person he was looking for was right before his eyes; he just couldn't figure out how to find him. A needle in a haystack, as the old saying goes. You see the haystack, and you know the needle is in there, but how do you go about finding the damn thing.

While he was going through the list, he would continue to monitor the current cases that came up across the scanner for anything that had any reference to a Volvo. He was sure his killer would continue to use the same vehicle.

Four thousand, one hundred and eighty-seven names. He would start alphabetically and research each person, methodically weeding through each and every name. The more in tune Sudhir became with the process of being a true detective, the better he understood how tedious the systematic approach could be. The painstaking attention to detail. The lifting and sifting of every angle, reviewing the same facts and details over and over again. Looking for the one small crack that would lead to the hole this sick individual was hiding in was what it would take. He now fully realized the need to return to the scene of the crime, as that was the one true connection he had with the killer. The actual place where the killing began.

He had strongly urged his captain to allow him to contact the FBI. Sudhir knew a local agent and felt that their profiling capabilities would come in handy—the murders were starting to spread. His captain refrained from allowing it, as there was no concrete evidence linking the two murders to each other. Besides, the random memory of a SUV might or might not actually be the abductors vehicle.

Sudhir started with the first page of his list of named Volvo owners. He sifted through and accumulated three piles. One group was a no chance, another group was a possibility, and the last group was a likely suspect. He sorted through names, calling some, asking about a dent in the back-end of their vehicle. He simply stated that he was with the police department and was worried that there might have been an accident. People who answered negatively went straight into the no chance pile.

He filtered race and age. The abductor had been described as definitely male and Caucasian. He also eliminated anyone that was below twenty-five and above fifty, giving himself a wide margin of error. He felt great after day one. He had managed to get through 650 names and had successfully eliminated five hundred of them relatively quickly. It continued to feel as if he were reaching into the ocean, his bare hands hoping to come up with the one pebble that he needed so desperately to find. He decided to call it a day and ensure that he arrived home on time to deflect any unwarranted hostility from his better half.

By day three he was half-way through the list and his initial first day ratio was holding true. He had eliminated 1,700 names from his list. He had 296 possibilities and he was left with four names of the first two thousand that had some issues. Unfortunately for Sudhir he got distracted. He was unknowingly close to a breakthrough, but across his screen came an alert about a shooting in San Francisco the night before.

A homeless person had been shot at point blank range in the head three times. Another homeless person was also shot, but in the midsection twice. Once right through the heart and once in the right lung. Both were dead upon arrival. There had been a third homeless person that had been hidden in the same alley, and he remained in his dirt filled trash receptacle sanctuary until after the killer had left. He did not see the wielder of death himself, but as he scampered out of hiding and peeked around the corner saw a man getting into a green Volvo and leave the scene.

While the two might again not be related it was odd that a Volvo had crept into all of these random crime scenes. Sudhir decided it was worth looking into and made the drive down to San Francisco that afternoon to see what he could find out. He talked to the local authorities, who gave him the flimsy file and said he could do with it as he pleased. The two murdered individuals were crackheads in and out of trouble on a consistent basis. Nobody would miss them. Sudhir thought to himself that at some point the two had families, and as misguided as their lives might have been somebody somewhere was going to feel some pain at their no longer having a chance at recovery.

The one lone person to escape that night in the dark alley was a local bum who had been on the streets for the past twenty years plus. He lived in that alley for most of the past ten and was well known in the neighborhood. He was an alcoholic but a decent soul who never really bothered anyone, and even in his most inebriated state was a pleasant enough person. The local hoods left him alone as he had become somewhat of an icon, and he seemed to be beyond reproach from the police or any of the low-lifes that frequented the area.

He was the Switzerland of Market Street and even the local establishments tended to give him scraps and keep him in good health. He apparently was well-known to the areas law enforcement and most everyone liked the old guy.

Sudhir drove down to find the homeless guy Samuel A. Adams, as he was known, and see if there were any further details that might have eluded San Francisco's finest. Nothing against the San Francisco police force. They have a great reputation, and Sudhir did think highly of them (although that is an extremely generic thing to say about such a large group of individuals). But in a case like this it would be given little to no priority. If Sudhir was not concerned nobody else would follow up.

Sudhir found Samuel A. Adams on a park bench sitting two blocks from the infamous Orpheum Theatre right on Market Street. Sudhir found a parking spot, paid his exorbitant fee to stay there for a short period, and went wandering up the street so he could converse with his eccentric witness. He had been given a description, but it wasn't hard to recognize Samuel—he held court for anyone who would listen that he had witnessed the next great San Franciscan killer. He and he alone was the sole survivor of what would be called the greatest killing spree of all time.

The crowd quickly dispersed upon hearing that Sudhir was a police officer, which allowed the two men to sit and talk quietly without interruption. Sudhir soon found out that Samuel was quite a talker. He had grown up in Chicago, on the South side. Had been raised in the projects and would have died there if it were not for boxing. He at one time was ranked as high as number seven in the light heavyweight division and would have gotten a title fight within a year if it weren't for the one bad hit to the head that dislodged something or other and after that he was banned from boxing.

He had flailed around Chicago for a while, but quickly found out that if you were a nobody then you were truly a nobody. People stopped caring about Sam very quickly when he could no longer fight, and he also found out how cold Chicago could be in the winter. He left in November, hitched his way out to San Francisco, and had been here ever since. He loved this city like it was his own, and although he had never given anything back, he was careful to recognize how nice the people of this area have been to him. He doesn't cause any trouble, and he never once has urinated anywhere outside of his alley. He has a spot specifically for that activity, and he goes there and only there.

Sudhir couldn't help but smile at the code of ethics that had found its way into Sam's thinking. Right or wrong, the man seemed genuinely good and had a decent heart. He was somebody that Sudhir felt he could grow to like, and if given a chance in another lifetime would actually be a great person. It was easy to see how a community could have adopted him.

They finally got around to the night of the murders and Sam had the story well rehearsed. By this time it was Sudhir's guess he had told the story north of one hundred times, and he immediately jumped into a dramatic showing that was not just a story but a reenactment of the events of said evening.

"The night was dreary and cold," he started. "I sat in the confines of the local trash bin doing my normal search and seizure mission for my nightly nourishment. Two of the local hoodlums were trying to move in on my territory and were attempting to take what was rightfully mine. I told them there would be hell to pay. This was my alley and everyone knew that. It was my territory and by them invading my space they were sure to face the wrath of the devil himself. He would swoop down upon them and strike them with his hammer and ensure that they did not see the light of the next day."

"They did not listen but instead started to harass me, and tell me that if I did not shut up they would make sure that I had no means to instigate another conversation after this night was over. I sat in my trash bin contemplating what to do. Looking out of the crack in the side devising my next move when he came."

"He walked into the alleyway. It must have been a little past 10:30 PM. The night took on a quiet calmness, and the noise from the street seemed to fade away into the darkness beyond. I sat and watching him, seeing the gun protruding like an additional appendage from his hand. Like it was part of his body, another limb that extended out unnaturally as he wielded it."

"The two morons did not see him until it was too late. They paid me no attention when I tried to warn them, and I sat stoically by as he raised his weapon of choice and pulled the trigger. Three times in the first one and then twice in the second. The one gentleman did not even hear the first guy go down. He had no idea what was coming. The weapon was longer than normal for a gun of the hand-held kind. It had a long stick on the end of the barrel and there was no noise to be heard save a slight swoosh as each round fired in sequence."

"He simply observed the two for a few minutes, after they fell into place. Watching them as you would a play or an enactment of historical proportion. It was as if he were committing the scene to memory so he could afford the luxury of replaying it over and over again in his mind in the safety of his home at a later date. After he had taken the surroundings in, he turned and walked back the same way that he had came. Retracing his steps, and slowly deliberately moving toward his escape."

"I stepped out of my bin after a few minutes and peeked around the corner only, to see him drive away in a Volvo SUV. I know it was a Volvo SUV as it is the same make and body type as the SUV on that billboard right overhead that has now been hanging there for the last several months. I know it was him that got into that car as I watched him for several minutes."

"He dismantled his weapon, and placed it in the back underneath a mat, then removed his coat and placed it in the back as well. He then went to the driver's seat, looked around, and got in. He started the car and slowly drove away as if nothing happened. No care in the world. The police asked me for a license plate number, but it was dark and I could not see anything that clearly."

"I think it started with a KY then something then ended in a six but that was the most that I got. I remember KY as it reminded me of Kentucky at the time. Isn't KY the symbol for Kentucky? I think it is anyway. The six is the age of my granddaughter that I will never see and miss more than I can ever tell you. You can't miss a granddaughter more than one you have never seen. Every time I think of her it is as if somebody is standing in front of me ripping my heart into tiny little pieces."

When Sam finished his story Sudhir contemplated what Sam had said. It seemed like a professional killing, yet that did not make any sense. The two individuals that were murdered were nobodies who floated around and paused for a drink now and then. It is as if Sudhir's killer had suddenly decided he no longer wanted to kill innocent women, but had now chosen a completely different path.

Was he randomly killing anyone or anything just for the thrill? Weren't serial killers supposed to follow some sort of consistent pattern? A mommy syndrome or hating their ex-wife or having been abused by their father. Didn't they look for individuals that fit a specific pattern, or at least kill them in a similar fashion?

His gut was again telling him this was the same guy but he had no idea how to sell this to his captain. He again felt he needed the help of the FBI, and at this point in time would try his captain again but if he refused would take matters into his own hands and ask for help—even if it was on the side, as they say.

He thanked Sam profusely for the magnificent recounting of the event and gave him $20 for his trouble. He would have to come back and visit him sometime as he had thoroughly enjoyed his afternoon story session and had taken an instant liking to the old guy. He made the trip back to his office and pored through his list of names and registrations. As was expected in this baffling case not one of his listed names had a license plate starting with KY.

It was as if this guy and his car did not exist. He found himself dreaming up images of the old cartoon character "Ghost Rider" and the recent movie with Nicolas Cage, "Next." How had "Ghost Rider" gone exactly? You suddenly turned into a blazing inferno skeletal demon and started killing off people the devil had told you to in some half-dream state of mind. You did all this with a whip of chain links that burned as well and laughed at everyone with your skull head.

Could it be possible that the motorcycle had been replaced by a Volvo, and the chain whip with a revolver? Nothing made sense right now. Sudhir decided to call it a day and head home. He would call the FBI agent in the next few days, but he needed to get his story together for his captain, and see if he could possible link the now four killings together somehow.

It seemed odd, even to him, and he knew it would be a tough sell. He would reserve the rest of his energy for the inevitable fight he was sure would be coming once he made it home. One thing in life he could always count: Janine being in a bad mood when he opened the front door.

Misdirected and Lost
Within Oneself

Hannah had woken up that Saturday morning to the familiar tune of the TV in the living room. Her two girls were already awake and had fed themselves on whatever they might have been able to scrounge up in the kitchen. It was difficult for her to get out of bed sometimes on a Saturday or Sunday morning. She at times lay in bed for a couple of hours, quietly crying to herself, as she lay lost wondering what the next turn of events might bring.

Occasionally her daughter Laura would find her in this state, and she would brush it aside and tell her it was nothing. She had simply had a bad evening. She knew that she could not effectively lie to Laura. She was too smart. She excelled in school, and was well liked. She had a good, core group of friends and had managed to stay away from drugs and alcohol. This would at some point be a problem, Hannah was sure, as all kids in high school seemed to fall to temptation at one point or another.

Laura took after her mom in a lot of ways. She was a rebel at heart and might have been labeled a part of the hippie generation had she been born a few years earlier. Unfortunately, she could also be swayed by the masses, and it scared Hannah to think of her beautiful darling daughter succumbing to the advances of some pathetic high school wannabe. Her youngest daughter Stephanie was gorgeous as well. They got along most of the time and relied on each other more than either would admit. She could also tell there was a level of normal sisterly tension that had built up recently as the two both reached their hormonal stage.

Hannah had also noticed that they had all managed to navigate to the same monthly cycle and for about three to five days out of every month. She tried to keep the household calm during this time. They all held the same feisty attitude and each of them could defend their positions quite skillfully when needed. She had not gotten into too many heated debates with Stephanie, but at times Laura would challenge her on some issues that were not worth challenging yet somehow always managed to be debated.

Dating was becoming more and more of a discussion, although as a freshman she still probably had about one more year to go before it became a bigger problem. At times like these she wished she had a man around. If only to scare would be aggressors. Try as she might she was just not that intimidating to boys of any age, and she held no challenge to a cocky sixteen-year-olds with an attitude.

The good news about Burlingame High School was its core group of teachers, its curriculum, and its after-school activities. The bad news was that the core group of students who were used to getting their way. As in all schools there was the right side of the tracks, and the wrong side of the tracks. Hannah had permanently cemented on the wrong side since she was a small child, and no longer held out any hope that she would be moving over. This meant her kids would never truly be accepted in the cliquish school but the education would be beneficial at a minimum.

Today seemed like it would be a typical weekend. She had some work to catch up on—she was continually given things to do during her "time off." She did not get paid for the additional work, and she was not paid a salary but by the hour. She was constantly reminded that she was lucky to have a job with her lack of experience and inadequate professional knowledge. She was not college-educated, and she was frequently reminded that there were other college-educated people out there looking for employment.

She would hang out with her daughters after doing her work, she thought to herself. She planned on going to church (they were Methodists), which they frequented about once a month. After church, Sarah had invited them over to her house for a swim in her pool. Sarah and her husband had a beautiful house in Pleasanton, and although Sarah hated the commute she continued to work so she was not strapped with staying home with the kids all day every day of every week.

Sarah loved her kids, and she loved her husband Hank, but as with all suburban households they had problems and issues that were never really discussed. Hannah had never told Sarah that Hank had hit on her one evening at one of the drinking bashes they had a few times each year. They had all been at Sarah's house, and had drank way too much. Sarah had passed out and went to bed. Hannah had planned on spending the night as she so often did.

After all the guests had left, Hank sat next to her on the lawn chair by the pool. He was always a little overly flirtatious, but he was that way with every lady, not just Hannah. She thought it was innocent enough, but that night he had tried to kiss her in an aggressively drunken way. He grabbed her head with his left hand and pulled her toward him.

He actually did kiss her. Hannah had let herself fall into dreamland—thinking this was all hers and she did not have to make the trek back to her small apartment. She simply needed to go upstairs and lay down with her husband—she relished this suburban dream. She had kissed him backed for that brief second, before sanity took control and she pushed him away.

He had gotten a little belligerent at the rejection, but they had never spoken of the incident, and she had never mentioned a word of it to Sarah. Hannah was 100 percent sure that Hank was not a devout husband, and he most likely had hit on several other women as well. After that evening she had simply been careful around him, and he with her. They were civil and polite, even friendly on most occasions, but there was always that tension. They both knew what kind of man he was.

This weekend had quickly passed, as all weekends do, and had gone basically as planned. The sun was just now starting to set and she was amazed that it was only 5 PM, as she watched TV with her two girls. She really did hate daylight savings time. The knock on the door came unexpectedly. She and the girls looked at each other and wondered who could be knocking on a Sunday evening.

Hannah got up and walked over to the door with her two girls in tow. They could not hold their curiosity but had to partake in the discovery. As she peered through the peephole she did not recognize this man standing on the other side of her door. It was at times like these that Hannah felt most vulnerable. She was well aware how flimsy the door was with the rattling handle, and the brittle chain barely holding itself in place. There was no way that it would keep out any intruder with a minimum amount of strength.

She asked who it was, and then stood there with her mouth open for a few minutes as she heard the answer.

"This is Duncan, the dad of a friend of Laura's. May we talk?"

Hannah looked through the hole again, and paused. Wearing biking shorts, holding a helmet and the plastic looking stick (Bike Pump), probably looked intimidating through that little hole. The sweaty clothes must have seemed a little unappealing as well, bike riding is big in the bay area.

Laura finally spoke up and said, "mom are you going to open the door?" Hannah brushed back her hair, closed her mouth, unlocked the chain, and opened the door.

I am not an extraordinarily handsome man, but I am not bad looking either. I work out but could probably still stand to lose a pound here and there.

Hannah invited me in, and I hesitantly stated would it be possible for me to talk to her outside. I could sense that she was leery, probably worried that Laura had done something wrong. I was now here to collect what I was owed for her transgressions. She stepped outside, and I cutely and somewhat shyly (I thought anyway) stated I would like to ask her to dinner or for drinks if she would be interested.

I explained that I had wanted to do so for a while, but my daughter had forbid me from speaking to Hannah. She was petrified of the possibilities of her dad dating the mother of somebody who was her friend. I went on to say ask if Hannah would also ask Laura not to mention anything to my daughter. If she found out I was here she would be beside herself, and I really didn't want to go through the drama that this would elicit.

This was all assuming that she was interested in going, of course. Any night that was convenient for her would be fine. I was flexible but did have to work around my kids' scheduled nights. They visited me two nights a week, and then every other weekend for three nights.

I then asked her if she was okay, and was she able to speak. It was at that moment that Hannah realized she had not said a single word during the entire interaction, and she had simply stood staring at me, perplexed. She did not appear blown away by me, as I stood there gawking at her waiting for a response.

Hannah was feeling like a schoolgirl being asked to the prom and wanted to run inside and call her friends. She had finally been asked to the big dance, and her only thoughts were about what to wear. She found her ability to speak and responded back saying she would be delighted to go to dinner someplace close one night this week. We settled on next Thursday evening together and decided to go to Straights, which was a local eatery/bar down on Burlingame Avenue.

Hannah explained to Laura the situation, and received her solemn vow that she would keep her mouth closed. Nobody at school would know anything of the impending date, and nobody would get an inkling of any news as long as Laura was filled in with all the details of how it went.

Hannah was a little worried about Laura at this point. It had been a long time since she had seen the flash of hope and sparkle emanating from her eyes. Laura, more than Stephanie, missed her dad who they had not seen now for several years. Hannah had little contact with anyone from her hometown and was not even sure that he was still alive.

Laura wanted a dad. She wanted pancakes in the morning and stockings above a fireplace at Christmas. She, more than Hannah or Stephanie or maybe even both of them combined, wanted that house with a white picket fence and the security of knowing a dad would protect her and ensure she was always safe. Laura loved her mother with her entire being, and Hannah knew this but Hannah also knew Laura wanted a father.

AN INTERESTING WEEK

I enjoyed the time with my daughters, and as usual the moment came all too soon when they needed to leave and would now spend the next two nights with their mother. I felt mixed emotions of relief and calmness, as well as anxiety over their being gone. God, I missed them the second they walked out the door. My oldest had decided to stay with me. She was not talking to her mother, and it was with trepidation that I allowed her to remain.

She seemed to be slipping into bad behavior, and was losing the ability to respect people. Back in my day it would have been a swift smack to the head, and all would have been healed, but in reality that did not adjust an attitude that needed help and nurturing. She was crying out for assistance, but both her mother and I were moving forward in a fog, lost at what to do or how to guide my beautiful daughter back to safety.

A ship is only as good as its captain, and the growing pit in my stomach was continually telling me that neither my ex-wife nor myself were any good at the treacherous waters filled with rocks jutting up at every angle. I could only hope and pray that my daughter was going to come out on the other side whole and at peace. It seemed the odds were against her, and all kids. I wonder how any of them make it through to adulthood.

I informed my daughter that she would be on her own for one evening this week. I had a work function/dinner in San Francisco, and I would not be coming home. She was fourteen and going to be fifteen soon so being on her own was not unheard of. I had misgivings about the timing of my dinner, but also knew that it was important to keep up the appearance of being a good corporate citizen. I also was completely aware that if I did not soon find a release for my anxiety that I would explode in a thousand pieces. My ex-wife had established a full frontal assault and was pulling out all the stops at deception and manipulation now that my daughter no longer wanted to return home. I still am utterly flabbergasted at her seemingly unending ability to lie to anyone and everyone we had ever known. Oddly enough the worst part is her extraordinary aptitude for convincing herself that her lies were actually truthful.

My work group outing included the typical gang of five. There was George the Cognos guru who navigated all of our corporate reporting. He was a recent addition, having only joined the company a few months ago, and was the level-headed silent leader of the motley crew. Samantha was our local EP expert, who helped with model building and data navigation. Ingra, who no longer worked at my company but was from Bulgaria had a knack for showing up at these events. Patel, who also no longer worked at our company but had come from the accounting side, and Dan who was the new guy on the block. Dan was recently from Apple and had the potential to really shine down the road. Linda our other analyst was not able to attend the evenings events, as she was currently occupied with her Navy husbands something or other event.

We all met at the restaurant House located downtown and were shown special seating. George's sister and husband owned and ran the local establishment. George was a San Francisco native and was well acquainted with the surroundings. He was a great guide to anything and everything one might want to do in the Bay Area. As was typical for our dining experience, appetizers were waiting and the exquisite taste and palate pleasing morsels were almost greater than the average man could handle. I have no idea how a restaurant like this goes unnoticed. It is extraordinary.

The evening went as expected. Ingra is wonderful company, somewhat earthy although she takes offense to the term. All the women try to avoid Patel as he is the touchy one grabbing, hugging, and feeling anyone or anything that is near him. It does make some people uncomfortable, if they do not know him, and at times even if you do. He has a good heart and is a devoted underappreciated friend. George is married, and has kids at home, but deep down still enjoys time out with a little kick now and then. Samantha is an anomaly. She has a sensual side yet at the same time has issues dealing with controversy or stress. Her life has been broken and hard, as she has dealt with a drug-addicted ex-husband, and the child that she gave birth to at the ripe age of sixteen.

She is the one who has overcome the most adversity in the group, and the one who also seems to have the most scars. Scars never really heal. I think they only fade, but resurface the minute old wounds are brought back to life.

As with most groups in my opinion, we are a bunch of misfits. Wanting and needing to feel connected, but not knowing how or what is missing in our lives. I play my designated role as boss to some, and friend to all. I appear as a wandering lost soul to everyone I meet. I wear my shortcomings as a comic wears his jokes, supplanting humor to avoid intimacy and leading with sarcasm the minute things get too tough. I, as are most, am lost in the world that seems too big to wrap my hands around most all of the time and am left wondering the vastness of what will happen next.

The night goes well, and we have several rounds of drinks and wine. We all do seem to enjoy each other's company, but at times that does lead to inappropriate feelings that have to be squelched before the night turns to day and regrets are felt at going too far. We say our good-byes and head back to our broken homes and shelved ambitions. We will see each other tomorrow, and with a pat on the back start the process all over again.

Everyone except me, that is. I take this opportunity, as planned, to seek out a small, dark alley with the hopes of leveling the playing field in my tumultuous mind. My volcanic side is building to levels of erupting proportions. I drive down Market Street and find a nice place to park. It is easy to find homeless people; they are everywhere it seems.

I park my car on a relatively lit street and get out of my SUV. I am careful now where I park in downtown San Francisco. I used to bring my ex-wife to plays in the theatre district. We enjoyed the live entertainment and a tasteful meal at one of the many top-rated restaurants that the city has to offer. We once had the bright idea to save on parking and found a great spot on a local street. I remember marveling at the amount of glass that was on the street as I was securing the car and how odd it was that there was an abundance of excess parking.

After dinner and the play were completed we returned to our car only to find our rear window smashed, and everything that was removable gone from the inside of our vehicle. The particles of smashed glass covering the asphalt beneath us now made perfect sense. I remember commenting at the time that at least the intruder was thoughtful and smashed the back window versus the front. It could have been worse. My wife took her typical negative route and complained nonstop about the event. You would have thought it was her car versus mine.

I looked around and marveled at the eclectic individuals that wander the streets late at night. I then removed the necessary essentials, and as again luck would have it, only need to walk less than five blocks before a perfect opportunity presented itself. Two bums in a dark alley appeared to be rummaging through the trashcans, looking for what must be their next meal.

It was not easy to see them in the dim lighting, but they appeared to be young adults prematurely aged well beyond their years. They didn't appear to be violent, but were absolutely high on something—that is never a good idea. To corner a cat and watch it brandish its claws is the same as cornering somebody on meth and assuming that you can beat your way out. Meth or heroin addicts are not people you would want to rile when they are in an agitated state—or as the term is nowadays "tweaking." I have a friend on the police force who tells me stories at times, and they are not stories you want to be a part of.

I observed the two for a while and caught glimpses of their black-orbed sunken eyes and their bony exterior frailly held together by a thin layer of translucent skin. They obviously must have track marks up and down their arms and seemingly have little ability to feel pain. One inadvertently picks up a shard of glass and doesn't even notice as the blood starts dripping down his arm running past his elbow to the ground below. They are bickering nonsensically about something that I can't decipher.

I walk into the dimly lit alley and simply raise my gun, deliberately aiming it at the first victim and pull the trigger three quick times. He drops quickly and easily, and I then move my now fully extended arm toward the other gentleman who is still busily rummaging through his stash of tasteful morsels. I pull the trigger twice, and he falls into a crumpled mass three feet from his recently dead friend.

I walk over to inspect each body, and look into the eyes of both. Sensing the relief they must feel to be free from their addiction and life of saddened hardship. I stop for a couple of minutes, taking in the scene and the surroundings, wondering how one wakes up and finds himself or herself a part of this environment. What happens to a person when drugs are the most important thing in his or her life? They give up all ties to family and friends, and relinquish any hope for a future all for the next stab of a needle into their scab-ridden arm.

I wonder about how many times the two have been in rehab, only to fail and wander back to their one true love. How many times have they stolen and lied to their families, and placed their siblings in danger. How much hard-earned money has been wasted on these two, as they continually made promises they had no intention or ability of ever keeping. The diseases that probably coursed through their bodies, as they spread STDs with their needles.

I place the weapon back in my coat pocket, and silently glide back to my car. I remove the gun, placing it in the trunk, and walk to the driver's side. I start my vehicle, exiting the scene, leaving behind only the salvation I have given these two leeches on society.

On the drive back home I realize the satisfaction I feel is much greater to me than anything else I have ever done. I feel justified in my actions. Unlike taking a life that is worth living, I have now forcibly reaped the just rewards on these two people that should have been sown long ago. I tried to imagine the pain and injustice they must have inflicted on their families. The lies they must have told to anyone who would listen enabling them only to get their next fix.

Their brothers and sisters would now be able to grow up in peace, without fear that their older sibling would return home and steal from their piggy bank just to by another tiny bag of stones. I should be getting a plaque nailed to city hall for the service I just performed for this city. I expunged a portion of a plague from our society and now felt like a true god that had found his calling. I did not know what my next event would be, nor could I foresee the future. I did know that I would from this day forth incorporate the eradication of any drug addict homeless person from the face of this planet. I was like the Lone Ranger who now stood up for justice when other people were afraid to face facts.

I made it home in my contained state of euphoria, and luckily my daughter was asleep. I jumped into the shower, which was slowly becoming a custom of mine after these events, and afterward threw myself into my newly acquired queen-size bed. I felt exuberant and was looking forward to sleeping soundly, having performed a civic duty.

The rest of the week was somewhat uneventful, save for my bike ride Sunday afternoon. I had finally decided to ignore my daughter's warnings and move forward with asking Laura's mom on a date. "Laura's Hot Mom" they called her. How could I not try and make a move on somebody with that acronym.

After a great bike ride I made it home and settled in to get cleaned up. My oldest was doing her homework (or pretending to) and stated she was almost finished. I decided to make some pasta for dinner and promised as soon as I was out of my shower I would commence the preparation of the feast. It had been a good week. I had managed to loosen the valve and free my built up frustrations, all the while making positive strides in my home life and on the romantic front as well. All in all I couldn't complain.

FBI

Sudhir spent the next morning pulling his facts together from the three different cases. He consolidated the four murders, laying out all his details, and had to admit even to himself that his theory was a little farfetched. The pieces just did not easily link one to another. There were too many holes in the bridges he was attempting to build, and he really only had his gut instinct telling him that somehow, someway this was the same man performing these different acts.

After a few hours he decided to go to his captain and lay everything on the table and get his advice. Who knows, maybe there was something he was missing in the pile of paperwork.

Sudhir's captain was a small balding man in his mid-fifties and was about four years away from retirement. He had seen a wide spectrum of events in his twenty-six years on the force, and his main goal at this stage was to make it to thirty, retire, and spend his afternoons fishing up in the mountains. He did very little to stir the waters and went by the book on most all decisions.

Sudhir got ten minutes with him as he was heading out to see the local district attorney on an issue with another detective, hoping to clear the air and stop a dilemma before it went any further. Politics plays a role in all occupations, and all companies in the world, as everyone is concerned with themselves first and foremost. Sudhir presented his hypothesis. He was very open in his description and agreeably stated that the odds were against him, but he also could not contain the continuing feeling that somehow these were all linked together. The Volvo was really the only key, which was flimsy he himself admitted.

Sudhir had not spent much time with his captain. He respected him, but in all honesty Sudhir had not focused that much effort in his job. This was the first time that he was motivated, driven to a resolution. His captain spent more time discussing Sudhir than he did the case. He told Sudhir how impressed he was with his dedication and how he felt Sudhir might have the makings of a good detective.

He also admitted that this was a surprise to him and everyone else. He personally could not remember how many cases had been solved by instinct and intuition. Sometimes filling in the blank spaces of a case with what you felt ended up being the only way to bridge the gap and move forward. In the end facts were needed, and you could not finalize a solution until your details added up, but getting there took more than just adding one plus one to get two.

He gave his permission to talk to the FBI and concurred with Sudhir that having the profiling skills involved at this stage might be the right thing to do. He also gave Sudhir a piece of advice as he was stepping out the door on his way to his next appointment. He stated it was the small things that solved cases. The little intricacies that could be overlooked or passed over. It might even be something that caught Sudhir's eye, but he was not giving it his full attention. The details are what catch a killer. Everyone is good at covering their tracks on the big issues, but nobody can think through all the minutia. Look at the mundane trivial pebbles and that is where you will find the killer.

Sudhir made his way back to his desk and called his friend Jason at the FBI. He caught him on a break and told him his story. Jason was a local. He was in the process of going through a divorce, had two kids, and his soon-to-be ex-wife was a very good-looking woman. They were currently working through custodial issues and living arrangements as his parents kept their house in a trust. It was proving difficult to figure out how to make everything work for everyone.

Jason was married to his job. He inhaled details of a case into his very being from the beginning to the last. The smallest piece of evidence was catalogued until it reached the final resolution. In the end, this had done in his marriage to Sherene. He just did not have the time or the energy to have two marriages in his life, and try as he might he was incapable of giving up on bringing killers to justice.

Jason had a knack for piecing seemingly unrelated events into a bigger picture. He was good at solving puzzles that nobody believed until in the end he always proved them true. He had started out in the Bay Area but was now a part of the national profiling team and if there was ever a highly publicized investigation he was involved at some level.

Jason agreed to meet Sudhir that afternoon for a drink and asked him to bring the details with him. He didn't feel that he could get the FBI directly involved but he personally owed Sudhir and would do whatever he could to help him out.

His debt to Sudhir had built like wooden blocks over the last few years. They didn't have much of a personal friendship, but Sudhir had allowed Jason the use of his couch on a few occasions when he had no business driving. Jason still loved his wife, and the separation was taking its toll on his mental stability. Jason was always fine when he was in the throngs of an investigation, and his attention was completely focused on the beams of building the connected structure he was forming in his mind. His downfall came on the few occasions when there was a lull in activity, and he realized how alone he was in the world.

Sudhir had started inviting him over to his house for a cookout or to watch a football game, but as with Jason's soon-to-be former wife Sudhir had soon found out Jason was just not around most of the time. Oddly Jason was coming to rely on Sudhir as a friend, and even though they only saw each other sporadically the feeling was mutual.

They agreed to meet each other at Valemar Station in Pacifica, and Sudhir planned on getting there a little early to scope out a table and organize his papers in a form that might make sense. He made the call to Janine, telling her that he would be late, and as he expected was on the receiving end of another verbal assault. At one point he was holding the phone three feet from his ear, as he patiently listened to the berating he was forced to endure from his loving wife. This provided a round of humor and applause from the other detectives as soon as he returned the phone to its appropriate cradle. This, he was sure, would be a station joke for several years to come.

Sudhir arrived at the designated meeting spot around 5:30 PM. He was planning on meeting Jason at 6 PM. He pulled off route one and pulled into the paved parking lot. He admired the dilapidated structure of the local bar. Valemar Station had not reached the level of dive bar as of yet. It was a local hangout and you tended to get to know the bartenders and waitresses rather quickly if you frequented the establishment at all. It was warm and inviting and the food was decent enough. The atmosphere was really the key and it kept the patrons content and left you with a feeling of home. Sudhir waved to Mike the bartender as he entered and spread out his paperwork on the table in front of him.

Jane (a middle aged women with white hair and a rotund belly) brought him over a Stella without Sudhir asking and said hello. Everyone in the bar was friendly. It reminded Sudhir of *Cheers,* the old TV show from the '80s, and he reveled in everyone knowing his name. He chugged down his beer rather quickly, and again without asking saw a few minutes later that it had miraculously been refilled.

Sudhir made the effort to pore over the paperwork one last time in the hopes that a different setting or different lighting might give him a new perspective. Unfortunately this was not the case. He remembered the often-quoted rule: the same actions and the same process does not lead to new results, and when we fall into that circular trap we find ourselves in a loop of craziness.

He was happy when Jason finally arrived—about fifteen minutes late. He was now already on his third beer and wanted to spend time reviewing the details before he found himself too caught up in the beverage portion of the evening. Jason greeted his friend hello, ordered his vodka and cranberry (smiling from the harassment he received from Sudhir and everyone in the bar over his feminine order), and got to work.

Jason liked the Volvo link in the cases, and although it was unusual it was not unheard of for a killer to jump around in his activities in the beginning of a new life cycle. Sudhir found it odd that Jason referred to the serial killers having a life cycle. As with all forms of life Jason believed that the serial killer was born at some stage when something clicked or snapped and pushed the individual into a new identity. He felt that in the beginning, as with all infants, a newborn killer might have to take time in finding his way and preferences. This was not always the case. There were several killers that immediately fell into their preferred routines but he had seen this same metaphorical cycle before.

He agreed with Sudhir that for now the vehicle was the best possible connection. Sudhir should spend as much time as possible pursuing any activities that involved a car of this type. Jason also suggested he would scan the FBI database and see if anything popped up. He didn't think it would. In his opinion this was an infant killer, and if the two of them were correct he was going to be difficult to catch. Jason still did not feel that it was enough to open a FBI file, but if anything else occurred he might push to have that changed.

They completed their work portion of the evening and moved on to personal issues. Sudhir was mildly disappointed in not learning anything he didn't already know but felt comfort in that he was going down an agreed-upon path. The conversation pushed around to Sherene, and how she was doing. Jason saw her sporadically. She had retained custody of the kids, but he had open visitation rights. With his schedule he had no ability to do anything routine from one week to the next.

They drank several beers and around 9 PM decided to call it a night. They both needed to get home and sleep it off. Sudhir looked forward to starting back into his list of registered Volvo owners first thing tomorrow morning.

Jason had agreed to run the entire list through the FBI reference checks as well and see if that gave any leads. He did not hold out much hope.

He felt strongly that they were witnessing the birth of a serial killer and only hoped that before he matured they were able to apprehend him. Killers only got more deadly as they gain confidence and in most cases became increasingly more difficult to catch the longer they were on the loose.

THE DATE

It was fun to hear Hannah describe the beginning of her evening and the preparation that occurred at her apartment. Hannah was clearly worried about Laura and how excited she was about us going out on our first date. It was cute how Hannah had talked about Laura helping her pick out clothes and doing her hair. Daughters and mothers can have such a wonderful relationship.

I was described as somewhat fashionable, so Laura really wanted Hannah to steer clear of her normal everyday attire that she adorned for several of her other dates. She needed something black had been Laura's main criteria. Hannah had settled on a nice below-the-knee silk skirt and a loose blouse. She went with some mid-sized heels, black as well, and topped it off with a silk scarf to bring the two together. It was easy for me to admit to liking it, as Hannah looked fantastic.

Hannah had enjoyed the attention. It had been a long time since Laura was into helping her prepare for a date, and even Stephanie had joined in on the festivity. They had both helped with her makeup. Hannah did not wear a lot, but at her age was in need of some touchups here and there.

She smiled having liked the outfit they had decided on, and she laughingly talked about putting the stacks of rejected clothes back in their proper place to avoid a mess in the morning. She was unsure how long our date would last so she had made the kids a pizza and went through the list of instructions, as was her habit every time she ventured out for an evening.

The kids had rhythmically mimicked her as they recited the instructions with her. All three had laughed at the fact that she felt she needed to repeat them every single time they were left alone. The most important one always being never answer the door. What if it is the police? "Then we call you but we never answer the door. We don't open it we don't go to it we don't say hi to anyone we don't even look at the door for fear it might burn us," Stephanie had laughed.

Hannah admitted to me she was paranoid, but she also knew that her two girls were the only two people she held dear in the world. If anything ever happened to them she had no idea how she would ever make it through the experience. She had made her exit with a couple of kisses and a nice big hug from Laura for good luck. Laura's overly excited anticipation had actually made even Hannah a little nervous.

She had made the short five-minute drive to the restaurant, which was located on Burlingame Avenue. It was a quick jump to get there, and she was glad that we had agreed upon a place that was so close. She really didn't like being out late at night during the week. On the weekend she felt more comfortable, but for some reason she had never shaken the school time rule of staying put Monday through Friday and letting loose Friday and Saturday night.

The restaurant was plush, catering to upscale patrons. The food, unfortunately, was just average and for the amount of money you would expect something more extravagant. It was well-frequented on most nights by a large amount of patrons, and its reputation of being the place to be allowed it to sway from quality.

Hannah had arrived at the side door and walked up the ramp spotting me at the bar, sitting on a stool talking to the local bartender. I was having a brownish-colored drink in a small glass with a few ice cubes. She had guessed was Scotch, but she was not a big drinker, and really did not know her liquor too well. She walked in my direction, and as I sat there I found myself staring directly at her. She was still a beautiful woman and you could tell that she took pride in presenting herself at her best.

I shook off my hesitation, got up from the stool, and met her halfway. After the initial greetings I spoke to Adrianna, a waitress that I knew, and she showed the two of us to a table. The hostess said hi on our way over, and Hannah asked me if I frequented here that often.

I did, but just within the last few weeks. I seemed to make a lasting impression rather quickly. Everyone in the restaurant knew who I was. The conversation for the most part centered on Hannah for the bulk of the evening, as I continued to inquire about her goals, her background, her hometown, her job, her hobbies, and her girls. I was genuinely interested in her, and she found herself getting lost in her historic past. She dug up old memories that she had not thought about in a long while.

She was born in Alabama, her parents were both deceased, and she had no close living relatives. She briefly touched on her tumultuous relationship, and the byproducts of Laura and Stephanie, but tried to steer the conversation away from her ex-husband and the bad memories dredged up from that dark period. I never mentioned the fact that I knew her background or that Sarah had released so much personal information. I felt that it was better left unsaid. She had never been skiing, but always wanted to go, she does love being outdoors and likes hiking.

Her favorite activity is to go for long walks. She likes company, but if nobody is available she grabs her Walkman and heads down to the path by the bay. She strolls along listening to REO Speedwagon and Sting and any other band from the '80s that she can drum up. She admittedly likes that period, even though she is frequently told it is not the best age for music.

She finds herself very relaxed talking to me and opens up more than she has to anyone in a long time. She shares about her friendship with Sarah, and although she has never spoken out loud about the incident, finds herself telling me about the night that Hank came on to her. It had filled her with disgust and guilt at who he was and what she had allowed to happen. Sharing did seem to lift a weight from her shoulders, but she had not anticipated discussing the situation with anyone let alone somebody on a first date.

Hannah had seemed a little off-guard, letting stories fly, and before she realized it the night was gone and it was time to part ways. Once outside she discovered that I had walked to the restaurant, so she offered to give me a ride back home. The night seemed perfect, and Hannah now had butterflies in her stomach hoping that I felt the same. On the quick trip home I did ask to keep all conversations about tonight limited where Laura was concerned. I was genuinely worried about hurting my daughter's feelings and Hannah assured me that it would be fine. I had made quite an impression on her darling daughter, but she would give no details and keep any future outings to herself.

She let me know that she was interested in seeing me again. We quickly arrived at my house. After pulling up in the driveway, she placed the car in park. I gently reached over and gave her a quick kiss on the lips as I said good-bye. She seemed like a schoolgirl again. Her knees looked weak and she seemed to have butterflies flittering in her stomach, threatening to break free and explode out to the slightly chilled starry sky.

She watched me as I pulled my key out of my pants pocket and opened the door of my pinkish colored house. I saw her slowly pull away once the door had been closed. I was sure that she was excited about the date and felt comfortable with her not telling Laura. I had also assumed that she would share the experience rather quickly with her friend Sarah.

I later found out She had called Sarah that night, and for twenty minutes sat in the car outside of her apartment describing her evening. She had been openly elated at the prospects of a future date, and hopefully more. Sarah had listened patiently and joined in with her excitement. Hannah was truly lucky to have her as a friend. At some point she was going to have to be honest with Sarah, let her know what a snake her husband was, and open up to her about the things that he had done.

Laura had been disappointed, but not completely diluted in her excitement when she was not given any details. Hannah had sat awake and dreamt about possibilities and our future. It is interesting how women get so excited about the prospect of happiness—they sometimes forget to enjoy the here today. That sounds sexist, as men are most likely the same.

Is There Any Hope?

The date with Hannah had gone splendidly. She was articulate, gorgeous, and easy to talk to. I found an innate ability to listen to her ramble on, without having to feign interest. I genuinely liked hearing her stories, and what had shaped her life to lead her to where she was today. It went so well that I felt the familiar rising of despair in the pit of my stomach. I was now beginning to feel that although happiness for me was a possibility, I would never allow myself the luxury of being whole and true. I needed a release of some sort. It had been a while since I had visited my friend's wife and I called her to see if she was still interested in hooking up. As in the past she was willing to make time. She really was an interesting if not sadistic person.

She was Indian, had tanned dark skin and jet-black hair of that typical nationality. She was a little tough to deal with, and I in no way enjoyed talking to her at any length. She was willingly available and open to allowing my deviant nature to run its course in our many encounters. We had been meeting periodically for the better part of two years, and it seemed uncannily easy for her to get away and us to sneak to a hotel room.

I made the quick trip up to Daly City and found her prepared and enticingly dressed in mesh stockings and matching panties and bra. She performed her skills masterfully, and as always had me satisfied and spent a short hour later. I lay exhausted breathing heavily staring up at the ceiling, while she cradled her head in my shoulder and relayed the activities of her kids and daily routine. I drifted off at some point in the rambling synopsis of her story and awoke some time later to find her in the same position snoring slightly in a soft way that only women seem capable.

I slowly moved her head and quietly dressed. I snuck out of the room and headed back to the warmth and comfort of my solitude. I was beginning to realize how content I felt being alone without the obligations and strings that come with serious commitment. Relationships come with ties that often hold you back from your true potential. One might successfully argue that a bond of support should be defined as positive and constructive, but I had never had the pleasure of being in a relationship of this nature.

I spent the next few weeks dating Hannah every few nights, sleeping with my tortured friend's wife in my sordid affair, and mustering enough energy to work and periodically spend time with my kids. My daughters were growing up quickly, it seemed, and having them only half of the time I was amazed at how they changed on a daily basis.

My oldest was going through major adjustment issues, had recently become very angry with me when I had inquired about her sinking grades. In a fit of rage she had decided to move back into her mother's house full-time and no longer wanted anything to do with me. My middle child summed it up in her delicate way: "She must feel conflicted, like, she has to choose between her parents and can't find comfort going back and forth with both."

Again, children amaze me. They have the ability to guide adults when our vision clouds.

I was finding myself complacent, comfortable with the killings that I had committed. I no longer felt the nagging tug of guilt and depression but instead was starting to feel complete. I knew that I would now kill again and that the missing link in my life was found once and for all.

My kids gave me the sense of normalcy that might otherwise have eluded me, but the true emptiness was only filled in my being by taking another life. I related it to the vampire movies where one is required to feed on the blood of the living in order to maintain one's own existence. I filled my essence with the souls of living creatures, as I continually needed the nourishment their death provided.

My relationship with Hannah was the confusing part of my life. While I did feel a connection with her, I knew that I would never again be able to feign the daily interests that marriage would require. I would never again make that commitment to another single human being. Life was too short to waste on the monotony that was required in this false belief of one partner for life. Again, God decreed us to go forth and populate the earth. What better way to do that than with multiple partners to saturate my palate of lust and carnality. My only worry as always was catching some disease, as I jumped from woman to woman to fill my lust.

I found myself lying in bed on a Wednesday evening in the midst of self-reflection when Hannah texted me. She was at a work dinner. She was several glasses of wine into the evening and wondered if it was okay if she came over. I reservedly agreed, as we had not yet moved into a sexual relationship. I was curious if this was what she had in mind. She was well beyond rational thought—muttering things in text that moved like a mosquito. She was obviously having conversations with her co-workers as well.

The next hour jumped by quickly, and I then heard tapping on my front door. I figured that must be her. I moved from the confines of my bedroom dressed in running shorts and nothing else and opened the door to a red-faced smiling Hannah. She held herself up by bracing one hand on the railing next to my stairs. I was a little concerned that she had driven from her nightly activity in the state she was in, but helped her through the door. I held her as we stood in the entryway.

I realized then how sad she must feel, needing to simply be held, and I gently caressed her shoulder-length hair. I ran my fingers deeply through the back of her neck, stroking her strands and letting them fall between each finger. I pulled her head away from my shoulder and gently touched my lips to hers. She was ready. We stood in the doorway for several minutes, kissing passionately, embracing each other for the first time. We explored the inner crevices each other's mouths, cheeks, and ears. Our hands were frantically moving from shoulders to back to arms then circling again.

We then moved to the bedroom where we continued our exploration, as we got to know each other in a passionate way. Making love to somebody for the first time is a truly unique experience. I often hear that the ocean is the last frontier of unknown space residing on our planet, but I would challenge that statement. Every woman you make love to is a move into a world that is 100 percent different than anything you have ever done before.

Each woman is exclusively unique, and each body moves and responds in a specific fashion. If you take your time you will find how amazingly true these words are. How can anyone who really grasps this concept stay committed to one person for life? Most men I feel are happy to ever find a woman who will accept them and allow them the sheer pleasure of making love. Most men lack the ability to give a woman what they desire and have the insecurity of not knowing what it is they need to do to please the opposite sex.

As I lay with Hannah, and she did the inevitable after-sex snuggling that all woman crave, I realized that my connection with her was moving to a confusing level. I did truly enjoy her company. She was incredibly beautiful, and as she lay in my arms I did love listening to her stories.

She worked with mostly men in a construction supply business. They sold concrete forms to contractors, and she was the all-around office person who kept the place going. She had been eating and drinking with all her co-workers for a holiday dinner, and she was with only one other woman in a group of twenty-plus men. A couple of suppliers had shown up as well, and the liquor was flowing freely. Hannah was not a big drinker, so it was unusual for her to get this far out of control.

I was surprised that she was not constantly barraged with offers from the several men that she associated with. She stated that all of them were married, but we all know that is nothing but an inconvenience. It is definitely not the deterrent that naive women think it is. She was also very excited at the bonus she had been given, which exceeded a thousand dollars in cash. Christmas was now quickly approaching, and she would use the money to buy the much-wanted gifts for her two beautiful daughters.

As Hannah lay in my arms, spilling her plans for shopping and recanting her stories from the evening, I casually asked her if she would be interested in the two of us taking a trip to Twain Harte where my cabin was located. The only stipulation I had was she could not tell anyone where she was going—I truly did not want my older daughter finding out that Hannah was there.

We debated the pros and cons of a weekend together, and after weighing everything out decided the short trip would be fine. She had never been skiing before, and with winter approaching the possibilities of Dodge Ridge opening up were gaining traction. I also felt with our relationship vaulting to a new level it would be a good test for what I wanted out of life. If I were ever going to have the semblance of a normal existence, then Hannah would be a perfect candidate. She was a far cry better than the sleazy women I had been hanging around lately. I was additionally saving money by not perusing the Internet for a quick fix.

I attempted to decipher the next stage of my existence. Where do I go from here? If my completeness was now true, and I only had to continue my recent string of extracurricular activities to remain content, then what else did I desire? Maybe we are all continuing the attempt to move in one direction or another. Maybe one is never happy or complacent with the same routine, but always desires more and more.

If that were true, what was next for me? Blowing up a building? That was not who I was. I needed the search for personal connection, and that only came from the taking of another life with bare hands. Watching the eyes cease, and creating an empty shell, drained of its energy lying in a stoic pose of death. That was the personal connection. Making love to somebody, or the concept of marriage, were only false placeholders for the connection one felt in the presence of another life leaving this planet forever.

Forever: the finality of it. Sex is fleeting, and marriage is rarely lasting in today's society. Even the marriages that do last are mired in a bitter, tangled web of deceit and sadness. Death is the ultimate lasting experience that once complete cannot be undone. Maybe this is why it held something special for me. Again, the feeling of power and godlike ability washed over me while

Hannah chattered away. This was becoming more of an occurrence every time I thought about taking the life of another human being.

I once again become excited with anticipation and rolled over to take Hannah for a second time before she needed to leave. She was surprised by my aggressiveness, but was accepting of my advance.

She then left, after hastily dressing to get home to her two girls. They were most likely waiting for her. I am sure she had not intended to stay out so late and most likely surprised herself at the latter contents of the evening. Smiling and happy, she left with a quick kiss good-bye and drove the short few blocks back to her apartment. Unaware of the tangled web she was inching ever closer to; and no understanding of the venomous ending that awaited her.

GOD, IT CAN'T BE TRUE

Sudhir had enjoyed his meeting with Jason. As confused as Jason was in his personal life, his work life was meticulously crafted. Jason continually achieved the always-inevitable goal of finding and putting his culprit in a cell far away. How many people had he held a hand in apprehending, ridding the world of the added sadness that might have been inflicted. Sudhir felt a tinge of jealousy at the thought of him not having felt this satisfaction and now realized that he was driven to the same end.

Sudhir was happy to be heading home. Janine was not in town for the next couple of days. He would be able to pick up his kids at his parents and spend some quality time with them on a foggy coastal evening. Every place you live everyone talks about microclimates, but in the San Francisco area it was never truer. You could drive a few miles in any direction and seemingly get twenty-degree variances in temperature. This was most evident on the coast during a foggy day, which was the majority of days out of any given year.

The sandy beaches were heavily burdened today with an overcast hue. The endless, vast darkness invaded without any sun present tending to wear people down at times. This was also the main reason the coastal community enjoyed a lower level of housing prices compared to the rest of the Peninsula. Where else in the world would ocean-front homes be less expensive than comparable structures further inland. It intuitively made little sense, but the fog was really the added detractor.

Sudhir paddled home through the thick substance after picking up his little ones, and, as usual on these days, his mother had packed him a very nice dinner. His mom didn't take to Janine for the most part, but she did spoil him and her grandchildren. What mom does like her daughter-in-law anyway?

Talk about a Freudian role issue, moms hated all daughters-in-laws. Nobody would ever be good enough for the son of any mother in her right mind.

After a nice prepared meal and the night's assigned homework, the three of them sat down and watched a little TV. Snuggling between the two kids on the couch, Sudhir could not help but feel how blessed he was. He had amazing children that loved and admired him to no end. He worshipped his kids. Lately with Janine going through her mid-life adjustment, they were the foundation that helped construct life into a meaningful existence.

They were watching the last taped episode of *The Amazing Race*, which had now become a family tradition. The three of them would make a huge bowl of popcorn and stay glued with anticipation on what couple would be the next one booted off the show. Sudhir was betting tonight on the two blonde girls not making it. The show seemed to always have one group of blonde girls, who were not the brightest on the block and made you laugh at the fulfilled cliché. It was either them or the frat boys that were sure to go. How the frat boys had ever lasted this long was truly amazing.

As the show neared its end, and the blondes came up short as anticipated, Sudhir prepared the kids for bed. Story-time was out tonight—supplanted by TV, a more often recurring theme as of late. Sudhir pushed the two into the bathroom for the tortuous task of brushing their teeth and washing their face before bedtime. How bad could it possibly be to brush your teeth that it brought about the bellowed yelps of protest every single night? You would think they were brushing with turpentine versus the bubble gum flavored sweet toothpaste that kids used nowadays.

He placed each child in bed. He then set a glass of water next to their bedsides, predicting their nightly requests. Funny how the glass never seemed to be touched, but the security of knowing the water was there every evening was the saving grace. This led each child into a peaceful slumber so it was well worth it.

After everything was quiet he poured himself a glass of Scotch on the rocks, which he had been thinking about since he first stepped across the threshold a few hours ago. He quickly gulped down the first pour. After preparing the second round, he sat down himself, placed the file he had been building on the coffee table, and spread out all the material. He knew he was not in a state to be much good, but maybe a different setting would give him a new perspective.

At times in your life an event threatens to rock your very core. The foundation that you have spent years building suddenly becomes vulnerable instantaneously. Everything you held true and believed in changes. Sudhir saw the name on the list of car owners, and he lost his ability to stand. He fell to the carpeted floor and hit his head on the coffee table as he went down. Like a beacon of light on a thunderstorm-ridden evening his eyes were drawn directly to the name.

The flow of information that flew like daggers into every crevice of his brain was the sudden realization of the truth and what that meant. Everything added up too easily and quickly but at the same time could not be true. The possibility was unimaginable, and therefore was not real. Not probable, and absolutely wrong. Could facts flow directionally to a point? Completely and totally implausible in every sense of the definition of what wrong must mean? Sudhir recognized this name. The name held meaning to him and was something he never thought possible.

Sudhir felt his legs starting to weaken and realized that he was gasping desperately for each breath. Oxygen was eluding him like a wasp you might try to grab with your bare hands. His failed attempts were coming in short gasps, like the rapid fire of a machine gun. He began to understand he must be hyperventilating. He stumbled into the kitchen flailing wildly and grabbed a paper bag normally used for packing his children's lunches. He fell to the laminated floor. He raised the bag to his mouth and lay there breathing in and out. The bag inflated and deflated with every burst of air that circulated through his overused lungs.

He lost track of how long he lay on the floor, as memories flooded his mind. They were too numerous to count, and he felt overwhelmed with the conflicting feelings at war with his disbelief of what might be possible. How had he been so blind? Had he allowed alcohol to deaden his senses so that he no longer consciously acknowledged the very things that were most important? What world was he living in that anything like this was even possible?

Sudhir felt the immediate need to connect to somebody and bring some sense back into what was happening. He was navigating the mundane tasks and was forever finding himself lost in the daily routine. It is usually at the moment of self-reflection with a forced dose of reality check that one reevaluates their lives.

Sudhir reflected back on a time when he was young. He and a bunch of friends were playing at one of their houses. Everyone was swimming in a pool and playing as boys do with adolescent abandon. The sudden fights that erupted usually dissipated quickly. If you were forced to narrow down the differences of boys versus girls, it would have to be that boys get angry and move on. Who remembers what yesterdays fight was about? Who really cares, when there are more important things to do today in the here and now.

Girls get angry and remain so for hours, days, and even weeks. The anger they feel builds up inside them. If they are not careful it can consume them from the inside out leaving them hollow and alone. Why can't girls agree to disagree without one of them having to come out on top? Does there always have to be a winner, and sadly enough always a loser? Boys in most cases can't even remember what a fight was about the following day as new adventures and unexplored avenues open. Boys hold simplistic ideas, like strapping a firecracker to the tail of your dog and watching him chase himself silly until it explodes.

Sudhir's mind wandered to the day when there were five of the neighborhood's boys running jumping and playing in the local pool. It was early, so nobody was around. Parents were still waking up. They had been playing for a couple of hours already and were sitting on the lawn chairs exhausted from the devotion being thrust forth in the latest activity. Life was simple then, not like now.

Sudhir was finally feeling a sense of control coming back to his breathing and felt strength returning to his limbs and torso. He slowly raised himself up from the floor, grabbing the metal arms of the kitchen chair, and bracing his stand back to fully upright. It was too much to handle right now, and he just needed to let things digest before he went any further.

He now frantically started looking for his glass of scotch, and decidedly filled it up with fresh ice cubes. He grabbed the entire bottle and sat down in his favorite recliner. He flipped on the TV after his now third glass for the evening and felt the numbness of total drunkenness filtering its way to the very tips of each finger. He knew he would not be in control of his drinking tonight. He would finish the bottle with utterly no care other than getting drunk and staying drunk for as long as he possible could.

He aimlessly flipped through channels not ever really stopping on any for longer than a few minutes. His vacant stare was sign enough that he was not really paying attention to the contents of what he was watching. He was merely using the background noise as a distraction from reality. He paused on one channel where a boy stood with his dog. They were playing fetch on some beach as the dog dutifully ran back and forth excitedly bursting off each time the boy raised his hand.

How many trips to the beach had he taken? Grabbing a friend's dog, tugging and playing in heaps of arms legs and tails. Sudhir often watched his friend's dogs. He would volunteer for the effort. Taking enjoyment out of the peace a dog brought with its joyful exuberance. Dogs were fantastic creatures. He only wished that Janine would allow him to have one somebody. Someday, before he was no longer part of this world.

The fogginess was now at full force and Sudhir felt his eyelids growing heavy as he sipped of his drink. The inability to feel has its advantages—though has sad permanent results. You will always wake up, come back to the real world, and be forced to face reality. The only perceived benefit is the postponement of dealing with the issue.

It is not always a bad thing to let the dust settle and approach the same formidable obstacle from a new angle. Sudhir knew what tomorrow would bring. He felt as though somebody had dropped a steel wrecking ball from several stories high directly on his head. The next day would require him to remove the ball and face the truth.

He would hold out hope that he was wrong, and his leap to a conclusion was the result of his own imagination baselessly freefalling out of reality. A person could fabricate all kinds of hypothesis, but only facts led to a firm conclusion. He would wake up tomorrow, filter through the facts, and not let his emotions sway him any longer. He was feeling isolated and alone. He could not tell anyone of his instinctual thoughts until he knew completely that he was either right or wrong.

Sudhir didn't feel the glass slip out of his hand. It tumbled to the carpet from his outstretched fingers. The contents seeped into the deepest recesses of the padded cushion beneath the Berber carpet. Sudhir's eyelids were now tightly shut as he snored, which was always amplified to the same level as his drinking.

Every drink he took of scotch seemed to have increased the volume knob one click on his labored nightly breathing. It would be another night in the chair for Sudhir. Troubled thoughts haunted his sleep as to what was to come.

How Can Everything Go Wrong

I find it odd how quickly at times things run their course and cease to have meaningful value. Kids are trained from the beginning to ensure that there is no single thing that can truly hold its luster for any length of time. Christmas is the perfect example of the throwaway society that we have constructed in today's materialistic United States.

Kids vigorously tear through wrapping, ribbons, and boxes to quickly attain the treasure hidden inside. The then only minutes later discard the object for the next attack on a nicely packaged item. We are inundated with programmed propaganda telling us how we need to move on and discard the old. Buy, buy, buy: it is how we are educated to keep the economy churning at full speed. The early 2000s were kept alive by the blatant disregard for thoughtful spending, as we continued to borrow money to buy things we did not need. We then worked harder to make more money to buy more things that were then tossed in a corner as a newer model supplanted the old.

I unfortunately was in the middle of this era and embraced its essence wholeheartedly. This had now led me in a few short weeks to start tiring of Hannah, who had only recently been the object that I actively lusted for and pursued. Now I was entering the stages of planning how to discard her for another model to successfully conquer.

I sat at a small local restaurant in San Francisco eating breakfast outside with the normal casual breeze blustering up a slightly cold stir of air. It is always so easy to spot visitors to the area as anyone west of Arizona relates all of California to the Los Angeles weather. San Francisco is just not the same, trust me. It maintains normal temperatures of between low 60s to occasionally hitting the mid 80s. It might be the one area that actually benefits from global warming.

As I was drinking my bland Bloody Mary I noticed a large family (in number and unfortunately in size as well) approach the restaurant and ask for a table. As they waited outside a local street vendor approached who sold beaded necklaces. The one attractive member of the clan initiated a conversation with the vendor forced by the prodding of her teenage son who desired a bracelet.

She had jet-black hair hanging loosely a few inches below her shoulders with tight curls. The curls appeared soft like a fresh towel that was just removed from the endlessly circular confinement of the dryer. I imagined the sweet smell that might emanate from her hair, as I would stroke it gently with a caressing hand as we possibly watched TV sitting on my couch.

She had a nice waistline and a perfectly proportioned curve in her hips and breasts like a model. Not stick-thin but extremely well-proportioned.

My guess is the beaded jewelry normally sold for around five dollars tops, and in all likelihood cost around one to make. In an odd set of events the boy ended up with a bracelet, and for some unknown reason the woman seemed to pay in the area of twenty plus dollars. A heated exchange began between the son and several family members. He humiliated his mother and questioned how in the world she could ever think of paying so much for a mere trinket. I actually agreed with him completely, but could also see the negative impact the conversation was having on the lady. I felt sad for her and her miscued decision.

After much bantering back and forth, they moved to their prepared table, sitting down with the woman enclosed in what was now a self-inflicted box of isolation. Normally I don't think or act on too many things, but suddenly felt inclined to inject my involvement. I would simply walk over to their table hand them ten dollars and state that I had negotiated a price reduction for her. Implying I had ascertained a refund from the manipulative entrepreneur she had dealt with. It was a brilliant idea—and a perfect way to start a long meaningful relationship with a perfect stranger. Everyone needs a great first encounter story, right?

I approached her table and felt the familiar churning in my stomach from the impending scenario. "Hello" I stated, "I could not help but overhear you transactional interaction. After you left I talked to the vendor and was able to reduce ten dollars off your original purchase and now would like to return it."

The look of shock and stuttered response was amusing to me as the two older women fumbled for an appropriate thank you. The gentlemen just gawked in my direction.

Oddly, my desired immediate effect on the zeroed in target was not what I anticipated. She appeared to get more annoyed that the subject was again broached and stood leaving the table. It appeared for a visit to the serenity of the restaurant bathroom.   I accepted the gratitude from the other family members and casually turned, leaving the mixed unit of various ages and sizes. I returned back to my table to finish my quickly melting Bloody Mary before it was completely devoid of any taste.

After breakfast I paid the check and stood in preparation to walk back to my car and head home. As I did so the woman approached me and in an apologetic tone introduced herself as Savannah. She was from Pleasanton and her family was visiting from Ohio and they were all out for the day sightseeing. She hoped I would accept her apology for being a little rude and even asked me to join them for the day. A few hours of wandering around aimlessly looking at the sites we had both seen on so many family and friend's visits.

She was an architect, and for some reason made several trips to Asia on a monthly basis. She had just recently broken up with her boyfriend of four years. He was a documentary film producer who lived in San Francisco half of the time and in Los Angeles the rest. She was in her early thirties would be my guess and indeed the child in question was actually her little brother. He had made the family trip out with her parents and was actually in his first year of college at Ohio State. I am so bad now at judging the ages of kids it seems. They all look so young I have lost the ability to differentiate between kids in high school and college.

After what can only be defined as the perfect meeting and the ideal day we parted ways so she could return her focus to her family. We had exchanged numbers and agreed to get together one week from next Friday for dinner. She decided she would make the trip over the bridge and visit me, as she enjoyed Burlingame and had not been there in quite a while. I felt a renewed vigor from the random encounter and quickly decided the ties to Hannah had to be removed quickly. I was now regretting the extended invitation I had given for her to accompany me to my cabin home.

Since the arrival day for our trip came very quickly, I decided to follow through on the proposed two-day excursion. As agreed I picked Hannah up at her apartment Friday evening and admiringly noticed how little she had packed. Women in general seem to have the ability to fill suitcases with items to the point of overflowing no matter how few days the intended stay is. I say in general, as you cannot correctly state the entire gender acts in unison but it does seem to hold true in the majority of cases.

Hannah had packed a small overnight bag and brought along a heavy coat as the temperature was now well into the 30s on most nights. This was a drastic change from the Bay Area. She reminded me that she had not told anyone where she was going, or who she was going with. This meant she would leave her cell phone close just in case her daughters called and or something happened.

Seemed like a fair compromise. I was still concerned with my oldest daughter finding out about our budding relationship and wanted to keep a lid on the entire thing as long as possible. I was hoping that with my now-planned severing of the romantic strings, she would hold true to this agreement even after we concluded. This would just have to be a chance I would take as we were definitely not going to move forward for a long period of time.

The trip up was uneventful, and I was now exposed to three plus hours of nonstop recounting of endless stories. These ranged from the raising of her two kids to the antics happening at work to her colored family life, which included a stay in a mental facility when she was young. This had been instigated by her parent's fear she was on drugs. Oddly enough, at the time she was not but later on in life she would do the normal level of experimentation and dabble in the area. Fortunately she had never seriously been in jeopardy of losing control.

Upon arrival we let Delilah out of the back of the truck, waved to Don who was outside with his dog Buddy, and with reluctance I introduced Hannah. She was the first female "friend" Don had met entering the house who was not my wife. They exchanged an awkward greeting, and Hannah and I moved to unpack our belongings and make ourselves at home. I gave the obligatory tour and found myself amused at the facial expressions Hannah displayed as we went from room to room. The enormity of the house became apparent in a very short time. I would guess you could fit her apartment in my house five times over and still have a little room to spare.

We had eaten a quick bite for dinner on the way up, so I started a fire and opened some wine in the TV room. I then sat down to enjoy some interaction with Hannah without the distraction of driving. We each went through a couple of glasses and then retired to the upstairs bedroom. This should have felt odd to me being there with another woman for the first time but for some reason felt more refreshing than uncomfortable. We made love in a strangely routine way and settled back to close our eyes and prepare for the next day.

It was probably more unnerving having a woman there at all with the enormity of my experiences over the last few months. The only other events were shared with my three girls as my wife had stopped coming to the house a long time ago. I casually fell into my normal position on my side with one of my arms straddling an extra pillow for comfort. As always, I drifted off to sleep very quickly. My sleeping position was a topic of continued discussion with my youngest daughter. She commented often on how cute it was that I snuggled a pillow while I slept. Her latest approach had been to positively encourage me in this endeavor as it allowed her when sleeping with me to snuggle a pillow as well from the other side.

As I drifted off my nightly snoring habit came into full-blown orchestral form, and since I had forgotten to mention this fact it must have surprised Hannah. I not only snore, but also gasp for breath. I suffer from sleep apnea and have trouble getting what is defined as a true good night's sleep.

I have taken the test where you sleep in a hospital bed and the multitude of straps and wires are fastened over your entire body. They are used to monitor the level of oxygen you push through all parts of your system, which is the key indicator of how well you rest. I failed all the tests and then after the prodding of my wife went to a nose and throat specialist where I promptly had my septum operated on. Apparently this was to remove some form of curvature. I also had the patella removed from the back of my throat during the same procedure.

This was theoretically supposed to help my sleeping disorder, but surprisingly my snoring remained. I even wore this Darth Vader look-alike mask to bed for a couple of weeks that forced a continuous flow of air into my lungs and mouth. It was scarily too much for me to use on a continual basis. Can you imagine inviting a date over, and after saying goodnight donning a huge contraption over your head? Flipping a switch, turning on the engine, and saying goodnight.

I had been daydreaming of my hidden room since we departed on our trip up and admittedly it was hard not fantasizing about taking Hannah there. These thoughts stayed with me and formed the crux of my nighttime dreams, while I sifted from one tortuous fantasy to another. All of them ended in the same finality of Hannah leaving this world and moving on to the next. I still had my small pile of bones and two remaining skulls from the last go around and thought it would be good if I could extinguish them completely this trip. I of course could not because of Hannah.

As my snoring must have reached a sustained level of nonstop blaring, I felt the familiar jabbing and prodding that my wife had continually abused me with. In her words it was to keep me from disturbing her precious relaxation. Hannah must have felt that was an appropriate recourse as well since she fell quickly into the exact same pattern that my wife had formed for years on end. As abruptly as the pellets from a shotgun disperse upon firing Hannah's one final prod snapped me awake. With the click of a tiny trigger I lost control as the memories of my former spouse pushed me over the edge.

I sat up and quickly subdued Hannah into a forced slumber with my hands and the use of the blockish alarm clock sitting on my side of the bed. I lifted it and smashed it into pieces over her once beautiful face. This act unfortunately left some blood on the sheets and blanket. I worried that I would not be able to remove the red circular droplets that would most likely stain. I carried Hannah to my secluded sanctuary, and after removing her clothes fastened her hands and feet in the now familiar bindings. After I was comfortable with her inability to free herself, I went back to my room.

I changed the sheets, placing them in the washer and after starting the cycle went back upstairs to prepare the bed for my next attempt at a good night's sleep. Even with the testing and educated synopsis the one obstacle for a full good night slumber is simply removing any of the distractions. Even if that removal has to be by force. I now lay down for the second time and unlike the first felt that the odds of being woken again were slim.

I was concerned that I now had no choice but to complete the addition of Hannah to my growing list of conquests, but this time my connection to her was too close. I could only hope that my luck remained true, and I would not be found out. She had not told anyone of her plans for the weekend, but she had told several people about her dating me. I had also introduced her to Don which as always was a problem. He had to know everything. It concerned me that he got into my affairs while I was here.

There was no turning back now. The deed had been started, and I would have to finish off the now-natural progression tomorrow. As I drifted off to sleep, I laughingly felt how strange it would be to state in a courtroom that the reason I was apprehended was I needed a good night's sleep. The poking and prodding that had occurred impeded that goal. I was simply removing the source of the contention and as all good deductions would conclude that was a great idea.

If I was convicted the poking and prodding I would receive in prison were most likely of another nature. Not that there is anything wrong with that. Still, I cringed at the thought of this as I fell back into my land of conflicted nightmares

JUST THE FACTS

Sudhir was finding it odd that his left cheek was so irritated. Why did he feel the thumping pressure, and what was the muffled noise in the background. His head felt like somebody had it in a vice:one short turn from popping it like a pimple on the end of a teenager's nose. He then heard the words daddy a few times, and he now realized where he was, and the activities that gotten him here.

He was still passed out in his chair in the living room with the TV blaring from the night before. His daughter was tapping his cheek and saying something about being late for school.

"You have to get up quickly." His evening's discovery and assessment came hurtling back like a bomb and exploded in his aching head, almost causing him to throw up on his beautiful daughter.

He lurched out of his chair, throwing himself down the hall, slamming the bathroom door behind him. He just managed to lift the lid and expunge himself of all bodily fluids in one brief violent seizure. Wow, he really fell off the cliff last night. Having his daughter see him in this state was possibly the single worst experience that made up his wasted life. How could he have allowed her to be the one to find him?

Unless he could invent a time machine it was now done and he needed to move forward quickly to ease any lasting affects this might have on her impressionable young mind. He opened the door, checked the time, and yelled. Please grab something to eat and make your own lunches today. Daddy is going to jump in the shower and will then drive you both to school.

Taking a shower was pushing it, he knew, but if he didn't do something he felt he would be driving his kids to school with the window down and dry heaving the entire trip. As anticipated, the water was able to soothe some of

136

the wrinkles in his tattered physical body. After making a quick pot of coffee he slammed down a cup and hustled the kids into the car.

He drove them to school, foggily trying to keep up with the conversation, and after making one deadline and missing the other he rambled back home and worked on getting into a reasonable mental state. Another shower helped, and a call to the front desk letting them know he would not be in the office was necessary. He told them he was working on some leads and this left him with some added time to forcefully pull himself out of his self-inflicted hell.

It had been a long time since he had actually gotten sick from drinking. One of the few benefits of consuming alcohol is that it affords you the ability to cope better than the average person with overindulgence. He knew he must have really lost count for it to have this effect on his battered old body. A couple of hours and four cups of coffee into the morning he felt aware enough to continue the investigation of the murders. He was still having trouble wrapping his mind around the murderer being someone he loved like a brother. How would he begin to move forward with something that ripped at his very soul? He was left baffled, but knew it didn't matter, and had to be done.

He started listing out the calendar of events, and in a diagram created a chronological flow of what had occurred. All the relevant details were filled in at each square. He had a nice flowing whiteboard of everything he could pull from the strewn out papers that made up his now bulging file of all four murders. He then added in details that he knew and studied how the two connected.

Suhdir then made a quick phone call and managed to track down the original man who had seen the Volvo in the parking garage. He asked him some specific questions on the dent he had remembered seeing. Oddly enough at the time it was not something that anyone thought about as a relevant item that needed further exploring when it had been originally mentioned.

Sure enough, the dent was described as a small intrusion like a rock had been thrown at the vehicle. Not more than an inch, and noticeable only from a close-up view. Again, the man mentioned the only reason he remembered it was that he had a sister who had the same dent on her car in the same exact spot. It was just an oddity that caught his attention at the time.

Sudhir decided to grab one of his many pictures that he had, and take it down to the restaurant where the waiter had thought he might have remembered seeing the man with Jill as they ate dinner. Sudhir was lucky enough to catch him, but the waiter felt that the man from his memory did not resemble the man in the photo. He could not recall exactly, as it had been so long ago, but the hair didn't match—possibly the wrong color—and the face looked a little different than he remembered.

Feeling a little relief, but nowhere near satisfied, Sudhir made his way back home and pushed all his work into the garage—his only true haven in the house. He didn't want to have everything exposed when his wife came home later that evening. Exposing himself to his wife ceased many years ago.

After a day of diving into the depths of his startling conclusion from the night before, he was now actively questioning whether any of this made sense. There were thousands of people in the Bay Area that had second homes up in the mountains.

People drove Volvos everywhere in the world, and he was still not even 100 percent sure that this was the car he was looking for. Everything he had was flimsily connected in a makeshift way. It just didn't add up, yet something inside Sudhir told him he was on the right track, though it made him feel consumed with sadness.

Sudhir's instinct was to have another drink, and while he initially fought this move, he admitted to himself that having one drink never really hurt anything. He still had the reeling headache from the night before. No chemical substance could completely mask the pain that jolted inside his head like a lead ball in an old-fashioned pinball machine. The pain reminded him of his previous night's debacle.

The only possible thing he could think of was to dig a little deeper into his friends' life, possibly even follow him around for a few days, and see if anything opened up a door. He couldn't tell anyone of his farfetched story just yet, as he didn't really believe it himself. He might just be pushed out to the front desk job monitoring the radio because he drank so much. He had to look deeper, and again he only hoped that he was as far gone as it appeared from his second view.

He decided to clean up the house and make dinner for the kids and Janine, which would hopefully be a nice surprise. She had again been gone for a few days, and he wanted to do something nice for her. See how she would accept it. He caved in to her strong will on all occasions. She ruled the house, he knew, and he really didn't care.

Little things in life are so worthless to debate when you take a long step back and evaluate them. Annoying habits make a marriage tick—and keep the spark flowing. If you pass them over and just accept people, life moves in such a smoother flow. Sudhir cared about his wife, and he felt he would have to attempt to be better at supporting her and getting them back to a comfortable state of cohabitation. They had been leading separate lives for too long now, and he knew that at some point the result would be too much for him to handle if she decided to move on.

As volatile as she could be, he still loved her, and in his mind marriage was a final commitment. As final as death—he would not bend on that. His relationship would not fail.

No Choice

I awoke early, and it was a slow, foggy climb piecing the events together of last night. What dimwitted act I had now committed? The only thing even remotely more stupid would have been if I called the police myself and said hey, look at what I have done. Please come and get me.

At this point there was no going back. Hannah was tied up in the other room, and I would just have to move forward. I have always operated with the realization that traveling back in time is not possible, so you deal with things as they are the best you can and take what is given. My father operates under the exact opposite set of rules. This creates frustration between us. He laments over every decision ever made, and his favorite mode of conversation is lecturing me and everyone he meets on the pros and cons of their past behavior.

I would have to stay indoors and avoid Don for the rest of the day and night. Hopefully I could sneak out of here tomorrow so he would not question his lack of seeing Hannah again before we left. Introducing them was a blunder, for sure, and I did not want to stir that pot any more than it was already swirling.

I ran downstairs to change the laundry. Since I was going to need my roaring blaze, I started a fire in the square, iron fireplace that was turning into my own little crematorium. I really wish I had thought to put a muzzle of ball and tape over Hannah's mouth last night. It was going to be very difficult listening to her voice, knowing what I would have to do.

The act of killing somebody with a knife or rope or anything else that requires direct contact is very personal, but the rancid idea of killing somebody you personally know and have made love to his horrific. I only hoped that it would not consume me and threaten my existence. God, this was such a mistake.

Lesson learned. I don't think I can bring a woman up to my cabin ever again not specifically intended for death row. The temptation is too great. What if you gave a starving man who was a vegetarian a nice juicy steak? Placed it on a beautiful table setting, and then cut each piece for him offering the tasty morsel up as resolution to his lack of sustenance. What do you think the odds are that he would not bite it chew then swallow and quickly ask for the next savory piece?

Temptation is an odd thing, and can sway men to perform acts that go against their better judgment. The very definition of an affair points that out in obvious clarity. I found myself caught up in the act of doing miscellaneous chores around the house avoiding the primary task of the day using dishes, laundry, and making the bed. Higher priorities loomed.

I finally opened the door to the chaotic event that was about to begin. Hannah was crying, and appeared to have been doing so for many hours. She looked up at me with a bewildered amazement of emptiness and fear. I wonder at times about the differences between man and beast. Animals really don't understand what the future holds. You can tell your dog you are taking him to the vet one hundred times, but he still will have no clue that is where he is going until you get there.

Hannah seemed to fully comprehend her situation and held the terrified recognition of what was going to become of her. She frantically started screaming and violently yanking with all her strength on the bindings that held her. I understood her frenzied reaction. I could see that she had full view of the small pile of bones in the corner. The two skulls sitting on top were both signs that Hannah was in a little bit of trouble.

Why did you die, Hannah? This might be a question posed her on the next journey to the beyond. The answer would be laughable. Because I gently prodded my boyfriend as he began snoring and he apparently really did not like that. I would be in prison and she would be dead, all because I could not keep my mouth closed at night.   Again, too late now to think about it. I patiently waited for her seizure to subside, as her energy level must drain very quickly from her manic episode. Surprisingly, the body does have unique levels of untapped potential. Adrenalin can be a very potent, instigating drug when you find yourself in a position of physical danger.

My knife lay on the table, so I gently picked it up and forcefully plunged it deeply into Hannah's thigh, twisting it slightly.

"I would like you to be quiet now," I said, "and if not we can ensure that your tongue is the first thing I cut out of your overused flapping verbiage spewing mouth." I surprised even myself with this curt statement, and how easily I inflicted pain on somebody I had held as a friend and lover a few short hours ago.

Stunned silence lasted for a few short seconds, as the shrieking shrill from the recently inflicted pain overtook her ability to control her screaming. Once again she crazily started the seismic seizure that would rate a scale of nine or higher and might topple a city building if she had any power behind her movements. This was going to be both easier and difficult, but with all things unknown you can anticipate potential outcomes—but you never know reality until you, well, face reality.

I firmly grasped the knife again, and this time plunged it directly into her other leg in approximately the same location as the first. With the constant movement of her gyrating thigh it was making it more of a pin the tail on the donkey game. I felt blindfolded looking for that spot I had just seen a few seconds ago.   This aggressive approach did nothing to slow down or mitigate her nonstop, hysterical whaling. I decided to sit back and just watch for a while neither continuing my own agenda nor disrupting her show. I can now understand the need for straitjackets in an asylum. With the potential for this kind of outburst from patients the need to protect staff and oneself would required an extremely tight hold on any appendage that could be used. Hannah had lost control of her limbs. They flailed in all directions and were held only by the metal shackles that limited her movements.

The only difference the last few minutes of our game of cat and mouse was the streaming flow of crimson from her two wounds on the table and a nice steady flow to the floor below. As happened previously the windmill-like arms were splattering blood in droplets.

I recognize in myself the weaknesses and flaws that I was given at birth and have accepted my inability to withstand high levels of screaming and fighting for long periods of time. Patience is not a virtue that I was blessed with, and although I can abide my tongue for short periods I have found this only leads to a voluminous eruption if held too long. My two little children bicker back and forth constantly, and it is like fingers scraping across a freshly cleaned chalkboard as the noise penetrates my essence. With the finality of my nerves extinguished like a candle, I grabbed her left arm, held it against the table. I very quickly slashed across her wrist a deep fresh cut. It instantly connected with her vein and opened to her inevitable draining. It would now be a matter of minutes, with the leakage spewing forth at full blast, helped along by her incessant fit that I now understood would never cease.

Although I had not planned on making love to Hannah I felt the familiar rising as her life squirted away in streaming bursts of red. I decided to enter her and hope that my timing was not too late, as her energy level drained in unison with her blood flowing down the circling hole in the floor below. As before, the excitement from the events had aroused me, and it took me a few shorts strokes to unload my gush of sexual pleasure with her blood squirting in bursts from the slash across her left wrist and legs.

It felt oddly like I was pushing the blood forward with each thrust. I collapsed in a heap on top of her, trying to balance myself in the slippery red mess. I caught my breath heaving from the unexpected exertion. Making love is a grand form of exercise, and once engaged it is hard to stop.

It reminded me of when I was a child, and my cousins and I were out in the backyard playing with my dog. He was a speckled beagle mutt of some kind. He ran away with a huge surge of energy. It took us several minutes before we were able to track him down a few houses over on another block. We found him connected to the back end of another dog on his hind legs with his front paws wrapped around the female dog's torso.

Try as we might we could not disengage the two, even though we planned on playing with him. He was thwarting our efforts. We ran back inside the house and explained the situation to my grandmother, who frowned at us and told us to leave them alone for thirty minutes. It was several years later that I realized what was actually occurring. I still laugh at that story today.

I must admit my early worry about conversation with Hannah making this more difficult was now lost in my thoughts. If she had taken the approach of conversing with me upon my arrival I might very well have broken down and cried. The road she chose, unconsciously, was appreciated at least by me. I was now taking great pleasure in seeing her simply shut up, as her energy receded as quickly as the tide pulls its water into the depths of the ocean.

The most interesting part of witnessing death is watching the eyes glassing over. The eyes are the true window to what lies inside of each and every person. Like a one-way mirror we spend most of our lives looking outward taking in all the daily activities that we are exposed to.

I loved watching her now quiet, muffled mouth forming the last remnants of speech and was amused that the only word she could muster was "why?" Everyone who is dying always wants to know why. How do you answer that question? Do I simply say because that is what God intended, and he created us each with a maximum span of years. You have run the course as you were meant to. Do I explain that God needs helpers now and then to do his work, and I am simply the conduit for his achievement in the circle of life?

I love that saying ever since watching the movie *Lion King.* "Circle of life" holds everything in three short simple words. God intended for us to give birth, consume what we need from the lives of others for nourishment, and then at some point have our lives taken. And so on and so on. I am just a simple employee doing the bidding of my God who picked me for my role in that circle.

God employs all types of individuals from priests to choir singers to wielders of death that take what is most precious. I continued to stare, as I was seeing the last flicker of light behind the two glassy openings enjoying the calmness that now engulfed the room. How quickly chaos leads to serenity. From the wreckage of tornadoes to the unexpected tsunami once havoc has been heaped in abundance the quietness that follows eerily overcomes the overwhelming event.

I now needed to allow the body to drain as much fluid as possible, making the burning process flow seamlessly. I left the room taking time to shower and clean myself off before I moved on to the next step in this now scripted event. Not really sure why I chose the shower since I knew I would only need another one after I sawed through flesh and bone, cutting my large morsel into bite sized chunks.

Just to clarify, the eating of human flesh is not something on my bucket to do list. I have no desire to add it to the accomplishments I achieve. I don't understand the desire to eat humans. A steak is fine for me. I will happily stick to the four-legged animals for sustenance and nourishment and leave the human meat for the movies and or sick individuals who in my point of view take things too far.

Ironically everything is perspective. My guess is the majority of the human race would lump me closer to the flesh-eating group than allowing my entry into the normal circles. Maybe I don't belong to either. I have never felt the compelling urge to need acceptance. I am fine being on my own ostracized from society in most aspects.

Granted, I don't think I would enjoy zero interaction. I do need the friendly night out for a beer with friends, but it is not a driving factor in who I am. I can take it or leave it, as they might say.

I was startled back to the present by my cell phone's familiar jingle, and upon looking at the screen saw that Sudhir was calling me. I had not spent much time with him lately. I should return his call tomorrow and see if we could meet for beers.

I liked Sudhir but he was really a lost soul. If I could do anyone a favor he might be at the top of the list for somebody who really needed to find out what the next step in a life was. His wife, although an annoying nag, was extraordinary and deserved much better. Sudhir was a good guy to have a beer with and he was always up for watching a game now and then but not much more.

I spent the rest of the day on my list of chores, cleaning up my self-made mess. I think once you cut a person into pieces you no longer have to address the pile by name. It takes on more definition of a chore as you separate each part and bucket it up for the trip to the disintegration chamber. I only ventured outside to let Delilah free for a urination break, and to gather additional wood. I was spared any verbal interactions with my neighbor.

All in all it was a good day and only the nagging remembrance of my closeness with Hannah, and the inevitable questioning that would be engaged left me any remorse from what occurred. I reflected back on my beginning episode, and the emotional turmoil that ensued from my regret. I thought how I had grown, or become more callous.

Callous denotes an inability to feel, and I had feelings. I just don't have the same feelings as say the vast majority of humans that inhabit our dying planet. Isn't the United States built on sheer diversity? That is the core of what we hold valuable. San Francisco is the crown jewel of being who you want, and respecting others allowing them to do the same. The one glaring difference in my segmented way of thinking was causing harm to my fellow man (or woman). Diversity as itself is okay, but taking your will and imposing it on women moves that into a dictatorial stance instead of true choice.

Ah well, I spent the rest of the day returning everything to order and cozied up for a night of burning and renting a movie. I had not watched *Burn after Reading* and thrust the DVD into the player, pausing only to insert another piece of wood or an appendage into the iron opening. I should let Delilah chew on one of the bones, I thought for a brief second, but that sounded too barbaric to me so passed on the idea.

She did curl up at my feet and snuggled up to the heat-induced sauna that always accompanied the cremation. Not quite the weekend I had planned, but it had turned out to be nice none the same.

JASON

Jason was born in the bay area, grew up in San Carlos where he still lived, and until recently actually resided in the same house he had known his entire life. He had one brother and several friends, and although not a perfectly charmed existence had to admit his life had been scripted better than most. His upbringing was a decent experience. He played two sports in high school (football and wrestling) and being above average in football afforded him a nice status in school. In wrestling he had gone to the state tournament every year and even placed third at his senior stint.

He was smart enough to realize he would never play anything professionally, and he really had no ambition to do anything in the physical area. He was bright and his inner desire was always something in law enforcement. Looking back at the time he had envisioned becoming a police officer in the San Francisco or San Carlos area. After heading off to Arizona State and making above average grades he had applied and tested well for enrollment in the FBI. Upon acceptance had felt at home from day one.

His parents had divorced when he was in high school. Some might have thought this would be traumatic, but he and his brother had not been very scarred by the event. His dad traveled to Washington, DC, on a weekly basis contracting for the Navy. Several years ago he had started an affair with a lady there, had a child, which nobody had known about, and subsequently divorced his wife. She, oddly enough during the beginning of his senior year, moved to DC as well in the hopes of salvaging the broken marriage. This meant leaving him and his brother, who was two years older, alone in the house at the peak of their exploration age.

The end result had been lots of parties, some sporadic involvement with the police, and his brother being arrested on one occasion for providing alcohol to underage minors. Luckily he himself had never been arrested, or his FBI career might not have gotten off the ground. His parents actually gave them one check a week for groceries, as well as needed supplies. His average Safeway trip ran in the five to six hundred dollar range. How could his parents have actually believed he and his brother spent that per week on just groceries was a little amazing. The checks were most likely payment for easing the guilt they felt for leaving them on their own at such a vulnerable stage.

Interestingly enough, both he and his brother had developed a knack and desire for culinary achievement and spent several weekends making elaborate dinners for close friends. His was probably one of the few high school groups to have real dinner parties that focused on seven-course meals versus simple beer binges. Their specialty had become homemade pizza with extravagant recipes for the crust and a nice tangy sauce.

They allowed everyone to add whatever ingredients they desired making some interesting combinations.

His older brother had not fared quite as well. He turned into an alcoholic, muddled his way through mediocre grades in school, and become an isolated social outcast. It wasn't until a family reunion that he met his first cousin (she was also a social recluse). They hit it off. She got him to stop drinking, and they eventually married. Granted, there were many in the family who frowned upon the union, but despite popular belief there is no physical evidence proving it can be harmful to child-rearing.

They now have two healthy, beautiful kids and are thriving in a small community in Florida. They don't attend many extended family gatherings, but are well-balanced and making it work. To sum up they are as well off as anyone can be.

Jason had met his wife Sherene at Arizona State, where she was a walk on for the tennis team and was quite active in school events. By college Jason had stopped sports completely, and focused mainly on his studies, but still enjoyed pickup games and continued his extravagant dietary experimentations.

After meeting his wife he took up tennis as an easy way to spend time with her and found he really had a knack for excelling in most all sports. He quickly became quite good. He began to realize at that point that things in general came easily to him. He studied, and was focused, but he never had to try very hard to be better than average in almost anything he attempted.

After making it through college with above average grades he moved up quickly in the FBI. He was now enjoying his current role in the limelight as one of the leads on The National Investigations Unit for the team headquartered out of the Bay Area. He was a master at picking out pieces and painting a picture long before anyone knew to even look in the direction of the canvas.

It was as if the images formed in his mind, and he simply placed them in the appropriate order.

His one failing was his devotion to his job, which now caused the failure of his marriage. As he reflected on his life he could say this was his biggest disappointment. In the beginning things had been great and it was no fault of Sherene's that they were still not a unit. He just could not de-commit enough of his mental fortitude from his preoccupation with catching criminals.

Neither of them had an affair or lost interest or fell out of love. It was just the lack of happiness from his not being home, or even when he was home from his lack of being engaged that severed the ties that had bound them together. Sherene needed to be happy and have a working family unit and he now knew that he was not able to be part of that.

He didn't really know his kids, was not a part of their lives, and although he loved them had no real knowledge of who they were. He was now drinking more than was healthy, but still not enough to cause concern. His little one-bedroom apartment was rented for the sole purpose of its proximity to his children. Sherene was still in the house his parents owned in trust, and he would put every effort in keeping her there until the kids were raised.

Ironically, he was now spending more devoted time with them than he ever had before. Distance makes the heart grow fonder, or something like that. Being separated from his kids had made him appreciate them more. His time with them now (when his job allowed) had provided more real connection than at any other point in his life.

Jason was not assigned to a case currently, but was consulting on a couple of active investigations, one in North Carolina and one in New Mexico. He took sporadic trips to discuss current findings, but other than a few guest speaking gigs at local colleges and some lectures at the FBI headquarters he was not overly taxed. He was still decompressing from the last case that had taken over six months to conclude and saw the end of seven lives. It was documented as being one of the more gruesome murder sprees on record, and had left him and his team mentally exhausted.

Even with the lack of anything directly requiring his attention, there were some issues that concerned him. One of which was the recent file his friend Sudhir had presented on a couple of missing girls that continued to tug at his mind. He didn't think there was a connection between the two, but for some reason his instinct, as was Sudhir's, was telling him otherwise. The two shootings seemed farfetched, having only the car linking the dots, but the two girls were more easily bridged. The only real problem was the vast difference in how they went missing, and the oddity of timing. He felt comfortable letting Sudhir move forward for now, but if another missing girl appeared he would get involved and raise the level of attention to his supervisor.

Most of their cases actually start out just like this scenario. The local police happen along a murder or abduction, link a couple together, and the next thing you know call the FBI for some advice. The unit gets involved, relieves them of the burden, and takes over from there. Simplistic, really, but the police are almost always the first ones finding the pieces. Depending on how good they do their job in almost all cases defines how long it takes to get to the end result.

Sudhir was surprisingly good at picking up on the normally missed details. He probably had untapped talent glossed over by his overuse of alcohol, and his submissive nature—beaten down by his wife for so many years. Jason really liked Sudhir a lot, and in another life with more time to devote to developing relationships would have been a close friend.

Ironically, time was the one thing he was not known for utilizing personally. It was only in the last month that he had even taken a vacation for well over three years. After the last case ended, his supervisor had insisted he leave for two weeks. Without the binding family ties he had spent one week with his kids, and one week alone in the Bahamas basking in the sun, drinking way too much. He had even managed to get to know a couple of the locals.

The main highlight from his trip had been on a sunny day as he was sitting on his balcony. It was right on the beach not more than fifty feet from the water's edge. He observed his recently moved in neighbors. They were definitely European, and the man had to be in his late forties while the woman must have been in her very early thirties. The age gap seemed to be ten years or more.

As is the European custom she removed her top to expose a nice pair of firm, tanned breasts that were definitely real and held an appealing attractive enticement. He had sat on his balcony basking in the sun for a couple of hours enjoying the view, wondering how lives were different depending on where you happen to be born.

She had fallen asleep. Her head was tilted to the right, and her mouth appeared to be open just a tiny crack. She was not aware of the approaching dog. Dogs are prevalent in the area, and for whatever reason seem to be more community owned. All are very nice in nature and usually docile because of the nonstop attention from the locals as well as the frequent travelers.

Still, as the dog approached her, he decided to give her a nice lick hello. The interesting part is it was on the nipple of her left breast. The lady stirred slightly, so taking that as acceptance the dog licked some more. The startled lady opened her eyes, and with a scream from seeing the dog, jumped up yelling something he had no understanding of at all.

It took all of his self-control not to burst out laughing, but he didn't want her to know he had sat there and enjoyed the entire scene. The rebuked dog made his way down the beach, and the lady then reluctantly resumed her position on the chair but did not allow herself to recommence her slumbering comfort. The eyes remained open.

The vacation had been a great reprieve from life, and as intended, drained some of the strain of personal issues and work related problems. He can't say that vacations always achieve success, but this one was well worth the payment and effort. Now as he was back and readjusting to life, he wanted to focus his efforts back on his natural talent and get back to his passion.

Jason looked through the file. The one thing that Sudhir had not pursued out of all the items was the license plate. Jason knew that if you were smart you would be changing plates on your car, or better yet not using your car at all. The easy way to make an abduction would have been to take a taxi to the location, use her car to leave the scene, dumping it later and not exposing your vehicle in any way.

That meant that the abductor was not sophisticated, but smart. This led him to believe that this was only the beginning, if it truly was a serial killer they were dealing with. As Jason always hoped, he wanted to be wrong.

He ran through the database looking for reported license plates missing in the Bay Area to see if anyone had reported an issue. Most license plates thefts are not even reported. People simply get another sticker or apply for a replacement. The expense is minimal, and the effort of reporting an issue is more trouble than it is worth.

Interestingly enough, there was an issue of a reported theft of a plate that began with KY in the Bay Area from a man in Redwood City. His report stated that he really did not know where or how the plate was removed. His front plate had been moved to the back of the car and his back plate containing the current sticker had been taken. He applied for a new sticker and plate, and wanted to inform the authorities in case anyone used his plate in illegal activities.

There was not a lot of follow-up, but Jason printed out the report and felt the familiar rumbling of concern that was emanated from Sudhir when they last spoke. This meant premeditation, which was not a good sign that this was isolated. Jill was not somebody that connected with people that might abduct and kill her. The missing plate issue meant somebody had stalked and or predefined her as a victim.

Jason decided to spend the rest of the day going through the file in more detail. He was now thankful he had Sudhir make a copy for him of at least the police reports of said crimes. He now wished he had a copy of all the details, as he knew Sudhir had pursued other angles and possibly had notes and or items that would be useful.

He went down to his supervisor's office and laid out the paperwork explaining the situation and asked for another opinion. While both agreed on the potential possibilities, neither of them were convinced it made sense to get involved. Jason was urged to keep in contact with Sudhir and have him update him on any new findings, but for now that was all. With their relationship that would be easy to do.

Jason gave Sudhir a call, told him of his discussion on an answering machine. He spent the rest of the next couple of days preparing for a guest speaking role on the last case they had successfully closed. It is common practice to slice up an activity and present it as learning material for everyone who wants to attend. Jason as the lead was normally asked to do the bulk of the material gathering and speaking.

He actually enjoyed giving presentations and the back and forth questioning and answering that followed. Unlike many of his peers, who were as reclusive as himself in their devotion to their job, he still enjoyed the varying opinions and questioning of decisions that often occurred. He kept his mind open to new ways of thinking, and some of his best approaches to cases had come from this.

He often started out his talks saying he had to give credit to the very people in these audiences for his team's success. He was only as good as the group and supporting cast that made up the entire FBI and they were all one entity. The core of his current five-person squad had come from this environment. He had plucked them out and after informal conversations and observation asked them to join.

His group makeup was an oddity in the FBI, but with his and their success nobody questioned it. They allowed him to run as he saw fit. He often acknowledged his supervisor for forward thinking and navigating the red tape to allow him to focus on his job of catching criminals—the only thing in life that he was currently any good at.

PREPARING THE STORY FOR HANNAH

After I had properly disposed of the pieces that used to be Hannah I now had a small pile of leftover—what I deemed my three trophies or the skulls from my recent harem. This was not my total set of prizes, as I could not have the heads of the two men that I had shot in the alley. Nevertheless I decided to build a shelf in my room and display them as one would his football or baseball accolades from decades ago.

I had never been much of an active sports enthusiast, although I did enjoy the spectator sport of watching others play. It was not that I lacked athletic ability, but I had never developed much as a youngster having to work most days after school instead. My father never fully understood the need for extracurricular development when there was a calling for a drywall job or repairing a sewer. The generous quarter an hour he paid me made up for the loss in childhood, though. (That was sarcasm by the way for all of you dimwitted people out their reading my diary.)

We had a leftover label maker from some art project the girls had used. After the shelf was properly installed and the trophies were in place I labeled each one appropriately. I could only call the second one blonde woman, as I never knew her actual name. I would have to remember to look online and see if I could discover this at some point. It seemed impersonal to not even know the name of somebody who had played such a pivotal role in the historical life and times of Duncan.

I left two open spots and labeled them man 1 and man 2 for the men in the alley. This reminded me of thing one and thing two from Dr. Seuss, and I suddenly felt connected to a kid's short story. The men had no lasting effect on my psyche, but again are now part of the story and played their intended role. From this point on I would have to really focus on knowing the names in order to finish off the display. It looked tacky otherwise, and who wants to display their accomplishments in a tacky way.

I wondered in the grand scheme of taking lives how my five stood up against the great villains of all time. This was no Hiroshima, and that would never be compared to what I was doing, but in the end it had the same result and finality for everyone involved. I wonder how warped our history books truly are, and if we went to Japan would it be labeled an atrocity versus a key event that brought the conclusion to a needless war. We vilified Germany and Japan, as well we should for their gross disregard for lives but were we any different really.

The men and women of that great city were not the cause of the aggression. In most cases they were simply following the misguided direction of the men in power who were forming public opinion and manipulating the masses in order to get what they needed. Germany as a nation was not bad and held many strong upstanding level-headed individuals. Sadly, in the end the majority had allowed unspeakable hatred to be leveled against people just for who they were and what nationality they called their own.

I could never hate a group of people as a whole. In mass is meaningless as individuality keeps the world moving. People do horrible, unspeakable things and yes individuals can sway groups to do the same, but in the end judging somebody for their beliefs can never be viewed upon as right. I realize fully that my actions are wrong, and what I am doing is one of the worst things possible against my fellow man. Does it matter that I am doing it without prejudice? That has to give me something right.

Anyway, I am losing myself in thought again. I closed up shop so to speak and prepared the area for my eminent departure. Once on the road I started planning and rehearsing my inevitable questioning about Hannah, and where she might be located. I felt most comfortable with simply stating I had not seen her this weekend, and although we had started dating we had only been out a few times. I by no means knew her whereabouts on a daily basis.

If she had told anyone where she was headed for the weekend I would have to live with my story and say they must be mistaken. My only real loose end was my neighbor, Don, who I had introduced to Hannah. If by some chance anyone ever did question my story, and followed up by talking to him I would be in a corner. I didn't really know how to get beyond this.

I contemplated driving back to Twain Harte that night, and unfortunate as it would be, shooting Don as he walked his dog, then heading back home. I think the odds of a killing in Twain Harte of that nature would bring more attention than I needed. In the end I decided to live with the first story and deny knowledge and hope that it ended there.

I had disposed of Hannah's cell phone and all of her clothes. After cleaning out the fireplace I felt that at a minimum the remnants of my actions were safely tucked away in the trashcan outside. While Don did have a tendency to go through my discarded refuge, I doubt even he would sift through the ash and remains of a burnt-out fire. The likelihood of something valuable being left in there had to be slim.

I made it home uneventfully and played with Delilah in the back yard for a while in utter awe of the dog's ability to fetch a ball with such chaotic energy. How the dog managed to ever sleep was beyond me, as she never seemed to tire.

I was surprised by my calmness and reflected back a few months ago to my first triumph with Jill, and how emotionally drained I had been. I no longer felt any remorse and had fully accepted what I had become. I had embraced my new outlook on life. I guess you might be able to say that the true definition of what I was now about was death.

Instead of jumping in the shower and wasting time lamenting over spilled blood I put on a pot of boiling water to make some tea and prepared pasta for a nice spaghetti meal. Tonight was Sunday, and I had two more episodes of *Californication* in the queue, and I was dying with excitement to see them. I had now decided my true idol was Hank, and if I could pick a single person to be it would be that character.

What better way to flitter through life than to do whatever you wanted and not care at all about the outcome or results of anything or anyone around you. Be true to yourself, and live for the moment. He did mix in the relationship with his daughter and in only the character's fashion loved her and wanted something good for her. He, in his own way, attempted to be a good father. Who can ask for anything more?

If you did a study on the fatherly attributes of American men I think you would be amazed at how inconsistent we truly are. Not only our thinking of right and wrong but also in our actions and how we approach things. One of my two sayings that I repeatedly emphasize to my three daughters is, "I only promise to do the best I can. Parents are never perfect and all we can do is love you and try our best." The other one is to promise to love them always no matter what.

The last part grows exceedingly difficult with my oldest daughter. She is definitely pushing the "no matter what" phrase. While I felt, and still feel, she is going through an extraordinarily difficult time I also now feel she is manipulating both her mother and I to maximize her desires to the fullest. I would never question how hard this has been on her, but I do now see that she is using the situation as much as she can to further her own personal goals as well. The sad thing is she doesn't know what her goals are. She is a lost girl, as are most of us, and I hope she can find her way. She has a good heart, and in the end she will be an incredible woman. If only she can make it through these difficult times whole and complete.

I can't blame her, really. She is a teenager, after all, and adding the hormonal upheaval they all go through with changing high schools and then throwing in the divorce is more than anyone should ever have to take. In retrospect I still do not know how I could have done things differently to make it any better.

Her mother's bitterness and attacking approach in the beginning would never change under any scenario. The hatred she still portrayed has left her bitter and sad. She denies this, of course, but pure anger oozes out of her pores every time we meet. Until she stops being so angry, she will never be happy.

Maybe I should tell her of my outlet. We could share a common theme and they would call us the "Bonnie and Clyde" of our generation. The only difference is Bonnie and Clyde actually loved each other. I would be in constant danger of lashing out against my wife, if she were ever in a situation where I was performing one of my conquests.

After dinner I dutifully completed my menial tasks, cleaning up the dishes and putting everything away. I then poured a nice glass of scotch, turned on the TV. I excitedly watched my idyllic character go through his endless array of sexual encounters. He continually was drinking with an aimless approach toward everything imaginable. I wish there was a way to be paid for actions such as this—oh wait, he is being paid for this.

The next couple of days were uneventful. Going to work and adding then subtracting then adding again only to finish something and redo the entire calculation. We are endlessly making sure that numbers matched anything that was presented previously. I failed to see the point of my job, at times. I felt I was constantly presenting data that was so obvious that anyone could see the trended outcome of where the company was going and what needed to be done.

Our CEO felt the accounting function was a useless tool as well. Sadly that was reflected in the overall viewpoint directed at our department. We were the bastard stepchild of the world and operated under those parameters. The only saving grace was our CFO was one of the smartest guys that I had worked with. He impressively knew details down to a surprising level and easily maintained them. He could continually regurgitate facts at countless meetings like he had just read them minutes before.

My memory is just not that good. I find nothing more impressive than somebody who can be presented with data and actively use that data at any point in time as needed. He easily rebuked our CEO on several occasions, pointing out inaccuracies that were stated with factual data. In the end nobody can really argue with facts.

I liked the boardroom drama that occurred when opinions were far out of alignment. It was easy to admire the political navigation where everyone felt the need to state an opinion and at the same time not state it in any way that truly offended anyone. After all the CEO is the CEO, and it is his company to run as he sees fit. He should have smart people on staff. Disagreement condones debate, which leads to better decisions but once something is decided everyone needs to rally and be part of the same team.

I learned this from my army days. Once the debate is over you don't question the decision anymore. You definitely don't question it in an inappropriate hierarchal standing. Loyalty is a must, and true loyalty comes from being able to disagree and still follow directives.

It was not until Wednesday that I received the call from Sarah. She inquired about Hannah, and asked me if I had heard from her. She was supposed to return on Sunday from a weekend trip, and had left the girls with her. Sarah had now been on the phone with all the area hospitals and the police. She was beside herself with worry.

As expected, this would be stressful to navigate.

Odd Night Out for Drinks

Sudhir was unsure of his plan. He had talked to several friends, and they had agreed to meet for Monday night football. There would be four to six going, and it would be nice to get out for a while with no strings or complaining in the background. The peripheral moaning was nonstop, and he was still unsure how to change the direction he and his wife were heading.

The dinner that he had in his mind thoughtfully prepared for his wife was a non-event. She hastily stated she ate on the plane and was in no mood to sit and listen to him belch at the table if she was not even hungry. This had not been the desired reaction, and his goal seemed unattainable. He had seen worse odds watching the Sharks game last night and they had come back from being three goals down to start the third period. Somehow they had squeaked out a one-goal win.

He, as always, enjoyed the dinner with the kids, but he was aware that stress was eating away at them all. Maybe a planned trip to the wine country for the weekend with just the two of them would be a good idea. Time away might push them back in the positive direction he so desperately wanted.

Throughout the course of the weekend his continual failed attempts at anything thoughtful were hastily rebuked. Breakfast in bed was the only thing that brought a slight smile to her frowning demeanor, and he made a note of this to try more often.

He pushed aside the ongoing investigation that was now becoming his obsession. He was a dad and husband again albeit briefly for the span of two days. He took the kids down for a movie rental and stopped at Baskin Robbins for a pick of one of the thirty-one flavors. Saturday had been pizza and movie night. With the family securely relaxed in front of the TV they had watched the latest Disney episode of some little robot thing that couldn't speak. Sudhir missed the point of this but enjoyed the microwaved popcorn and soda with the family. The dawning realization of missed opportunities and the unappreciated blessings of life washed over him as he simply smiled for the hour and a half they enjoyed together.

As with all family activities, they quickly end and the participants hastily dissipate to their designated personal preferences. Janine headed off to read while the video game in the boy's room was flicked on. His cute, beautiful daughter curled up in the chair with him, offering to snuggle as they watched a couple episodes of the latest *Hannah Montana*.

He actually didn't mind the childish bantering that the show projected in the simplest form of TV entertainment possible. That is what TV is for. It was pure enjoyment of mindless stimulation to garner a laugh or make you jump in your seat. The shows produced oohs and ahhs at the incredibly stupid things some people might attempt to win a hundred thousand dollars or a million or whatever prize was being touted on the latest reality craze.

He might still be in the minority, but had and would always prefer a show about something. The shows that were forced upon this generation of "real" actionable items were a sickness that hopefully would soon be purged. Like all things, he was sure it was a phase and would be coming to a conclusion. He didn't hate them all, just to be clear, but by far the majority could be eliminated and he would not even be aware.

After enduring a couple of episodes his daughter gave in to the night and offered up going to bed. He tucked her in, and told the boys they had only thirty minutes left. He went back to his familiar chair, poured the comfort of his much-needed glass of scotch, and began the random cycle of flipping in the hopes of finding something tolerable. Sudhir was not sure how much exercise the population would receive if you didn't count the hand movement it takes to push the remote frequently through the hundreds of offered channels. It was good practice for him, as he used the same hand to provide the only sexual pleasure he held in this house.

True to his nightly custom, he found himself waking up around 2:30 AM still sitting in his chair. The TV was talking about some magical chopping machine that could basically do anything you ever wanted in life with but the push of a button. All of this for only three monthly payments of $29.99. He was sure that people buy these things. Otherwise why would the commercials remain on TV? But who? He just wanted to know who.

He made his way to the dimly lit bedroom with the nightlight as his guiding beacon. After a quick bathroom break quietly slipped in under the sheets and snuggled up by himself as he prepared to doze back into the land of dreams. He liked waking up just at the edge of something good, trying to remember what fantasy his body had been partaking in that was not possible in the land of the living.

Monday mornings, as always, were a little chaotic. Nobody really wanted to get moving. The kids did not want to get up from their cozy pillows and blankets. By attempt number three, the threats were unboxed, and very quickly the covers were thrown back while the morning ritual began anew. Sudhir actually even enjoyed this process. The bickering was minimal, so it didn't reach the level of annoying.

After he dropped the kids off, he headed to the office. He had stuffed his attempted chronological mapping in the trunk with the thought he would make use of it in his tasks for the day. He actually ended up not even removing it from the coffin where it lay stranded. He instead preferred to muddle through work doing very little as he anticipated the nightly activities.

He had no agenda, and did not even know if he would broach the subject in a subtle way. He tried to weed out any facts that might slip through that would either help eliminate, or at a minimum, clarify assumptions. He doubted more and more the very plausibility of his hypothesis. His years of friendship were undermining the weekend's farfetched ideas.

They had planned on meeting up at a little Irish bar on Third Street in San Mateo, which was a frequented gathering place for male bonding activities. Jeff and a couple of guys would also tag along. He couldn't even remember who was playing at this point, but was excited about not having to face Janine. She was becoming increasingly more annoying and difficult to live with.

Sadhir thought of asking the group for advice. It seemed like a good idea to him, and if the opportunity arose he would do just that. The guys know Janine very well (one very well, indeed), and it would be odd to try and talk to about his marital problems to say the least.

Sudhir arrived at the bar early and was the first one of the designated Monday night gang to show up. He ordered a single beer waiting for everyone else before starting in with the pitchers. Not very many places seem to serve a nice large pitcher of beer anymore. With the hundreds of microbrews and choices abounding most people nowadays steered toward individuality, beer connoisseurs were now as prevalent as wine snobs. Sudhir was fine with Coors Light, as his beer of choice. The crowd arrived in tandem. The table Sudhir had secured worked fine, and everyone all settled in for a night of cursing, drinking, and manly talk about the many annoying habits of everyone's wives.

If you were able to listen in on the same circle of friends only supplanting the male figures with their counterpart female figures the conversation would be similar in nature. Women most likely don't understand men much better. How do we as a race cohabitate at all with our visible differences and strikingly annoying habits?

The group of gangly men meandered through halftime in a low-scoring, poorly played game and spent more effort on conversation than watching the event. There was a brief moment when Twain Harte popped up as a peripheral topic, but it was only used as a reference point and led to nothing conclusive. Sudhir did notice that one friend seemed preoccupied, and the best description he could come up with was nervous.

As the game ended the crowd dispersed quickly. As Sudhir was reviewing the evening he noticed that they had drank very little. Everyone seemed guarded.

Sudhir did mention the desire to talk about Janine, and although the response was subdued he did agree to go to marriage counseling. Who could say for sure if Sudhir was imposing his own delusional manifestations or if anything he was picking up was actually real? The mind plays so many tricks on you. You can convince or talk yourself out of things that are perfectly rational or absolutely crazy if given enough time. Thankfully, he did not know the answer as of yet.

Sudhir managed to drive home easily enough. Since everyone normally stopped the alcohol flow at the end of the third quarter he felt like he was following his civic duty by not driving while inebriated. He was a law enforcement official after all, and if he didn't obey the law then who would?

The odd thing about the West Coast was on Sundays and Mondays when football was in full swing the games are all played at times not normally associated with drinking beer and cursing. Starting Monday night football at 5:30 is such a quick rush from work to wherever you might be going. Sunday morning at 10 AM was quite early to have people over if there was a specific game of interest being played on the East Coast.

It was still early when he arrived home. He took fifteen minutes to tuck the kids in, and as the nightly ritual required, he got them both a glass of water and told them a quick bedtime story that he made up on the fly. As long as there was a once upon a time and a princess in it you couldn't really go wrong.

Janine was surprisingly quiet that evening and made it very clear when he approached her that her preference was to keep it that way. Sudhir took the subtle direction and headed off to the family room to watch some TV in his well-worn favorite chair. If this kept up much longer you might have to start defining his chair as a bed with him sleeping in it more hours than settled in next to his wife.

He perused through random channels and with his customary glass of scotch he for once didn't feel like watching anything. He bid his time until the bedroom light was extinguished. Giving Janine ample time to fall asleep, he quietly moved into the bedroom and was annoyed at her having again taken his pillow. Not wanting to rouse her he made do with one of the less appealing alternatives.

It didn't take him long to move into the darkened fantasyland. He rustled through the night with troubled dreams, as his once peaceful world was having trouble staying calm.

Answering Questions

It was less than a week later on a Tuesday afternoon I received a surprise visit at work. As usual for any day of the week, I was in my office with the west-facing windows soaking in the bright afternoon sun. I sat facing my computer trying to decipher another mundane spreadsheet.

Spreadsheet software reinvented the accounting world and brought with it an even greater focus to the mundane boring life that all detailed anal accounting personnel face. Oddly enough I don't think that most people employed in the accounting area are even aware of how sad and repetitive our lives are. The same numbers each month followed by the same processes each quarter followed by the same annual audits that are exactly the same as the quarterly.

If you do not like repeating yourself continually then you had better hope for a better life than the accounting/finance field. I look back on my life and still wonder how in the world I ended up in this job in this area. Don't get me wrong, I made good money, had a great CFO, and our team was an eclectic group of misfits. We enjoyed each other's company and in the casual atmosphere I projected we tended to have a decent time at work.

It was only the work itself that seemed meaningless and un-appreciated. I would have never remained in this path if it weren't for some ability to succeed, and then after doing well getting promoted and continuing to make more money. My wife loved money. She outwardly expressed the support for me to change careers but once the front door to the house was closed it was another story.

Nobody in the world truly knows what happens once the front door to a home is closed. Families are locked away in isolation, which allows their true personalities to come out. Wives and kids are beaten, alcoholics drink, drug users inject their next fix and affairs are fostered. The shutting of doors empowers people to throw away their false projected personalities and be who they truly are. In most cases this is an alter ego of their social shell they project.

My wife's appetite to continually acquire more stuff meant we always needed more money. Happiness to her was shopping until she ran out of corners to jam things in then having a yard sale or simply a purge of past purchases and then filling the space up again. In this endless cycle of craziness I found myself tied to a merry-go-round on a playground. You stepped into this world only to find a crazy big brother spinning it with exuberance that could only end in somebody throwing up. Our circular path was headed for destruction, and neither one of us had the power to stop the continuing cycle of doom.

One of the prizes of my divorce when finally complete was going to be the ability to throw myself into some unexplored desire that I had always wanted to do but was restrained from participating by the chains of holy matrimony. Writing was one avenue, and was actively being explored, but there were others as well. Dealing drugs or starting a prostitution ring were possibilities but might require an expertise that I did not hold. The world was finally open so nothing was going to be ruled out until given the proper attention.

As I diligently go through my spreadsheet, adding, subtracting, dividing, formatting, I get a call from the front desk that the police are here in the front lobby. They would like to talk to me if I had a few minutes. There are only a few moments in your life that you can truly say, yes that is where that saying comes from and completely be able to define the feeling without doubt. "Shitting oneself," was now added to my list as I felt like somebody had come by with a prized Electrolux vacuum cleaner, stuck the end of the hose to my mouth, taped it down, and sucked every drop of air out of me instantly.

After I failed to respond, the question was repeated and I garbled out a "sure thing, I will be right down." Bracing myself with both hands I pushed myself up. Being on death row gives oneself time to reflect and prepare for the long walk down the row of cells containing fellow prisoners who can all relate to what you are going through. You have the ability to mentally say, "Yes I know what day they are coming to get me." I know what hour they will push the button and zap the life out of me snuffing my existence on this planet.

I wonder what the responses would be if you said to each inmate "you are slotted to be executed and that will not change." "We will surprise you with the exact time and date and leave you here wondering when it might occur." How many inmates would mentally fall apart with the ticking of each second wondering if today would be the day or would it be the next or the next? How could you live knowing your life was going to end, knowing how it was going to happen but having the insanity of being played with?

I made the walk down the long hallway to the elevator and felt as if I was one of those inmates who had just been told today is your day buddy. See you in hell and laughed as the button was pushed. I imagined my body spastically fried to a crisp like a chicken leg left to long in heated oil. I stumbled into the bathroom next to the elevator door and made a quick trip to the toilet where I did end up losing all my lunch and something extra I didn't recognize. I knew my time was limited, so I quickly rinsed out my mouth throwing water across my face and headed downstairs.

I started wondering on the way down, why. Why at work? Why couldn't they have come to my home and talked with me there? Why would they come to me here and embarrass me in front of everyone I knew jeopardizing my reputation? As I pondered the questions, the answers eluded me like a little toy crane in one of those video game arcades that searches for the toy over and over again. It never seems to have the capacity to grasp those damn stuffed animals with those flimsy tentacles. My kids always demanded to play those games, but I have never once seen anyone actually win anything from them.

As I stepped out of the elevator it dawned on me instantaneously like an epidural injection as it quickly relieves the pain and suffering of the first childbirth. They wanted to catch me off guard. They preferred to have me unnerved and rattled in the hopes that I would let something slip if I were indeed the person they were searching for. This was a little juvenile police game that was being played from the "How to be a detective for dummies" workbook that must be standard issue in all academies for police training.

As I stepped from the elevator the anger rose up in me, threatening to explode, but gave me renewed energy and focused my attention on the issue at hand. The adrenaline flow felt like an intake of speed. The color came back into my chalky face. I once again used the anger that had guided me on my past adventures and felt invincible sauntering over to the two waiting detectives.

They showed me their badges and suggested that we find a place to talk, assuming that I had a few minutes for them. They assured me the entire process would only take a small amount of time, and was a formality. They simply needed to follow up on all leads and were here in regards to the disappearance of Hannah Thomas and my recent relationship with her. I admitted knowing her briefly over the past few weeks, expressing my hopefulness that she was okay. I walked them through our cumbersome ineffective security screening to the second floor conference rooms that were frequently used for unexpected meetings.

We closed the door behind us, and they began the scope of apparently routine questions about my relationship with Hannah. How long I had known her, what was the definition of our association (friendship/romantic) and how many times I had recently seen her. I answered everything truthfully and casually, stating that it was the beginning of a friendship. We held the possibilities of moving into a closer intimate form for companionship, but it was far too early to tell what the true outcome might hold.

They then began asking me about my whereabouts over the two to three days that marked the disappearance of Hannah. Upon hearing that I was at my house in Twain Harte during said time period, they asked if there were people that could vouch for my activities. I had seen my local real estate agents that weekend as I always stopped in to say hello on most visits. I had also seen a past work associate at the grocery store and both could vouch for seeing me. The time period they were covering was rather large, and I had been alone in my house most of the weekend so there was nobody who could attest to every minute. The people I had mentioned would place me in said location over that given period.

We spent about an hour, and I began to see the pattern of questions being asked in different ways, but with the same desired goal or outcome. I sensed that this was page two of the "detectives for dummies" handbook as they were looking for any inconsistencies in my responses. As you are growing up your parents continue to tell you how much easier it is to tell the truth—telling a lie only leads to more lies. The underlying philosophy is you have to remember a lie, but the truth is simply the truth. It is what occurred and your mind knows this and naturally navigates toward this in reflection.

I simply told the truth to every answer. They did not ask me if I abducted and killed Hannah or if I had tortured her in any way. I would have lied to both of those answers, but my location and activities were easy to recall. Keeping with the truth and only adding in or changing what you absolutely must is a key to survival, I decided. Let them think what they will of me, and what I choose to do in my personal time but don't cover up meaningless embarrassing facts as it overly complicates things. Lay all the cards on the table only holding back the one or two that are hidden up your sleeve, which you are not supposed to have anyway.

My energy level fueled by my anger and adrenaline lasted for the hour-long questioning. The two detectives then left their hopes for finding a culprit behind as I escorted them both to the door. I offered them my help if they needed to contact me again and asked them to keep me informed of Hannah's status. I was now very worried. I watched as they walked to the parking lot and then turned to head back to my office once they had made it a comfortable distance.

Having three kids I have had on more occasions witnessed them inject themselves with soda, candy, cake and any form of sugar they were able to stuff into their mouths as quickly as possible. I find it humorous how kids never understand why adults don't eat cookies at every meal once they grow up and can make decisions for themselves.

I have also witnessed the freefall crash that occurs after the sugar has run its course and inevitably loses its toxic energizing ability. You see your child plummet down the abyss of emotional reasonability. Birthday parties are the perfect example, and why almost all of them last three to four hours. Stuff them with as much artificial toxins as possible. Then send them home so the parents can go through the detoxification process of returning them to normal stability.

As soon as I walked back through security my energetic rush lost its power, just like sugar being drained from my veins. It was all I could do to make it back to my floor, hobble to the bathroom door, and once in the stall continue the purging process of anything residing in any form in my stomach or anywhere close.

I was sweating buckets and felt like I had just taken a shower with my clothes on. They were now clinging to my skin. My hair was soaking wet, and the only part of my body that seemed dry was my mouth from the constant flow of heaving. I knew the right thing to do was to return to my desk and gather my senses, but I also knew that I was incapable. I needed to find a way to exit the building, get to my car, and get out immediately.

I stayed holed up in the toilet stall making noise and commotion for about thirty minutes. Finally, once my need to heave uncontrollably had subsided, I splashed huge fistfuls of water from the sink on my face. I then made the long walk back to my office for my laptop and my belongings so I could head home.

I passed two coworkers as I made my way down the never-ending pathway, both of whom commented on my looks and asked me if I were okay or needed help. I stated that I was fine but had just received some bad news. It had affected me harder than anticipated. I was going to leave for the day. Luckily, they were the only two I had to interact with, but unfortunately they were also the two defined gossips of the department. I was sure before I had even made it to my car there would be rumors flying.

Does every office have those one or two individuals who seem to know everything that happens before it is announced, and have the inside scoop on all activities? Isn't it odd how much time in company politics is spent on the gathering of knowledge in the background through non-official channels? Whispers happening in the hallway or hushed conversations in the cubes. Everyone talks about who Sally is sleeping with or that Bob might finally be fired or Betty in receiving is having a baby but she is not married or is married but it is not her husband's.

Even with the invention of the Internet and online gaming, which have to be two huge productivity sucks from the corporate bottom line, I still think that the tried and true gossiping has to remain crowned in the top tier of corporate distractions. Everyone is involved at some level. Even those of us who try to abstain get sucked into conversations at times that in retrospect should have been avoided. We are all human, and as such our curiosity can be piqued and once saturated has to be appeased.

So with this I left the office. It was Tuesday afternoon, and I knew that I could not stay for the day. At this point I had no idea when I would return. I called from my cell phone on the way out, leaving a message for my boss, stating that I felt ill and had to leave early. I would call him tomorrow morning and give him a status update on what I thought tomorrow looked like. My voice was horse and cracking from the recent regurgitation activity, and helped my cause. With the story most likely being spread I was sure that everyone would have me in handcuffs before the night was over.

I made it home in one piece, went straight to the liquor cabinet, and began to drown myself in scotch as quickly as possible. My kids were coming over for the night, and I luckily remembered this two drinks into my quick gulping. I called the au pair stating that I was sick and would not be able to see them until tomorrow evening. She said she would inform my ex-wife. I was sure to get berated as my ex-wife liked her evenings out and would be pissed to have her social life disrupted.

I no longer cared about anything. I just needed to escape and alcohol was the vice of choice as I now downed my third glass of scotch. With my empty stomach and the quick intake I was flat out drunk in less than thirty minutes of stepping through my front door that I now noticed remained opened. I laughed at that, and slowly stumbled over closing and locking it. Right after, I tripped backward and fell to the floor hitting my head on the way down. I would spend the night there, waking up around 4 AM in the morning with a headache. I was left to deal with my fragile now broken mental state that was on the verge of irretrievably leaving me forever.

Too Much to Handle

The definition of insane according to Dictionary.com is "not sane; not of sound mind; mentally deranged." I think it is safe to say at this point that I was definitely not of sound mind and deranged, demented, and distraught. It is one thing to be psychotic and lose the line of black and white or to even know what the line is and knowingly cross it with disregard. It is another thing to lose the ability to function in society. To keep up the pretense of being normal while harboring activities is an art.

In order to be a successful serial killer, one must understand how to deal with the normal daily functions of life and project the pretense of normalcy. "Normal" being defined as acceptable practices that are allowed in standard society, I would assume. While this might sound easy, the oddity in this situation is the self-inflicted stress caused by our mental capacity to understand the difference between right and wrong. Knowing that I have crossed the line and the guilt associated with those activities is the issue.

Guilt is the wire that keeps humanity intact and allows us to interact within the guidelines that have been preordained as acceptable. God gave us guilt to ensure that we did not disregard the fabric of social interaction. Imagine a world where nobody felt guilt, and remorse was undefined. We would all act on our whims and fleeting desires caring nothing about the consequences.

Billions of dollars are funneled into the very religious factions that prey on our guilty consciousness of things that we have done or even things that we think of doing. Thou shalt not covet thy neighbor's wife is a great example. Shit, even if you don't sleep with your neighbor's wife, just thinking about her large naked breasts is defined as a sin. You should feel guilty about doing so. It eludes me as to the gray area of when this became a true sin and when the leeches of society simply saw a way to make money on our fragile coexisting lives and thwarted that for profit.

As I lay on my hard wood floor, slowly stirring out of deep sleep, I rubbed my head and felt the large bump from the fall of the night before. I struggled with my own guilt of what I had done, and what that meant to who I was, and what I was becoming. I tried to define the wording and understanding of what it was that I had meant to accomplish and if these activities were truly making me whole.

I think that guilt was not an appropriate label for my feelings and thoughts, as I did not feel remorse for my acts. I felt that what I had done was the essence of who I now was. I was no worse than the man who reads your meters and sends the information to your gas company, creating a bill that self generates and is then mailed to you for payment. I had my role in life that fulfilled who I was meant to be.

My feelings were more stress defined from the possibilities of being caught. I did not feel guilty for my actions, but instead simply felt stress from the fear of the ramifications if my actions were exposed to the world at large. Unlike the meter reading gas occupation, which is accepted by society as normal my actions were not socially correct. I had no desire to go to trial, or God forbid, go to jail. I am not a large man, and would not function well in the type of prison that I would be sent. Wasn't Jeffrey Dahmer killed in jail? If you are labeled a killer you are then housed with other killers. While I enjoyed being on the giving side of this activity I did not want to fathom the thoughts of what might happen to me in a maximum security prison.

I felt that I needed to find out how to deal with my stress and develop good stress-coping exercises. My anxiety level was only going to increase and drinking might temporally relieve the pressure but it was not a positive way to deal with issues. Counseling seemed like a great idea. Wasn't the show *The Sopranos* made with just that very core thought as the theme? This was a show about a mobster who couldn't deal with his actions and needed to work through his guilty/stressful thoughts.

I was not chartering new ground, but I needed to deal with this quickly. My mental strength was taxed by work, divorce, kids, murders, police, friends, and affairs. It was too much to handle and more than any one person should have to cope with.

So it was with this newfound direction that I pulled myself up from the floor, which I had so uncomfortably slept on, and showered and attempted the daily grind of going back to work. The holidays were approaching, and I would have some time to take off and gather my thoughts. I needed to try and focus through the next few days, and make the appearance of being a good corporate citizen.

As always, the shower helped me gain my composure as the warm water washed away my anxiety and let the air back into my deflated nerves. I gathered my belongings in my backpack, and as I had now started to ride my bike to work, I prepared for the energetic boost that always came with my forty-minute ride. I had decided to focus on getting into shape, and did pushups and sit-ups in the morning attempting to do 250 of the former and three hundred of the latter. The only thing I had found that subdued my stress-filled life was a nice warm shower, and the isolation that came with putting on my headphones and riding recklessly through traffic. The self-absorption of listening to music while pedaling through automobiles is therapeutic in nature. You lose yourself and forget about the outside world for a while, as you pedal in rhythm to the latest pop tune. There is nothing like the beat of Pink or Rehab as you weave through cars while thinking about a girl who has just kissed a girl, and how oh so good she feels at doing something so taboo.

In just a few short weeks it had achieved a portion of its designated goal. I was continually complimented on how good I looked and everyone asked me if I had lost weight. At the ripe age of forty-one I was now starting to feel physically better than I had in the last twenty years. My only issue was the mental instability that my stress was weaving throughout my mind.

I made it through the day, and I had my daughters for the night so I decided it would be a good idea if we went shopping. I needed to start the process of gathering Christmas presents that should be delivered in just a couple of weeks. Having three daughters presents me with limited knowledge on what their desires are for gifts. I have now found it is easier to ask them and let them help me pick things out versus trying the guessing game.

I do have to give my wife credit in this department. She used to do all the shopping, and even though I disagreed with her approach of quantity over quality it was much easier having her take care of all the gathering of items than doing it myself. My oldest said to me one time "dad it is nice but you are the only one who has ever really gotten me a name-brand item that was not from a discount store." Her reference was to the jeans that I had purchased for her at Nordstrom's on or around her birthday.

I don't think my wife had ever stepped in Nordstrom's, as she preferred the knockoffs that were equal in value—she wouldn't pay the high markups. She failed to realize that every once in a while it was nice to just have the real thing. Kids especially in high school are so in tune with what who is wearing. The groups you associate with are so often plugged into your status in the clothing line.

I took my two younger ones to Limited Too they tried on jeans and shirts and sweats and sweaters and even with the 50 percent discount that the store was promoting still spent close to $400. I must say that the bulk of the shopping was complete, and it was nice to head home and start the process of wrapping presents.

For the first time without their mother the following Saturday we expeditiously picked out a Christmas tree, and after strapping it on the truck we headed home to set it up. It was a great week to soothe my nerves, having the distraction of decorating and the excitement of the holidays that only comes through the eyes and mind of a child. We had spent some time together going to yard sales this summer, so with forethought I had purchased some Christmas decorations. We had the ability to spruce up the house in holiday spirit, and it looked very festive.

We were a little short on tree ornaments, so we took construction paper and with scissors and a stapler made a great streamer that wrapped around the tree in multi-colored fashion. We hung stockings over the fireplace, and with the few knick knacks from the yard sale, the house was transformed into holiday mode.

After much debate I had conceded to giving my wife the kids on Christmas Eve. She had them for the rest of the vacation holidays after. I took the kids for the week before Christmas Eve. While the house in Burlingame looked festive, we had planned on spending the actual holiday up in Twain Harte. The little ski resort Dodge Ridge was opening up the weekend before Christmas, so it would be a nice outing to take the kids out for our first ski trip of the season.

My seven-year-old had become quite the accomplished skier, and while my oldest was naturally athletic, she had spent less time on the slopes. She still had some learning to do. All three kids could go down all the blue slopes, so it was always fun hanging out with them. It was a very good athletic family activity. So many family events are sitting around eating and or watching TV or a movie. It is nice sharing something that is active, and allows the interaction and involvement that skiing together does. Granted I still boarded but we could all go down and up the hill together.

I wonder at times what I would do without my kids keeping me in tune with what is important and the constant reminder they give me about the simple things in life that provide happiness. At times my seven-year-old while I am driving will reach up to my shoulders behind my seat and rub them softly as only a child can do. It still melts my heart every time she does this. She is attempting to reach out and do something for me to express her love in a kind gentle way.

My older daughter looks at me in the eye every once in a while and asks "dad are you okay, is there anything wrong that you want to talk about." Their intuition and perception is uncanny.

The holidays with the kids were uneventful. We skied as planned, saw a movie, and set up the fake Christmas tree in Twain Harte for the first time that had come with the purchase of the house. The two little ones didn't understand the concept of the fake Christmas tree no matter how many times I explained it. They had never seen one in their entire lives. We and everyone we knew always went through the process of cutting down and or purchasing a live tree.

Even though the tree was fake it was quite life-like, and I think that confused them even more. It was a far cry from my days growing up with my grandmother where we annually pulled out the silver wired tree and set up the translucent limbs. I, as my kids, had never known anything else as a child so it was not until I grew up that I realized not all Christmas trees were silver. The fakeness takes something away from Christmas, I believe. Even though I don't mind the pretend trees that are green I strongly feel that on Christmas there should be no tree in the living room that is shiny and silver.

As with my kids and all kids it is ironic how traditions and isolation of childhood keeps you from knowing the differences that are prevalent in the world. I am sure there are millions of kids that have never even had a Christmas tree, nor a present under it. Wouldn't they be happy with a warm meal on the table to eat versus crying at not getting the latest fad toy that was being marketed as the "can't do without holiday treat". All a matter of perspective and luck of the draw on where you were born and what status you fell into as the egg happened to hatch and you were created I guess.

It ended up being a nice holiday, and was much less stressful than I remembered it having been in a long time. My ex-wife always operated under the mindset that the holiday season had to be perfect and worked that point to death. Perfect presents, perfect meal, perfect wrapping. She warped the holiday into a stress-filled week of last-minute shopping, and continued complaining of not finding this or not getting that. It was nice just relaxing and going with the flow this year and not dealing with the turmoil of her family and her never reachable lofty expectations.

I did try to be aware of the kids being pulled in two directions this year, as it was the first Christmas that we spent as a divided unit. I think it went well and the kids seemed to enjoy both celebrations with me and with their mom. They in turn gave me the distraction that I needed at such a tumultuous time in my life. The plan was to spend that week with the kids dropping them off Christmas Eve at their mom's parents and then head out that night for my planned trip to the Dominican Republic. It would be my second trip and my first one had been an eye opening experience that injected me with thoughts that had led me to where I am today.

The only disappointment I believe was the kids were a little distraught in the quantity of gifts as most of my concentration had been on clothes. Money was all too tight this year, and the normal inundation of needless trinkets went by the wayside. I did manage to get them a couple of Wii games that were Karaoke-oriented. The two little ones enjoyed being the center of attention and they always liked putting on a show. I had just gotten my younger one an American Girl doll for her birthday in November. That was number one on the list for both of them but I felt it was unneeded to indulge them in one yet again. $100 plus dollars for a doll seemed extravagant.

I instead tried to focus on hot chocolate, making pies, and spending time together watching Christmas movies and reading Christmas books. One tradition that my wife's family had instilled in me was the watching of *White Christmas* and I still enjoyed that with the kids this year. As I get older I have more respect and admiration for older movies, and the simplistic nature of how they are approached.

I do enjoy the special effects of *The Dark Knight* and the elaborate scenes that can be played out now in computer animation, but the older movies are just easy to watch and bring you back to a time in life where things didn't seem to be so complicated.

I dropped the kids off at my ex-wife's parent's house, and she was not there yet. She was attending church service with her mother. Her father coldly let the kids in the door. I tried helping them up the stairs to the condominium he shared with his wife of fifty plus years. The exchange was awkward and sad for the kids, as he was rudely non-communicative and horrible to deal with. It is not that hard to understand, since he had been filled with lies from my former ex-spouse and with her being his daughter most likely felt protective of her.

My wife never seemed to understand the effect that her lies had on her, the kids, and on me as well as everyone she spoke to. She spread deception as easily as creamy peanut butter, and lies flowed from her with no thought or concern. This was probably the single biggest surprise in my divorce was her ability to distort facts so fluidly until she herself believed the words that came from her mouth.

I tried to put this behind me as I kissed the girls good-bye, giving them both huge hugs, and headed off to my week in the Caribbean. The sunny beaches and removal of daily distractions would be a nice reprieve from the grind that I had been going through. I would miss the girls but it would be nice to just get away.

Still Doesn't Add Up

Sudhir awoke to his normal routine, and once he arrived at work went about trying to figure out how to look busy. He checked the finance section on Yahoo to see how things were shaping up, read the latest headlines of how Obama was facing a tough uphill climb on the economy, and how tax cuts would save the day. He had to admit that he considered himself lucky in his conservative approach to investing. He didn't risk anything and he didn't gain a lot but he also had not lost much in the recent downturn.

His job was secure, and he couldn't say the same for several of his relatives and friends. Sudhir would always have a job as long as he had seniority, and there was a need for a police officer. This was one good thing about working for the city.

Sudhir had spent the last several months doing odds and ends, while everyone knew he remained focused on Jill's case and the missing person aspect. He was now starting to get pressure to move on, and let the case die by the wayside. There were other activities surfacing, and he had proven his skills with the big assignment. His captain now wanted to see if he could apply those skills as other crimes surfaced.

Even with the jump-start in his career, and the newfound respect, he couldn't help but feel the failure that he had let Jill, her family, and himself down by not apprehending anyone. He still kept his prime suspect in the back of his mind, but the weekend work that he had put together remained in his truck sealed away as he still refused to believe that the fragile strings holding the pieces together actually made any sense. That, added with his direct knowledge of certain activities made it impossible for him to fathom that his hypothesis was anything more than a drunken fluke of coincidences that in the end didn't add up.

Still, he refused to relinquish the file. While he had stated he would accept new assignments he would never give up his hold on the hope that someday he would find out the truth about Jill and what happened. He was sure by now she had moved out of this world and into the next by some torturous method that he was unable to comprehend, but he would never be able to live with himself if he gave up hope for finding out the truth.

Sudhir instead focused on his personal life and waited for the next case to be passed his way. He helped out with minor infractions in the meantime. People tended to fall back into their normal daily routine activities. He did the same calling on his retail owner disputes and domestic violence eruptions that had evaded the everyday patrol personnel.

He planned a weekend in January to the wine country, and had plans of giving the trip to Janine for Christmas. He had found a great bed and breakfast for a two night stay, planned dinner Saturday night on the wine train, and had lined up his parents to watch the kids. The details were all in place down to ensuring that there was a hot tub, and he had a planned wine tour booked at one of the larger wineries.

Neither he nor Janine was heavy wine drinkers, but it is beautiful country. They both enjoyed getting away although they had not done a weekend stay in years now. Kids tend to distract you from your marriage and personal life as all your focus stays upon them. Ironically one day you wake up and realize they don't want to even talk to you let alone have you in their daily activities.

Then they go away to college and come home one day married and suddenly they have the realization that you were not as stupid as they thought you were. You then develop a mature relationship, and the next thing you know you are a grandparent then die. He had life all mapped-out from beginning to end it seemed. He loved his kids, and still appreciated them allowing him to be so involved in who they were but it was easy to see that in a few short years they would not need him in the same way they did today.

It was in this deep thought that Sudhir went about checking the activities for any missing persons that involved a Volvo SUV or where a lady from the ages of twenty to forty had disappeared. He had added this to his daily routine about three months ago after getting nowhere with Jill's case. While it had led him to Manteca on a wild goose chase involving a blonde girl named Brenda he had not found anything else that had connected to his cases in any way. At least in any way that he was able to see from the facts that he viewed off the daily wires.

He pulled up the last week's activity including the last couple of days having neglected this for a while. He noticed an oddity that felt somewhere along the lines of getting hit by a semi-truck. There was a case of a missing person in Burlingame. A lady named Hannah had allegedly been abducted, and had not been seen for a couple of weeks. She fit the profiled age range and was attractive from what he could gather off the dot matrix photo, but that was not what had caught his eye.

Apparently she had been known as an acquaintance of Duncan's, and it noted that he had been questioned. The report stated that he appeared odd, but seemed to hold up well during the interview. They had no reason to believe he was of any further use in the case. Sudhir fell into his seat and instinctively reached in his drawer and without even hiding the fact poured himself a shot of whiskey. He downed it in one quick gulp.

They say an oddity is one thing but recurring coincidences at some point form a pattern. Even if that pattern is something that does not initially make sense there is most likely a reason for the pattern having formed. Duncan surfacing again like this was not expected, and it shocked Sudhir into now thinking again that there was too much circumstantial evidence starting to add up pointing at him being involved in this circle of issues.

Hannah had two girls and had lived in the area for several years. Her good friend Sarah had been watching the girls for a weekend as Hannah was going away and was expected to return on Sunday afternoon and pick them up.

When she had not returned Sarah had called into the police station worried and upon further investigation Duncan's name had surfaced as having been dating her a few times over the past recent weeks. He had been questioned had a good alibi and seemed like a straightforward person, so the two detectives had moved on. Her ex-husband was also in the process of being questioned, even though their association had not been recent. He was not the most upstanding guy and was not diligently paying his child support to say the least.

Life is a mixture of circular events that travel around and around and around. The earth circles the sun, while the moon is circling the earth, and they both spin upon themselves leaving you wondering at some point where it is that you really stand in life. Everything is constantly moving directionally toward its end, so how can you ever know for sure at what point you are currently residing. You don't know the timing of your death or what tomorrow holds or what will happen a mere split second from the time you read this single word until you move to the next word and so on.

Sudhir felt his world crumbling around him as the disintegrating pieces were piling up at his feet. His puzzle was being pulled apart. His wife was living a different life, his friend was adding up slowly to look like a killer, and Sudhir couldn't keep his grip on what was happening. He remembered his last visit to his parent's house and the gossip session that ensued.

His parent's friends who had two boys were recently in the mix of trying to give back their grandchild to one of the boys who had just gotten out of prison. The boy had shot somebody over a drug deal, then taken the body to a reservoir, tied a few bricks to it, and dumped it in the water. The only reason the body had surfaced was due to the low water levels from the lack of rain.

The boy had then spent the last seven years in prison, while his stripper girlfriend had dumped off their child to his parents for safe keeping. His parents loved the child but were in their late sixties and the burden of keeping a child full-time was taking its toll. This was a boy that Sudhir had watched grow up. He had seen him in church camp, attended youth group with him, and watched as the boy blossomed into a young adult.

Sudhir had moved on and lost track of the specifics of several younger kids, but now to find out he was getting out of prison for murder. Who are these people that we call friends in life? Who is the person that lives next door to you that you wave to as you pull into the driveway? This is the same person that you feed the dog for as they go on vacation.

Does anyone know who anyone is, or is everyone some fake shell of a human being that hides away their true feelings? Only allowing the beast out of its inner sanctum when the lights are turned down and the door is shut and nobody knows what is occurring in our individual sanctuaries called home. Internet porn is so lucrative, and do we even have to ask ourselves why? How many husbands scan the Internet for seduction as their wives lie in bed pretending not to hear the fluttering of the rhythmic beat of masturbation to some dark seductive enticements that can be viewed for $19.99 a month?

God, this world that we live in seems like such a lie of false propaganda blown through a television tube telling us how great things are. We condemn the Islamic community for their harsh treatment of woman, while we in the civilized world treat them like mere fixtures to be viewed at will for pleasure.

Sudhir now realized he could no longer keep Duncan out of the limelight. He needed to be listed as a primary suspect, if only for himself. Duncan should be fully investigated to the smallest detail that Sudhir could imagine. He would have to follow him, stalk him, and find out the seedy underpinnings that no one person should ever know of any other individual.

Ask yourself as you are sitting at dinner with your group of friends that you went to college with. Sharing wine and reminiscing on stories of who was with whom and the formal dance that you all attended at the junior prom. If you knew the thoughts of everyone at the table, knew what they were thinking about you and about the person sitting to your right and to your left, knew what they were truly thinking of what you looked like and what you said would you still be friends?

Sudhir thought about a time long ago. He was in high school as a senior and he was in the backseat of a car as three of his good friends who happened to all be girls were in the front. Somehow the topic of rape was brought up and all three girls admitted to being in a situation where they had said not only to be forced to do things they had no intention of doing and fought not to. All three girls admitted to this, and they were only in high school.

What does it mean when you can't make it out of high school without a boy who you know and trust and who you play baseball with and football with and sit next to in algebra turns into this person that can force himself on a girl without remorse? Who shows up the next day with his homework done and sits next to that same girl as they talk about the civil war or the last historic world battles.

These are the good kids. The kids who are going to college and will be our future leaders in society. The guy doing your taxes and who invests your money or sells you the house that you live in. We concentrate so much on the Middle East or on the slums of Los Angeles, and who is to say that down the road in the high school classroom our kids are any better than the scourge of society that we lift our nose to. The only factual statement you could make is that some are more transparent in their feelings and beliefs while most of us hide who we really are.

Sudhir felt himself getting light headed, and the room seemed like it was spinning as everyone moved in slow motion. The sluggish mire of being in quicksand as it holds your limbs and you go limp trying not to sink into the oxygen-sucking pit of blackness. He raised himself up slowly and heard somebody ask him if he was okay. His face was turning paler than the white paper on his desk that held the news that was pushing him into his imploding despair.

He shuffled down the hall, bracing himself with his hand on the wall, aiming for the bathroom and the closest stall to the door. He heaved the second the lid was pulled up as the door rang shut behind him slapping against the latch again and again as he had failed to lock it closed. With every gasp, his backside banged against the door causing a loud crack as it rang back and forth.

The cold water from the white-stained porcelain sink was refreshing as he splashed his face. He dumped the water from the top of his head letting it flow down his forehead dripping from his chin and nose. He felt the color slowly creeping back as his body as the flow of blood resumed. He made it back to his desk, pulled out his keys from the drawer and headed for his car. He heard somebody asking him something about where he was going or what was wrong, but felt his mouth slur as he mumbled an incoherent response.

He drove to the closest bar and spent the next several hours drinking himself into a drunken stupor of scotch-induced numbness. He slowly forgot what it was that instigated his demise down the road of inebriation. He knew he was getting louder and louder with each passing hour and it was only his familiarity with the nighttime crowd that kept him out of trouble. Eventually Nathan the local bartender of the night cut him off and called him a cab insisting that he not get behind the wheel. A regular crowd in a bar frequented routinely resembles a dysfunctional family of sorts. They do take care of each other to the best of their limited abilities.

The cab dropped him off in front of his house, and he seemed to take money out of his wallet handing him back the worn brown leather container. Sudhir seemed to manage to put it back in his pocket. He then stumbled up his concrete drive as the cab pulled away, tripping over the familiar crack that raised up a couple of inches, and hitting his head as it impacted against the hard surface.

That is where he lay for the evening. He was passed out in the 55 degree California weather. His kids lay tucked warmly in bed having dreams of innocence and happiness that they felt might still be within their reach. They did not yet have to face the morbid reality of life as an adult where you come to understand that this is it. There is nothing more and disappointment is the only truly God-given right that you are guaranteed to obtain.

ANOTHER TRIP TO
THE DOMINICAN REPUBLIC

My second visit to the Dominican Republic was anticipated with trepidation. I couldn't help but wonder if my lofty memories from a few short months ago would hold up for a second round. It is like eating a moist piece of white cake with creamy whipped frosting that is smoothed to perfection. The bites melt in your mouth as you eat fork after fork, chewing slowly to savor every morsel. At the end of the first piece you wait a few minutes and decide against your better judgment to dive in again and take another. How can anything that good not be consumed until there is nothing left but crumbs.

Unfortunately, as we all know, the second piece always leaves you feeling slightly bloated. The excess sugar forms a small army in your stomach that declares war on anything else within reach. Before long you understand what "too much of a good thing" means. Still, I was looking forward to the trip. After my modest exercise regime I was in decent shape for the beach, and well into writing my memoirs. I felt that this would be a great venue for loosening my artistic ability and hoped that I could focus some energy on my ever-growing self portrayed on the page. I only hoped that it would not be too much of a good thing, and force me over the edge.

The biggest change would be that my friend Jean was no longer around. He had lost his ability to make any money on the island and had been forced to return to Canada to try and find a job. He hoped to return at some point in the future. He had set me up with his island wife, who was meeting me at the airport and would drive me to my hotel on the beach. She had offered to help me navigate the now more familiar terrain.

Upon arrival, Jean's wife had a sign and met me with her twenty-year-old girlfriend, her son Junior who I had met, and her cousin who was the designated driver. We stopped at the local grocery store on the way into

Caberete, where I purchased some beer and loaded up on candy and snack foods for my new entourage. We then headed to my hotel where my new tour guide promptly charged me $55 for the cab ride over. This was after I handed her a $50 bottle of perfume and eight shirts for Junior that had been requested by Jean as gifts for his family the last time he and I had spoken.

I enjoy giving gifts, and I like the fact that I can freely give something to somebody that they in no way would ever be able to afford themselves. Going to Dominican Republic again puts me in my place. No matter how bad off financially I am or will ever be I will still have more money than most anyone on the island. I am careful to say more money, as I realize money in no way buys happiness. The people of this island live in paradise and have no money. Most people in the states have money, but dream of living in paradise. It is a paradox of nature that we always want what we don't have. Still, it is one thing to have money and another to manipulate or take advantage of somebody with money in the hopes of ascertaining more than a fare share for services rendered.

Once on my honeymoon with my wife of the past tense, we arrived in Spain. We left the airport, got into a cab and were given a verbal tour of the countryside on our way to Seville. He was a wonderful historian of facts and fiction and eloquently passed the time pointing out sites and explaining their origin as well as present significance. He did all this as he manually manipulated the meter, charging us a grand total of $120 for the ride to the hotel.

As we were getting out of the cab I had my wife enter the hotel and ask what a normal cab fare was from the airport to the front entrance. I was told it should be no more than $20 to $25 door-to-door. Upon hearing this I handed the driver $30, which seemed more than adequate and entered into a heated verbal debate on what it meant to be honest in society and not take advantage of tourists. We ended our duel of words quite angry. He cursing me in his native tongue as I flipped him off and headed inside. This wasn't a great start to the trip, but in retrospect was the low point. The rest of the vacation turned out to be wonderful.

I felt as taken advantage of by my friend's wife, and although I paid her the total requested fee I stated that I would not need her services the rest of my stay. I promptly told Jean via text that I was disappointed in her and did not like my generosity being abused. He apologized, but since they were only married in title he had no control over her and who she was. It was very sad for me since I had planned on getting to know them. In the end they lost much more than they gained. I could have been very generous over the course of several days.

After checking into my room, which had a balcony sitting right on the sandy beaches no more than one hundred yards from the edge of the ocean, I ventured over to Elvis'. His place was only a five-minute walk from my hotel room door, and upon arrival I said hello to my old friends. Elvis remembered me instantly. The girls were acquaintances of mine from the previous trip and remembered me as well. It was like walking into *Cheers*, and, yes, it is nice when everyone knows your name.

I like the aspect of extended families; older generations influencing younger generations on a day-to-day basis. I think in the materialistic society of the United States that is our one biggest loss. As young adults get jobs and venture out on their own they quickly gain the ability to pay their own way through life, and sadly relegate their once-protectors to an afterthought. A phone call on every other Sunday, while they look for excuses to get off the phone as quickly as they can to concentrate on their important afternoon events.

In the Dominican Republic, as in most third-world countries, the extended family acts more like a unit. Kids have babies at young ages and the parents (now grandparents) take them on as their own. Children having babies when they are teens is not ideal, but it does force the broader family group to unite and act as one. Elvis had a very large extended family. Most worked in the bar/restaurant seven days a week as they all chipped in keeping the business running smoothly.

As I do in most cases I blended in quickly, and it wasn't long before I was being invited to dinner and greeted like a distant uncle who was visiting. All of this occurred without me knowing even a tiny fraction of Spanish. If I only had the drive and mental ability to learn Spanish I think I would have moved beyond the distant uncle stage and taken the next step to being a brother. Who knows if they share the same feelings, but I like to think they did. We shared many experiences in a few short days.

My fondest memory was a Sunday afternoon playing softball. I had been working out, and although not in perfect shape had to say that I was gaining definition in my shoulders, arms, and chest. My stomach had started to flatten out as well. I was now down to an average weight, in the 175 range, and with my height that is close to ideal. I say all of this knowing that I still am forty-one, and was just a few short days from turning forty-two. Even the most arduous athletic group can't compete with those twenty years younger.

A couple of nights before, Elvis (the coach of a local softball team) had asked if I was interested in going with him and his team for their weekly league game on Sunday. Since I love experiencing anything local, I happily accepted. Around 11 AM Sunday morning I ventured over to his bar, happily anticipating what the day might bring. Nothing happened in haste on this little island, and it took a couple of hours for everyone to get organized. It was around 1 PM when we finally jumped on the back of several motor scooters and headed off to the field.

Elvis had lent me an old pair of baseball pants, and I was allowed to borrow his son's retired sneakers since he and I had about the same-size feet. We zipped off down the road, and about twenty minutes later arrived at the field. I use the term "field" loosely since it was more of an unused dump than a true baseball field. It had ankle-high weeds that were intermittently splotched with brown dirt patches where the only access was a dirt/gravel road about a mile off the main highway.

It seemed as if somebody had taken a monster truck, and in the middle of a muddy rain had zig-zagged doing donuts, digging up ruts and trenches wherever possible. Home plate consisted of a white rag that was held down with a couple of bricks. Right field was partially blocked by a seven-foot concrete wall that jutted out about ten feet into the official playing area. It was always a guess on whether the ball was caught or dropped, until you saw the right fielder jog around the wall with a smile or rushing to throw somebody out.

Left field was left open in plain view but held a 20 x 20 mound of dirt about two feet above the rest of the normal playing level. It was like running through a minefield as you tried to shag down fly balls. The practice session before the game began consisted of a round robin with each player taking a turn at each position. Once an out was made everyone rotated to the next spot and so on. Both teams interjected members sporadically in the mix, as it was a free for all so everyone could get ready for the real thing.

The average age of the players would have been in the high twenties to very low thirties. I was probably the oldest person within shouting distance of a couple miles. Additionally, as I began my indoctrination into Dominican sports, I would have to guess that most of these guys had been playing baseball since they were all old enough to throw a ball or pick up a bat. I, on the other hand, had played two seasons of old-man softball where drinking was the primary goal a few years back and had never played as a kid.

Starting out with this big of a disadvantage might have frightened some, but to me it was just part of the adventure. I held my own as I went from position to position not embarrassing myself too badly until I hit the pitcher's mound, and it all unraveled quickly. I have the arm of a five-year-old girl, if you gave her a bowling ball and said throw this overhand. I just can't throw a ball to save my life. After about fifteen attempts to get the ball over the plate, and several rounds of belly rolling laughter the coach for the opposing team yelled something at me in Spanish (which I didn't understand) and took the ball away from me.

He then supplanted me on the mound and pointed me toward the bat so I could take a turn at hitting. The spectacle I created was most likely the mealtime conversation of many dinners that evening. I dribbled a ball to third base, on my one swing, ran as fast as I could to first but was thrown out. I spent the rest of the day on the bench watching as the true game began, and I was no longer needed as a clownish distraction.

I met several guys that day and would remember most of them as we all frequented the same bars. It was nice feeling part of a group. A couple of my fellow bench warmers went on a rum run (after I volunteered to pay), and we then shared a glass that got passed around as shots throughout the afternoon. Now that was my kind of participation. I immediately felt at home with the warmth of alcohol in my bloodstream.

The one glaring difference from that day and when I played my two years of beer ball in California was the community participation, and the difference that I emanated from the crowd. As we sat there that afternoon, you began to see people drift by and then stop as the concrete wall and random bricks became seats for spectators who just wanted to watch a game. At the peak of the day nearly fifty people watched the baseball players not anywhere near good enough to make the majors, but could crush most any middle-aged softball team that I had ever seen in the states.

It is rumored that the minor leagues are populated by nearly 50 percent of Dominican Republic personnel. They live, breathe, and die baseball, and it showed in how fluidly they played. It was an amazing afternoon. I felt blessed to have participated. It was sad at the end when after losing two games our team got eliminated, and we headed back to the bar for my evening ritual of drinking and, well, drinking.

Dinner was fresh fish that one of the players had caught earlier that morning by spear fishing off the coast in the ocean. He apparently did this quite often and promised to take me the next time I went down to this little island paradise. I wish I had known this earlier. What a great experience that would have been. The evening went as most, and we got very drunk. We headed down to the beach bars around 10 PM and drank more as we harassed the local ladies and tourist girls equally.

The only night that was significantly different was New Years Eve. I hope that for as long as my aging body can handle the torturous after-effects of alcohol that I am able to spend every New Years Eve in the Dominican Republic. If it equals or exceeds the wonderful experience that I had that evening I will count myself blessed. It started out like most nights at Elvis' bar, and it was precluded by an afternoon of sleeping on the beach and napping on the balcony in my room. I had been smart enough to realize I needed to conserve my energy for the all night events that were to ensue.

As a present, I had bought Elvis a 1/5 of black label. He as well had purchased a 1/5, so we worked on bottle number one starting at around 6 PM that evening. In retrospect, that was a little early to begin, but alas it is hard to hold off the anticipated events of a night filled with debauchery and alcohol. Elvis and I plowed through bottle number one, and while doing so enjoyed the company of his stunningly beautiful bartender and her mammoth boyfriend.

Luckily, the fourth member of our group that evening would be the bartender's friend who lived in the mountains and had ventured down for the all-night party that awakened the island on an annual basis. She was about 5' 3" and couldn't have weighed more than 100 pounds. She had chocolate skin, and her hair was course and straight as she sauntered around the bar in a tight, form-fitting thigh-length dress. Other than a slight overbite she was an above average specimen that could rival most twenty year olds from the United States with her natural beauty.

The four of us, along with Elvis, spent the next several hours drinking and lightly eating until it reached about 11 PM. We then decided it was time to head down to the beach. The beach had been worked on all day in preparation for the several thousand visitors, as island locals came down from the hills and tourists ventured out from their rooms. All were bent on spending the evening and early morning hours bringing in the New Year. There were numerous temporary bamboo bars that had been erected through the sandy area, as each restaurant extended its reach in the hopes of reigning in as much capital as possible from the drunken horde.

As the clock struck midnight, I embraced my friend for the evening. We passionately kissed, as my tongue deeply penetrated her luscious smooth lips. With us both having been drinking for several hours it was as much the alcohol as anything, but the feeling of connection roared up inside my loins. I held her tightly, rubbing up against her small petite frame.

The rest of the evening was a mix of kissing and drinking, as we meandered through the crowds talking and mixing with various people that we both or at least one of us knew. It amazed me how many people I had become acquainted with over the course of now two short trips. As the evening turned to morning around 2 AM the last thing I remember was seeing an American across one of the temporarily erected beach bars and screaming at him "I know you." Not sure if I did or not in retrospect, but he reacted warmly and bought me a shot of tequila.

That was where my evening went blank.

Waking up after eight plus hours of heavy drinking is never a fun experience no matter how old or young you might be. As would be expected I rolled over in my bed with my head exploding in pounding beats. I was mildly surprised that I was in my room and had no recollection of how I had made it back. I was completely naked and lying face down. As I looked around I noticed that I still had my companion from last night with me and she too was totally 100 percent de-clothed.

The only thing that I can imagine more unsatisfying than never having made love to a beautifully perfect twenty year old when you are in your early forties is making love to a twenty year old, and not remembering a single thing that happened. One might ask how I knew that I had actually taken this young girl and inserted my manliness into her taut supple body. Well, I guess I couldn't be sure but there were no less than three spent condemns strewn about the bed. My guess was they were remnants from the night before.

I stumbled out of bed and shakily hobbled to the bathroom. After relieving myself from last night's liquid intake I stepped into the shower and stood there for twenty plus minutes letting the warm water wash away as much of the pain from my overtaxed aging body as it could. I then grabbed a bottle of water and decided that I could not let the experience escape me. Even in my taxed state I felt the familiar rise of excitement as I lay down on top of my gorgeous companion and commenced to arouse her with my fingers hoping for another try down memory lane.

She continued to be accommodating, but needed a break to the restroom before allowing me another go. It took longer than I would have hoped. My limited energy threatened to give out right before I felt the familiar release spewing forth inside its gloved container deep inside her moist tight pleasurable opening. I collapsed, spent, resting my sweaty head on her firm round breasts.

This I would remember, I thought, as I felt her pushing me off while rolling me to one side. She headed for the shower wiping away my memory from her young overly used body. I thought about joining her, but realized that I lacked the ability to move and started wondering how I would rise and prepare to leave in just three short hours. Today, January 1, was my departure date. Even though my flight didn't take off until 5 PM my hotel would be kicking me out at 12 PM. They were not known for allowing you to stay beyond check-out time.

The most difficult part of vacation is the preparation of going home. You are still in paradise, but you are packing your belongings to leave. Your mind exits before your body does leaving you in a paradox of emotional turmoil. I started thinking of my troubles, what I would face upon my return, and it was too much for me to handle. I thought how odd it was that I had been here for several days, and my desire to kill had been extinguished upon arrival. If I lived here would I tire of this place as well? At some point would I face the same overwhelming desire, allowing it to consume me as it had back where I called home?

I tried my best not to think about what awaited me, but focused on gathering my belongings. To the best of my limited ability I navigated my way back home. Everything was as I had left it. I interjected myself back into a routine rather quickly, not understanding the events that awaited and would again alter the course of my life.

THE WAITRESS
(TURNING FORTY-TWO)

The odd thing about returning home from the Dominican Republic is facing reality, which is so different than vacation paradise. On the island twenty-year-old girls flock to middle age men in all venues. It doesn't take many brains to realize that the physical attraction is not the drawing factor, but the enticing aroma of another life where being poor is not a waking reality. Again, no matter how little money you have, it is substantially more than most of the island locals will see in a lifetime.

The other oddity is conversing with somebody who holds this cavernous age gap. I admittedly do not even understand the language at times. The "dude," "whatever," "sick," and other slang that flows from teens' mouths is indecipherable. If you are after anything beyond a quick encounter, I wish you luck.

In the United States twenty-year-old girls look upon middle-aged men for what they are. Middle-aged men. No matter how much we in the over-forty crowd might lust after the tight, hard bodies that predominately make up the opposite sex of twenty years younger, we just don't have that much to offer. I myself was now just a few days away from turning forty-two. With my birthday fast approaching I was trying to figure out how to celebrate my first annual passage as a single man in several years.

As my working crowd of friends knew first hand, I looked for any excuse to go out on the town. Being the center of attention was just an added benefit. With that in mind, I circulated an invite letting the normal drinking group know that it was my birthday. I asked if anyone would like to join me for an evening of drinking and dinner at my local hangout, Straights. The food was average and the crowd was a little on the young side, but by now most

188

people there knew who I was. It was a comfortable environment for me to have a drink now and then.

Truthfully the biggest draw that Straights had was a twenty-one-year-old brunette waitress with a killer smile. Her hair was full and wavy, hanging down to her middle back. Her eyes held an inner glow that seemed to hold secrets not normally found in somebody of such a young age. She, as most of her counterparts in the service industry, dressed in tight-fitting shirts and paraded around in skirts that took only a tiny fraction of material to make.

The two noticeable traits she held upon our first meeting several weeks ago were her smile, and the nylon stockings she had worn at the time. Her legs seemed to be endless, as they reached up from her black high-heeled shoes. You traced the dark triangle patterned stockings up until they disappeared underneath the form-fitting miniskirt that barely hid the forbidden treasure underneath. She seemed a little off from the normal waitress, and had a wild glint about her that beckoned you to talk to her. Still, you knew her only goal was simply piling on the percentage of tip that you added to each bill she handed out.

The idea of gratuity in today's society has taken on a saddened likeness to begging, it seems. No matter where you turn everyone has a tip jar waiting to be filled, even if they have done little to nothing to service you or anyone else for that matter. There are tip jars at self-service restaurants, at coffee houses where the serving attendants never move from behind the counter, and a nonstop endless amount of service oriented establishments. It seems that you have to do very little to request a tip in our materialistic money-hungry me-oriented world that has done such a disservice to those who truly do deserve special consideration.

Adriana, the waitress in question, was one of those deserving souls who demanded to be compensated not by her requests or by a jar on a table, but simply by her presence. Allowing us the sheer pleasure of her serving us our drinks pushed the money from my wallet. I showered her with the only thing that seemed socially acceptable.

She was not the normal physical build that attracts my eye. She was a little overweight: possibly ten pounds or so. She looked like she lacked a physical desire to keep in shape. Although she possessed healthy curves and an eye-catching body when you looked closely, you could tell that she was soft around the edges and did not possess much muscle underneath her revealing attire. The blessing of being in your twenties is that even without exercise your body maintains the tightness of age. You don't have to be a workout fiend to look great.

She drew me to the restaurant, and without her my attendance would have drastically declined. Every time I suggested the restaurant it was met with protests from my fellow employees, as they cited the expensive drinks, average atmosphere, and less than stellar menu items. I continually made excuses and explained why it was the place to go, but on this occasion it would be my turn to pick with limited protests—this was my night out on the town.

The normal eclectic group had decided to come. George, Samantha, Ingra, Patel, Dan (and his girlfriend of five years), and Camille (who attended at times but was not a member of the core social drinking club), made up our motley crew of dinner attendees. Camille had started to show an interest in me as of late, and after several months of hinting at an attraction I admittedly was not opposed to taking our relationship to another level.

Camille was a petite, Asian girl closer to my age. She was in her mid-thirties. She possessed a spunkiness that would either lead to passion or to many angry, bitter arguments. I agree with the thought that love is closely matched to anger. How can you feel such strong emotions about somebody if they are lethargic and hold no true fire inside them? It is only how people manage that fire and passion that defines who they are as a person.

The evening started on cue, but threatened to take a wrong turn when the hostess informed me that Adrianna was not working that evening. It was always disappointing not seeing her. The thought of organizing an event with the sole desire of ogling her, forcing everyone to come to my trough of choice, and not having the magnetic force present that drew me here would be a drain on the evening. Luckily, somehow, she was at the bar and through some possible coercion appeared at our table. With that electric smile, she asked us what we would like to start our evening with.

As was customary, Patel and I ordered scotch on the rocks, while George was a gin and tonic guy. Dan and the ladies ordered a mixture of drinks that held multiple colors. They were garnished with umbrellas and various other oddities that should never adorn a drink in front of a man. Dan had opened himself up for ridicule with his fluffy drink of choice. We ensured that he was properly ridiculed as the night progressed.

We were placed at a small round table in the corner close to the entrance, since we were originally unsure how many people would attend. It was somewhat of a tight fit, but made for cozy conversation as the evening progressed. I had been lucky enough (or strategically managed) to sit next to Camille. She spent a lot of the evening touching my arm and leaning in close to me as she discussed the topics we filtered through.

The standard subtle signs of attraction that our society has endorsed as acceptable were used with abandon that evening. We are all so tentative to show our cards before the targeted goal shows theirs first. It is odd how we are so insecure and afraid to take a chance without knowing the outcome.

Flirting is like walking on a frozen pond and slowly inching toward the center. Each step looking down and around, listening for signs, making sure that the ice will hold our fragile consciousness. Hoping it won't crack and break, dropping us down into the icy fathoms of frozen darkness.

The humility of rejection keeps so many people apart, as neither party holds the courage to take that first step. I am one of the few who hold myself out in the dredges flirting endlessly with anyone who will allow me to. That attribute is either found attractive, or is endlessly annoying to people who become acquainted with me. This night I was focused on the waitress, while trying to keep my less than subtle advances hidden from my other possible object of affection—Camille. Flirtation with the waitress was fairly safe. I knew my advances would never be reciprocated but would be rebuked the minute the check had been paid. With Camille I was unsure.

I find it relatively easy to get to know people. Asking questions and freely giving up personal information is always a sure way to allow people the comfort level needed to divulge information ranging from who they are to their desires and goals. Adrianna was twenty-one and her goals at present remained rather simplistic. She spent most of her days/nights working and had no real interests outside of her job. She was attempting to change her occupation and had hopes of working on a cruise ship. She had applied as a bartender/waitress on a couple of the main cruise lines. The job contracts were doled out in six-month increments, and she was hoping to snag one for the next cycle.

Like most young people, she held a desire to travel and see the sights of the world. But, as with most young people, did not have the needed financial backing that would allow her this luxury. There are so many of us that trudge through life and are not allowed to reach our goals. When we are young we have energy and passion, but lack the funds to let us explore our desires. As we get older we have funds, but are saddled with the blessings of raising children. Once our children are grown we lose the passion and are left with funds allowing us to find our way, but our energy has been sucked dry by the trials of life.

I like the recent movie *The Curious Case of Benjamin Button*, I think it's called, that explores the possibilities of starting out life as an old man moving into infancy. The backward progression through time gives you the exact opposite perspective on natural tendencies, and you have a diametrically opposed approach to normal life obstacles. How interesting it would be to flitter down life's path in the completely opposite direction as everyone around you. Age and desires offering different perspectives, more than anyone could imagine.

I have recently been told that I have a great body for somebody my age. My workout regime of the last few months is starting to pay dividends to my outward appearance, but one cannot thwart the natural progression of age. The key words in that compliment are "for my age." I still cannot be compared to somebody twenty years younger—people in their twenties naturally have great bodies. The telling signs of wrinkles and gray hair cannot be reduced by riding a bike or doing push-ups each and every morning.

So, the flirting with my waitress was just that. Flirting and nothing else. As is my normal stance, I must take it to a level where I know for sure, so I did ask her if she was interested in buying me a drink. I like the slight twist in that approach. There is no real rejection to having somebody refrain from buying you a drink. That thwarts the natural progression of advancement. Guys don't ask girls to buy them drinks.

Adrianna gave me a flash of her exotically perfect smile and brushed off the request without really acknowledging it. She was, after all, twenty-one. She had no desire to buy me anything and very little interest in talking to me outside of the scope of gratuity that the restaurant atmosphere provided. Alas, I would have to resign myself to admiring her from a distance never having the pleasure of allowing her to fulfill my lustful needs.

The evening was fun, as is always the case with my working/drinking bunch of misfits. We drank ourselves into a stupor with our boisterous ranting increasing in volume at every tip of the glass. The evening progressed, and we decided to make way for the cleaning crew with part of the group talking about coming back to my house for a brief visit. Surprisingly, Camille seemed interested in joining the after-hour party and was open to exploring the evening, not ready for it to yet end.

The crowd stayed only a few minutes, like most after-hour gatherings at our age, as once in the cozy confines of a home the eyelids droop rather quickly. Camille was the last one to leave, but had showed her discomfort when she found herself now alone with me in the unfamiliar territory of my home. She lingered by the door as I showed her out, so I decided to test the boundaries of our relationship and see what the possibilities might hold for future encounters.

I cupped her petite head in my hands and slowly brought my lips to hers, as she readily accepted my advances. We embraced in a passionate, deep kiss. I remember the movie *Hitch* where Will Smith stated the importance of a first kiss. The idea being that every time a girls kisses for a first time, it could potentially be her first last kiss and what the importance of that moment might mean.

That is a lot of pressure, if you think about it too long or too often. I fortunately was doing little thinking at the moment. I had lost myself in the soft sweetness of Camille's lips. Her lips were Angelina Jolie type lips, full, yet soft, seeming to fold in yet wrap around my own all at the same time. I had not rated kissing at a high level but found myself lost in the pleasure of these lips that seemed to embrace mine in perfect sync.

Too quickly I felt her pull away, as reality seemed to be injecting its claws back to her thoughts. The numbness of alcohol could only sustain our embrace for so long, and she said she needed to go. She abruptly stepped back and then headed out to her car. I realized there was an obvious attraction and now held open future possibilities. I was surprised at the inner desire and warmth that the three kisses we had held for me. I was moved in a way that I had not expected and felt stirrings inside me that were not funneled by the demon that I had become.

Unsure what to think about the encounter, I headed off to bed to contemplate the interaction and hold on to the feeling those luscious lips had stirred. Going to bed with that connection catapulted me into dreams of happiness, as I drifted off into a quiet slumbering calmness.

ANOTHER RANDOM KILLING

New relationships keep our minds wandering. What she might be like in bed, or what it might feel like to hold her in your arms or how it must feel to kiss her softly on the lips and caress her soft, flowing hair. The fantasies of the wild mind! Interestingly enough, it is similar to reading a good book with the anticipation and imagination of the words forming pictures in your head.

I was debating with my oldest daughter the other evening about the difference in artistic talent it takes to write a book versus paint a painting. A book is nothing more than painting a picture with words. A writer hopes to help the reader visualize images and explore the imagined feelings of characters as they interact in some make-believe world. Each person looks at a painting and pulls out different formulated pieces. We all focus on different aspects. Everyone conceptualize different pictures that leap from the pages as a good book weaves its way through the written story.

One of the downfalls of today's society is the trend to take all good books and form them into a movie. I was recently reading *A Beautiful Boy* and enjoyed it so much I insisted my daughter read it as well. Eighty pages into the book she looked at the jacket cover, which had a picture of a man. She asked, "This is not the father, is it?"

Everyone forms various images of reality from reading the exact same words on the same pages, yet the imagination runs in different directions. While this is interesting and the exploration of newness has a profound effect, there is also the reality of images cutting off your imagination. The mindless raw pull of physical needs versus fantasy that once tasted leaves you with the satiated desire to eat again.

With my new relationship possibilities still in budding infancy I knew I could not squelch my inner desire for the taste of blood and sexual pleasure. I decided to explore the streets of San Francisco again in the hopes of appeasing myself with a quick fix of hidden ecstasy. I was worried about my recent encounters with the local law enforcement agencies, and what that meant, but had not heard from them in several days now. The immediacy of my lust moved my concerns into the forgotten realm of the past.

San Francisco is an interesting place. The moderate temperatures and the scenic views of Angel Island, The Golden Gate Bridge, and Golden Gate Park make it one of the most enticing cities in which to live. As with all pleasures and positive attributes, it is has a negative side. The city attracts a large group of homeless people that frequent the streets.

Having rid the city of two such vestibules of emptiness not long ago, and gaining pleasure from the act, I felt that taking this path again was logical. Many could admit that it was a needed service. It was a Wednesday evening, and having left work a couple of hours ago, I was now home alone. I was fully energized from my frozen pizza dinner and small toke on the rarely used marijuana pipe from my college years.

Being middle-aged I was pretty conservative and rarely partook of the mellowing, smoky substance, but in my latter high school years and during college admittedly inhaled far too often. I had many experiences that should have swayed me to understand that I was wavering to close to the edge of the abyss. As most young people I felt the strange invulnerability that encompasses youth allowing them to pursue things without thought.

I once remember crossing a street in Carbondale, IL. It was a four-lane main road. I was walking to a friend's house having decided that I was no longer in a state of mind to enjoy the festivities of Halloween. Our years in college were the last ones where the city actually shut down the main street and embraced the holiday, while it inhaled the inflow of thousands and thousands of people creating a weekend long party.

Everyone would dress up in costumes and wander about the city streets. Bands played and kegs flowed and anything and everything seemed to not only be allowed but was encouraged to be explored. Having never been to New Orleans, I think this is the closest thing to which I would compare the event—decadence was openly displayed and promiscuity was embraced.

Along with several friends I had decided to ingest not only many mushrooms, but also pot from a bong multiple times. This had left me with the whirling energy of the drug-induced fungi that was softened by the subtlety of marijuana. In my altered state the streets lined with people had been too much for me to take. I forcefully pushed and pulled my way out of the crowds into the openness of the peripheral grounds beyond.

As I made my way to my friend's house and crossed the four-lane road there was a group of four young adults walking on the sidewalk at the other side. I heard one of them say in a boisterous voice "dude did you see that guy, he walked right in front of that car and didn't even flinch. I can't believe he didn't get ran over."

Having piqued my curiosity on what kind of idiot would walk in front of a car that was speeding down a main road, I turned to see the event first-hand only to realize that the "dude" in question was me. I had apparently sauntered into the road, oblivious to my surroundings, and had come very close to becoming a permanent fixture embedded into the pavement for all time.

The ironic thing of being young and letting invulnerability flow through your veins is that reality knows the difference. How many young people purposely or accidentally lose their lives by the stupidity of their actions? They don't understand the consequences of certain activities. I wish I could say that the event sobered me up and left me with a new outlook on life but, alas, the shaking feeling was fleeting. I resumed my self-destructive agenda for a few more years. The City of Carbondale did wise up eventually, though, when some of the students got out of hand one Halloween and a couple of kids got killed. Afterward they closed down the festivities the raging street parties stopped.

Having gotten slightly wiser my rare indulgence of the smoky relaxing substance was always minimally consumed with one or possibly two hits at the most. I now remained in control of my actions and was able to cross all streets safely reaching the other side.

I had ventured out to the SUV, and was now making my way into San Francisco along with hundreds of other cars. I navigated down to Market Street again, which seemed like a logical place to move forward with the evening's plan. Predictability is never a reality in the world. I think the word should only be allowed usage in the confines of scientific experiments, and should be banned from use anywhere else. Nothing in life is predictable. You can play percentages but you always have that chance for an oddity to arise and throw everything out of whack.

As I arrived it was easy to find a parking spot on one of the side streets, which is not usually the case in San Francisco. I veered in and made my way to the back of the vehicle to gather the tools I would need for the evening. In general, it is really just the one tool that mattered. There is nothing like the respect you gain when you hold a gun at point-blank range and jam it in somebody's face.

It reminded me of the movie *The Grand Canyon*. In the opening scene the gangster wannabe stated something to the affect of if I don't have the gun you don't respect me so in essence you only respect the gun. He was talking to Danny Glover's character at the time. Great movie, by the way. I stowed the gun and strolled through some of the back alleys, looking for a likely conduit to fulfill my present needs.

As I made my way down one specific alley I was entranced by the pull-down stairs, and how eerie the lighting sifted up through the iron railings. Ironically, as I stared enamored with this oddity, I saw a slight movement and realized I was not alone. A young woman sat half-naked underneath the top railing, and leaned against the brick structure. I found it odd that even in her unclean state her exposed breasts were very attractive and firm. I would have thought that a woman in such a degenerative state, obviously drugged condition would have more wear on her physical form.

As I tried to decipher the extent her nipples were erect, I received the surprise that can change the course of your existence if you allow it to take control. A sharp twang resounded throughout the alley as I was struck by what must have been a shovel of some kind squarely between the shoulder blades on my back. My knees buckled as I felt myself slowly slipping to the ground.

I find it odd how some guys feel they are so tough, and yet have never actually felt the blow of another person's fist to any part of their body. Call me lucky or unlucky, but I have had the experience of being hit on several occasions. I know full well the end result of the impact and how it feels on the body. I admittedly until now had never been hit by a shovel and I would have to state that the feeling was not something I was desiring to repeat at any point in my future life.

As I slowly fell to the ground, I began to realize the situation that I had wandered into. This was no random act of violence. The girl was there to attract my attention and to distract me from the man who was now my attacker. I hypothesized this was an attempted robbery. The scene was most likely played out quite often for unsuspecting men who didn't mind stopping to observe a half-naked woman curled up in a dark alley.

Luckily for me my attacker was not the smartest guy in the world. Instead of delivering a blow to my head, which might have rendered me unconscious, he had aimed for my back. While the blow was definitely going to slow me down, it was in no way leaving me unable to react. I was now almost completely on my knees and feeling the pavement connect with my kneecaps. The sharp pain raced up my legs but also brought my awareness to a heightened state. My nemesis reared back his crude weapon and prepared for another blow.

It must have been surprising to him, as I had put my hand in my jacket. I pulled out my weapon and simply allowed my body to fall completely on the ground turning to one side at the point of connecting with the surface. At that moment I let out two quick bursts of flashing scenario-changing bullets that he was not expecting. As astonished as I had been my now victim was indeed sharing my dilemma, but he was not going to recover quite as fast as I had.

The two bullets each hit home directly in his mid-chest section, impacting dead center in his heart. He appeared to lose life before he had even fallen to the ground. The shovel clanged against some metal behind him, as it fell from his lifeless hands and rattled to a resting spot in the darkness. He dropped back from where he had hidden, no longer a threat to me or anyone else again.

I now turned my attention to the young lady, who was curled up in a ball in the same place she had been when the entire thirty-second altercation had began. Most fights you will find are over so quickly that you don't even have time to contemplate the end result. My back would be sore for weeks, I was sure. In my current heightened adrenaline pumping state, I could not feel the bruise that I was sure would be forming quickly.

As I walked closer to the girl, who seemed to be attempting to curl inside herself so tight that she was hoping I could not see her, I was admiring her even more. She would have been extremely attractive at one time I was sure, and even now held remnants of her beauty that would never be completely removed. She spoke as I approached in a garbled tone and seemed to be begging me not to kill her.

She had felt fine being the bait for the brutal beating and possible killings of how many men in this scene from some act that her friend had concocted. Only now as the play had changed directors she fell to begging for her existence. She was probably better off not continuing down this path she had chosen of drugs and prostitution I thought. What hope did she have, really? Unless somebody took mercy on her, she was doomed to die as a drug-infected pest in some back alley like this one, if not this exact one.

I decided that it was dark enough and my actions had still gone unnoticed (probably why they had chosen this alley). I unzipped my pants and pulled them down, along with my boxers. With my staff already growing I pointed it in her direction while holding my gun no less than an inch from her head. She opened her mouth and took me in, grabbing my butt with both hands, as she forcefully swallowed me whole over and over and over again. She showed her experience in her technique. I was sure that she had been coerced into this situation several times in her young life.

There is something to be said for having oral sex with somebody who seems to be doing the act to save her life. The enthusiasm and energy injected is a direct result of trying to give the best blow job ever. It is given in the hopes of staving off what might end up being the last sexual act she commits. I found it was hard to remain alert, as she was providing such pleasure with her mouth. I grabbed the top of her head with my left hand holding a fistful of her hair, as I pulled and pushed her head moaning with delight.

It did not take long for me to explode in her mouth, as I shoved myself into the deepest part of her throat that my penis would allow. At the instant when I felt the last drops slowing, and the subsiding orgasm was just reaching its finality, I pulled the trigger on my gun again twice. I actually saw one of the bullets exit the other side of her head, apparently going all the way through. The ricochet of the projectile off the brick building echoed slightly. I was now left holding up her head solely on my own by the still fistful of hair that I had not yet released.

I let her body limply fall to the ground and started gathering my belongings. I made sure that I had not dropped anything in my haste of the last several minutes. I again realized that I was leaving my DNA all over this young ladies mouth and face, but I could not think of any way to properly dispose of her. I again decided to just leave things lie and take another chance. My chances were going to run out soon, I was sure, but until they did I would continue fulfilling what was now becoming my legacy.

I could feel the soreness in my shoulders and wanted to get home to take some pain medication and sit in the tub and relax. The evening had been somewhat of a success, and I had gotten more out of the night than anticipated, but again I would have never been able to predict the events as they had unfolded. I was becoming a hardened killer, I thought. For better or worse I was reaching the end of my metamorphosis. I had enjoyed the evening immensely.

As I was stepping away it occurred to me that I would be without the heads of my victims, and my ever-growing trophy display would now yet again have two empty spots. I was not warming to the idea and decided to try the shovel out and see if that could be used to be-head the two bodies. It would be easy to wrap them up in some plastic, with the alley being full of discarded bags strewn everywhere.

I was surprised how easy both heads became detached after a couple of swift downward plunges from the shovel. It took a little footwork and some rocking back and forth to remove the last tangled attachments but all in all not too difficult. I had my gloves on, so I was not worried about fingerprints. Taking the heads would also remove the bulk of my DNA that was still warming the inside of the girl's mouth. I quickly grabbed a black plastic bag and tossed my trophies inside. After looking around I proudly took them to the SUV, and quickly packed my belongings.

It was a successful night, and I had enjoyed the much-needed release. This would tide me over for a while, as my memories of the events unfolded. I did have to get home now as quickly as possible. My shoulders were stiffening up and the soreness was quickly turning into a sharp pain. I would have said "I could kill that guy for what he had done," but as I sat behind the wheel laughing I had actually done just that. Ah, the simple things in life that can amuse me.

On a Whim

In the midst of a great dream, it is always hard to fight your way through the fogginess and reach the surface of reality. This is especially true when the land of your dreams is so much more enticing and refreshing than what you will face upon your departure from the realm of fantasy. I wonder how many of us would remain forever subdued in the placid tranquility of this made-up world if given the choice. I guess that is why we have drug addiction. What is being addicted to drugs but simply the choice of not wanting to face reality?

Sudhir was running with his dog through a field on a slightly cloudy day. The warmth of the sun was still shining, keeping it close to perfect. It was one of those days where it is not too hot yet not too cold, and at this young age you have no worries and no cares about anything. Your main goal is to entertain yourself, and your dog as always plays a very important role in this endeavor. It seems that you can do anything and be anywhere, and life is just perfectly sublime.

It was odd to Sudhir that on this exquisite day it seemed like it was starting to rain. Yes, it was definitely raining now, and he was getting soaked. His head was beginning to hurt, and he suddenly felt like he was getting sick to his stomach. It was as if the water had been sucked from his body, and instead used to form these relentless drops that were now completely drenching his clothes. The edge of his field became dark and the fogginess began to engulf his world then start to lift. He opened his eyes slightly, and tried to adjust to his surroundings.

He saw his wife standing on the front porch. She appeared to be holding the watering hose, spraying it in his direction. He could hear her yelling obscenities and telling him he was a loser who was never going to amount to anything. His mouth was dry, and he rubbed his eyes and removed the caked layer of mucus that had formed at some point in the evening. He then instinctively reached for his head that was feeling like it had exploded in the last few minutes and all that remained were the leftover pieces glued back in place.

Yesterday's events were slowly coming back to him. As if a floodgate had opened, thoughts gushed into his consciousness, causing increased pressure on his already aching throbbing brain. He pushed himself up on all fours, and then slowly erected his body as his shaky legs carried him past his still-screaming wife through the front door to the bathroom. He spent the next thirty minutes heaving the poison out of his mouth expunging the cause of his current state. He then showered for what seemed like decades.

He ignored Janine's rants, while he spent most of the morning in the bathroom gathering his senses. He heard her state that she was leaving today on a trip after dropping the kids off at school. She still had some time before her eminent departure. She had woken him up quite early, once discovering where he was in order to avoid the kids seeing their loser dad in such a state of demise. He did appreciate this small token, as he did not want his kids to see what he had become.

He managed to focus enough to get dressed and inhaled his first cup of coffee like it was the only cup he would ever be allowed to drink in his lifetime. He had quickly downed a huge glass of water as well, and this enabled him to slow the process enough to appreciate his second cup of black, soothing liquid more slowly. The kids were in their own world as usual and sensed that their dad was not operating at 100 percent, but in their innocence had no idea why.

Have you read the book *Blink*? It is a fascinating book that focuses on the ability to make snap judgments. It points out that quick decisions are actually the calculated conclusions that our experience has allowed us to make based upon our minds ability to formulate a hypothesis very quickly. I think the statement "on a whim" is in reality the same general philosophy. We as people can never turn off our minds. They are constantly working, even in our sleep, which is why we have dreams to begin with. Imagine the fact that your mind never stops functioning. In everything you do your brain is sending waves throughout your body, moving on its own. Guiding you in aspects that you have no ability to understand or control.

It was on this whim that as Janine pulled out of the driveway on her way to take the kids to school, and then off on one of her business trips that Sudhir decided he would follow her. He didn't know why or couldn't explain the reasoning but nevertheless "on a whim" he got into his car and pulled out at a safe distance and trailed her path without her knowledge. It felt odd following his wife, but he needed some direction in his hung-over state.

Maybe a distraction was a better term versus direction, and he felt that this was an easy route to take.

Janine made her way down the familiar route to both schools. Dropping off the kids with little fanfare, made consistent by the daily routine so many parents are a part of. The monotonous ritual of making lunches, getting breakfast, fighting with the brushing of hair, and insistence on actually cleaning themselves and brushing teeth always makes for interesting parental tales. How can kids possibly fight so hard against brushing their teeth? The entire concept escapes the logical ability to understand.

After Janine dropped the children off, she headed north toward Daly City, which was an interesting way to the airport. Sudhir was sure she had stated she was heading out to a business trip. Maybe she was going on an errand before she navigated to the airport, off to her flight. Women constantly have things they need to do, from getting their hair done to getting their hair cut to getting their hair highlighted to nails then toenails, waxing, eyebrows. It was too much for any man to keep up with.

Her next stop was puzzling as she pulled into a parking lot, and exited her car. Suhdir noticed that she removed her suitcase out of the trunk. Why was she taking her suitcase inside an extended stay hotel in Daly City? It was as if she were checking in and staying, but in Daly City. If she had business in Daly City wouldn't she be doing that business during the day then coming home at night. This was merely twenty minutes from their house. Sudhir's mind was entangled with webs from the previous night's activities, and he knew he was not thinking clearly. He was unable to decipher these events into a scenario that made any sense.

He waited in his designated spot along with several other automobiles for forty-five minutes, sitting staring at the front door of the hotel trying to piece together what was happening. He puttered around with anything he could find, and as luck would have it there was a pint of vodka in the glove compartment from a few weeks ago. He took a couple of swigs and felt the welcomed warmth as the liquid penetrated his throat and stomach, cascading through his limbs as the pain from his dehydration seemed to subside.

They say (I have no idea who they really are but they seem to say a lot) that a sure sign of being an alcoholic is using the numbing effect of alcohol to thwart the pain of the previous night's hangover. Suhdir had just been through too much to care. With the events that had recently shaped his life, he knew he was beyond his limit. He was becoming afraid that what he was about to discover might push him irretrievably over the edge. He wondered if he lost his footing and took the plunge would he ever manage the ability to find his way back. Maybe some people are better off not knowing the deep dark secrets that they are surrounded by. Living in happiness, if it is living a lie is bad? Maybe but maybe not as well, happiness is the key right? No matter how you get there.

Sudhir exited the car and walked through the front door of the hotel into the lobby. It is about what you would expect from an Extended Stay establishment. The flowered print hanging on the wall, and the indoor/outdoor carpet that was time warped in straight from the '60s. The Formica desk that housed the twenty-year-old pimple-faced attendant sitting behind the make-shift furniture with his iPod stuck in his ears, paying very little attention to anyone that might have a question. The lobby was void of humankind, save the two of them. The quiet held an eerie foreboding silence as Sudhir watched the boy beat his hands against his legs in rhythm with the song blaring, which only he could hear.

Sudhir racked his knuckles on the plastic covering that for some reason was in place to protect the Formica desktop. The boy annoyingly took off his earpiece and asked "can I help you." Sudhir opened up his wallet to show his police identification badge, and the boy sat up straight and this time in a politer tone asked if he could be of any service. Sudhir simply stated that he was looking for Janine Takhar, was wondering about her stay, and how often she frequented the hotel.

The boy opened up the books without hesitation and stated that she had checked in a little less than an hour ago. She was staying for two days, and she did frequent the hotel on a somewhat regular basis. Sudhir asked for a copy of the last few months' records, and the boy gave him a printout of what was readily available. It was enough for Sudhir, as it dated back close to two years.

Sudhir stumbled back to the car, not really in control of his bodily limbs. He opened up the glove compartment and guzzled down half of the pint of vodka in one swift inhale. He called his parents and asked them if they would mind watching the kids for the next couple of days. The kids stayed over there frequently enough, so they agreed to pick them up and take over the parental duties.

His mother asked him if everything was okay, saying he sounded odd. He reassured her, the best he could. His goal was more focused on getting her off the phone and allowing him to think through what the next step in his fast disintegrating life might be. Janine had never had business trips out of town. He tried to think back on when this had all started. His memory muddled the dates so he could not pinpoint a time where she had begun this charade.

It didn't seem fair that his life was imploding. He felt like an aging boxer that was getting pummeled, hit after hit, and he was unsure of when the knockout blow was coming—but he did indeed know that it was coming soon. He contemplated going to a restaurant and ordering a huge, juicy rare steak.

If he was going to be punished to this severity, he needed to feel like he had wronged God in some way. He never fully understood the reasoning on why God did not allow him to eat beef in the first place. Everyone else in the modern world did. God his head was aching, what had he done to deserve this life?

In his trance-like state he realized that he had actually started the car and driven to his local bar. His autopilot apparently functioned quite well, but was programmed with only one destination. As would be expected this time of day, the restaurant portion was open, but the bar was still shut down. The waitress agreed to his request for a drink and poured him a glass of scotch. He had handed her his credit card, asked for the bottle. She hesitantly obliged giving over a bottle three quarters full, wishing him luck.

The first three glasses slid down like shots. The liquor found a home next to the ingested vodka from less than an hour ago. He could feel himself already losing the ability to speak, and he was quickly hoping that he would lose all functions. He did see the waitress put down a plate of unordered food, and thanked her for her proactive reasoning. He was luckily in a back corner booth of sorts, knew everyone who worked in the bar/restaurant and most of its frequented patrons. He felt he would be left alone to wallow in his self pity for hours if he could keep from making a scene.

Have you ever painted a room in your house completely on your own? You walk through each doorway, observing the furniture, the style, the décor. It all provided the atmosphere that you had created from bare brick, drywall, and wood. Once you have taken in the essence of your home you then venture out to Home Depot to spend an hour or two perusing through the paint samples, picking out that one color that will fit perfectly on your wall. You might even bring a pillow or two to match colors, as your memory gets muddied when you look at hundreds of colors at one time.

You select the perfect brushes and rollers, buying all your peripheral gear. You then head back to your house where you carefully mask the doors and windows, taping the trim as well. Then commence to paint with the hopes of upgrading the room to a new level. When you first start the rolling process the yellow you picked out seems a lot brighter on the wall than it did in the store. You comment to your spouse questioning whether this is really a good idea.

You both agree that the paint is wet, and once it soaks in it will bring you the much sought after change in your lives and future. You roll and roll then trim with the brush as the sun goes down. After a full day you are both tired so you head to bed. The fumes fill the house, spreading the aroma of paint throughout. You crack a window allowing the fresh air a sneak attack on mitigating the smell.

The next morning you both casually stroll into the room. After spending a few minutes looking at the walls and then back at each other you express your displeasure with the color you chose. This was not the intent. This bright, obtrusive, overwhelming aberration. What were we thinking, you both express as you lament over the choice trying to figure out if it is worth the effort now to go through the entire process over again.

If it is this difficult to pick out a color for a bare wall in a house how do we expect to ever pick out a spouse to spend our entire lives with? Sudhir sat in the booth drinking himself into oblivion, as he felt the stabbing knife of betrayal being pushed deep inside his chest. Was she having an affair? Most likely, he thought. Why would she spend her days and nights in a hotel? Nobody was home most days, so it made no sense for her to seek escape from an empty house.

Was she trying to simply obscure her life? Was it so horrible to even be in the house that she couldn't stand the thought of staying there with or without him? How long had she been having an affair, and with who? Did Sudhir know this person that his wife apparently preferred to hold and snuggle? Did he wrap his arms around her as she lay there in bed talking about how horrible her life was, and what kind of an idiot she was married to?

His thoughts were interrupted by two men in their twenties that were making a small scene pointing in his direction. They were complaining that he was drinking. They did not accept not being served a drink themselves, no matter what time it was. Sudhir watched as his body slowly rose up from the seat taking an advantaged viewing point from what seemed the ceiling above.

He watched as his body walked over to the two gentlemen. His arm move forward in a balled fist as he connected with the back of the head on the young man who was closest to him. He knew that this was wrong, but couldn't stop his arms from flailing punch after punch in the direction of anyone that was moving near or within his vision. The two young men ran from the restaurant as Sudhir saw the waitress standing two feet away from him. Her mouth was wide open having just dropped her tray of dishes that were in route to the dishwasher in the back.

Sudhir simply sat down on the floor as she continued to gape at him with her wide eyes. Once there he curled up in the fetal position and started to cry. He didn't make a habit of crying and couldn't remember the last time that he had. He was not a man who never cried, but it didn't occur that frequently. He watched as his body shook in convulsions. He was heaving with each inhale, no longer in control of his anything.

He didn't care anymore about what people thought or what people saw. He was finished with pretending to be something he was not. He simply just wanted to cry, so that is exactly what he did.

DIVORCE IS FINAL

I was finally forty-two. When you are young, you listen to the ranting of generations that are older than you. How they talk about time whisking by and your years seem to run into one another leaving you standing one day doing nothing more than reflecting back on where time went. You don't really listen. You are young, invulnerable, and invincible and there is nothing that can stop you. Then one day you wake up and realize that you are no longer young and yes things are different.

Forty-two years is a long time, and reflecting back on the good and the bad is an experience that can make you wonder how anyone ever makes it through life. The interesting part is for sixteen years I was married to one person. I shared the good times and the bad, just like it stated in the vows. The vows I was not allowed to say verbatim because of my wife's instance on warping them to her self-centered view. But still, sixteen years of the forty-two that I have been alive I spent with this woman who was now the mother of my three children.

I wish that I could remember the wonderful times that we had, and how much we loved each other. If I am truthful with myself, we had a rocky road from the very beginning. There was one instance before we were even married when we got into a heated debate. I was trying to remove myself from the situation until it blew over as I so often did. This was a typical exchange between my ex-wife and me. Anger would bubble up like lava flowing to the surface until she erupted. We lived on the outskirts of Chicago. Still close enough to have a Chicago address, but far enough away where no real native would readily accept the fact that this near Western suburb was truly part of the city. We had rented the top-level three bedroom apartment from a Hispanic family. The family had somewhere in the neighborhood of fifteen people living in the downstairs apartment and were dumbfounded at why two

206

people would rent such a large space by themselves. The dad was ecstatic at having such a small family unit or couple rent the place that he readily did anything he could to help us settle in.

It was an older home with a spiral staircase that circled up as you entered the front door. The entrance to our apartment opened into a hallway and to the left was a large living room with a non-working fireplace on the north wall. As you entered to the right was the dining room, which emptied to a kitchen, and from there was a sunroom that let you out to the back staircase.

We kept the larger bedroom for ourselves, made one bedroom into an office, and my ex-wife kept one bedroom as a walk in closet. I am close to anally neat, not a freak, but I do like things put away in their proper space. My ex-wife could not have been more of the opposite. She threw her clothes down wherever they happened to fall. The bedroom was littered with discarded garments all over the floor in piles of some discerning system that only she could figure out.

As the argument ensued I remember trying to enter the bathroom and shut the door, locking myself in solitude, until she found the ability to control herself once again. I continued to attempt to close the door but she blocked it with her feet and hands holding the door open while she hurled cursing screaming vulgarity at me. I don't want this to sound like I am innocent in our war of words, as I was anything but. It always takes two people to argue but in my defense on most occasions I was the one trying to keep peace or just stop the exchange. I was tired of the constant fighting.

My ex-wife at the time was holding a glass of red wine in one hand, the bathroom door in the other, and was throwing dart after poison dart in my direction from her slandering description of me. Who she thought I was and what kind of a man she felt that I was not. I countered with my opinion of her, and as usual this was froth with hurtful descriptions of her body that seemed to cause the most pain. As the last words left my mouth her hand holding the wine glass flew forward, and I felt the cold showering gush as the red liquid jumped from the container and landed squarely in my face. On that happy note I had finally tired of this and forcefully pushed the door closed. With her in the way, she was knocked backwards in this physical stand-off which I had now brought to closure.

Unfortunately my wife had long ago lost any athletic ability or grace and once the door was moving shut, which removed her brace she lost her footing and stumbled. As one might expect the wine glass went with her. In her fall to the floor, as luck would have it, the glass broke into several pieces of which a couple found their way into her hand causing a rather large nasty cut.

As somebody that grew up in a household of harsh physical discipline I have never and would never spank my kids, hit my wife, or physically abuse anyone. I have anger issues and have on occasion been known to kill a person here or there lately but I have never physically abused anyone in my family. If I did have this in me then I would have been beating my wife long before we were ever married. God knows if anyone did deserve this type of treatment (and they don't) she would head the list.

With the spill to the floor and blood now flowing freely from her hand the screaming in anger quickly turned to screams of pain. I slowly opened the door to take in the newly created scene. As angry as I was, I still knew my civic duty and helped her to her feet taking her into the bathroom. We worked on stopping the blood from flowing. The cut should have received stitches, most likely, but she chose to simply wrap it at home. She sucked it up while working the sympathy angle to ensure I felt as guilty as I possibly could.

This exchange seemed to closely define our marriage. Through our sixteen years there were many exchanges that could just as well be used as examples and would be as typical as this. We had a volatile union, and with her relentlessly tense disposition there was never a time to just sit back and relax and enjoy each other. Most people who met her for the first time commented on her intense approach to even saying hi. While she knew this she preferred to reference herself as passionate.

She would constantly say how she did not argue; she passionately debated her feelings. I never knew how to respond to this. Passionately debating how I didn't tell her thank you for making dinner one evening that was burned beyond recognition? Leaving me wondering what it was that I was even digesting seemed odd to me. For the most part I would listen to her as I continued to dig deeper into my hole of solitude and resentment.

I should have known from the beginning that our compatibility was an issue, but when you are young your eyes get foggy—you can only focus on specific things. One time when I jumped into bed I heard a crunching noise. I lifted the covers and found remnants of popcorn, potato chips, and crackers littered throughout the sheets. I blew up. That was the point in our relationship when eating in bed was banned. She had the ability to place her hand in a bowl of popcorn then remove her hand with the popcorn. Once she made the arching movement to her mouth she lost track of half the contents in her hand. Only later we would find it spread sporadically throughout her body and on her side of the bed.

Isn't it sad that after so many years when I reflect back on our time together, these are the types of memories that stand out? The violent examples, the angry moments, and my inability to let go of the hurt that was inflicted in my direction during the bulk of our verbal exchanges. It is all my mind can conjure up. As I sit here writing I am purposely trying to think of a time when I genuinely felt close to her. What happened to bury that feeling so deep that I can no longer bring it to the surface?

I guess in the end it doesn't matter. My divorce was final, and with it came the relief of finally closing out this chapter forever. Now being able to move forward with the renewed hope of finding that person that can fill whatever it is that seems to be lacking in my life. As I am sitting in bed in my little two-bedroom home listening to the quietness that comes with no kids, I start to cry.

It is hard when they are not with me. I think of the life that they nor my wife and I will never know. Having two parents is every child's right, and to deny this is one of the hardest decisions that I have ever made. I will continue to try and work toward giving them this right to the best of my ability. Sadly, even now it is still so difficult interacting with somebody who is so filled with hatred and remorse. I told her recently that I worry she is still in the midst of a depression. She denies this instead, explaining how great her life is how her happiness is propelling her forward.

She expresses all of this while telling me that she has recently been fired from her job. The main reason is she lost her focus with the distraction of the divorce and the mental toll it has taken. Isn't that a pretty big sign that somebody is in need of a little help? It is one thing to be laid off, and given a nice package as part of a large group. If you are shown the exit which you have most likely walked in and out of for a few years after being fired it is a completely different story.

That is somebody telling you point blank that they need your services, but you are simply incapable of providing them. They will have to look elsewhere for an employee who is bright enough to give them what they are looking for. In my mind the ultimate slap in the face is being fired from a job that you were originally qualified for, but for some apparent reason you just can't perform.

Who really knows? I sit and reflect back, and it seems my finger is pointing out toward her as much as hers is pointing directly back at me. As always, in the end, it takes two people to argue. I have never seen a single person sitting in a room yelling—and then pausing to yell back at himself.

The focus needs to remain on the fact that my divorce is final. Getting that piece of paper stating that you are free is a welcome relief. Knowing that you are no longer tied to another individual, but you can now yell out to the world yes I am divorced. The mistake I made had been cut out of my life. I can now move forward and hopefully find somebody to fill this hole that should helped dig.

Martin arrived, interrupting my self-reflection, and stated he was taking me out for a pre-drink, drink. Getting me drunk before I started the real party is an Irish tradition, I believe. Martin originally talked to me about staying with my wife. He feels that once you make the commitment, and there are kids involved you should do anything you possibly can to make the marriage work. Kids are the victims in every divorce. They have no choices; they make no decisions. They simply get dictated to that their life is going to be torn apart, and they better get ready to adjust.

His thoughts were leaning toward helping me reconcile, until he had his first exposure to the person that my ex-wife had become behind closed doors. She had apparently been contacting him on several occasions via e-mail and over the phone. At home and on his cell even writing him a letter at one point stating the importance that the two of them meet. Martin did not mind meeting with her but he was a close friend of mine. He did not want to cross any lines or be put into the middle of an awkward situation.

Finally he relented and agreed to meet her at a restaurant so they could talk and work through whatever it was that she felt was so dire for him to be involved in. The conversation basically went with her telling him how wrong I was, how much trouble I was in, how unstable I had become, and that she was worried for my mental and even physical health. He repeatedly tried to tell her that I was doing okay and that even with the stress of starting my life completely over with nothing (my wife had kept everything) I was doing rather well.

This went back and forth for several hours until he finally had to end the discussion. He explained to her that he needed to leave for an appointment. Martin had promised my ex-wife that he would never mention this conversation, and she had given her word as well. This would remain between the two of them, and they would agree to leave the topic here at the restaurant— nobody would know any difference.

Unfortunately Martin did not know my ex-wife that well. It was less than a week later in the midst of an argument with me when she stated that not only had she met with Martin but she suggested to me that he was not really even a friend of mine. He knew me, and we were acquaintances, but he would never consider me a friend. She, of course, was only telling me this because she was concerned for me. She didn't want to see me get hurt thinking that I had a friend when I apparently did not.

I spoke to Martin about the conversation. For the first time I saw the enlightened look in his eye as he finally became aware of how manipulative my ex-wife could actually be. He was furious at first, but then after he calmed down actually stated that he now agreed I most likely was better off without her. How could she blatantly lie to him? She had betrayed his trust and then manipulated his words to hurt me and push me into isolation purposely.

Having him acknowledge this was helpful for me. Knowing that somebody else saw the real person that I had been dealing with for so many years was a relief. At times you question yourself and your judgment. It felt good to have it substantiated to such a degree. My next step was to just let go of the hatred and disgust that I felt for her. To move forward with my own life leaving her behind.

Happiness cannot be found down the path of hatred. Being pissed off can only lead to discontent. I still had no idea how to completely release the bitterness that had taken years to grow. She had done such a good job fertilizing the seed and ensuring that the root structure was firmly in place.

Anyway, that seemed like enough reflection, tonight was not about the past but about toasting to the future. I had cried on Martin's shoulder way too many times, and now I needed to relax, get drunk, and have a good time. My future was wide open, and I had closed a chapter to my past.

Is Life Really That Bad?

It had now been twelve years that Jason had been a part of the FBI. It had taken twelve years for his career to supplant his wife, and one could argue his kids as well. The most important thing in his life should be his family, but for some reason his job always came first. Twelve years doesn't sound like a lot of time in the realm of the world as a whole or even in comparison to how long the United States had been a country. Was twelve years long enough for the justification of losing the things that he now understood he valued the most?

He could never leave his job. This was something he knew, and in the end had also been the deciding factor in his marriage dissolving. He understood that he could not live with himself if he allowed certain deviants to roam free in the country, butchering and killing people needlessly. He also knew that his job was probably the only thing he would ever be great at. How many people enjoy their job? How many people enjoy going to work each day? Sitting down behind their desk as their middle-aged boss with a round belly and a focus on meaningless tasks hovers over them, demanding more final product than anyone could ever deliver?

Jason loved his job. He lived and breathed his job. His job was the mental focus of his very being twenty-three hours out of every day. He slept five to six hours on average and out of those five to six hours he guessed he dreamt of his job four to five of those hours. It meant everything to him to close a case, knowing that he had saved the lives of people he would never meet and never hear of. It didn't matter that those people didn't know he had helped them. He received no pat on the back from the families who never knew that they were the next ones on the list of some sadistic murdering psychopath.

Jason did appreciate the distraction that his kids provided. They took him away from the everyday life of killers and death—to pull him in the direction of softball and baseball and his daughter's social life. Jason was the assistant coach now of his son's baseball team. It was a pleasure seeing the look on a twelve-year-old boy as he turned a flawless double play or hit a ball so hard that it made an arching swoop over an outfielder's head.

He was not a religious man, but he did attend church on occasion. Since he had been diagnosed with leukemia he had become a touch more acquainted with the priest at his local Catholic church. He was luckier than some, he realized, with the medication effectively fighting back the disease for several years now. His blood work every six months was receiving praise from his doctor.

He never considered himself a handsome man, but his wavy hair leaned toward a natural blonde. He had been lucky enough to have several beautiful ladies in and out of his life. His wife Sharene would always be the best in his book. She wasn't perfect, but she was as close to perfect as any woman he had ever met. He still spent many nights dreaming of her, and she was the frequent object of his affection as he lay alone in the dark relieving himself of wasted sexual pleasure.

He found it interesting how most of the middle-aged women that frequented the kids' sports circuit always found the time to sit and talk with him or offer their help if he needed an ear to listen. This was not only the single or divorced women, but many of the married women were readily available to help him navigate the waters of the shark infested single's ocean if he were interested. He realized that being in decent shape, and still having a full head of hair left him far ahead of his competition in the middle-aged men category. It didn't take a lot nowadays to be in the lead pack.

He just couldn't find the interest yet. He knew that at some point Sherene would move on (she was far to beautiful to remain single long). He would as well but he needed a push from somebody or a sign or something that would pique his interest. He had never been a serious aggressor, but he had never had to either. The women for the most part had come to him throughout his life. Sherene had been different, and he pursued her back in college, but even she was not somebody that he had to work hard at swooning.

He had once heard a girl say that she had been in four relationships in her life, and she had not picked any of the men. They had all picked her, and they had navigated their way into her life until she relented and took a chance. Could it be possible that life always found a way of working out? The balance of good versus evil, pursuers versus pursued, and so on and so on. It seemed too easy to think that in the end when the score cards would be tallied for the existence of man that everything would be equal.

Jason had always enjoyed a good *Seinfeld* episode, and it brought to mind the show on balance where everything Jerry did evened out for him, including his friends. Elaine had lost her job, and became a loser at the same time that George had gotten a job for the Yankees and started dating a gorgeous woman. Jerry had lost a $100 bill only to find a $100 bill a few hours later in the pockets of his pants that he had retrieved from the cleaner. If this were the case in reality, then did it mean that if Jason quit his job that an appropriate amount of killers would simply never materialize because there would be no Jason to pursue them?

If that were true then he was doing nothing more in life than perpetuating the very thing that he worked his life to destroy. The paradox stumps us all at times with its emotional implications. Jason was wrapping up his work, and there were a few people from the office that were going out for drinks tonight. After several situations of getting himself worried about his drinking, Jason had not been ingesting alcohol for a couple of months now. He had instead decided to focus on himself and work on getting his life back on track.

He wished he could say the same for his friend Sudhir. He was worrying Jason with his self destructive nature as of late. At some point Sudhir's wife was going to break him into several pieces of kindling then throw some gas in that direction and light a match. She was becoming more vicious, and Sudhir was becoming more submissive every time Jason saw the two of them. Even without heavy alcohol consumption tonight would be nice, because Helen was going with the gang and Jason had felt some attraction for her when she first transferred in.

He had chosen not to inquire about her or instigate anything, but she was extremely attractive and very athletic. Apparently she had just turned thirty, and having moved from Oregon to the Bay Area did not know a lot of people just yet. With her looks it wouldn't take long, but she didn't appear to be interested in men at this point. Jason seemed to remember hearing about her moving because of a bad break up, and she had wanted a clean fresh start.

They had exchanged the normal water cooler banter, since Jason had been in the office more than normal lately without a case of his own to monopolize his time. In that period he had actually gone as far to request she be placed on his team. Who knows if it would happen, but Jason usually got what he desired from his supervisors. With his reputation now growing and his casual demeanor he was listened to at an unusually high rank.

Helen was athletic in stature about 5' 5" and had brown shoulder-length hair that was naturally wavy. Not curly, with tight kinky folds, but full and rolling like the waves of the ocean on a calm, slightly breezy day. She worked out frequently, and he was sure that she could hold her own against all of the women in the office and a very large percentage of the men. Jason was normally attracted to softer, more subtle women like his ex-wife who was athletic but not as muscularly toned with definition as Helen.

He felt happy that unlike most of the men who were now becoming acquainted with Helen, he did not feel intimidated by her in the least. He had dealt with all kinds of people in his life, and he was unsure if he would ever meet anyone again that might make him feel uncomfortable. It was not a cocky attitude, as he was always pleasant, but it was the self-assurance that came with his association to the dredges of the cesspool that he dealt with in his career.

They were heading out to a local bar down the street from their office called O'Reilys. It was an Irish bar, and it held the appeal of several law enforcement officers from the FBI, so most of the group was well known. Jason, who was gone from the city as much as he lived there, was not a local but going out with the large group he would be accepted easily enough. It was a great bar to relax in after the interesting days they all put in at the office.

The walk was a few short blocks, but Jason could not help notice Helen was sticking close to him and initiating a conversation. She was asking the basics of where he was born, where he grew up, and asking about his brothers, and sisters. The kind of small talk that two people begin a life with. I wonder how many people really care about who you were when you grew up so many years ago. Did the effects your childhood had on you in that process and your environmental influences and how they helped shape you into the person you are today really matter?

My guess is that in our self-analyzed society of today that is so preoccupied with the warped beliefs that therapy should be engaged every time you break a nail would answer absolutely to all of these questions. Jason was a more practical guy, who approached the here and now. He, of course, answered all the questions politely and followed up with the same generic garble in response so he didn't leave a bad impression. The entire time he spent wondering who originally established the list of top ten questions to ask when you first meet somebody.

He was interested in Helen, so he did inquire about her stay in Oregon, where she had decided to live in San Francisco, and her transfer to this office. What did she like to eat, and what activities did she navigate to, or were there any hobbies that she enjoyed?   He took his time admiring her, as she walked in sync with him, and her athletic self-assured stroll that exuded confidence and intelligence. He wondered who the man was that could have let her escape his grasp once he had her close enough to embrace. Probably somebody not confident enough to feel secure around a woman of this caliber. Somebody who might have been successful, but needed to feel dominant in his personal life, and with Helen that would never be an option. She was an equal and would not let herself be controlled, but in this brief conversation seemed to be wanting a connection with somebody as well.

They reached the bar in a few short minutes and found a couple of open tables toward the back of the room. They all ordered a round of drinks ranging from beers to scotch to wine. Jason and Helen both ordered red wine, Jason because he was no longer on the track of drinking too much and enjoyed red wine, while Helen just plainly enjoyed red wine. She had most likely never lost control in her life, and with her stylish, casual beauty was becoming more attractive to Jason with every passing minute.

They spent a few hours in the bar, and as the early evening was beginning to pass them by realized that most of their working crowd had dispersed. It was now just the two of them. They couldn't remember anyone having left. They had been engaged so deeply in their conversation that they somehow had become engrossed in each other not keeping track of their surroundings.

They both laughed at the same time, as they realized what had happened and agreed to take a walk in the hopes of finding a bite to eat before heading home. They spent a couple more hours at a little Italian restaurant a couple of blocks from the bar and after finishing dinner walked back to Jason's car. Helen normally took the bus to work, so Jason agreed to give her a ride back to her apartment on the north-west side of the city.

It was close to Golden Gate Park and the winding hilly drive took about twenty minutes. Helen invited Jason in, but he declined while emphatically stating he had a great time and would love to do this again. He didn't feel comfortable yet having just recently ending his marriage and hoped that she would understand. He did walk her to her door, and as she turned from getting her keys out of her purse gently cupped her head kissing her lightly on the lips.

He had not expected to do this and felt his cheeks getting bright red as she lightly held his shoulder pausing as she looked into his eyes. She said what a wonderful time she had. She was looking forward to doing this again so he better not renege on his promise. She was going to hold him to it, so he better start making plans as soon as he left for home. He paused as she walked inside closing the door behind her. He stood for a minute just staring at the oversized mahogany wood door that was almost archaic in its original form after years and years of use.

He finally left. During the drive to his apartment he reflected over his unexpected outing and smiled for the first time in a long while. Jason was always a decent guy and had a good life, but he had not felt a genuine deep true smile in so long. He had forgotten what it made you feel like. He had a rumbling in his stomach and was giddy like a teenager, as he put himself on autopilot for the drive. Hopefully, this would be a routine he would be making many times in the future.

Lose Job

I sat in my favorite reclining leather chair in my small living room in the little two-bedroom house wondering how the saying "it always happens to me" came about. We always tell teenagers they act like the world revolves around them. If we are honest with ourselves the world revolves around each of us. Do we have any concept of what goes on when we are not here or there or wherever we happen to be? Everything we do revolves around ourselves. We are all the center of our own story, as there would be no story if we were not here. We would not know it.

I looked at the flat-panel TV hanging above my painted white brick fireplace, and tried to understand why anyone ever paints brick. Was it a fad at one time? Somebody suddenly said let's take some white paint and cover everything we possibly can? Didn't they even start to make paint for bricks? Why use brick if you are just going to cover it up? The TV was the symbol of my frivolous behavior. I had only bought it about ten months ago, and although it was one of the cheaper, more affordable, models it was beyond my ability to afford at the time of purchase. America, and their credit cards, right? I did not understand the concept of living within my means.

As I leaned back, staring at my belongings, I reflected on my day. It had only been less than a week ago when I was celebrating my divorce, reveling in the release that I had sought for so long. I admired the fact that not only had my wife lost her job but she had lost her marriage as well and the balance in society was finally becoming real. I know I shouldn't be happy in her misery, but in the bitter battle of divorce it is sometimes the only consolation prize you receive. Her losing her job also affected me as well since the kids kept us intertwined financially and emotionally through their upbringing.

The attorneys are really the ones who get all your money in a divorce. In today's economic times there is not that much money to go around. We had lost our home, as she was required to sell it. I was in jeopardy of losing the house in Twain Harte, but knew that somehow I could not allow that to happen with my special room so deeply embedded in my happiness. The kids are torn apart and your friends are divided up even if unequally.

The one thing that I could relish in was my wife falling so far so hard. I, at least, was still perched a few notches above her on the descent into the catechism of darkness. That is what made it so difficult when earlier today I had received the summons. Don't you hate the summons? Your boss comes in and states that he needs to talk to you, and you say sure not a problem. You walk with him as he passes his office, and you wonder why you would not be directed there as you so often have discussions in his or your office.

Why would he be going down the hallway, and you blindly following assuming maybe you were making your way to one of the conference rooms? Oddly, there is no conversation during the long stroll and he is not forthcoming about where you are going or what the purpose is. Just the silence, as he walks slightly ahead of you so you are sure to follow him to the designated spot for the summons. Maybe there was a meeting that you had forgotten to attend, or maybe there was some office party that was quickly being thrown together for somebody's birth day or a baby shower or anniversary that you had somehow overlooked.

Then as you make your way further you see the HR representative sitting in one of the smaller meeting rooms, and your boss enters, pausing for a minute, as you walk by then shutting the door behind you. You wonder if you did something wrong and start quickly reflecting back over the past few weeks trying to figure out if you said something inappropriate or directed a wrong e-mail as you forwarded a joke.

The sun was shining in through the westward facing window, as it reflected off the tan table. I sat down in one of the four chairs thinking that we only had three people in the room, and we didn't have use of the extra metal chair with the seat that was wrapped in brown fabric. I saw the sheen of the light, as it jumped off the EFI folder that was sitting on the table in front of the HR representative. With that final clue I knew that for whatever reason my time as the Director of Finance was coming to a close quicker than I had anticipated.

My boss went into his rehearsed speech about how times are bad, and with the economy everyone is cutting back blah blah blah. I lost track of what he was saying, as my mind wondered to bills and no savings account and the lost chances that I had squandered over the span of my forty-two years. I had never liked my jobs, and hated accounting, but it was a good paying occupation. Where else can you make a large salary and sit in front of a computer simply adding up numbers then subtracting them and then adding them up in a different way.

My self esteem seemed to be getting sucked through the vent that was on the floor behind our HR person who was now rattling on about extra weeks, and how with my almost five years at EFI I was eligible for blah blah blah. It was really hard to focus on the contents of what she or my supervisor was saying as my mind was flying in so many different directions at once it was difficult keeping up.

How many times had I invited this same HR person for drinks, asked my boss out so he would feel included in the crowd, and organized events for our team? Companies are callous and unfeeling. In the end it is all about the bottom line. There are some that are more compassionate than others, and none of this was personal. It was my time to go. I was the next expendable rung on the ladder of profitability and just a fixture that needed to now be discarded. It wasn't that they didn't need my services they just could no longer afford them.

When times were good I had negotiated a substantial increase in salary. The extra money I had made over the last couple of years was a driving factor in my current demise. I was now priced out of the market place. Some of this is just an excuse. They didn't ask me if I was willing to take a pay cut, or if I would renegotiate my current status. It was black and white with companies. You were either expendable, or you were not expendable. I unfortunately had been labeled in the previous category.

I wondered what I would now do with my family in its current status. My wife without a job, me without a job and no savings to speak of between us. What little we had in our 401ks had shriveled up like a dried prune left out in the blazing dessert heat for several days. The economy had taken away my savings and now my job as well. The first step in finding a solution to a problem and the first step in all celebrations and the first step … well in almost anything was scotch.

I got up from my relaxing position of pent up anxiety and stress, grabbed a full bottle of McAllen 12, and filled a glass with ice. I ventured back to my familiar spot. I poured the soothing liquid then tipped it slowly back sipping the beverage so I could savor the slightly biting warmth as it flowed through my lips swirling around my tongue then inching its way down my throat spreading warmth the entire way. Scotch was one of the best discoveries by man. Who cares about going to the moon or cell phones or the ability to fly, Scotch is the beginning and end of all aspects of life.

I flipped on the TV and navigated through to my DVR box and instinctively gravitated to my favorite movie *PS I Love You*. How many times had I watched that movie? I was not a big Hillary Swank fan, but she held her own in this romantic comedy. She was always a little to boyish for me after that one movie she did pretending to be a boy who was a girl who thought she was a boy. In this movie she seemed to come back to her feminine side, and was perfectly cast. I was frequently admitting to crying every time I watched this movie. It was the truth despite that fact that nobody believed me.

The opening scene alone with the perfect music and the passionate argument followed up by the emotional embrace and obvious display of affection was a glaring example in my belief that love is so closely entwined with hate. Two people who feel so deeply for one another can and do hurt their spouse but they also feed their spouse with support and love. The trick in life I guess is to make sure that the support and love far outweigh the hurt or hope that your spouse is one of those people who are unnaturally patient.

I had been laid off once before in my career, and that was after I had moved to Chicago. I had a job at a trade show exhibit manufacturer that was privately owned and operated. I was living an apartment with my future wife, and had watched for two years as the company had sunk into oblivion. The owner was an elderly man in his late '80s who was at the tail end of his life and had trouble walking to and from the car. His ability to run a company had long ago demised.

About ten years prior he had married a trade show hostess from Las Vegas and she was now running the company with the official title of president. I am not sure that I have to continue the story as you can pretty much guess the outcome from here. She was your typical blonde hostess, and it was not that she was dumb but let's just say she wasn't bright either. She had managed to take the company that he had started from nothing, and run it into the ground mounting up huge sums of debt in the process.

Sadly, she had also used his personal funds and his home as collateral for business loans, so he not only lost his business but he lost his home and all his belongings as well. I would imagine he left the world pretty much the way he came with very little to show for his endeavors. She on the other hand was still in her early forties at the time of the bankruptcy, so most likely went after another old man who she could entice to take care of her as she entered middle age. I don't know the specifics of their outcome, but still remember how sad it was to watch the company implode. One week after I had been let go they closed the doors on the business for good.

I had been the last of twelve in the accounting department to be let go and had seen the writing on the wall for a long time. I had been searching for a job, but had just not found anything that was a good fit. I had prepped my ex-wife (girlfriend at the time) as well so she understood the situation. She had actively helped me with my resume and in the job-hunting process.

This is why her reaction when I told her should have been my final red flag that sent me scurrying to safety fleeing from her tyrannical grasp.

When I informed her that I had been laid off she was angry at first, blaming me and asking me what I had done wrong. I tried to explain to her again the company situation telling her that we had talked about this, knew it was coming, and it should not have been a surprise. She would not accept this, and I now realize that her reaction to being scared or unsure of her future or unsettled in any way was to react with anger. That anger I would grow to learn was very often directed at me. When you say for better or worse in the marriage vows you are assuming that it will be more better than worse but that is not always the case. Never assume anything.

I realized I would not be able to get a job making near the money that I had been making, and since I was unable to keep up with my bills for the first time in my life had no idea how in the world I was going to move forward. Without winning the lottery I was screwed. Maybe this was my punishment for my recent sins. Most people would argue that losing your job does not equate to murdering several people, but it was devastating to me.

I decided tonight I would do nothing. I would drink my bottle of scotch, watch my movie several times, and once sufficiently inebriated would pass out either on the chair or stumble my way to bed. With my stocked-up vacation and my severance package I was good for five to six months, so I was not destitute yet. I didn't want to plan my self-inflicted death until I had exhausted all hope of finding my way back. I still had the kids to think about. The absolute worst-case scenario still had me better off than a lot of the people in today's environment.

Killing Really Can Be Therapeutic

Waking up with a hangover is something that I will never get used to, no matter how experienced I am. The pounding beat of your skull like somebody is taking a hammer and playing taps on your head from every side can be excruciatingly painful. I had fallen asleep in the chair, and it was now early in the morning but still very dark outside. My guess was in the 4 AM range, as I stumbled into the kitchen, grabbed a bottle of water, and sucked half of it down on the first swig.

I managed to make it to the bathroom and dropped a couple of Advil down my throat as I swigged the rest of the water. I drained the bottle entirely. In a way, it was always better falling asleep in a chair or on a couch. You tend to wake up so very early, which enables you to drink water, take aspirin, and then head off to bed for more sleep. The only issue with alcohol, really, is the dehydration effect. It makes your body feel like you have been stranded in the blazing sun for several days, and you forgot your backpack of supplies.

I woke again at 7 AM the second time, and as hoped felt much better. Still not operating on all cylinders, but definitely clawing my way out of the sand pit. I took a shower and grabbed another bottle of water, downing this one as I let the sprinkle from the showerhead flow down my face to my body that seemed to soak it up like a sponge. I stayed in the shower for close to thirty minutes and admittedly was feeling okay by the time the pain relievers began to work.

After watching a movie and spending the morning relaxing, my next step was to get dressed and drive to the city. I would hit a local bar and start the process over again without restraining myself to the confines of my living room. As helpful as the alcohol was, my hidden desire was hoping that luck would pass my way. I hoped to stumble into an opportunity to quench my other thirst, as the only thing more enticing than a drink was the fresh flow of blood from a new victim.

There is nothing like killing somebody to renew your hope in life. Ironic, isn't it. My hope and energy comes from watching somebody else lose their life. I am like a vampire in a way. I don't have to actually suck the blood dry from the bodies of my victims, but somehow their death gives me the energy to focus and continue forward down my path. I would not be that picky tonight. I headed to a seedy part of town, close to the strip clubs, in the hopes of finding something that would appease my thirsting lust.

There is something to be said for hitting a bar and heading to the strip clubs in the latter part of the afternoon. Most do not even open until after 4 PM, so you can't spend the day watching breasts flop around on an oily stage. You are regulated to the evening and night for this type of activity. It was still a little early, so I stopped in at a pub, ordered a beer and settled into camp waiting for the real activities to begin later.

Local bars are so much more enticing than clubs and trendy establishments that encompass the younger generation of San Francisco. Everything has its place, and the overpriced, posh settings that attracted the hip crowds were appealing to a large portion of the population. For losers like me the bar down the street with the torn seat cushions and an overweight bar-mate is like home. Sit me down on a stool that hasn't moved in fifty years where I can lean my arms on the sticky used bar top. Suddenly I feel like this is where I grew up.

I sat at one end, admiring the square-box tube TV hanging on a platform at one corner perched above the bottles. I reflected on it as one would an antique. It was fast becoming extinct, with even the plasma TV now going by the wayside, as the flat panel was taking control of the market. It was blaring an East Coast NBA basketball game with the Celtics up by a large margin. I was not a big basketball fan, but would watch a game if it were on. Football was my preferred choice of spectator sport, but I also enjoyed a good game of baseball.

Being from Illinois, I was and would always be a Cubs fan but had navigated toward the Giants having lived out here for so many years. I couldn't believe the great teams the Cubs were fielding in recent years, and how they always managed to somehow choke once they reached the playoffs. How could a team year after year fold like a wet paper towel every time the stakes increased and the pressure mounted? It was becoming too painful to watch.

There were about fifteen other people in the bar. My guess was half regulars and half in for an afternoon drink session, for whatever reason.

There was nobody in the place that I would be interested in getting to know any further, so I simply hung out for a couple of hours, had a few beers, and watched the end of the game and the meaningless commentary afterward. There are some sportscasters that are worthwhile to listen to, but most of them are hacks that either couldn't make it in the sport or were publicity-mongering fools who would speculate on any aspect of the game to try and make a name for themselves.

I finally closed out my tab and paid with cash. Someone might follow me or recognize me or trace me back here, so I didn't want any hard evidence. I was careful not to make a scene or spend too much time talking with anyone. I just sat in silence watching the game and sipping my beer. I remember one of my friends (back when I was married) actually said to me when the split occurred how it was too hard on him to remain my friend, so we no longer associated. Can you believe an asshole I had known for several years of my life and shared some of the most memorable moments actually said to me during my divorce that it was too difficult on him?

He had mentioned one time during our friendship, while I was still married, the reason he never felt close enough to me was my personality. It was the type where I could never go to a bar by myself and comfortably sit and have a beer, talking to nobody that I had previously known. His criteria of friendship was a little warped, since he was an alcoholic, but what an odd way to judge your friends. I should have known then that he was a balless hack that was too pathetic to waste my time on, but I continued to associate with him for whatever reason until the demise of my personal union.

I left the bar, sauntered into the closest strip club, and was immediately greeted by several of the working women. All of whom wanted to vie for my attention, and most important, my wallet. I told them that I was taking my time and wanted to cruise through the joint to weigh my choices before proceeding with anything further. San Francisco has an odd foray of strip clubs with most of them having private back rooms that you can utilize for your personal dances. Most of these rooms have some type of closure, be it a curtain or something soft that allows the girls to give you as much as you are willing to pay for of their services.

The first time that I ventured in one I was a little taken aback as the girl reached into my pants fondling me as we had just entered the room asking me if I wanted her to pleasure me in an oral fashion. Coming from Chicago, where you are not allowed to even touch the women in the middle of a lap dance but are required to keep your hands to your sides, it was a drastic change in environment. There were several very attractive women there for an afternoon so I figured the nighttime workers had already entered and they were preparing for the arrival of their prey.

It is all about the money with these women. From the second they look at you and saunter over in their seductive clothing their only goal is to suck as many dollars (and I don't mean dollar bills) from you as they possibly can. My guess is that a gorgeous woman in an average weekend can easily pull a couple thousand down in tips alone. I wonder if they even make a paycheck from dancing. It would have to be paltry wages, as their true payment comes from the naive guy who pushes money out before he even negotiates the services.

I have seen my brother-in-law enter one of these rooms the second that we had arrived one evening with a small group of guys as we celebrated my birthday. We all remember that moment—it is a standing joke that we tell and will tell for several years to come. Fifteen minutes later he exited the curtained enclosure, raised both of his hands, and yelled "I am done." He then left the strip club. He and one of the other guys spent the rest of the evening drinking beer as me and a couple of friends did the more generic women watching from the chairs spread around the stage. The joke was most likely on us, as I am sure we spent more money than he did and left far less satisfied.

I sat down at a table and scanned the group looking for somebody that might fit my taste. I settled on a tiny brunette that had small, perky breasts who was wearing a purplish-colored piece of silk lingerie. I had to fight off a few girls before she caught me eyeing her and shook her way over to my table. Her ass moved in ten inches each direction with every step that she took. How do some women shake their ass that way as they walk? Is it a class that some of them take? Did others miss that day, so they are unaware of the proper form to move in that sultry, slinky movement?

She sat down and introduced herself as Cherry, which of course I was sure was her real name. I shook her hand and said that I was Dirk Digler, and it was very nice to meet her. She didn't even smile at the reference, my guess being that she was at most nineteen to twenty and probably had no idea who Dirk even was. She asked me if I was up for a private dance, and I honestly told her that I would be but she would have to put some time in here at the table getting to know me. Since there were few other men in the place she was most likely not going to be losing any money.

I could see her calculating in her mind if it was worthwhile, and she then asked me how much I was willing to pay to keep her company at the table. She could then judge her desire based on the dollar figure. Everything is about money, isn't it? I had no intention of paying this girl any money but instead was planning on shoving my four-inch knife through her Adam's apple. Watching the blood squirt out as she held her throat unable to talk right after I released my sexual explosion all over her gorgeous brown hair.

I stated that if she was willing to talk to me for a while, and then perform whatever act I wanted in the back room, I would take up no more than two hours of her time. I was willing to pay her $500 for this service. I could see her eyes light up a little. There were a lot of women here tonight, and odds were low that she might be able to make that much for the entire night. If I gave her that in one sitting she could most likely double her intake for the day as the place got more crowded into the later hours of the evening. She agreed, and we started the small-talk portion of getting acquainted.

I shouldn't spend the time boring you with the details of the interaction, as she stumbled over her facts throughout the conversation. I am unsure of what was true and what was simply a made up history for the benefit of "Cherry's" normal patrons. She started getting antsy, and had now asked me if I was ready to go to the back room. She stated that she would only feel comfortable proceeding with our deal if I were willing to give her some of the money up front.

Let's get the party started, I said, getting to the meat of our transaction so to say. I followed her back, again admiring her ass as it flowed from the left side of the room all the way to the right side of the room, as she walked slowly in front of me. She couldn't have been more than 5' 2" in her five-inch heels, and she probably weighed no more than ninety pounds, but she had a perfect full ass that cried out to be cupped with both hands. She would be termed a spinner, which is a term so often used in the porn section on the Internet.

As I entered the room I had to pay $100 just to reserve it for the thirty required minutes. After handing over the deposit, and then giving her the payment she demanded (she would not start without full payment, and I would not give her full payment so we finally negotiated on half up front) she removed her lingerie. Standing completely naked in front of me, she unzipped my pants.

Negotiating time with a stripper/prostitute is an interesting process. I can stay in the room as long as I like. Once she has induced me to climax her job is done and she will most likely leave telling me that she is finished but I am welcome to remain until my time has expired. They have one goal in mind—to complete the process then move on to the next guy so they can rack up the payments that they are whoring themselves out for to begin with.

She moved with gazelle-like speed placing the condom on me as she worked her magic hoping for a quick few minutes to force me into submission with her seductive ways. As she was going through her routine, I looked around the room. The curtain was well shut and covered both sides of the door all the way across. It would be easy for anyone to open, but there was no way that it was possible to view the inside without moving some portion. I looked carefully for any lights in the walls or ceiling, and saw nothing, so I assumed there were no cameras.

You have to be very careful nowadays as there are several of these places that have installed video monitoring equipment to ensure none of the girls get hurt. This was an older building, and it was not the most upscale, so it seemed to operate in the old-fashioned way with a gumba sitting outside that would kill me if anything got out of hand. I was leaning back on a black leather couch and was thankful that it was not sticky from past experiences. There was a half-full trashcan with paper towels and condoms strewn about it in one corner from either today or recent customers who had attended the party before me.

It was dark enough in the room, and the music was blaring through a black speaker hanging from the ceiling in one corner. It reminded me of those drive-in speakers that used to hang on your window back in the eighties when they were so popular. What a great concept that died out before its time. How could you not love the drive-in movies and why did that business model not work? Some failed concepts baffled me. She was working up a sweat now, and I could see she was losing patience, but unfortunately for her I still had a few minutes to go.

I started telling her how great it felt, making the noises of ecstasy so she understood her job was close to completion. These girls sure didn't like physical exertion, which seems stupid to even say. It was all about easy money to them. I then started to feel the stir of excitement and grabbed her hair with my left hand to help her movements keep the correct pace in the process. With my right hand I had reached into my jacket pocket and flipped open the knife blade exposing the metal from its encasement.

I was close now, and just as I was exploding I drove the blade home in her back as it connected with her spine forcing me to plunge it in with all my strength angling the blade down in order to inject it fully into her spine. As I did so, I held myself inside her with my left hand keeping her mouth fully occupied as I completed the task that I had come for. I removed the blade, and drove it home several more times as she grew limp in my arms. She finally slipped to the ground, as I was unable to hold her up any longer.

This was not completely as planned but very fulfilling. It was exquisite to climax at the point of death with some young beautiful girl. I contemplated how much money I had saved for how many guys that she would not swindle tonight, and for all the nights in the future. She would have continued this occupation until one day she woke up and realized she couldn't in her haggard old body make money doing this anymore. She would by then be on several forms of drugs and probably OD. How long would this process take? Five years, or maybe in her case because she started out so beautiful, eight or ten years at most.

I left the condom on, so I wouldn't leave my evidence in the room. I pulled up my pants, checked to ensure that I had my wallet, took back the money that I had given her and exited. I walked out the front door, making sure that I did not make contact with anyone on the way out, and admired how I had managed to spill not a single drop of blood on any of my clothes or even my shoes. I was still pretty stupid in this process, but I seemed to be going undetected and unnoticed in all circumstances to date.

I sat in the coffee house across the street for about thirty minutes and watched as floods of strippers, customers and large bulky men ran from the front of the building like ants that have just realized their home is being flooded. Once the police arrived, I left the coffee house and made my way to my car that was parked in a self-service lot about ten blocks away.

I might have lost my job yesterday, but I felt damn good today.

FOLLOWING ALONG

Sudhir woke up in his own bed, and again as was becoming quite the custom his head was pounding with the aching relentless reminder that he had drank far too much the night before. He remembered being picked up at the restaurant by his brother and driven home where he had stayed by his side for a while. Sudhir had woken up at some point to find himself alone and had attacked the liquor cabinet again with a vengeance. This wasn't the first time that he had dove into a drinking binge before even recovering from the hangover caused by the last one.

He fell into the bathroom, catching himself with his hands on the toilet and threw up on the lid. He violently heaved his insides up like a fountain spraying even the tile surrounding the white porcelain receptacle. He now felt he knew what stepping over the edge felt like, as his memory flooded back into consciousness, and his renewed disgust mounted at what this life had become. His marriage was over, he felt. They were already in a rocky area before, but the betrayal burning inside him was never going to heal.

He would have to be careful to remain in control, he realized, as the memory of screaming at the top of his lungs in the restaurant that he could kill his wife burned in his mind. He never said he was going to kill her, only that he felt he could, but in court that would only be a matter of semantics. He knew that physically he could never hurt the mother of his children, but the rage had taken control in one of the rare instances of his life—combined with the alcohol he had been beyond recognition.

The next few hours were focused on bringing reality back to his fragile existence. He showered, drank coffee, showered again, and took another nap. He did all the things you would normally do to give your body what it needed to overcome the intake of too much alcohol. Once he felt whole enough, he got dressed in one of his better pair of slacks and his favorite shirt.

He always liked this shirt with its subtle stripes that blended in slightly with the black fabric.

He combed what remained of his hair, and admired himself in the mirror. He wasn't looking too shabby. The perpetual drunkenness as of late had done him one favor. He seemed to have lost a few pounds. All that vomiting was like a self-induced bulimic diet that resulted in his pants fitting a little looser than they had in several years. He looked around the house, fighting back the tears that started forming, as he reflected on his kids and their life and what might have been if only things were different.

After walking from room to room, and pausing for a minute in each one, he knew that it was time to leave. He opened the garage door only to find that his car was not there, nor was it out front in the driveway. He remembered then that his brother had brought him home, so it must still be sitting in the parking lot of the bar he had visited yesterday. Quite a scene he had played out for the mid-day working shift he thought. He was on full drama patrol yesterday with the open display and the non-stop crying, as he curled up into a little ball on the floor. Everyone must think he was crazy, and at this point they were probably all correct.

He called for a taxi, as the bar was about five miles away and the rolling hills of Pacifica didn't lend well to walking for a hung over out of shape middle-aged man. He didn't like walking, anyway. As he waited, he renewed his stroll through the house, thinking of the memories that were stored away in the walls and with each piece of furniture. They had been married for so long it was as if every corner of every wall contained a small piece of who they were as a couple. He had failed to look at himself individually in so long it seemed foreign to him to even approach the concept.

The taxi pulled up in the driveway, and as Sudhir was shutting the door he contemplated writing a note but then decided against it. They would be able to find him, of that he was sure, and what would he say. Nothing really mattered. He closed the door to his house and stepped off the front stoop heading to that taxi. He smiled as he saw the Indian driver behind the wheel, and again wondered what his life would have been like if he, too, would have gone that route.

The driver navigated the hills and curves and dropped him in the parking lot of the structure that held the embarrassing event from yesterday's activities. Sure enough there was his car sitting in one of the spots like it was laughing at him. He paid the driver $50, and was thanked profusely for the generosity. What did money matter, really?

He opened his car door and sat behind the wheel for a few minutes, again fighting to control his emotions and keep the tears at bay. His eyelids felt like the Hoover dam as they worked diligently to keep the liquid bottled up behind their thin enclosure. He felt a few sneaking through, unfortunately, and wiped his eyes with his fingers as he worked his will and self-control, purging the action once again.

The car started fine, and he felt himself pulled in the direction of the kid's schools. He first stopped by Matt's and slowed along the curb watching the kids playing behind the fenced in field. Schools are like little fortresses today, with their fences and security guards and in many locations metal detectors are a way of life. In most schools these are all protective measures against the scum of the earth that prey on kids and have no concept of what is right or wrong. In some cases it is simply to protect the kids from themselves, as so many have now turned to violence at such a young age.

He sat and just watched for a long time, having lost track of what time meant. It had no relevance to Sudhir anymore. He didn't see Matt, but at the same time felt he had connected with him in some form of conversation by just being here. He would never be able to explain to Matt what was going on. A child should never hear those things about a parent until they are much older, and have already lost the innocent view of the world. Every child should hold onto their belief that parents are perfect for as long as they can.

The car seemed to start up by itself, as Sudhir made his way to Tracey's school now and followed much the same process as before. The kids were not playing organized sports at this school, but were still utilizing playground equipment. They were left on their own to devise what school kid games they might to exert the endless energy that every child is blessed with. He was lucky enough to see Tracey in the playground, and that alone broke the barricade he had just recently erected, and he again felt the flood of tears streaming down his cheeks landing on his shirt and pants. He didn't attempt to stop them this time.

It was now getting close to time for school to end, and the last thing Sudhir wanted was to meet his parents here or to actually have to talk to Tracey and or Matt in person. He didn't have it in him to face anyone in his current state. He started the car and headed for The Golden Gate Bridge.

The bridge is a magnificent structure, and in today's economic times would be too expensive to even build. Isn't that such a weird thing to say? One of the ills of our worldwide industrial revolution is that many of the wonders we visit and admire could never be built as they cost too much at today's labor rates. That alone should tell you what is wrong with our economy. No wonder we were facing the worst recession ever seen. It was inevitably going to lead to a depression in Sudhir's mind. How ironic really. In his case he had already bridged the gap to depression. He must be ahead of the curve, he thought.

Sudhir had decided the bridge was as good a spot as any. It might require some walking, which he didn't enjoy, but it was a beautiful view looking back over the city. The view out to Angel Island or even just gazing in the direction of the ocean with its vast unexplored depths of secrets that might not ever be discovered was amazing. Parking was easy to attain, and he pulled into the lot, stopped the car. Again he felt the floodgates being compromised as the tears renewed their assault bent on escaping the confinement that was so flimsily holding them at bay.

He gazed out over the scenery, and just didn't feel right in the next step of this process. There was an oozing burning inside like something was still left undone. It was like he was jumping from the beginning of act three to the end of the play. Even though he knew he was on the downside of the scene you couldn't leave out the important parts as the ending wouldn't make any sense.

Janine he guessed was sitting in her self inflicted fortress, either alone or with somebody. He knew that he would have to confront her and at least bring to a conclusion this charade that was being acted out before he could close the curtain on the play itself. It was approaching dusk at this point in the day where again time had lost its hold on Sudhir. He was wandering from hour to hour with no more time table to drive his actions.

Don't you love those vacations where you just lay around, and there is no place to be and no appointments. You wake up, sit by the pool or lounge in the ocean-side chairs, as people serve you drinks and food. There are walk-up massages that cater to your every whim, and the only thing driving you to ever move is the fact that there is no restroom built into your lounge of luxury. Sudhir felt himself in that vacuum of time right now. He had purpose and was moving forward even though he was operating in this void of seconds/minutes/hours.

He started up the car and made the drive back over the bridge weaving in and out of the congestion that had now formed from rush hour timing. People were attempting to hurriedly move from work to home so they could spend the designated thirty minutes seeing their loved ones before everyone turned on the TV and lost themselves in the world of entertainment. "I am bored." How often did kids utter those words, and we annoyingly can't believe where they come from. We ourselves train them that they must be stimulated twenty-four hours a day seven days a week. How pathetic.

There are TVs in bathrooms and kitchens, and have now been for a very long time invading the bedroom. The act of making love to your wife or husband has been supplanted by re-runs of *Friends* that are still played non-stop on peripheral channels, endlessly repeating themselves over and over again and again. We as a society would rather watch something that we have seen hundreds of times, than spend time with the person that we are committed to for the rest of our lives. Conversation is a lost art form, and yet we ponder why we are so alone in this world that we give nothing to and make no effort to change.

Sudhir was finally pulling into the familiar hotel parking lot that he had only exited yesterday from his stark discovery that had been the final blow pushing him into his new world. He was ready to explore new adventures and test the water of the world beyond seeing the next step in the evolving cycle of existence. He had only one last thing to do before his journey would be thrust forward in the exhilarating unknown of the next frontier.

It was now dark outside, and he opened the car door, feeling his hand shaking on the handle. He pulled it toward him unleashing the latch that had held it firmly in place. The metallic click that signaled the movement as he instigated the release from the confined protection of his metal carriage rang in his ears. He didn't pay attention to little things anymore. He simply took so many things for granted, and it wasn't until everything was lost and it was all taken from him that he could reflect back on what the little things meant.

Who pays attention to the sound of a car door opening? Nobody does, would be the answer. It is simply one of the things that work. You know it works, and it does not garner the magnitude of an event that needs to be contemplated beyond that. We are always lost in the big picture, and it was only now that Sudhir was realizing the big picture was only a conglomeration of tiny events. You had to see the tiny events before you would ever fully understand the picture as a whole.

He started the walk to the front door, and in his mind had now memorized the room number. He was ready to face the truth. He was only going to have to deal with it for a short time as the rest of his plan would be carried out quickly after. He showed the attendant his badge, received a key to Janine's room. He then made the long walk down the dimly lit corridor where the cause of his happiness and now his demise unknowingly waited.

Hotel Confrontation

I received the frantic phone call from Janine, and she was insistent that I come over and see her tonight. I had feigned sickness the night before, but she was relentlessly badgering me. Having known her now for several years I realized that she was not going to give in so I agreed. I had decided that this had to be the last time we would ever see each other. I wasn't going to give her a choice. It was finally time to start cleaning up loose ends, and she was at the top of that list.

I had filled a few glass bottles with gasoline, placing them carefully in a duffle bag, and had several lighters with me as well. I figured once I shot her in the head in her room I would then simply burn the hotel down and hope for the best. Sudhir would be devastated, but the poor bastard would be better off even if he didn't know it. She was a leech on him, and was now trying to drive her fangs into me as well. What she didn't realize is that I was not anywhere close to the same man Sudhir was.

Our affair had started a few years back accidentally. We had all been drinking one evening, and as usual Sudhir had passed out in his chair in the living room. We had continued drinking, and for some reason had decided to watch a movie but the only unoccupied room with a TV had been her bedroom. We both went in, turned on the TV, and shortly thereafter I found myself making love to my good friend's wife. This episode had been followed up by the appropriate levels of guilt from both parties, but in the end it had happened again and then again and before we knew it a pattern developed.

It provided for some awkward times, but if you detached yourself from the sexual events and looked upon them as a couple during the barbecues and restaurant outings it proved doable. Several weeks ago when Sudhir had asked me to talk to him about Janine it was a little odd, but I felt I had successfully avoided that issue as he hadn't brought it up again recently. Come to think of it, I had not seen Sudhir in a while now and was curious what he was up to. I was guessing that tomorrow morning when he woke up and found out she was dead in a hotel room in Daly City that would change. He would need somebody to confide in as he tried to piece together what happened.

I got my pistol and needed supplies then packed up the Volvo. After putting Delilah in the garage I headed off to my adventure. A few months ago, killing Janine would have been difficult. I am not sure that I could have managed the feat, but I was a different man today than I was back then. I was the new improved Duncan who was a killing machine—nearly invincible. Okay, that might be a little much, but I did feel the energy flow of adrenaline as I got pumped up in anticipation of the experience I was about to have.

As usual, I parked in the side parking lot not wanting to go through the main entrance. It was a habit that now served me well for my new purpose. Over the years as we had wanted to avoid detection. I called her to let her know I was entering the hotel, so she could open the door for me. Sometimes hotels have those annoying locks on the side doors so you can't access anything, but through the main lobby without a key. Too many homeless people sneaking in and sleeping in the halls, maybe.

She let me in the door dressed in a tight-fitting pink lingerie outfit with silk stockings that ran up to her thighs. Sadly she was destroying the look with her incessant bitching of Sudhir and his loser habits. As we walked back to her room I was admiring the contrast of the fabric with its neon color next to her dark tan skin. I love women with dark skin. Maybe it has something to do with them being completely opposite myself, as I make love to them with my chalky white body next to their flawless smooth dark flowing outline.

Even the coarse hair that so often accompanies somebody of darker tones is wonderful to hold in the act of making love. The darker hair held in my white hands as I run my fingers through it holding it in both hands. Imagining myself making love to the young supple bodies took my mind back to the Dominican Republic. I was losing concentration, and tried to bring myself back to reality. That was somewhat easy to do with Janine, as her voice was her main obstacle form being a perfect female specimen.

God, if she would only shut up. As I so often did I informed her that while I did want to commiserate with her and listen to what the latest occurrence was that had her so worked up I as usual would be unable to concentrate until I could relax. The only thing that would make me relax was the sensual release of her beautiful touch. She smiled, and said of course, and we then embraced in a long passionate kiss that bordered on frantic as we tore at each other in the throngs of mutual pleasure.

I stood next to the bed, and she began to please me using her mouth for the one purpose that did not annoy the hell out of me and everyone around her. I had my bag on the bed, and as she was busy she didn't notice me pulling my pistol from inside the contents and laying it on the nightstand with my right hand. She attempted to pull me to her, but I insisted that she finish not wanting to make love to her tonight but preferring instead the sole gratification of being pleased.

She reluctantly agreed, and continued her work, as I felt the familiar initial twinge of my climax inch its way up from the depths of my toes. I was now grabbing a fistful of her hair with my left hand. I had reached for the pistol, and was going to attempt to mimic my experience from a short few nights ago since it had been such a memorable one. I was now thrusting in unison, and at the moment of truth lifted the gun and felt myself exploding with excitement as the flash of the discharged entered her left ear and with it slightly pointed up must have lodged itself somewhere inside her skull.

At that exact instant I opened my eyes to see Sudhir standing in the short hallway with his mouth open and looking like he must have just urinated in his pants. His slacks were forming a liquid pool all around his crouch that was growing quickly. He just stood there as Janine's body became limp in my hands, while I raised the gun pointing it in his direction and fired off two short blasts. The silencer that was permanently attached to my weapon purposely kept the noise to a minimum and I walked over to see if the door remained closed.

I will never forget the look in his eyes as the bullets seemed to trace every inch from the gun to his body in slow motion. He just stood there transfixed as if he had no idea how to digest the scene that was playing out before him. He was obviously in shock as he vacantly stared in my direction. His lack of reaction had me confused. It seemed he was truly playing out his life in the seconds he had left to live like watching a movie in fast forward jumping from picture to picture.

I had not heard him walk in the room, but saw the key on the floor as the pool of blood coming from Sudhir's body worked its way in that direction. It was forming a growing pond of dark red liquid encircling my former friend of many years. It was odd looking at Sudhir and thinking of what had just occurred. The surprise that not only was his wife and I embraced in a compromising passionate sexual position but that fact that she was also now deceased. He had seen the entire event standing helplessly by.

I wonder if he had known that she was dead or if it was simply the sheer act of what she was doing that had stopped him in his tracks keeping him immobile. He had seemed to be asking for death, as he blindly willed me to turn my weapon in his direction and fire it ending his misery from what he was forced to have witnessed. I sat down in the chair and tried to inhale the scene, not understanding what Sudhir was doing in the room in the first place.

Had he finally, after all of these years, become wise to Janine and our extracurricular activities? What had thrown him into the fray? He had kept a blind eye for so long it was as if he didn't want to admit what was occurring let alone face the truth. He was one who lived in his world and did not have the strength to face reality on his own. Without a crutch he was a small man, and the honesty that he held close had done nothing but doom him to failure. His soul mate was the deceiver that had undid his frail hold.

Still, he had been a friend of mine since we were kids. He was somebody I could always count on, and now my actions had directly led to his exit this evening. He would no longer be there for drinks or to catch a game or to simply listen when I wanted to rant about the latest crazy thing that my wife had committed. I was now understanding that I was isolating myself, ironically, the single thing my ex-wife had attempted to do I was doing for her.

Either by alienating my friends, or simply by killing them off, they were dropping by the wayside as my journey was moving forward by myself with nobody else around. I wish that I had planned this out a little, but the surprise of Sudhir had now left me with a predicament of uncertainty toward the next step. He was a police officer, and as such the investigation into his and his wife's death would be a full-blown heavy duty inquiry. He had friends in the FBI, and they as well might get involved. I was most likely either going to be caught, or I would have to flee and be hunted. My life was going to be changing very soon I thought.

Obviously not to the extent that Sudhir's had changed, but nonetheless different all the same. I made a couple of trips to the car and brought in the bottles of gasoline that were needed and started spreading the contents across the room. It was important as much evidence burned into ash as possible. It would have to be a quick burst of flames to overcome the sprinkler system and drive home the destruction. I carefully stepped around Sudhir's body, not wanting to get blood on my shoes.

I had not even gotten undressed, as I glanced over one last time and saw Janine's head hanging over the side of the bed where it had dropped when I disengaged with her to focus on Sudhir. I gathered up my bag and the emptied contents making sure that I had left nothing behind, and I opened the door a crack to peek out ensuring nobody was in the hall. I dropped the lighter to the floor and saw the instant swoosh of flames that immediately engulfed the room.

I closed the door behind me, and walked to the exit. I left the familiar hallway of the Extended Stay Suites for the last time. The bag felt a little heavy, and I realized I had one more bottle that I had failed to empty. Seeing Sudhir's car now in the parking lot, I dropped the contents over the hood and lit that on fire as well. Might as well destroy as much of this memory as possible, I thought. I heard the alarm blaring as I opened my door. While driving away I saw the flood of people flowing from the exits wearing all sorts of clothing as everyone was in a different stage of the evening.

It was like rats fleeing a sinking ship. Everyone was running and screaming, pushing their way to the safety outside. The flames were doing a great job, as they leapt from the structure grasping at the sky above. In a huge burst they appeared to attempt flight only to be pulled back toward the building in a large explosive sound. I would like nothing more than to sit and admire the work that I had created, but knew that I was already out of luck. I did not want to be anywhere near this place in the next few minutes.

I slowly pulled onto the highway and made my way home, stopping only at the local grocery store. I emptied the contents of my bag in the garbage can in the back. I wanted to get the evidence as far away from me as possible and as quickly as I could, so I didn't attract unneeded attention. I was going to lay low for a while. If by some miracle I wasn't compromised I would continue my mission down the road in the future.

The killing spree of Duncan was not at an end but simply pausing to take a breath so everyone could take a break and replenish their snacks and soda for the next stage of the game. Nothing goes on continually without pause for reflection and the need of another beer or possibly a glass of scotch taking precedent at times.

PICKING UP THE PIECES

Several days had now gone by, and I had not heard anything from anyone. It was in all the papers, which stated that the cops were looking for the murderer of a local law enforcement agent and his wife who had been spending a romantic evening in a local hotel. The spin that people put on things always amazed me—or maybe that is what they thought had actually been occurring.

I went to the funeral as they both were close friends of mine, and played the role of the concerned citizen as was needed. Oddly enough, when I was at the viewing and needed to use the restroom was when I first began to see the spotting on my boxers. It was an odd, green color, and appeared sticky and was somehow coming from the tip of my penis.

The next day I called my doctor and since she was not in I agreed to meet with her father who shared the practice. I had seen him several times before during the ten years that I had been going to them. He fit me in that day, and I went in to show him what was occurring. I had since looked at other pairs of my boxers and discovered this must have been going on for at least a few days. All of my underwear held that same splotching staining discoloration that seemed to be permanently scarring my underwear.

The dirty pairs were worse, as they were stained, but it was much more sticky. The clean pairs held only the small, spots of foreign coloring that must now be imbedded in the fabric as some reminder of one of my past deeds. My doctor went through the physical exam ritual, since I had not been there in a while. Even to the extent of having me bend over so he could examine all parts of my body with those latex-gloved hands and that scary lotion gel that is frequently used. He stated that I had a definite problem and lined me up to get the familiar tests for HIV, gonorrhea, syphilis, and chlamydia.

It was surreal going through the motions and anticipating the worst as with my lifestyle it was most likely going to hold true. How many women had I been with in the last year? He asked. I honestly couldn't answer the question. "Ten?" He asked. I said "definitely." "Twenty?" he asked. I said "yes, at least." He asked me how many I had been with and not used protection and I stated two, which I believed was close to the truth. I honestly could not be sure.

When you find yourself drunk on scotch or even beer and in the moment of naked ecstasy, you don't always think that now should be the time to protect your penis. All those commercials, and even the talks I had with my oldest daughter seemed ironic if I couldn't follow the same basic rules myself. The women that I associated with were the ones most likely to have issues. It would be from them that I should protect myself the most. How stupid could I possibly be?

I left his office in a trance as I walked down the long hallway to the front lobby that held a couple of couches and some chairs all of which were filled by ladies and men in their eighties or nineties. It was like walking in a dream that I was trying to wake from, but couldn't shake the feeling of being unable to rise from the bed.

The next two days were long, painful, and slow as I spent the time with my daughters, enjoying my stint of the custody rotation. I had planned on some parent teacher conferences with my oldest, so I went to those as well. My ex-wife attended with me and embarrassingly showed how little she knew about what my daughter did in school or how her studies were progressing. She really was out of touch.

I went through all of the motions, making dinner and helping with homework, reading books and snuggling. My oldest is perceptive and asked me several times if I was okay or if something was wrong. I wear my emotions on my sleeve most of the time, and while I enjoy being transparent there are times when I wish I could hide them better.

It was on the third day that I called my doctor to see if he had heard any news. He stated he wanted to see me in his office if I could make some time as quickly as possible. I agreed and told him I could be there in ten minutes. He confirmed that would be acceptable, but wanted closer to twenty to prepare my file. The ticking of a clock doesn't change from one second to the next. A minute is a minute and an hour is an hour, so how is it possible that some minutes fly by while others move like a snail inching its way across a busy freeway?

As a rule, if a doctor agrees to see you on short notice, and then additionally wants to see you in person, it will never be good news. I jumped in the Volvo, made the quick drive to San Mateo, and quickly ran up the stairs to his office. I was shown directly in not stopping but for a second in the waiting room, long enough to only give my name. Again, none of the above can possibly be good. The receptionist simply looked at me in a detached sympathizing glance that oozed pity and foreboding.

As I sat down in the small chair in his office with him reviewing my charts he closed the door. "Duncan, there is no easy way to say this," he stated. "You have tested positive for Chlamydia for which there is a cure. Unfortunately you have also tested positive for HIV for which there is not. There are several drugs that are now on the market that can keep the virus at bay for years if not decades but…."

I started to lose track of what he was saying at that point. The entire room instantly became engulfed in a fog, and I drifted in and out of reality. Pushing my way forward trying to understand the words that were being directed toward me.

I was in his office for about an hour, but I can't remember what was said after the initial news. How many new cases of HIV are reported per year in the United States alone? I was now simply part of that statistic. I was one of the percentages that had drawn the short straw and would now have to face the future that was unknown. I had felt so invincible just a short time ago, and now I was face to face with what most likely would be the cause of my death. Did I not reference myself to God? God doesn't catch HIV, does he?

There were so many things that I didn't know and would have to learn quickly. Were my daughters safe? How did the disease really spread? You always hear not to fear people with HIV, but is that truly how anyone feels? If you knew that in the office down the hall or in the cube next to you there was somebody with a life-threatening illness and that illness was something that could be contagious would you not have a twinge of anxiety no matter what you were told?

Kissing, is that still allowed? Can I kiss my daughters anymore? What about the times they are sleeping at my house and want to spend the night in my bed or snuggle in my lap? Do I have to now tell them no, as daddy doesn't want you catching his germs. Daddy's germs are now fatal sweetie, and there is no second chance. I went home and sat in the darkness in my favorite chair. I did not watch TV or read a book, but just thought about the price you pay for your actions.

Everyone knows to wear protection, yet not everyone does. Why is that? Could I answer that question myself? Why had I chosen to take a chance for a few minutes of pleasure with somebody I would never see again, and didn't even know her name? I would now be forever connected in life, and then in death, to this unknown person. My trips to the Dominican Republic, where I now know has a prevalence of HIV in the women prostitutes were froth with almost daily encounters. Apparently the government keeps a tight lid on the true statistics in that country, so nobody is sure what to believe in the percentages.

Homosexuality is frowned upon in the tiny island nation, so they are not as open about their sexual preferences. Who knows if it is more prevalent in that group of people or if it is just widespread? Does it even matter? You hear that HIV is the disease of homosexuality, but what kind of person even says that. I can't stand other people telling me or anyone else how to live their life. Who are these pretentious groups that seem to think they can dictate who can and who cannot be married.

Isn't it ironic that in the face of my death I now feel most human? More human than I have felt in a long time. I understand that I have caught the virus early, and that is a positive for me. I also understand that with the knowledge we have today it is possible to hold off the metamorphoses to AIDS for several years. At my age I might very well die of something else before HIV gets its tentacles in me to the point of turning to AIDS and I then die. I could have a heart attack just as easily in my early sixties.

Still, it is an odd feeling not knowing what is coursing through your veins, and how your body will change and be affected. How will I live, and will people see me differently? Should I tell my ex-wife, or should I keep it a secret? What about my kids and the stigma that comes with saying I have HIV. Will they look at me differently? Even if I can hold them, will they be to scared to be held? Will I feel like I have the plague, and my only recourse is to move away in isolation?

I need some help understanding this, what it means, and how to face the next day. I have to go to a help group and start gathering facts or get some support before I lose my ability to mentally function. The speculation will kill me faster than the disease itself if I don't stop my thoughts from taking off on these tangents of ridiculous speculative unknowns. The one thing I knew for sure—my life was going to change.

My trip to the Dominican Republic had opened up a door for me to begin my hobby, and start the killing spree that had made me feel alive. The trip had also been the instigation of where I most likely picked up the very thing that would ensure my demise. Life is so closely coupled with death, and the two are intertwined in ways that I will never fully understand. One thing I knew is that the tiny island nation was now an integral part in shaping who I was.

I sat crying uncontrollably. Crying and reflecting on what kind of monster I had become. I didn't like myself, and didn't like my path. If my historic demise was known to the public how would my kids perceive me? Would they remember the father who read them books and snuggled them when they were sick, or the father who butchered and murdered innocent people, calling it his hobby. I was sick in so many ways, and the fallacy that I was in control and functioning normally was a paper-thin veil that was now cut in shreds.   •

I couldn't stop crying. Would I ever be able to stop? Please help me.

I grabbed my head, as the pounding would not cease. I heard myself screaming, but had lost control of my body. I was throwing anything within my grasp in whatever direction it could be hurled. I saw the vase leave my hand. It impacted the flat-panel TV hanging above my fireplace shattering it to pieces. The chairs were flying in different directions as one squarely hit the glass door to my wine refrigerator, disintegrating it to pieces. All of this as I continued to scream.

I was human, after all. I was being punished for my sins by a god that was merciless. Was it time I begged forgiveness? Should I go outside, grab my gun, and start shooting anyone that came within my site? Is it fair to take out my pain on random people, or is that not what I was already doing. The screaming would not stop. It could not be stopped. The furniture continued to fly, as pieces were now littering the floor of every room in the house.

The screaming was continuous. One long scream of death and destruction. One unbroken note that held steady as my head pounded, listening to the scream echoing constantly.

The screaming kept going.

The screaming kept going.

The screaming would never stop.

Epilogue

Out of the blue, Sharene called me with a pressing desire to go out for drinks. I had not talked to her now in a long time, and although the call was odd I welcomed the distraction that going out with a beautiful lady would bring. I had not told anyone of my new predicament, so she was unaware as was everyone else save my doctors who were focusing on helping me prepare for my changed life.

I agreed to the request, and on the designated date picked her up at her house. Jason was there watching the kids as we went on our date. I felt a little awkward making small talk with her ex-husband while she placed the final touches on her preparation, but left with no choice made the best of it. I had waited outside, not wanting to intrude in the home they had built together for several years and for some odd reason he waited outside with me.

He was admiring my Volvo and asking how long I had it and how much I enjoyed it. He even commented on the small dent I had in the back, and I replied it was from Sudhir's son one past camping trip. He had dropped a can of something on it causing the dent that never did get repaired. It was an odd conversation, and at one point he mentioned that even though he and Sharene were not together they were still friends. He personally would kill anyone that ever harmed her. He still loved her very much.

I didn't know what I had done to provoke the exchange, but felt that I was very much in the dark with how he felt about me and what exactly he was trying to imply. Sharene walked through the door wearing a form fitting black dress and calf-high black leather boots that matched her dark, kinky-curly hair. She was stunning for somebody her age. She wasn't in her twenties anymore, but she was a vision to behold.

I opened the door for her and walked around to the driver's side having to navigate around Jason who was standing very close to the vehicle. He seemed to be threatening me in a non-verbal way. As we pulled out of the driveway he stared after us with his arms crossed. His eyes never wavering from our direction. It was a creepy feeling, but Sharene and I were now off and the smell of her alone was enough to make me forget the odd beginning.

LaVergne, TN USA
30 November 2009
165429LV00004B/1/P